Three Trillion Drops of Water

Vietnam, a Hero, and Home

A novel based on a true story

CYNTHIA BABERS STAFFORD

Published by Cynthia Babers Stafford.

For more information,

visit www.cynthiabstafford.com

First Edition

Cover Design by Lindsay Heider Diamond

Library of Congress Cataloging-in-Publication has been applied for.

ISBN 978-1-7360004-0-3

Three Trillion Drops of Water is a work of fiction. Any resemblance to actual events or
persons, living or dead is entirely coincidental. The author changed names and iden-
tifying details to protect the privacy of individuals. However, the events in Quang Tri
Province, South Vietnam are based on authentic letters written by a Marine Corps officer
serving in the war zone between January 1966 and September 1967.

In Loving memory of
BFDO and Roberts, LSAC
Died on 18 Sept 67
at the Cam Lo Bridge, Quang Tri Province, south Vietnam.
He gave his life so others could live.

Deep calls to deep in the roar of your waterfalls;
all your waves and breakers have swept over me.
By day the Lord directs his love, at night his song is with me—
a prayer to God of my life.
Psalm 42, 7-8

Chapter 1

Ellie stared at her distorted reflection in the deep, dark water surrounding her rubber float. She leaned forward and peered over the edge, hoping the lake's sandy bottom might appear, but all she saw were the opalescent fans of sunbeams fading into the blackness. The water hadn't been scary before, but it was now, same as in the nightmare that woke her up last week. She looked up at the ruffling surface around her float and imagined her brother's body sinking into the depths as she had seen it in her dream.

She had seen him drowning before he made it to shore.

The lake—a spring-fed, raggedy oval three football fields wide—had looked smaller when she stretched out on her new pink float to drift untethered just offshore. Now she bobbed alone in deep water, carried there at the whim of the breeze, like a bit of cork broken off a fisherman's line. She stared at her family's lake house, a distant square under the trees that ringed the water. Short, rapid breaths burst from her lips.

She had started close to shore with her twelve-year-old brother, Hank, nearby. A few hours before, he had raced across the worn planks of the dock and done a cannonball off the end, landing in the water with a *kuh-*

thoom. A crystal-clear, five-foot liquid wall shot into the air above his entry point. Ellie ran close behind him, her eight-year-old legs pumping hard to keep up before launching herself off the dock at full speed and piercing the water, feet first.

They had surfaced at the same time, laughing and squirting water through their teeth, then he put on his snorkeling gear while she settled back on her float, ankles crossed and hands behind her head. Ellie had gotten lost in the never-ending show of cloud formations in the bright blue sky, where the puffs became whatever she imagined as the whisper of a breeze rocked her pink island. It was 1956, and this lake house her grandfather had built near Tallahassee under hundred-year-old live oaks was the only place in the world where she could be free from the constraints placed on her by polite southern society. The lake was the only place Ellie could float alone in her make-believe world and watch the waterbirds fly overhead. But when she heard the rumble of distant thunder, she lifted her head, expecting to see Hank and the shore close by; instead, she discovered that the lake house was a far-off square on the horizon.

She slid her feet into the water, then sat up, straddling the float as if it were a horse. A steel band closed around her chest as her breathing picked up speed. She squeezed her legs around the float and gripped its sides, straining to see Hank's snorkel sticking out of the water. Then she heard a soft hissing sound, and tingles prickled her arms and legs. She stared at a row of tiny bubbles just above her hand, clutched on the left seam. Alone, too far out in the lake, she felt like a speck of lint on Mama's winter jacket. To her horror, the hiss grew louder, the bubbles got bigger, and the float began to soften under her.

The lapping waves disappeared as the water settled into a deep, deep stillness. The only sounds disturbing it were her heart's *thud-thud* and another roll of thunder in the distance.

"Hank! *Hank!* Help!" she yelled. Her voice rang across the water, but Hank did not respond. Frantic, she yelled again, her voice tight and higher. Hank still did not respond.

Something snapped in her mind. She had to get to Hank. Head down, she thrust her arms into the water and paddled with all her might toward the shore. The inky liquid pushed back, preventing her from going anywhere. She yelled again and again while her tired and burning arms splashed into the water.

When she had a chance to look up again, she saw Hank standing by the dock in knee-deep water. He stared in her direction with the mask pushed up on top of his head. She took in as much air as she could to yell for his attention.

Two figures stood at the end of the dock beyond Hank. Ellie could tell one of the people on the dock was Elmira in her gray maid's uniform, its white collar and cuffs bright against her mahogany skin. Elmira, who became "Mira" when Ellie's baby lips tripped over the whole name, shielded her eyes, her hands and face dark against the sky.

The other figure on the dock was Daddy. He stood, feet apart, in Bermuda shorts with his shirt sleeves rolled up and his fists planted on his hips. He turned to look at the approaching thunderhead, then back at Ellie. She was almost chest-deep in the water when she yelled again as loudly as she could. This time it was a scream.

Hank shouted, threw off his mask, and splashed over to Grandpa's old rowboat hitched to the dock. After quickly untying the rope, he climbed into the boat and yanked the outboard motor's cord in one smooth motion. Ellie heard a low, deep growl in the distance as the motor came to life. Hank sat down, then jerked the long steering handle, and the boat headed toward her, its bow throwing arcs of water from each side.

She took a deep breath and began to paddle harder. After an infinite moment, Hank was close enough for her to see his eyes fixed on her, his brows knit together in concern. He slowed the boat, cut the engine, and let inertia carry the craft to her. She still straddled the float even though its ends were the only parts visible above the water. Wide-eyed and winded, she held out her arms toward Hank. He glided closer, then reached down and grabbed one end of the sinking float with both hands. The rubber made a muted noise and wrinkled around his fingers.

"Grab my arm, El," he urged. "Get next to the boat, and pull yourself up."

Ellie held tight to his arm until she got near enough to grab the boat's side. With a mighty heave, she swung her right foot and then her right arm over the edge. She hauled herself up, rolled over the top, and landed with a flop in the belly of the boat. She sprawled breathless on the bottom boards with her eyes squeezed shut and the back of her head canted against the bow seat.

"You made it, Little Sis!" Hank said from his place by the motor.

"H-hank! I was so scared!" She swallowed hard, pressed her lips together, and tried not to cry.

"Guess the wind carried you out," he said. "Glad Grandpa told us to keep this old boat nearby when we're in the water. You okay?" Their eyes met, and she nodded.

"Yeah," she said and climbed up on the vacant seat facing him. She looked down into the water, but all she could see of her float was a pink shadow descending into the depths. They sat without talking while the boat rocked like a cradle.

Hank started the motor again and turned the boat toward shore. "We'll get back before the storm hits," he assured her.

Ellie turned to face forward so she could see ahead. Mesmerized, she watched the bow cut across the water and once again remembered last week's nightmare. In it, she and Hank were in water that began gushing—powerful, uncontrollable, pulling them apart. She fought it, and Hank tried to grab her. She reached for him—a fingertip away—but he went under, swirling foam in his wake.

Shaking off the chilling image, she glanced over her shoulder at Hank. He was at the helm with his eyes focused on the shore as the wind blew stronger. He was okay. It had just been a dream.

Their family always retreated to the lake during hot Florida summers. Most of the time, Mama read on the porch while Daddy studied medical journals or napped in a yard chair under the trees. Neither paid much attention to the children. Even at the lake, Mira kept an eye on them from the big kitchen window, the same way she had done for as long as Ellie could remember.

As Hank slowed the Evinrude to trolling speed, he said, "It wasn't your fault, El. The storm made the breeze pick up. It carried you out."

"The peacemaker fish," Ellie murmured to herself, remembering all the times she and Hank had watched the fish in his aquarium at home in a town near Tallahassee. Big brother and little sister often sat side by side in the comfy bucket chairs Mira had put there, watching the fish and talking. Hank had told her he learned a lot from his fish.

"Every tank has a boss," he'd explained. "That big one"—he pointed to a yellow fish with a red belly and muted gray stripes—"it's my peacemaker fish. It makes sure there is harmony in the tank. It helps the rest of the fish get along."

Ellie's thoughts of harmony disappeared as the boat neared the dock. Mira wrung her hands in the apron tied around her waist, but Daddy stayed put, not moving an inch. Thunder boomed, and Mira took a step toward the dock's edge.

Hank cut the engine and let the boat coast the rest of the way to the dock. A familiar, unpleasant heaviness formed in Ellie's chest, then grew into a huge ball and spread to her arms and legs. The feeling came over her the same way a panther had crouched, then pounced on a baby antelope in a film she had seen at school. The panther held down the tiny calf while it cried out and struggled to get free, but the calf was no match for the beast intent on killing it. As the boat bumped the dock, Ellie felt as if her panther were ready to strike. Then Mira's voice interrupted.

"Lord, chil', you gave me a start. You okay?" she asked, reaching toward the children.

"What in the world were you thinking, Eleanor?" Daddy's booming voice made Ellie cringe, just like that poor baby antelope. "You know not to go out that far! You know better than that. You didn't think, did you?" He glared down at her.

Mira turned to him and gestured toward the house. "Go on now, Dr. Mark," Mira said. "I'll see to her. Miss Lela is up on the po'ch, and she'll want to know what's goin' on. B'sides, it gonna be rainin' in a minute."

Ellie held her breath, relieved when Daddy turned and strode away down the dock. He stepped onto the sandy path and headed to the house, turning to look back as he passed under the trees. Then he yanked open the porch's screen door and disappeared as it slapped shut behind him while Mira waited for the children by the water.

As Hank put the boat back in its mooring place, Ellie got out and waded to where Mira stood on the shore, little clumps of wet sand on her shoe tops. She grabbed Ellie and bear-hugged her.

"Ya brotha done a good thing, baby," Mira said and kissed the top of Ellie's head. "Did you say 'thank you' and hug him? You is lucky to have him. Need to let 'im know that!"

"Oh, Mira," Ellie sobbed from her safe place in Mira's arms. "I was so scared! The lake was so big—I didn't think I was gonna make it back!"

"Don't worry, Baby E—you is okay now. I gotcha." Ellie let her small trembling body sink into Mira's hug as the first huge raindrops plopped into the water.

Mama fired Mira a month later. Hank was playing baseball at the park that day, but Ellie witnessed the whole thing from her place at the kitchen table. She was about to take a bite of one of Mira's fresh biscuits when Mama came to the arched doorway and announced she had something to say. Mira slid the roaster pan back into the oven before straightening up and looking at her.

"We don't need you anymore, Mira," Mama said. "I have to let you go. I can take care of my children without help. Anyway, you're making Ellie too soft and sensitive."

As Mira stood motionless by the stove, a hot mitt in each hand, Ellie's world stopped. Her heart sank, and her stomach turned sour, but she knew better than to question Mama or go to Mira for a hug. The only warmth in the room came from the biscuit, melted butter and honey drizzling down its side. She looked at Mira and watched the sweet brown face turn shocked, then sad.

Mira looked down at her shoes and squeezed her lips together, but she never uttered a word—not one word—even after she cleaned up the dinner dishes and gave the children extra long goodbye hugs. Hank wore his serious face, and Ellie cried, heaviness invading her.

That night, she fell asleep wondering if Mira had to leave because of her, wondering if she had caused the firing because caring for her slowed Mira's housework too often or because of the day at the lake when Hank had rescued her. *Was it because Mira comforted me that day? Was that what Mama meant by making me too soft?* Either way, guilt held her down like the panther on the tiny antelope because Ellie believed she had caused Mira's firing. It was a staggering weight for an eight-year-old to bear.

Three years later, eleven-year-old Ellie was sure she was an add-on, a second child born to make the family an even number. Without Mira, Hank was Ellie's only ally, the sole person who understood how much his sad-eyed, wispy-haired sister struggled under the weight of her lot in life. He had even tried to lighten her load by whispering to her that after Mama fired Mira, Daddy had secretly given Mira a job at his office.

The news helped a little, but it was the South, and Ellie was expected to be a good girl who followed the rules no matter how unfair things seemed. Rule one was that girls did what Daddy and Mama said without back talk or questions. The reply was to be "Yes, sir" or "No, sir," "Yes, ma'am" or "No, ma'am." Nothing else.

On one especially hot, humid Sunday morning, Ellie and Hank hurried from Sunday school to meet Mama and Daddy for church because Daddy said that good Baptists should always be in their pew on time—before Mrs. Winslow started playing the opening hymn. Ellie tried hard to do what Daddy said.

Hank smiled down at his little sister. "We won't be late," he said, patting her shoulder. "Don't worry."

Physically, there was no mistaking they were brother and sister. They were both lean, well-proportioned, and taller than average—but that's where the resemblance stopped. Hank's light brown hair was short, cut military style, while Ellie's blonde puffs framed her freckled, heart-shaped face, and flaxen strands touched her shoulders. Even so, the main difference between them was their eyes. Hank had green eyes that saw into a person's soul. Ellie's eyes were large and blue, dipping downward at the outer corners. She had sad eyes, some said. Thin lips and a solemn expression made her look waif-like—a lost little girl.

Hank, on the other hand, knew exactly where he was going. When he finished military prep school, he'd go to college, and then, according to Hank's plans, a long and memorable military career as an officer in the Marine Corps would follow. But wherever he went and whatever wonderful things he accomplished, Ellie knew that he'd always be there for her.

After Hank and Ellie joined their parents, Mama went into the pew first. She touched Hank's hand and shot him a small smile as she passed in front of him. Daddy gave his son a congratulatory pat on the shoulder on the way by, then took a seat next to Mama. Daddy motioned Ellie to sit down beside him, so she slipped in, small and skittish as a fawn in a clearing, then settled back between Daddy and Hank.

Ellie smoothed her skirt over her knees the way Mama had taught her and looked around the sanctuary at the bald men sitting beside their wives in the pews in front of her. Smooth, rounded, evenly spaced, the bare heads reminded her of eggs lined up in a carton.

The preacher talked longer than usual, and Ellie began to squirm. She crossed and uncrossed her legs several times, trying to get comfortable. Her skirt had hitched up, leaving the exposed backs of her legs stuck to the wooden pew so they made a squeech sound every time she moved. Embarrassed, she looked down the pew and caught a glimpse of Mama on the other side of Daddy—head tilted forward, eyes cold and piercing, glaring at Ellie.

"Stop wiggling. Sit still," Mama mouthed from across Daddy's chest, a frown visible on her otherwise pretty face.

"I have to go to the bathroom," Ellie whispered, scrunching up her nose.

Daddy leaned close to her ear and said, "You should have gone before church. You'll have to wait."

"B-but, you said . . . " Ellie sank back against the hard pew and sighed. "Yes, sir." There was no use trying to explain why she hadn't taken the time to stop at the bathroom.

Hank tapped her leg and shot her a conspiratorial look. He cocked his head toward the end of the pew. A moment later, the congregation rose for the final hymn, and he took her hand. They slipped out of their seats, and he led her up the aisle to the bathroom off the vestibule.

"No one noticed. We can meet Mama and Daddy here when they come out," he said.

"They'll be mad," Ellie worried.

"I'll handle it. You better get going!" As she started toward the bathroom, she heard him add, "You just have to know when to make your exit, Little Sis—that's all! Don't worry. I'm the peacemaker fish, remember?"

His words brought back another water nightmare the night before. She had woken up sweating and afraid when angry currents carried a yellow striped fish away to the depths, its red belly turned up as it sank. She'd felt worse when she remembered that Mira had told her to pay attention to her dreams because they could be about things to come. *Why do I keep having these horrible nightmares about water?*

Chapter 2

In September, 1966, eighteen-year-old Ellie forced herself to step into her future at Carter College, not far from Tallahassee. Mama had said Carter was close enough to commute from home, and she didn't think Ellie would make it in a large school like FSU. Daddy had said he didn't care where she went as long as she got good grades and didn't waste his money.

Hank had been more encouraging. "Look at it this way—your freshman year is an adventure no matter where you are," he said, his green eyes intent. "I had a ball during my first year of college. You're on your own—plus, you can explore! You'll figure things out. I got faith in you, Little Sis."

Ellie didn't agree that starting college was exciting or adventurous. Clutching a campus map and a schedule card, she set out to find her first class—English 101. Half an hour later, she was in front of the building she needed. When she had first started searching, she wasn't the only freshman with a map and a card, but the others had evaporated and left her alone, stranded on the sidewalk, staring up at the vast brick and stone building. A sign on the front proclaimed it "Eddings Hall, English Department." She shuddered, rechecked her card, and forced herself to go up the steps.

The classroom she was looking for was down a long, dark hall. She stood outside the door, took a deep breath, and—only because Daddy would be mad if she didn't—willed herself to walk into the classroom. She stopped two steps inside and looked around at a cavernous lecture hall that buzzed with conversation. Every part of her wanted to run away. She stared at the rows of small, flat-topped desks set less than an elbow's length apart in semicircular ranks, each row higher than the one in front of it. It looked like a battalion of soldiers marching into battle. A podium in front faced the ranks like a single adversary.

Ellie looked around and saw a few available desks sprinkled among students who sat upright, leaned back, or slouched in their seats. A few faces turned to look as she tried to disappear while she scanned the rows, only to discover there was no way she could sit by herself. She finally spotted two vacant seats on an upper tier, partway down the row. When she reached the row, she started toward the empty places, muttering apologies and attempting not to step on anyone's toes. She edged past the first empty desk and eased into one next to a clean-cut guy on her right. A dimple caught her eye when he smiled up at her, and she managed a meek smile, but neither said anything.

The closeness bothered her, so she tried to scoot away, but the desks were bolted in place. Forced to stay put, she clenched her teeth and looked around, listening to nearby conversations, trying to take in her new life.

A long-haired girl in flared pants and a loose blouse flopped down in the empty seat to Ellie's left side, interrupting her thoughts. The girl said something that sounded like "hey," but nothing else.

Ellie noticed other girls wearing slim pants or skirts with pressed blouses like hers, but a group in front of her wore gauzy, loose-fitting tops with well-worn jeans or one-piece dresses that flowed to the floor. It was apparent that a couple of the girls didn't wear bras.

"Yeah, it was a great party," one was saying. "That guy—the one with the long, blond hair—I don't know his name, but he was a great kisser!" The others giggled and said they hoped he'd come to their next party.

A guy leaned over the seats and said something that made them laugh. He flashed a two-finger peace sign and said something about an anti-Vietnam War demonstration. The girls nodded, and he sat back in his seat. Ellie listened to the conversation turn to drinking or getting it on—having sex, Ellie surmised. She had little in common with them because she had not partied nor gotten drunk in high school, and her constrained, sheltered upbringing said that under no circumstances did young ladies talk about sex. This scene, these people, their styles, their words—they were foreign to her. She fidgeted and looked at her watch while their words bounced around in her brain.

Ellie slumped against the back of her seat, crossed her ankles, and tried to disappear while she waited for class to start. Being a college student didn't signal adulthood or a time to break free; it meant she would be alone, adrift, without a familiar course to follow. She shifted in her seat and wondered what might lay ahead.

To Ellie, it seemed her misfortune was to start her future when political and social chaos reigned and long-held beliefs and traditions were being challenged, and like most Americans, she felt caught in the turmoil of society's changing rules. Three months earlier, Hank had told his family he was to deploy to Vietnam. His news had left Ellie certain the Fates had spun her life of heavy cloth. That very night, another water nightmare had woken her up, and it was worse than the others because Hank was swept away—completely gone—in black, angry, dirty, rushing water. *Did that mean anything?* She hoped not.

As a child, she had felt as if she were a dinghy tethered to her parents, dragged behind them with no power of her own. Bobbing along in their wake, she was forced to follow, no matter how rough the seas. Hank was her lifeline then, a ray of sun touching her shoulders, warming and reassuring her. She had no idea what would happen to her when he was gone.

Ellie stumbled upon her "special place" late one September day after class. As she wandered across campus in a sea of chattering students, she looked ahead and noticed a majestic oak tree in a football-field-size area at the edge of campus. Huge, gnarled branches reached almost eighty feet into the sky, and getting closer, she saw that the oak grew on the banks of a pond nestled in the junction of two sidewalks that formed an L-shape near Eddings Hall and the biology building. Ornamental vegetation and a grassy fringe encircled the water. The stark campus buildings dwarfed a bubbling spring in the pond's center that sent concentric circles rippling across the surface to end in tiny waves that lapped against the bank under the tree.

There Ellie found a wooden bench leaning against the base of the knobby tree trunk, and she sat down under the branches. She looked up through the fluttering leaves and felt calm begin to overtake her fear. She wondered how something as mighty as that tree could soften life's hard edges. *Why is this spot so compelling?* she mused.

Like the click of a View-Master, an image popped into her mind. This place felt the same as being under the trees at the lake house. She rested her head against the rough bark and stared into the water. Campus noises faded. Her world was still, and she felt invisible to students on the sidewalks or people crossing the street beyond the pond.

She watched antiwar protestors gather and get ready to march down the street. Their loose clothes adorned with feathers or beads—fashions that were becoming the norm on campus—fascinated her. The panther breathed in her ear and said the allure wasn't right because Daddy had said the demonstrators were draft dodgers, disloyal cowards, but Ellie could not take her eyes off the display.

Ellie felt a heaviness in her chest. The panther was getting ready to strike, but then the trembling leaves drew her eyes up to sunlight sparkling through the branches. She took a deep breath and relaxed. Her tree offered calm, not criticism or judgments, so she was safe in its shade. It was her thinking tree, her place to sink into oblivion, watch the world, and examine her thoughts without worrying about pleasing anyone.

She recalled the family dinner when Hank had told them he was to be in Vietnam by January 1967. His girlfriend, Patti, had joined them for the meal, and with her beside him, he gave details about travel, then said it took about a week or more for letters to go back and forth, depending on combat conditions.

"I want you all to write as often as you can," he said, then cleared his throat, stood up, and held out his hand to Patti. She rose beside him, her tanned skin and strawberry-blonde hair glowing.

"We have an announcement," he said, looking from Mama to Daddy to Ellie. "We're going to get married in November after I finish Basic School in Virginia." Hank kissed Patti's hand, and she moved closer to him.

"What do you think, El?" Hank asked.

"I'm happy for you both," she said, a lump threatening to close her throat. She shifted in her chair as reality set in. Too soon Hank would leave Florida's oak hammocks and spring-fed lakes for the tepid, tea-colored rice paddies and jungle canopies of Southeast Asia that she'd heard about, where the vegetation was so thick noontime was as dark as midnight.

No one said a word for a moment. Daddy pushed his chair back as a grin broke across his face, while Mama looked at the couple and smiled politely. Ellie leaned back against her chair and looked at her lap. She raised her chin a bit when Hank continued.

"We both know that I have to go to Vietnam right after the wedding. Patti understands why I chose the Marines, and she knows this is part of being an officer's wife." His voice was clear, unwavering. He studied his family before he turned to Patti, who spoke with the same clarity.

"I know he has to go overseas because communism is a malignancy destroying everyone and everything in its path," Patti said. "Hank's mission in Vietnam is to stop the spread of that cancer before all of Asia is lost." Then she put her arm around Hank's waist and pulled him to her.

"We have everything planned," Hank said. "I'll be at Basic from July until November. I'll come back here, and we'll be married the day after Thanksgiving and then have a couple of weeks for a honeymoon. After that, we'll go to California, where we'll have our first Christmas and New Year's together. I'll deploy to Vietnam from there. Patti wants to stay here until I come back, so we'll need to find an apartment before I leave." Hank looked at Ellie for a moment, then turned to his parents.

"We'd like to spend our honeymoon at the lake house," Patti said.

"No problem," Daddy chimed in. Mama smiled and said it would be a bit cool at the lake in November, but she would be sure the house was clean and ready for them.

Ellie didn't add to the conversation. All she could think about was that with Hank gone, she would be on her own, and this was different from him going to boarding school or college. Those absences had been brief, and he was back home in the summers. This time he would be on the other side of the world. Totally absent. Something in her wanted to pull free of her family's tether, to search for her mooring, but stronger was fear of the endless sea of unknowns ahead.

"We've been talking about who we want at our wedding. And Mom," Hank said, turning to his mother, "I want Mira to be there."

Mama's smile disappeared. "Absolutely not," she stated.

Daddy grasped the arms of his chair and set his jaw. He stared at his wife while Hank and Patti sat down. Ellie was mute, her hands in her lap, squeezed together so tight they hurt.

Eyes on his mother, Hank inhaled and spoke without hesitating. "Yes, she will be there, Mama. I don't mean any disrespect to you, but she took care of Ellie and me from the time I was a baby. Plus, I talked with her practically every week during the summer when I helped clean up around Dad's office. She loves us, and I want her at my one—and only—wedding."

"Well, to have her there is disrespectful to me." Mama murmured.

Hank put his arm around Patti and stared at the table. Ellie's heart pounded so hard she thought everyone could hear it. She wanted to help Hank and tell Mama she felt it was right for Mira to be there, but the panther had her by the throat.

Hank shifted in his chair and said, "No, Mama, this has nothing to do with you. Patti and I wanted to have the wedding at our family's church here because the sanctuary is large, and the guest list will be long since you and Daddy are obligated to invite everyone in town. We know that." He waited for a heartbeat before continuing, "But we can just as well have a smaller wedding somewhere else. We explained everything to Patti's mom, so she's happy to come here, but I think she'd be just as happy to go to another place." Hank kept his eyes on his mother, who inhaled and spread both hands flat on the table on either side of her pie plate.

Mama exhaled and said, "So it means that much for you to have Mira there. Is that right?"

"Yes, it does, Mama," Hank said. He and Patti stared at her.

"Well, in that case, I won't say anything else. Just know it's not my wish."

"For God's sake, Lela, I don't think anyone could ever misunderstand what you wanted," said Daddy, his cold eyes boring into Mama's. That was the end of the conversation.

Later, after Mama and Daddy had gone to bed, Ellie found Hank and Patti still on the porch. "I came to say good night," Ellie said.

"Hey, Little Sis," Hank said. "Listen, I'll be away at Basic for twenty-one weeks, but time will go faster if you help Patti with the wedding plans. Besides, you can tell me all about your freshman adventures when I get back!"

Chapter 3

Ellie discovered that her classes temporarily distracted her from her worries about her brother's absence and she found another distraction in helping Patti with wedding plans. Reality kicked in only when she heard news reports or read a newspaper containing unsettling reports of body counts from the war zone. Such stories inevitably brought sleepless nights or terrifying nightmares.

Mercifully, the nightmares stopped when Hank arrived back in town just a few days before Thanksgiving, and Mama's traditional turkey and dressing took a back seat to the joyful homecoming and pending marriage, planned for the day after the holiday. The ceremony was simple, elegant, and bathed in the scent of fresh pine from holiday decorations in the sanctuary. From her place with the other bridesmaids, Ellie watched—torn between joy for her brother and fear for his future—as he vowed to love, honor, and protect Patti until death parted them. Ellie prayed that Hank would be an old, old man before that inevitable parting came for the happy couple.

After the ceremony, she lingered close to him, enjoying how Hollywood-handsome he looked in his blue dress uniform, while the photographer concentrated on placing Patti in front of the altar for a formal wedding portrait.

"I'm glad you married Patti," Ellie said. "I want you to be happy, but I miss you already."

The photographer beckoned to Hank, who smiled and whispered, "You'll be okay, Little Sis." She felt a soft squeeze on her elbow as he stepped around her to take his place beside Patti.

At the reception, Ellie studied her parents as they greeted the guests and wondered if anyone but her noticed Mama's icy stare at Daddy when he shook hands, laughed, and kibitzed with people passing by. On the opposite side of the room, Hank stood next to Patti, her hand tucked into the crook of his elbow. When Ellie came over to join them, Hank reached toward her with his free arm.

"Hey, Big Brother," she said quietly. "Patti looks beautiful—not even tired after shaking so many hands!"

"Isn't she marvelous? I'm so thankful she's my wife!"

Ellie started to say something but was interrupted by one of Hank's Marine buddies who pushed through the crowd, squeezed in close, and began pumping Hank's hand.

"Way to go, pal," the other Marine said with a wide smile. "You two make a great couple. Thought that ever since you told me about her at Basic School. Glad you made her a Marine Corps wife before we deploy. Oorah!"

Ellie stepped away, left the crush of guests, and found a quiet nook with a couple of chairs in a bay window on a far wall of the large room. She sat down and watched the crowd until she saw Mira making her way toward her. Ellie jumped up and wrapped her arms around her beloved maid.

"You're here! I'm so glad," Ellie said, comforted when Mira's arm lingered around her waist.

Mira's curls, shiny with pomade, set off the pink floral design of her Sunday dress with matching wide-brimmed hat. Ellie thought she looked beautiful. Still holding Ellie's hand, Mira eased into one of the chairs but kept her eyes on Ellie as they sat down.

"How ya doin', baby?" Mira's voice was soothing, welcoming. "You look so pretty. Bet you is gonna miss that big brother of yours."

"Yes, I am."

"Hank tol' me you was still livin' at home."

"So far. I guess it's okay for now, but Patti and Hank said I could have the extra bedroom in their apartment if I want to stay there. It's not far from campus."

"Well, that's good." Mira said and shifted her eyes toward Ellie's parents. "Are you thinkin' about that?"

"I guess. Hank said he's worried about Patti being alone, so it would help if I lived there too." Ellie shrugged and looked at her feet. "I don't think Mama and Daddy would miss me anyway."

"Oh, they'll miss you plenty, even if they don't show it," Mira said warmly as she lifted Ellie's chin with her forefinger.

"I guess," Ellie mumbled, "but I've never thought they liked me very much." Mira lowered her hand to pat Ellie's knee, and Ellie shrugged again. "Mama's hard to figure out—that's all."

"Oh, but she loves ya, baby." Mira's head tilted, and the corners of her mouth curved up as she assumed the Old South dialect she reserved for speaking to blood kin or those she loved like kin. "She jus' diff'rent from us cause she from the No'ph, 'n' she keep everythin' inside, 'fraid to let her feelin's show. She don't get southern ways. All her life, she jus' done what she s'pposed to do, 'n' that be hard 'n' made her hard— on the outside, anyway."

"I don't understand that, Mira," Ellie said, picking at her thumbnail with her finger. "Hank always tells me the same thing. He says it isn't my fault Daddy and Mama act the way they do. So why do they act that way? I don't understand, and I don't think I ever will."

"It's cause if she say how she feel, she's 'fraid she'll show folks how to hurt her. Ya' mama's sof' on the inside—same as you, same as me—'n' she reckons it be easier to close up like a clam do to protec' its sof' insides. She never wanted you to git hurt the way she been, but she didn't know how to teach you any better. Bein' a mama is a tough job, 'n' I fear she 'bout ready to jes' give up."

"I remember overhearing Mama and Daddy arguing a few years ago," Ellie said softly, staring at the floor. "She told Daddy that some woman had scolded her, saying she should just enjoy Daddy's wealth and make a comfortable home for him and his children, which ought to be enough for any woman. When Daddy agreed with that woman, Mama got angry and told him she didn't want to stay home and keep house for him and us; she said she wanted to accomplish something on her own. Daddy kept asking why taking care of a family wasn't enough for her, and she yelled and said he would never understand her—never." Ellie paused as she looked back up at the milling crowd. "It was awful to hear them fight about such things. I wish I'd never overheard all that."

Mira waited a moment before asking, "Did you know my mama tended ya' daddy's mama when she was laborin' to birth him? I was fo' years old. Him and me, we go way back. We was raised in the same way, together, in the same house, 'n' we get along cause we understan' one another. But ya' daddy and ya' mama, well . . . it ain't the same for them."

Ellie stared at Mira, then said, "Weren't you angry when Mama fired you? Hank said she didn't even let you come visit when you asked to see us."

"No, chil'. Life too short to hol' grudges. You gots to forgive. Ya' mama come here 'n' had to give herse'f up, which got her all resentful 'n' angry. Hank's the only one she let inside her head. Guess that's cause he was her firs' baby—or mebbe cause he a boy. She don' know how to teach you south'n-lady rules or what else to do wif you. Ya' daddy and Hank had a nat'ral father-son relation. I saw it grow every summer when Hank was home. It growed more man to man the older Hank got, 'n' I know'd that even tho' they disagree sometime, Hank can cut through Dr. Mark's hard words 'n' draw out the best of him. Us women ain't got that same opportunity. We taught not to argue, but to sweet talk in order to git what we want."

"Well, according to what I hear on campus," said Ellie, "that's changing."

"Lotsa good things is happenin', but ya' mama got stuck livin' wit' th' old ways. Only thing is, what kin she do about it now? I 'member once when I was fixin' dinner, I hear her tell Dr. Mark she din' wanna be the cause of a broken home. She said her chil'ren deserve better. That's why she took a back seat to yo' daddy's wishes even tho' it grates her down."

Mira patted Ellie's arm and studied her stunned face for a moment. "Hank said he tol' ya' mama that he knew she be the one keepin' the fam'ly together. He say he know his daddy be easier on other people but hard on his own fam'ly, but she 'n' ya' daddy musta loved one another once 'n' she ought not forget that. Hank tol' her he 'preciated her being a good, strong mama 'n' that you would, too, in time."

Mira paused, smiling a rueful smile. "On'y reason I'm tellin' you all this is to he'p you unnerstan' you ain't the problem."

Ellie lowered her eyes and asked, "Did Hank tell you what Mama said after he told her those things?"

"Yeah, he sho did, 'n' when he did, I was so s'prised I near dropped a plate! Ya' mama tol' him to go 'n' live his life. She say, 'Find someone who don't have to prove herse'f to you. Love her as she is, 'n' she'll love you back the 'xact same way.'"

Mira lifted her chin and nodded to herself. "I b'lieve that conversation is what keeps ya' mama goin'. Hank was a gift that keeps her going year after year. I fear fo' her when he goes off to th' other side of the world."

Ellie choked back tears. "I'm afraid for him too."

Ellie and Mira stayed in their private corner, talking until it was time to throw rice, wave goodbye, and give the newlyweds a happy send off. Ellie fell asleep that night with Mira's words tucked safely away in her brain so she could revisit them under her thinking tree.

Two weeks passed before Ellie saw Hank again. She was standing outside their parents' house, waiting and watching for him with her feet rooted to the cold, hard cement driveway. Her heart pounded, beating as hard and heavy as a pile driver. It was time to say goodbye to her brother, knowing it would be thirteen months before she saw him again.

Soon Hank would board a plane and fly to the other side of the world, and Ellie felt powerless. Even worse, she was scared and worried about what might happen to him. He had been with her her whole life, and she had believed he would be safe and sound forever. Her nightmares had changed that, and for the first time in her life, dread overcame her like a river overflowing its banks, flooding her senses, nearly suffocating her.

Her chest tightened when his car turned into the driveway and stopped. *No, no, no! It can't be time already!* Ellie watched as he paused, took his hands off the wheel, and turned to Patti to say something that made her nod. Looking every inch a Marine in his crisp travel uniform, he stepped out of the car and came toward Ellie.

"I'll be right back," he said, laying a hand on her shoulder for a moment before walking past her and going up the front steps. He disappeared into the house, and Ellie's throat closed. She wanted time to go backward and all of this—the war, body counts, nightmares—to go away, but he emerged a few minutes later with his jaw set, his eyes straight ahead. He paused on the top step and looked at the treetops lining the street, then stood still for a moment before he lowered his eyes to meet Ellie's. Time slowed to a crawl when he strode to Ellie and embraced her.

"Goodbye, Little Sister. I love you."

"I love you too," she said, barely getting the words out. She buried her face in his shoulder and held her breath to keep from sobbing.

He let her cling for a moment before putting his hands on her shoulders, easing her away so that he could look into her eyes. "Listen. You take care of yourself. Write me lots of letters, okay? And don't let Mama and Daddy's stuff get you off track. Their problems have nothing to do with you. Hear me?"

She lowered her head and mumbled, "Uh-huh," struggling to hold back the tears.

When she finally lifted her eyes, Hank smiled and hugged her again before turning to get into the car. She waved, the tears now rolling down her cheeks. She kept waving as the car turned, went down the street, and left her alone on the driveway. She didn't stop waving until the car was out of sight.

Staring at the spot where Hank had been a few minutes ago, Ellie heard a car coming and her eyes jerked to the street. *Maybe he's coming back!* When the car went past, she began to sob and turned to run into the house. She stopped short when she saw her stricken parents sitting in the living room. There they were, Dr. and Mrs. Dennis—stone-cold symbols of success in this affluent community. Surrounded by beautiful, costly furnishings, they sat like a two-faced Mount Rushmore in separate chairs—not touching, mute, and sharing nothing as their only son's goodbye hung heavily in the air between them.

Ellie didn't know what to say, so she ran upstairs as tears flooded down her cheeks and her breathing hitched. All she wanted was the safety of her lonely room, where she flopped across her bed and tried to push away her choking fears—fear for Hank, fear for herself, fear of the future.

Most brothers teased their little sisters, but Hank never had. Years ago, when Ed Sullivan showed a film about the communists dropping an A-bomb on New York, Hank had let her curl up next to him and cry for a while. The children in the film were about Ellie's age, and the images of nuclear destruction had scared her to death, but even then, Hank's arm around her felt strong and steady.

What will my life become without him to lean on?

She remembered how Hank had told her life was like a river flowing along a course it had carved for itself out of a rocky landscape, always finding new paths because nothing could withstand its pounding force. Without her big brother to help her navigate the conflicting currents and treacherous undertows, Ellie felt adrift, powerless, and she feared she would soon be swept away by the wild and raging whitewater.

After Patti and Hank left for Camp Pendleton, Ellie's holidays were a jumble of lights, music, and a couple of frightening dreams of water that slid away in the early morning light. Christmas and New Year's Day quietly came and went, and when Winter Trimester classes resumed the second week of January 1967, louder anti-Vietnam sentiments began to take hold across the nation. Protests erupted on college campuses, and Carter College was no exception. Hank was in Vietnam now, and Patti had returned to their apartment, but Ellie felt a hole in the middle of her life. When she saw antiwar placards proclaiming Vietnam a lost cause or our military doomed pawns in a deadly, unjust war, her world darkened and the empty hole in her life deepened with each passing day.

The lawn outside her parents' house looked like a dull, winter-green shag carpet stretching from the driveway to the front steps. Ellie parked by the garage just as Hank had done a month earlier and rushed up the steps to her parents' front door. Mama didn't like it when she came home late and ruined dinner—Mama's main source of pride—so no matter what she was working on, Ellie always hurried home from campus because she didn't want to cause problems.

She ran her hand over her hair to be sure it looked good when Daddy saw it, because it was so different from her usual permed, teased, and hair-sprayed style. She'd had it cut only an hour ago in a Mary Travers–style, which left her shiny blonde hair swinging loose and free below her chin. Taking a deep breath, she pushed down the thumb grip and pushed open the door. The heavy brass handle was cool against her palm, and the dark living room was cave-like compared to the warm afternoon sun of the bright January day.

Daddy sat in his easy chair reading a news magazine under a floor lamp that illuminated his forehead. His frown was visible above the publication's masthead, and his fists were gripping the magazine so tightly the pages wrinkled. Ellie entered the room quietly and moved closer to get a better look at him, studying the deep furrows of his brow. Downturned lips, pressed tight, left no question about his mood, and she knew this was not a good time to speak to him.

He began muttering, and, before she had time to retreat, she heard a few words that grabbed her attention. One was "Vietnam." And another was "Marines." *What is he reading? Is it something about Hank?* She inched closer but stayed behind the bulwark of his footstool.

"This is unbelievable," he growled louder with his eyes glued to the pages. "Good God—they put these boys in an impossible situation."

She had heard confusing statements about the war on campus—some stated as fact and others as opinion—but she wanted to know what was really going on. The thought of asking her father about anything put a knot in her stomach, but she needed to know—she *had* to know—about Hank, so she took a breath and spoke.

"W-what's wrong, Daddy?"

The magazine collapsed onto his lap, its pages smashing against his leg. He closed his eyes and bowed his head as one hand clutched his temple. He could have been praying, but that was unlikely since clenched teeth worked his jaw. Ellie stood still and felt preadolescent again.

Daddy did not answer. *What's the matter? Why doesn't he say anything?* His hand fell onto the mangled magazine, and he looked up, finally acknowledging her, but his eyes swept over her like he was taking inventory. When he spoke, his voice dripped antipathy, his eyes drilling into her.

"What have you done to yourself?" he barked. "Your hair makes you look like one of those horrible hippies on the news. Don't you know they hate your brother and all he stands for? I don't want you looking like one of them!"

Stricken with self-doubt, Ellie touched her hair and wanted to run away, but she was in too far to back out of the confrontation. She stared back at her father, too afraid to reply immediately, and the panther attacked, spreading its weight over her body. Hank's voice rang in her ears: it was not her fault Daddy was mad. She hung onto Hank's words and struggled to survive the painful encounter.

"M-m-maybe I shouldn't have gotten it done this way, but it's easy to take care of," she stammered. "That's all, Daddy. All the girls are getting their hair cut this way." She paused a moment, trying to find a way to get beyond the ridiculous subject of her hair. "I can always just put a scarf on, Daddy, but I want to know what you were reading. Is it about Hank? Where is he? Has something happened to him?"

"You won't understand what's going on over there any more than other idealistic college students," Daddy hissed. "You've never been in a war. You can't understand—not the way I do. I was patching up soldiers fresh off the front lines back when nobody asked stupid questions like whether we should be there. I patched up our boys, then sent them back to fight the Nazis whether I liked it or not. Some were so badly hurt I couldn't save them, so I watched men—young men like Hank—bleed and die. That's reality. That's war."

Ellie wondered for a minute if her father even remembered she was there as he stared blankly at the magazine before he continued more quietly: "This thing in Vietnam is not going well. Hank's up against two enemies. One is the North Vietnamese Army—the NVA—and the other is the VC, the Viet Cong. We're finding out they're skilled jungle fighters. Better trained than our military or political leaders thought. That puts Hank in more danger."

Daddy looked up, unblinking, before adding, "And now antiwar demonstrators are howling that our boys are baby killers. Does *that* answer your question?" The rage in his eyes dared Ellie to question him further.

His cold stare made her take a step back, but she needed to know about her brother. "Well, I understand that war is bad and this war is really bad, but what I was wondering is if you even know where Hank is." She was shocked by her persistence, and even more shocked by her father's answer.

"Your brother is headed for the thick of it. The Marines are defending Leatherneck Square. Con Thien. Almost in North Vietnam. He'll be in the jungle, but how in God's name can they fight when their weapons don't work, tanks are useless, and there aren't enough men to get the job done right?" His eyes moved past her and took on a distant look, but only for a moment. "This is a politician's war with no good military strategy to win." He raised the magazine as if he wanted desperately to go back to his reading. "Why must you be so intent on upsetting me, Eleanor? You're simply making things worse. Just let it go."

Ellie knew that was all the information she would get, but questions continued to plague her. *What kind of danger is it? Where exactly is*

Hank, and who is there with him? She opened her mouth to ask, but Daddy looked up and glared at her above the pages with such a wild look in his eyes that Ellie knew better than to ask any more questions.

"Yes, sir. I understand," she whimpered and looked away. The tiny antelope was no match for the panther, and she was no match for the guilt that Daddy's words brought.

A piece of white paper open on the table beside him covered with familiar handwriting caught her attention. *Is that Hank's first letter from the war zone?* Before he left, Hank had explained that it would take about ten days for letters to go back and forth, so his news would be old by the time letters arrived. Patti had said she would write every day. Mama and Daddy wrote to him individually, and Ellie planned to write her own letters, but Hank said he doubted he'd have enough time to answer each one separately, so he would send one letter addressed to all three of them. Ellie was content to read Hank's letters after her parents finished with them, but tonight she was anxious for dinner to be over so she could read this one.

A clatter from the kitchen made her and her daddy both wince.

"Stop talking about the war—both of you!" Mama called out. "Words won't do any good. Besides, dinner is ready. Come to the table."

Ellie heard the clink of ice against glass and knew that Mama had poured rich, brown liquid into her water glass. Ellie could almost smell the alcohol because Mama had had a drink in her hand most of the time since Hank left.

Daddy stood up and brushed by Ellie. "Your mother is an ostrich," he muttered.

Denied peace of mind and forced to comply, Ellie grabbed Hank's letter and shoved it into her pocket, then followed Daddy to the table. She shouldn't have to fight for information about Hank, and a nagging feeling crept up her spine. She wondered if things with her parents would ever change.

An internal buzzer went off, and she knew the answer. She could not stay here, but when—how—would she tell them? The winter trimester ended in April, so maybe that would be a good time, a natural time, to make the break. But could she stand it here until then? April was months away—a long time. She didn't think she would make it.

Chapter 4

Safe in her room, Ellie held her breath and pulled Hank's letter from her pocket. It was a week old, but old news was better than no news at all. She had to find out what was happening to Hank, so she propped her feet up and started reading.

5 January 1967
Dong Ha, Quang Tri Province, South Vietnam

Dear Mom, Dad, and Ellie,

How is every little thing? Got here just fine and am getting settled in. Flew over from LA on a commercial jet so we were pretty comfortable. Man-o-man, was it hard to leave my Patti waving 'bye on the tarmac. Had a short stop in Hawaii but no time to enjoy it. Took 13 hours to get to Okinawa from there. Got my gear and had enough shots to protect me from anything a person could possibly think of before we took off for the short hop to VN with a little over 150 other 3/4 Marines. Flew into Da Nang, and that's the last I'll see of human comforts for a while. At least that's what the old timers say (those who've been here for six months or so). I'm up in Dong Ha now. It's pretty far north, not far from North Vietnam, so I'll have a little time to write while I'm here getting adjusted. I'm kinda getting used to the weather. It's hot now and it rains a good bit.

Dong Ha's up North in Quang Tri Province near Leatherneck Square where most of the USMC has been since the beginning of this year.

Alarmed, Ellie looked away from the page, then hugged her knees because she had heard news reports mention high body counts in Leatherneck Square. But this letter was not a broadcaster's dispassionate voice stating a fact. It was her brother telling her he was heading into danger. She steeled herself before reading the rest of the letter.

Dong Ha is a big combat base and LZ (landing zone) with lots of aircraft coming and going. Choppers (a.k.a. helos) fly in and out all the time and so do fat-bellied C-130s that bring supplies—pallets of them—to be unloaded so that material and equipment is stacked & ready for distribution to troops fighting in the field. Dong Ha is a huge tent city with Quonsets, roads, and stuff. This place is a prime target for NVA & VC—the enemy—but I won't say what Marines call them because I'm a gentleman! When it's time to join the jungle fight, we'll get on a helo and move from here to field positions closer to the Square or the DMZ.

Gotta go, short on time tonight. I love to get letters because it feels like being home for a few minutes when I read them. I'm gonna write Patti letters of her own so if I run out of time to write you all, she can fill you in on my whereabouts. No one has a better family than me!

I love you and miss you,
Hank

PS They make sure we get our mail even when we are in the field, so I'll get yours no matter what's going on. It'll take longer for my letters to get to you when I'm in the jungle, but please keep those cards and letters comin' my way. I need them.

Ellie woke next morning with Hank's letter still pressed to her chest. As she swung her feet to the floor and sat on the side of the bed, she couldn't stop thinking about what Hank had written, so she decided to get going and spend the day on campus in hopes that would distract her from her worries. Besides, she wanted to be anywhere but home after last night's confrontation with Daddy, so she showered, dressed, and focused on making a stealthy exit out the front door.

The aroma of coffee greeted her as she tiptoed down the stairs and past a strip of light under Daddy's den door. Then she hurried toward the front door, but the phone rang an instant before she reached for the doorknob.

"It's for you, Ellie," Mama called out. "Pick up the extension."

Ellie stopped short, shifted her load of books, grabbed the receiver, and heard a welcome voice greet her.

"Hi, Ellie!" Patti said. "I know it's early, but I wanted to catch you before you left this morning to ask if you'd like to come to the apartment for dinner tonight."

"Oh, wow, yes. I'd love to come!"

"Okay, good," Patti said, sounding upbeat. "Don't rush to get here because I'm going to fix something simple so we can have time to talk over a glass of wine. You don't mind having wine, do you?"

"I'll try a little," Ellie said. It felt good to allow herself that decision, so her day looked brighter already. Dinner with Patti would be relaxing, but first, she had to tell Mama her plans. Ellie hesitated, hoping her mother wouldn't get upset, but excitement overcame her doubts, so she went to the kitchen.

Mama was at the table, and the smells of smoke and coffee hit Ellie before she got through the door. Mama looked up when Ellie told her about the dinner plans with Patti.

"Then I won't expect you home this evening." Mama's eyes swept over Ellie from head to foot. "It's a good thing you had enough sense to wear a sweater this morning," she said with a dismissive wave of her cigarette.

Ellie watched the confetti of ashes litter the floor and said, "See you later, Mama." She walked to her car with her mind on her mother's wave. *Bet she won't miss me tonight because she doesn't care, and so what. Neither do I.* Ellie drove to campus feeling emotions swirl around her and the panther growling in her ear.

That afternoon Ellie visited her thinking tree instead of going to the library to study because she couldn't concentrate on anything. She wasn't sure what Hank's letter meant or what dangers he faced by now, and she didn't know what to do about moving out of Mama and Daddy's house. She settled on the bench and pulled her sweater closer around her chest to let random thoughts, like the tiny leaves on the pond, float through her mind before coming to rest on the December day when she, Mama, and Daddy had driven to the lake so they could spend a day with Hank and Patti before they left for California.

On that day, Daddy had gripped the stirring wheel, the sunlight flickering on the tight muscles that worked above his jaw. Mama, beside him in the front seat, had been looking out the side window with one of her shoulders scrunched up against the glass, the other arm extended across the seat back as if she were pushing him away to create as much distance between them as possible. Ellie had closed her eyes and sunk into the rich, brown leather of the back seat, but this luxury could not take away the poverty of her spirit as her mind spun, thoughts about Hank tangling as tight as a backlash from an amateur angler's bad cast.

When they arrived at the lake house, just as the sun set over the wetlands, Mama went to the kitchen, and Daddy walked to the dock. Ellie found Hank and Patti on the porch, cuddling together on the old couch. Patti had leaned against Hank's shoulder with her eyes closed, her palm on his chest where his heart beat. When he kissed the top of his wife's curls, she smiled up at him. A moment later, they saw Ellie and invited her to sit in the rocker next to them.

Ellie let her head drop back against the back of the rocker and looked at the lake. Quiet settled over them until Hank said suddenly, "Patti will be by herself when I leave, and my gear will be out of our extra bedroom. So it will be yours whenever you want it. Plus, having you there will help Patti while I'm gone."

"Isn't my Marine something?" Patti asked, proudly. "He's watching out for me, even though he'll have his hands full making sure his men stay safe! I guess you and I have to do our part and take care of each other while we wait over here—okay, Ellie?"

"Oorah" murmured Hank, nuzzling the top of Patti's head.

"Oorah, Lovie," she had whispered against his shoulder as the trees sighed in the evening breeze and frogs and night birds began their songs.

Two days later, Ellie's life had changed forever when Hank hugged her and said goodbye, but that December day now seemed surreal from her place under the thinking tree. Noise from passing students startled Ellie out of her reverie, and she looked at her watch. She didn't want to be late for dinner with her sister-in-law, so she gathered her books and purse and walked to her car with her mind full of questions.

"Something smells really good," Ellie said as she followed Patti through the living room to the kitchen.

"I made lasagna and a salad, so we can eat whenever we feel like it," Patti said over her shoulder. "Would you like to try a little Chianti first? We can nibble on chips and dip and see how the wine suits you!"

After some sips, Ellie's head felt a little buzzy, her body began to relax, and the panther seemed far away as Patti's soft classical music filled the room. "We got a letter from Hank that he sent from Dong Ha," Ellie said.

"I got one too. It was pretty long and told all about the base and his duties."

A mellow Ellie looked at her near-empty glass, bit her lip, then said, "What did you think of what he said about going into Leatherneck Square and the DMZ?"

Patti didn't answer right away, but finally she said, "The Square and DMZ are risky places—even to be near—but at least he had time to write. That must mean he has downtime when he can relax a bit. That makes me happy." After a long moment, she continued. "Remember the spare bedroom is yours when you want it. Might do you good to be on your own."

"Thank you, Patti," she said, deeply grateful. "I might take you up on that soon."

"Trust yourself, El. You'll know when it's time to make a change. I'm here when you decide."

After dinner, Ellie drove home feeling good because Patti was right: a place of her own would be the exact opposite of living at her parents' house. *Maybe 1967 will be a good new year after all,* she thought with a smile.

The next morning, the English 102 lecture hall seemed less overwhelming. The dimpled guy who had sat silently beside Ellie throughout the first trimester had returned to reclaim his seat. The girl who had regularly flopped down in the seat on Ellie's other side also returned. The girl—whose name was Susan—had struck up a conversation with Ellie within the first week of fall classes, and though Ellie had said little, there seemed to be no end to Susan's before-and-after-class chatter. By January, their odd, lopsided classroom friendship was well established, so Ellie had wanted to share it with Hank in a letter:

> *Oh my gosh, Hank. Susan breaks more taboos than I can*
> *count, but truth be known, she is fascinating. She's usually*
> *late to class and wears long, wrinkly "granny" dresses, loose*

*skirts, harem pants, or bell-bottom pants with peasant shirts
and halter tops. I don't think she even wears a bra (oops, sorry.
Mama wouldn't approve of me saying that.)*

   *Anyway, she always has on tons of different necklaces or
single strings of beads with crystals dangling from them.
She never carries a purse but has a cloth bag thing she calls
her "satchel" and goes barefoot or wears sandals she calls
"Birks." Her hair is long and wavy, sometimes held back by an
Indian headband or decorated with a flower tucked behind her
ear. She says she's done with fussy hairdos.*

Ellie went on to tell Hank that Susan was uninhibited and straightforward and had declared honesty and acceptance were her best qualities.
She regularly assured Ellie that she was happy to be far away from
home in California.

   Ellie had added a postscript to her letter:

*But Hank, even with all those inhibitions, I admire her confi-
dence and hope some of it will eventually rub off on me!*

A few days after dinner with Patti, Ellie was on her bench under the
tree when she saw Susan on the sidewalk nearby, her Birkenstocks—
Birks—dangling from the fingers of one hand. She moved along with
the crowd, but when she stopped short to gaze into the pond, a student
behind her nearly knocked her over. Oblivious to the near collision,
Susan stepped onto the narrow apron of grass between the water and
sidewalk, scanned the pond, then looked up at Ellie's tree, from top
to bottom. When she saw Ellie sitting on the bench at the base, she
waved, yelled something, and adjusted her satchel's cloth strap across
her body before starting toward the tree. A hippie dress, filmy and flowing, fluttered around her legs in the breeze. The upper half of her hair
was tied back with a leather strap while the rest flowed down her back
and across her shoulders in an ode to randomness.

"O-o-o. This grass is so soft and cool," Susan said, when she got closer. She ran her toes across the emerald blades, but she didn't sit down on the bench. "Let's go get coffee. I could stand something warm." She gestured across the street, dropped her sandals, and slipped her feet into them. "That's my favorite coffeehouse. Come on, El!" Her energy was a tidal wave, and Ellie could not help but be swept away.

Once inside the coffeehouse, the two young women made their way through a gray fog of smoke floating like a mountain haze until they reached a table by the window. Susan dropped her satchel on the floor, while Ellie put her purse and books on an extra chair. The waiter, wearing plaid bell-bottoms and a turtleneck pullover, ambled over with an order pad in his hand. Ellie ordered hot tea; Susan asked for strong coffee, then reached down and pulled a pack of cigarettes from her bag.

"You smoke?" asked Ellie. "You don't look like the kind of person who would smoke."

"And what kind of person would that be, huh? Look around. See everyone smoking? Do you see one particular type of person doing it? And what about the waiter? I know him. He doesn't smoke. Not this stuff, anyway." She put the cigarette to her lips and popped the lighter, then took a drag, lifted her chin, and sent a smoky stream billowing over Ellie's head. "Use your critical eye to answer that."

"Uh, well, I guess I never thought of it that way," Ellie said, turning to look. "I guess you can't tell which people do what."

Susan was uncharacteristically quiet for a moment, then turned the conversation to family. She said she was an only child and both her parents were physicians. "But I refuse to be known as 'Dr. Rigeltry's daughter' with no identity beyond that," she declared. "I may be a girl, but I want people to know I am a unique person. I'm not going to do things just because that's the way they've always been done. That's why I chose a school so far away from home."

"I know what you mean," Ellie murmured. Slightly uncomfortable thinking about her own family, she decided to change the subject. "I have Cameron DeMarco for biology this trimester. Have you heard anything about him?"

"I sure have," Susan snorted. "Dr. D. has quite a rep for his ways with students—especially girls—who have trouble with biology. You gotta watch those handsome profs!" A puff of smoke erupted from her lips in a vaporous exclamation point.

"This is all new to me," Ellie said, "because I was born in and went to high school in a town near here called Timpana Springs, so I had the same classmates all the way through school. We all knew each other pretty well, and there wasn't much excitement. Besides, Mama and Daddy always kept a close rein on me."

"Well, it was different for me," Susan replied, holding the cigarette in one hand and picking up her coffee cup with the other. "I wasn't given many rules, and there was plenty of excitement. The best boyfriend I ever had was the quietest but most adventurous guy in school. To look at him, you'd never guess he knew so much about sex and alcohol. That's why I'm warning you that it's the quiet ones you need to watch!" Susan grinned without embarrassment.

Ellie's eyes widened, and she squirmed and cleared her throat. "I didn't date much in high school. I went to my senior prom with my next-door neighbor. He was into someone else, but she already had a date, so we ended up going together because he wanted to keep an eye on her. He knew I'd go 'cause we were neighbors and I didn't have a date."

"The prom?" Susan laughed. "Geesh. I don't even remember mine. Well, I guess I sort of do. Let's see . . . I put on my little black dress and heels, my boyfriend picked me up, and we went to the school gym. That's all I can recall for sure, except that the prom theme was Mardi

Gras, so the gym was decorated to look like New Orleans—or what the prom committee thought New Orleans should look like. Didn't really matter as far as I was concerned, though, because the rest of the night is a blur."

"Why?"

"My boyfriend—you know, the quiet one—had brought some really smooth weed, so we went outside to get high, and that was it. I don't remember anything else after that." Susan tapped her cigarette against the edge of the plastic ashtray and watched the ashes fall, adding to the pile already there.

"So you smoke cigarettes and marijuana?" Ellie leaned back, shocked almost to the point of gasping.

Susan studied the ashes for a moment before cocking her head to the side. "I don't mean this to sound ugly," she said, "but you're pretty naive, aren't you?"

"My parents would have killed me if I did things like that. My brother, Hank, told me some kids do marijuana to get high, but Daddy is dead set against it because it's illegal. I know that much."

Susan mashed her cigarette into the ashtray and held it there. She stared at the smoldering ashes and was quiet so long Ellie thought she must have said something to make Susan angry. But Susan didn't seem angry at all when she finally asked, "Does your brother go to school here, too?"

"No," Ellie answered. "He's in Vietnam. He's a Marine officer, and he's going to be a rifle platoon commander. He's over there fighting communism, which means he won't be home for thirteen months. We were the only kids in our family, so I really miss him." Ellie stared at the ashtray sadly.

Susan's lips became a straight line. She leaned her chin on her free palm, looking up at Ellie, brows drawn together. "I've marched against that war, you know. I don't like it one bit. But even though I do like you, Ellie, I don't want to pretend I approve of what we're doing in Vietnam, because the whole thing is wrong. I think any and all wars are stupid, and all I can say is I hope your brother comes home safe and sound."

Another long moment passed before Ellie dared to reply. "I . . . I don't know much about the war, but I know Hank believes in helping the people. He told me that's why he's there, and I'm proud of him. He means everything to me. And I . . . I want him to come home safe too." Ellie's voice was barely audible as she sat back in her chair, eyes locked on her interlaced fingers in her lap.

Susan lit another cigarette and sighed. "I can tell how much you love your brother, and I'm sure he's a good person, so let's just leave it at the one thing we can agree on: we both want him to come home as soon as possible, okay?"

"Deal!" Ellie murmured. She was relieved when the conversation turned to class assignments.

Early the next morning, Ellie awoke with a start, breathless and trembling from distorted images of protest marchers driving Marines into murky waters filled with floating bodies, so, it took her a long time to get her heart to stop pounding. Since she could not hope to get back to sleep, she got up and took a long, hot shower, got dressed, and grabbed the book required by her English class. Her eyes were on the pages, but her mind fixated on body-count reports and Leatherneck Square so she couldn't stop wondering what was happening over there right now.

Chapter 5

By February, Ellie knew her second trimester biology was, hands down, the worst experience of her life, but if she wanted to get a college degree, she had to pass it. Every time she tried to study the textbook, her mind rebelled and refused to focus on the images of dismembered worms, frogs, or larger animals. She couldn't stop thinking that the two-dimensional, flat pictures were specimens that had once lived and breathed. Because she cringed at the thought of cutting up the rubbery things that were once defenseless creatures, she dreaded Monday—Dissection Day.

So far this trimester, Dr. DeMarco had merely lectured about lab cleanliness, proper use of materials, and approved lab techniques, but according to the syllabus, it was time to do an actual dissection. Ellie slipped into the biology lab, oblivious to the conversations that hummed around her, and took her assigned place in the back row of the large black tables. She put her things under her chair and avoided looking at red-faced, pimply Paul, leering at her from his seat next to hers.

Every Monday she had scooted away from him to avoid his prattling and pawing, but undeterred, he smirked and kept trying to flirt, leaning in close and touching her while he talked. On Dissection Day, she moved her chair away again as Paul's eyes swept over her from head to toe. He winked and said, "You look fab, Ellie-baby. Tomorrow's Valentine's Day. Do you have someone to celebrate with?"

Ellie felt rude, but she ignored him and stared down at the square of particle board in front of her. It was covered with green intersecting lines that created precise one-inch squares and had a shallow, half-round tray running along its sides where liquids were to collect. A group of large, T-shaped dissection pins stood in one corner, like spectators at a medieval execution.

"Gonna be a fun lab today—dissecting real specimens!" Paul proclaimed.

"Right. Dissecting lab," she muttered, then stiffened when she noticed the slit-eyes of a large frog staring down at her from a poster on the wall.

The room got quiet when Professor DeMarco strode in pushing a wheeled cart with a large, covered container on top. His collar-length auburn hair was gray at the temples and complemented deep-set, dark-brown eyes surrounded by thick lashes. Ellie wondered if those were the bedroom eyes she'd read about in novels. Wrinkles across his tanned forehead and a strong jawline made his face intense, focused. A trimmed mustache and goatee framed his soft, yet masculine lips.

Muffled thumps sounded from inside the clear plastic container as its contents sloshed around in the liquid under the lid. Ellie leaned forward on both elbows, with her hands covering her mouth.

Pulling on elbow-length rubber gloves, Dr. DeMarco greeted the class and, with intermittent finger-pointing between the drawing in front of the class and their dissection boards, he described the dismemberment process, emphasizing that this activity was a major portion of the biology grade. Ellie tried to convince herself that a frog was small and manageable. *At least it isn't something larger, like a sweet little pig!* she told herself.

Her internal pep talk worked until Dr. DeMarco reached in the container and pulled out one of the lumps. Her dreamy, cool professor held up a puffy, seven-inch-long dead frog, its front legs splayed and unseeing eyes bugging out above Dr. DeMarco's fingers. The slimy thing was as big as his hand. He held it above the tub while he talked, and opaque liquid dripped from its floppy feet, webs stretched between stiff toes, as the noxious, musty smell of formaldehyde filled the room. Ellie opened her mouth and tried to get a breath of untainted air to settle her stomach.

"Cool," said Paul, leaning closer to Ellie. "An American Bullfrog. Not as big as a Beelzebufo—they can get as big as a beach ball. But this one will do." Paul was clearly eager to begin until he looked at Ellie. "You look pale. You okay, El?"

"I'm not sure," she murmured. Her stomach was roiling, and she was dizzy, her hands sweaty. The room started spinning, and she tried to stand up but fell against the closest thing to her, which happened to be Paul's shoulder. "I . . . I'm sorry," she said, squeezing her eyes shut.

"That's okay. Stay there as long as you want. My shoulder is big enough to share." Paul grinned and put his arm around her waist.

Dr. DeMarco pushed his cart along, talking and handing a frog to each student on the first row of lab tables. He repeated the instructions about how to spread the frog's legs out and use the pins to secure it to the board. When he reached the end of the second row, he looked up and stopped.

"What's going on?" he asked, staring at Ellie and Paul.

"Don't think she's a fan of *Rana catesbeiana*," Paul answered.

The professor's eyes lingered on Ellie. "Uh, is she okay, Mr. Butler?"

"She said she was."

Dr. DeMarco turned to Paul and said, "You seem comfortable with the task here—I'm sure you can catch up, Mr. Butler. Please escort Miss Dennis into the hall where she can recover. She appears to be a bit green."

"But . . . aren't you going to give me my frog?" Paul sat straighter and removed his arm from Ellie's waist. With his support gone, she wobbled, nearly falling.

"Yes, I am," Dr. DeMarco said, looking at Paul distastefully. "You surprise me, Mr. Butler. Do you prefer frogs over women? I thought you'd be happy to help her."

Ellie struggled to regain her balance. "I . . . I'm sorry for the interruption. I think I can make it myself," she said, shuffling toward the door, holding onto each lab table as she passed until she made it out of the classroom. She leaned against the wall by the door and took several deep breaths. As her stomach began to settle down, she wondered what would happen next. She would fail the class if she didn't cut up some kind of animal. *Why am I the only person in class who couldn't do it?*

A few minutes later, Dr. DeMarco stepped out of the lab. "How are you feeling?" he asked, concerned.

"I think I'll be okay," she said. "Guess it was the smell that got me." She tried to smile but failed and looked away from his eyes. "And the only frogs I know about are the little ones, like tree frogs. The ones you were passing out are the biggest frogs I've ever seen." She slumped against the wall and studied the floor.

"Well, I'm glad to know you'll recover," he said. "You're the only student I've had who got sick before we made the first cut. That's some kind of record!"

"Sorry. But what can I do about the assignment?"

"Come see me next week during office hours. We'll figure out something. Do you know where my office is?"

"Okay . . . I mean, yes, I can find it," she said, lifting her eyes to his.

"See you then. Don't worry about coming back into class. Go get some air," he said. He gave her arm a reassuring pat before he returned to the classroom. She pushed off the wall and headed to the place where she could think.

Ellie slid onto the bench—her bench—and replayed the conversation with Dr. DeMarco. He was going to help her figure out how to get through biology. *That's good, isn't it? Or is it?* Susan had said to be careful of him.

Ellie closed her eyes, leaned back against the tree, and let the weak winter sun warm her skin, while patterns of limb shadows quivered red behind her eyelids. She sighed and tried to relax, but her thoughts ran away with her.

What am I to do about Dr. DeMarco? About biology? Do I even belong in college? And what about Mama? Is she drinking too much? Will I ever stand up to Mama and Daddy the way Hank did? What about moving to Patti's? Why am I not strong like Hank when he had told Mama that he wanted Mira at his wedding?

"Hank told me over and over that I was not the cause of Mama and Daddy's problems," she murmured aloud. "Will I ever get away from them? Is college too much for me?"

The question hung in the air as she left the bench and went to the library where she found a quiet place to write a letter to Hank:

> *Oh, Hank, I thought I knew the rules, but everything is changing. I make sure I'm on time to class and stuff like that, but I don't know what to think about college. I hear my classmates talking*

*about pot parties, women's lib, free love, or getting it on with
someone they just met. Those things seem like nothing to them,
but they say how much they hate the war. I can't stand what they
say, but at least they voice their own opinions. The girls don't act
the way ladies should, but they seem more confident than I'll ever
be. If only I had one tenth of what they have. I don't know if I'll
ever get there. It's just so confusing here.*

She finished the letter with a humorous version of the frog story,
hoping to give Hank a laugh. She stuffed the letter in an envelope,
addressed it, and dropped it in a mailbox on the way home, hoping to
find a letter from him there.

Mama always took Hank's letters from the mailbox first, so Ellie
figured she'd find her mother with a letter in one hand and a drink
in the other, but Mama was nowhere in sight when Ellie got home.
There was an opened envelope and trifolded pages lying beside it on
the kitchen table. Ellie picked up the pages and saw that the news was
almost two weeks old, but that didn't matter—she was happy to read
anything from Hank. As usual, he had made it a newsy letter and put
a positive spin on everything.

2 Feb 1967
Dong Ha, Quang Tri Province
South Vietnam

Dear Mom, Dad, & Ellie,

*I'm kinda getting used to the weather. Just to orient you
about where I am—look on a map, find the South China Sea
and Gulf of Tonkin. Look inland, a little south and around 10
miles west . . . voila! There it is, Dong Ha!*

*From here, supplies go out to the field for our guys in the
boonies—meaning jungles with rice paddies in between. We
do sweeps (search & destroy operations) of certain areas to
look for enemy movements and sh-- stuff, I mean. We take enemy fire at Dong Ha cause they want to destroy our supplies*

& reinforcements and this is where they are. My duties will multiply as time goes on. I took over as assistant plt (platoon—that's 42 or so men) commander of 81s (mortars) last month. The commander is a good guy. Working out fine 'til I get a rifle plt. I'll be happy about that, but that'll be in the jungle. I'll need my machete for sure.

Somebody in command decided it would be a good idea for us to stop bombing north of the DMZ when the Vietnamese celebrate Tet, the lunar new year, and apparently, the Allied forces thought it would be a great idea to let them do it in peace. So we're supposed to cease fire while they have a nice, quiet new year. Interesting, huh?

Gotta quit. I'll be back—something's come up.

OK, I'm back, but I don't have much time. We'll be bombing the North before long. No surprise the NVA & Cong used the "free" time during Tet to go back and forth across the DMZ and build bunkers, fortify positions, store rice & munitions on the south side. They are all over Quang Tri Province, especially Leatherneck Square.

Patti says she's keeping you posted on what's going on so you'll know everything's OK when I don't have time to write everyone. Will try not to use abbrev you might not understand, but no promises! Dad knows what they stand for, so just ask him.

I love your letters. When I read them, it feels like being home for a few minutes. No one has a better family than me!

I love you and miss you,
Hank

Hey, El, how's school going? Your favorite classes? Don't worry, things will work out. Don't let anyone bug ya!! Just remember you are kind & a fine person. Smart, too. You'll find your way.

After several nights of fitful sleep, Ellie set out for campus and found Dr. DeMarco's office in one of the 1940s-era buildings that flanked her tree. She went up the wide stone steps into a dimly lit hallway where patches of morning light reflected off smooth, dark flooring buffed to a sheen, with the aroma of industrial floor wax hanging in the air.

Sunlight squeezed through tall, narrow windows and made bright, rectangle-shaped stripes in the dark hallway that led her past a row of heavy wooden doors with brass name plates until she found the plate engraved with "Cameron DeMarco, PhD, Associate Professor, Biology" by an open door.

Dr. DeMarco was at his desk, his chair tilted back and his legs crossed at the ankles on the edge of the desktop, which was littered with papers and books. His fingers stroked his goatee as he read a book propped against his knees.

Ellie paused and touched her hair, then adjusted her blouse and glanced down at her new hip-hugging pants. She hoped her outfit looked right and respectable. He was doing her a favor, after all. He didn't look up when she took a step inside the doorway, and she wondered if she should have knocked. She didn't want to startle him, so she cleared her throat, which was enough to make him look up and swing his feet to the floor.

"Oh, there you are, Miss Dennis. Right on time. Come in and have a seat here," he said, patting an empty chair beside the desk.

His office was large enough to accommodate the desk, two guest chairs, and a floor-to-ceiling bookshelf behind his wooden swivel chair. A large window took up the remaining wall. There were diplomas and certificates on the wall above the desk, and books lined the shelves behind his chair, with preserved specimens in jars among the books. Plants of all sizes filled the windowsill above a soft-looking leather couch, and a lit candle gave off a spicy scent. The room was masculine, appealing. A green-shaded banker's lamp cast light on the papers and books strewn across the desktop, and a pen and yellow legal pad lay within Dr. DeMarco's reach. To Ellie's surprise, the only area free of debris held a silver-framed picture of a smiling blonde cradling a child in her arms.

Ellie perched on the chair facing the window. Outside, a bushy evergreen muted the natural light, but happily, she was still able to see her tree in the distance. "Thank you for seeing me, Dr. DeMarco," she said, her eyes fixed on his lips. Surprised to feel her heart pounding and her body tingling, she realized she had never felt this way before. She was overcome by his presence and stared at him, paralyzed, until something inside told her she needed to act.

Gathering herself with an "ahem," she said, "I'm really sorry I had to leave dissection lab. I don't know what happened."

"Don't worry about it, Ellie. It happens sometimes. Have you ever dissected anything before?" he asked.

"Well, in high school we did a worm, but that was about it."

"Nothing big, huh?" Dr. DeMarco leaned toward her, elbows on the chair arms, hands clasped in front of him. "Obviously, you weren't prepared for our frog!"

She fidgeted under his gaze as warmth climbed up her neck. She quickly looked away, hoping he wouldn't notice that she was blushing.

"You're no different from lots of people who don't care about studying the way living creatures are put together, so don't beat yourself up over it. You're not majoring in biology or anything related to it, are you?"

"No, but Dr. DeMarco, I know I need to get over my . . . uh . . . problem so I can pass biology," she said, her throat tightening.

"Please, Ellie, call me Cameron or DeMarco or something less formal. I encourage my special students to get to know me. Some even call me Cam."

As he spoke, he stood, brushed by her, and closed the door, then sat back down, and faced her with a smile that set off a crease in his left cheek just above the edge of his goatee. More tingles raced through her body, and she realized she had rarely talked to a grown man alone—never mind behind closed doors. Was this something young ladies should do?

She pressed her knees together and folded her hands in her lap. She knew she looked prim, but Mama had said that's the way ladies should sit. She squeezed her palms together, in order to control the trembling. Focusing on a safe subject, she said, "Do you have any suggestions about how I can pass your class?"

His face turned serious. "I've been thinking about that, and I have a solution for both of us," he said. "I can exempt you from dissection, as long as you do extra academic work related to biology. Also, you'll have to pass extra written tests with images of dissection.

"I am working on a book," he continued, "and I could use your help with directed research." He looked at her and smiled, the statement hanging in the air.

Ellie finally began to relax. "Research sounds like something I could do, and I don't mind extra tests. When do you want me to work?"

"Let's say you work for me three hours a day, two times a week to start with, and I'll fit your extra tests in during that time. Six hours a week should do it."

Dr. DeMarco shot her a sly grin, reached out to pat her knee, and let his hand linger there for the briefest moment. Ellie stiffened and looked down at the plain gold band on his finger until he drew back his hand and stood up to look down at her. The warmth of his hand remained on her knee the same way sand stayed between her toes at the lake.

"Take a look at my lecture and lab schedules, then pick your days," he said. "Let me know which are best for you, and I'll have everything ready." He stepped past her and opened the door, standing aside so she could get by.

"Thank you so much," she said, rising on unsteady legs. A hint of cologne tickled her nose when she passed by him.

Ellie walked away knowing she shouldn't like the feeling she got when Dr. DeMarco touched her because his ring said he was a married man. But something felt good about a man noticing her in spite of the fact that guilt—the panther—was closing in. At war with herself, she passed through the sun patches and walked out the heavy oak door. She headed toward her tree and spent an hour there with her head back and her legs extended so her toes touched the water while she thought about her forbidden attraction with Dr. DeMarco.

"Okay," she said to herself, "I'm going to have to get used to being around him. No more silly attraction. It all has to be about the business of passing biology. It's the same as a job, and Dr. DeMarco is my boss." One foot tapping out each syllable, she began repeating the vow, "It's only business, it's only business, it's only busi—" And then she heard someone call her name.

She sat up and blinked. Her eyes cleared, and there was Susan, coming toward her.

"Hey," Susan said, standing beside her. She looked up into the branches and said, "I love this tree. It has a good spirit." She sat down on the bank in front of the bench and put her feet in the water. "My friend's having a party Friday night," Susan said, leaning back on her elbows. "It's gonna be a happenin'! Wanna go?"

"That sounds, um . . . good. Where does your friend live?"

"In an apartment in the Ville."

Ellie had heard of the Ville. It was a neighborhood of older, Victorian houses that had been converted into apartments, and her parents—Daddy in particular—complained about families moving out of the beautiful homes and letting the neighborhood get run-down because college students were taking over.

"They don't give a hoot about our town's history or traditions," he had declared. "They're ruining the whole place. It's a shame."

Ellie had not been to the Ville, but she had overheard classmates talking about loud music and the pot parties the hippies had. Still, she wondered if it was as bad as Daddy said.

"Uh, thanks, Susan," she stammered, "but I just remembered I can't go. My mother wants me to do something at home." It was a lame excuse, but she couldn't think of anything else to say. A party in the Ville would be interesting, even exciting, but she couldn't make herself say yes.

"Well, the guy has a party nearly every Friday night. Maybe you can make it another time." Without another word, she rose and threw her satchel over her shoulder.

"Yes, I think that would be nice." Ellie said, but Susan was already walking away. "Hope you have a nice weekend!" Alone by the pond, Ellie watched her new—her only—friend slip on her Birks, stroll across the street, and go into the coffee shop.

There were more and more people like Susan on campus. They gave peace signs to each other and marched down the street in front of Ellie's tree to demonstrate against the war with chants and placards that hit Ellie like a prize fighter's punch. Susan and her friends hated what Hank was doing and blamed Marines like him for the bad things that happened in war. But Ellie knew differently. She knew that Hank did not hurt innocent people. He did not burn up children or old people. *Am I betraying him by even talking to Susan?* Ellie didn't know. She had many more questions than she had answers.

It was close to dinnertime when Ellie made herself stand up and start for home because she didn't want to make matters worse by being late. There was a letter from Hank, and she was eager to read it until she saw where he was when he wrote it.

10 Feb 67
Close to DMZ

Dear Mom, Dad & Ellie,

Been a lot of action around here. Marines do recon & sweeps to secure the area around Con Thien, a small mountain 2 miles south of the DMZ, 12 miles from the South China Sea. You can look that up on the map I sent.

Con Thien ("The Hill") is strategically important for us to make secure because it's high enough for a 360° view and we can see north of the Ben Hai River. In other words, we can see North Vietnam. We keep an eye on their activities from The Hill. NVA want it too. In order to keep it, we endure shelling by thousands of rounds of artillery & get ambushed in the field. Snipers everywhere. We need to get them outta there cause they kill too many good men. There are a couple of other hills west of Con Thien that we need to secure, too. They are Hill 117 & Hill 174. Both are to the southwest.

Getting in and out of action is challenging. Like I said, they get us into a combat zone on helicopters, so as long as the recon is accurate, we can set up and stop Charlie fast. We take fire and the jungle gets in the way—a good place for them to hide—but that's part of it.

I read a good article on the plane coming over; it was "Reporter at Large" in the Dec. 17 '66 issue of The New Yorker magazine. Pretty long, but tells you what 3/4 has been doing over here and will give you a good idea what we're up against.

When I get my platoon, we'll no doubt go up North after Viet Cong. We can't cross the DMZ even though they go back and forth whenever they want! Until then, I'm busy doing what I'm assigned. We get enemy shelling attacks regularly. Gio Linh (northeast of here) gets it worse though.

Mostly just waiting for my plt, getting used to the heat and terrain, and my Vietnamese is getting better. Northeast of here the jungle is thick with a triple canopy that makes it slow going on patrols or when the companies try to link up. Elephant grass is huge and cuts you like a knife. In the field, your boots and feet stay wet most of the time, so we have to take care of that because things get infected fast here.

Sorry if this jumps all over the place, but there are lots of interruptions here. Ha, ha!

I love you and miss you,
Hank

PS Ellie, Sounds like things are getting interesting. Huge frogs, huh? Keep workin' hard. Don't let anyone get you off track and you'll be OK!

Ellie put the letter down, closed her eyes, and—risking Mama's wrath—waited a minute before going to the dinner table. She and Daddy were already there when Ellie took her seat with her mind filled by images of Hank slogging through the jungle until Daddy's steely voice broke through.

"Can't you even say hello tonight?" he asked.

Ellie's head jerked up. "Oh, sorry, but I have a lot on my mind. I'm sorry."

"Well, we do, too, but we're still not rude," Mama chimed in. "Pass the vegetables, please."

Ellie handed the bowl to her mother and tried to smile even though she didn't feel like it. Her only thought was escaping to the peace of Patti's apartment.

Chapter 6

The lecture was half over when Susan eased into her desk one Monday morning in mid-March. "Hey," she murmured, flashing a peace sign.

Glancing at her, Ellie whispered, "Do you have any idea how late you are?"

Susan returned a weak smile and shrugged.

"You missed most of the lecture," Ellie continued, "but you can copy my notes if you want."

A few minutes later, a pencil fell to the floor, and Ellie glanced at her friend again. Susan was sound asleep with her head on her desk. When class ended, Ellie had to shake her awake. "Why are you so tired, Susan?" she asked. "Are you sick?"

Susan yawned, stretched, and rubbed the back of her neck before the two girls rose and followed the crowd out of the lecture room. "Guess I stayed up too late last night," Susan said as they entered the hallway. "I was uh-h-h, studying. Thanks for letting me copy your notes." She held out her hand, and Ellie gave her the papers, staring at her friend's red-rimmed eyes.

"O-o-o, studying will do that to you," a male voice said from behind them. Ellie turned and saw the guy who sat at the desk on the other side of her. He glanced down the hall and said, "Hey, would ya look at that! Heck of a crowd. I'm gonna wait for a path to clear before I head outside."

Ellie stared dumbly at the young man who had never said anything beyond "hello" a few times. She had sneaked peeks at him and noted that he looked hip, but he dressed so that his long-legged, athletic body looked casual, not messy.

"I'm Joe," he continued. "Couldn't help hearing you ladies." His smile and cobalt-blue eyes grabbed Ellie the way magnets draw metal.

Susan tilted her head, righted it, then nodded once in his direction. "Overhearing, you mean," she stated. "You sit next to Ellie, right?"

"Yup, been right there for two trimesters," he nodded. "Well, the crowd's thinning. I'm gonna take off, but let me know if you want my notes too. See ya later." He merged into the stream of students flowing down the hall.

"Cute guy," said Susan as she stuffed Ellie's notes in her satchel. "Thanks for bailing me out. I owe you."

"No problem," said Ellie, eyeing Joe as he disappeared into the sunshine along with the stream of students. He sure was cute, and she hoped he didn't think she was stupid. She looked at the floor and shifted her weight, then wrapped her arms around her books, hugging them in front of her like a shield.

"Hey, my friend's having another party on Friday," Susan said, interrupting Ellie's thoughts. "You remember? The one who lives in the Ville. Why don't you come with me this time? I'll pick you up. It'll be my payback for the notes."

Ellie stared at her disheveled friend. Part of her wanted to go, but another part remembered Daddy's warning. "Uh-h-h . . . thanks for inviting me again," she said. "I would like to go, but I'm not sure what my parents would say."

"No big deal if you can't. I just thought it would be groovy if you

went, that's all. You know, help you unwind," Susan clutched her satchel's strap, and her face hardened. "But if you have to worry about what
your parents want or what anyone else says, I'm gonna quit asking ya,
ya know."

Ellie felt like a fifth grader standing in front of the principal's desk
looking at the floor, shoulders sagging, textbooks tight against her chest.

"Listen, don't feel bad," Susan continued, her voice firm. "I want you
to make up your own mind for once, that's all. When are you going to
stop asking everyone's permission and live like you wanna live? Unless
you want to let other people decide who you are forever." Susan shifted
her weight from one hip to the other.

Ellie looked up, still hugging her books like a kid. "I understand,"
was all she managed to say.

Susan turned and started down the hall but stopped and looked back
over her shoulder. "It's not what you should or should not do, it's what
you *want* to do," she declared. "You can't please everyone all the time.
Call me when you make up your mind. Thanks for the class notes," she
said and walked outside.

Later, at her thinking tree, Susan's words ran through Ellie's head
over and over. They hit hard every time. Hank had told her to give herself credit—to trust herself—and to remember she was made of good
stuff. Wasn't that pretty much the same as what Susan had said, in her
usual blunt way? Ellie was paralyzed, unable to decide anything because she didn't want to get in trouble with Mama and Daddy, but she
didn't want to make Susan mad or disappoint her either. She had to
make a decision to go or not go to the party. She felt like a water-skier
being pulled behind a speedboat with the ski jump ahead—the long,
forbidding ramp reaching upward, getting closer and closer. It was time
to take the leap or stay on shore, time to sink or swim, time to hold on,
steady her skis, and shoot up toward the sky.

She walked into the kitchen before dinner, but Mama was nowhere in sight. Relief swept over Ellie, and then she paused as a thought exploded: *A daughter shouldn't feel that way. She should not be relieved when she doesn't have to talk to her mother!* The panther gripped her, held her down, and compounded her angst. But when she saw Hank's letter on the table, her worries faded, and the panther let go. She grabbed the folded paper, leaned against the counter, and started reading.

7 Mar 67
Dong Ha

Dear Folks,

    Lots going on up here now. The RVA loves to shell us and run. Like I said before, this is a huge supply base so we make a juicy target. Today I was transferred to L company (still 3/4 Marines). Got my rifle platoon (plt from now on). Now I'm a plt commander with 36 men under my command. They're good guys and I'm responsible for their well-being so I have to make good decisions. I re-read all your letters today and then had to burn them. It's hell having to do that, but I have no room to carry them anymore. I was thinking that I'll be home for Mama's birthday next year. We'll have a good time! Gotta go.

I love you and miss you,
Hank

Ellie put the letter back on the table and thought about what the letter really meant. It was over ten days old and a short one. She wondered why he'd not written more and why he'd said there was "lots going on." He had gotten a platoon—something he'd said he wanted—so she guessed that was good, but platoons in the jungle were "a target," and that was bad. Yet, even with all that, Hank remembered Mama's birthday. Amazing!

Ellie sighed and pushed off the counter just as Mama appeared and grabbed a casserole from the oven. "Dinner's on the table," she snapped.

The next morning, Mama came to Ellie's room and stood in the middle of the doorway while Ellie was gathering her things and getting ready to leave for campus.

"Patti makes an effort to stop by to visit during the week," Mama said. "She doesn't stay long, but at least she acts like she makes time to talk to me." Mama's voice was flat. "Seems like you're always coming or going. You're not here much. Seems as if you're avoiding us."

"I have to study, Mama. I'm trying to make good grades."

"Your father told me to tell you he wants to know what you're doing, so please try to be here before dinner more often and talk to him. You'd make it easier on me if you did that." Mama delivered her message, turned on her heel, and disappeared.

"I suppose I'll have to be here earlier, then," Ellie said to the empty doorway.

Mama was right—Ellie was avoiding her parents, and her work for Dr. DeMarco had given her an excuse to stay on campus late doing research and eating from the vending machines most nights. Ellie felt safe in the hush of the library, and when she was at her favorite table, snug and tucked away in a far corner near the periodicals section, she forgot all about family conflict. But how could she stand her ground and stay away from home now, knowing she would cause trouble for Mama? *That would be selfish*, the panther breathed in her ear.

Days after Mama had confronted her, Ellie walked in the front door and heard loud voices coming from the kitchen while Walter Cronkite's evening news played in the background. Afraid of becoming a target, she leaned against the front door and stayed quiet.

"That dutch courage helping you get through these days, is it?" Daddy's voice rang out, commanding attention. "Just listen to that, will you, Lela? Cronkite's talking about our son! Just like those other Marines, Hank is hacking his way through the jungle, slogging through polluted water, and getting shot at and ambushed, and all you want to think about is what? That he says he's fine? Do you really believe that, Lela?"

Ellie heard the clink of a glass against the counter, then the sound of liquid being poured.

"I don't know what you want me to say," Mama whimpered. "I can't see how to get through this any other way than to believe what he writes. I don't dwell on bad things. He's there and says he's fine, so that's what I spend my time thinking about. Not the bad things."

"How can you do that?" Daddy's voice was tense. "Don't you worry about him? Didn't you read today's letter?"

"Of course, I worry. I'm his mother. I just don't like to talk about what's happening to him. That's all," Mama said.

"Well, that's perfect," Daddy said. "I have a daughter who's turning into God knows what at college and a wife who refuses to talk to me."

"What's wrong with what Ellie is doing?" Mama asked, her voice getting louder.

"I hardly know the girl anymore," he answered. "She sleeps here. She comes around to read her brother's letters and have a meal sometimes, but she says nothing and acts like she doesn't have a brain in her head."

"You never were here when she was a little girl. Why should she talk to you now?"

"Because she is my daughter; that's reason enough. Besides, I doubt if she understands where Hank is, much less why he's over there. She's happy and ignorant as long as I pay the bills."

Ellie heard a smacking sound—like a hand slammed down—followed by the sound of Daddy's footsteps leaving the kitchen. Then she heard Mama swearing an ugly word and the clink of ice against glass.

Ellie tiptoed toward her room, but a riser board popped when she was part way up the stairs. She froze when Daddy called to her from his den. "Ellie, is that you? Come in here, please." It wasn't a question. It was a command.

Her shoulders hunched, and she wanted to swear too. Still holding her books and her own newly purchased satchel, she turned around and went to the den door.

"Yes, Daddy," she said.

Braced like a prize fighter ready to deliver the knockout punch, her father stood to the right of the doorway next to his huge wooden desk, holding what looked like a letter. A big leather easy chair and footstool dominated the opposite corner of his den. Wrapped in dark paneling, Daddy's den, like Dr. DeMarco's office, was a man's room. The only seating was his oversize chair, its footstool, and the desk chair on brass wheels.

A wall of bookcases beyond his big chair held his treasures—the classics and medical literature. A window stretching from floor to ceiling opposite the doorway provided a clear view of his manicured lawn, trees, and the horizon beyond. Ellie knew he sat in his chair for hours with his feet up, looking at the world outside.

Daddy looked at her and said, "Ellie, do you remember I was a combat surgeon in France during World War II? What I didn't tell you was that the sound of aircraft and artillery explosions is a permanent part of me and I can't forget the hundreds of surgeries I performed on young soldiers. My memory is full of the faces—unconscious and serene or awake and twisted in pain. I have nightmares about those distorted faces. Young faces, like Hank's. The sounds and images wake me up at night, sometimes."

Ellie didn't move from the threshold when Daddy paused and stepped around to his desk or when he pushed the chair aside with his foot and leaned over, his palms flat against the desktop. Large pieces of rumpled paper, scored into even squares from folding, were spread on the desk, and when Daddy continued, his eyes remained fixed on the papers.

"Hank sent me these military maps because he knew I could read them and keep up with where he was. All these green and brown squiggly lines and the coordinates along each side mean something. Come over here and look." She obeyed and joined him at the desk.

"This letter"—Daddy shook the paper in his hand—"This letter says Hank is in Leatherneck Square." Daddy placed an index finger on a small circle on the map. "This is Con Thien, a high spot close to the DMZ"—he tapped a red dot—"and it anchors the northeast corner of Leatherneck Square." He moved his finger up. "North of the Square is the Demilitarized Zone, the DMZ. The Ben Hai River runs through there." Ellie watched as Daddy traced a wavy line in the middle of a wider, darker swatch he'd marked "DMZ."

He pointed back at Con Thien, then moved his finger as he talked: "If you go east toward the South China Sea, you get to Gio Linh. Drop down south, and you get to Dong Ha, where he first arrived in Vietnam. Go back west and, as you can see, there's a river, the Cam Lo River. Then back north to Con Thien. The square I just traced is Hank's Leatherneck Square. Know why it's called that, Ellie?"

"No," she whispered.

"Because that's where the Marines—Leathernecks—are fighting. Marines like your brother have been there since the beginning of the war, and it's proven to be the deadliest place Marines can be. More Marines have died there than anywhere else." Daddy straightened up, put his hands on his hips, and glared at the map.

"It's my opinion that human political ambition, pure and simple, is the reason we're having problems in Vietnam. When politics drives policymaking, bad military decisions are made. I have a file full of your brother's letters—I save every one—but all I can do is read them and pray. I'm helpless to change anything. Political wars like Vietnam cause conflict among policymakers at home which hampers combat strategy overseas," he said. "Our war is here, in our government. Our boys are the victims."

Ellie watched her daddy go to his easy chair and sit down, but he left the letter on his desktop. He leaned his head back on the soft, pliable leather, then closed his eyes. She waited a few moments, but he didn't say anything else, so she reached over and picked up the letter, then left him and went to her room, quietly closing the door behind her. Safely on her bed, she read what had happened to her brother and knew why Daddy was angry:

18 March 67
Leatherneck Square
(Dad can show you where this is on his map)

Dear Folks,

   Been awhile since I wrote, but we've been pretty busy. I wrote Patti about the specifics. Hope she filled you in. Our artillery's been firing into North VN from Gio Linh, but the enemy hit back hard. We took "a long walk" in the jungle down south looking for them. About 2.5 clicks (1.5 miles) southeast of Con Thien used to be a hamlet called Phu An. At one time, it must have been a beautiful little place with a French style Catholic Church in it, but there's nothing there anymore cause we had to hit the phooey out of the place because NVA built well-established bunkers all around there & used them to hide in & kill too many Marines. One is too many, but there were lots more casualties. We suffered so many that we had to regroup.

   I told Patti that I had gotten a Purple Heart. She may have told you by now. Don't worry. It's just a little half-moon shaped scratch near my right eye. The corpsman cleaned it up, rubbed a little methylate on it, and bandaged it. He said it wouldn't leave much of a scar so it's nothing at all to worry about. He didn't even send me to Dong Ha for triage, but said he wanted

to report it for my PH. I'll heal the Marine way, and it'll be
gone by tomorrow. I'm OK, just a little tired.

Gotta go. I love you and miss you,
Hank

It was past midnight when Ellie fell asleep with the letter pressed against her heart. She drifted off reminding herself that he said he was okay—all he had was a scratch by his eye—but nightmares kept waking her up.

Susan had invited Ellie to several more Friday parties, but so far her "Don't go" list had won, and she made an effort to be home well before Friday dinner. One early April evening, she rushed in and took her chair just in time to grab a serving dish that Daddy shoved in her direction. She took the dish, served herself, and passed it to Mama.

"Sorry I'm late, Mama," Ellie said, trying to send a smile her mother's way. "I was at the library and got involved in research. Plus, I had to finish an assignment for English. Lost track of time."

Daddy did not look up when Mama handed him another bowl, but instead he uttered something unintelligible, guttural. Serving dishes slid by, silverware clinked, and ice dinged in the glasses, but no one spoke. Walter Cronkite's baritone filled the void. Tonight's news was mostly talk of high body counts and difficult jungle warfare. Ellie forked a brussels sprout and tried to block images of Hank hacking his way through the jungle in the sweltering heat from invading her mind.

She stared at a full plate of delicious food and felt sick to her stomach. *What did he have to eat?* Did he have enough? She flinched when Mama's icy voice rose above Cronkite's: "Ellie, stop eating. Your father has not asked for a blessing yet." Mama sat straight in her chair, hands folded in her lap, staring across the table at him.

Daddy grabbed his napkin and jammed it in his lap. Ellie followed suit, then turned toward him. He looked up, eyes drilling into Mama's.

"Bow your heads," he commanded. Against the backdrop of the evening news, he spat out a string of sounds followed by "Amen" while Cronkite's voice droned on louder than God's.

The newscaster said General Westmoreland wanted more troops to serve in Vietnam, then turned to reports of escalating anti-war unrest at home. Another reporter commented that President Johnson had decided to delay sending more troops to help in the fight because it was political suicide.

"Lyndon Johnson is a snake," hissed Daddy, talking over the newscast. "Why can't they just tell us the truth about Vietnam? Give our boys what they need to win or bring them home."

Ellie raised her eyes toward Mama and stopped eating when Mama asked him why he thought Johnson and General Westmoreland were not telling the truth. He didn't answer her and continued eating in silence for a few minutes.

After a moment, he said, "Our boys went over there thinking they had a mission to defeat communism, but I don't think we have a winning strategy for that because we get nothing except enemy body count numbers, and that's supposed to mean we're winning. They say we're killing more than we're losing, but that's not how you win a war. It's a fight that can't be fought like World War II. It's jungle warfare. We didn't fight in the jungles and never have! A Sherman tank wasn't meant for a rice paddy, but we're using them over there.

"On top of that, the politicians and generals don't want the country to think we could lose because they have to save face no matter how many of our boys they sacrifice." He stabbed a piece of meat, then bit down hard on it. "They want us to think things are going well, but anyone can see the ground war is getting worse."

Daddy's words hung in the air, daring Mama to respond. Her eyes narrowed and her lips parted, but she did not utter a sound. Instead, she turned her attention to Ellie.

"How were classes today?" she asked, her tone casual as she picked up a piece of bread, then put it down a second later without taking a bite.

"Nothing to shout about. The usual," Ellie said, watching Mama dab her eyes with her napkin. At that precise moment, Daddy looked up and reached for his drink. When he saw Mama wiping her eyes, he turned a stern face to Ellie.

"You need to give your mother a decent answer. She wants to know more about what you're doing in college. Look what you've done—you made her cry." Daddy's accusation planted a lump in Ellie's throat.

She looked across the table at her brother's empty place and longed for one of Hank's reassuring looks, but all she saw was emptiness. She slumped back in her chair and rested her fork on her plate.

Mama's eyes traced Ellie's line of sight across the table until hers, too, landed on the empty chair. After the briefest moment, Mama turned back to her plate and stabbed at her food but remained silent.

Cronkite's famous "And that's the way it is" echoed through the cavernous hush in the dining room. Something snapped in Ellie's mind. A cog fell into place, and words emerged from deep inside her.

"No, I didn't make her cry," said Ellie, voice steady, not raised. "You did. Don't you know how hard Mama tries to make dinnertime a good part of the day?" Ellie straightened up and continued: "We miss Hank just as much as you do. And we're worried too."

She was as surprised as her parents but regretted the words as soon as they were out. No doubt what would happen next. She braced herself and looked at Daddy while he remained silent, still facing her. Time clicked into slow motion.

Her father turned from her and stared at his plate for a second, then put down his fork and rested his forearms on the table. It was like watching a great white circle a swimmer. When he raised his head, Ellie sensed the flare of controlled fury, so she waited, expecting the worst.

When he addressed her, his words were carefully chosen: "Well, that's it then. You have finally done it. I knew you'd let yourself be corrupted by all those crazy people on campus. You think it's okay to say whatever you want whenever you feel like it, and now you've made dinner most unpleasant, Ellie. I had hoped this would not happen."

Mama remained silent as she stared at the glass she held in her lap.

"You're not going to have to worry about unpleasant dinners anymore, Dad," Ellie said, the last word a low, hammering syllable that made her breath catch in her throat. What had she called him? He had been her daddy until a second ago. Little girls always said "Daddy." It was the southern way a child showed affection for a father, but in that one word, spoken that instant, Ellie told her parents things had become different between them. He was "Dad" now. No more adoring little girl.

There was no going back, so she continued: "I've decided to move out. I'll get my things together tonight."

"Ellie!" Mama's voice was soft, but strong. "Are you serious? Where will you go?" Her brows drew up in concern—a response Ellie was not accustomed to.

"To Patti and Hank's apartment. Before he left, he said I could live there. Patti wants me there too. I'll be fine, Mom."

"Are you sure this is a good decision, Ellie?" Dad's voice was cold, clinical, as if he were checking off a square on a patient's medical history. Diabetes? No. Heart problems? No. Good decision? No.

"Yes, it's the right decision," said Ellie without wavering.

"Time will tell, I guess," her mother murmured.

A steel band encircled Ellie's chest, and her heart raced, but she forced herself to stand up, pause, and look down at her mother. Then she turned and walked out of the dining room, leaving her parents sitting there, Dad red faced and Mom stunned.

Chapter 7

It didn't take long for Ellie to unpack and settle into the bedroom across the hall from Patti's. The apartment was in a quiet complex filled with married students and young professionals, an easy twenty-minute commute to both Patti's work and Ellie's campus. They fell into a routine of having breakfast together followed by easy conversation while they fixed dinner at the end of the day. The best thing for Ellie was that Patti asked questions about campus life and listened—really listened—to what Ellie said.

"I'm so happy you decided to move in with me!" Patti said one day. "It gets kind of quiet here, especially on weekends."

"I-I was glad you still wanted me here. Things got overwhelming at home."

"I understand. Your parents are complicated, but I think your life will settle down now."

Patti had found a job at a small flower shop called Eden's Beauty on Timpana Springs' Main Street. She chuckled when she told Ellie that Tommy, the manager who cooed when he talked and dressed like a hippie, hired her because of her inexperience.

"I told him I majored in art and knew the elements of design but didn't know a thing about flowers except that they always made people feel better and I wanted to be a part of that. Tommy said floral designers are simply artists in love with flowers, and he could teach me all I needed to know about doing things the right way, so I love the job. Besides, it helps pass the time."

Patti did not complain about waiting for Hank to come home and never mentioned that the wait would be over a year long, but she kept a calendar held to the refrigerator door with a U.S. Marine Corps magnet. Every evening before she went to bed, she made two strong strokes in an X through that day's square and said, "One day closer to when he gets home!" Once in a while, usually on weekends, Ellie heard Patti's voice catch partway through the sentence.

The microfiche reader dinged, and pages swooshed by in the dark microfilm room where Ellie lost herself in her research for Dr. DeMarco. She knew the research—as well as their relationship—would end in a few weeks when winter trimester was over because she was definitely not taking biology when the spring trimester started in May. After their first meeting, she had allowed herself to enjoy being around Dr. DeMarco and even dared to think of him as Cameron, but she still wasn't sure it was proper to like the way she felt when they met in his office to go over her notes.

"I'll miss him," she said aloud, then ducked her head when the guy next to her, his face ghoulish in the dim light, put his index finger to his lips. "Oh, sorry!" she murmured and focused on the film running through her machine. *White type on a black background, the opposite of normal—just like my life.*

The idea faded when she found the article she wanted to show Cameron, so she sat back to read in the glow, forcing herself to concentrate on the report.

Later that afternoon, she went to Cameron's office with the annotated bibliography she had prepared. Sitting quietly in the guest chair by his desk, she breathed in his now-familiar spicy aroma while he studied the list.

He put his feet up, turned pages, and read while the thumb and forefinger of his right hand ran down opposite sides of his mustache, smoothing the whiskers from under his nose to the corners of his mouth. There the fingers opened, moved back up to his nose, closed, and slowly traced the path down to his mouth again. The pattern repeated over and over while he read, and the rhythm drew Ellie in. She wondered if his fingers were strong. Or were they soft and gentle? What would it feel like if he stroked her cheek that way? He took his hand away to turn a page, and she swallowed, then made herself look out the window where birds played among the trees.

Months before, he had explained he was working on a book about behavioral genetics, and they had met every week after that so he could review her notes, ask questions, or discuss what she had read. He said her grade depended on how thorough, accurate, and useful her research was to him, but to her dismay, she began to look forward to their meetings—almost like dates—so it was unsettling to be there while he assessed her value based on her work, not on her as a person.

She waited, picking at the ends of her hair and watching the birds while he examined the pages. Her heart jumped when he looked up, and a broad smile spread across his face.

"Great job!" he declared.

Emboldened by his compliment, she replied, "I've become intrigued by human behavior. I mean, it's fascinating to think about how surroundings influence a person's genetic makeup."

"The problem of nature versus nurture is captivating," he responded, "but the difficulty is determining whether environment influences behavior or vice versa." Ellie hoped he was talking to her, but he seemed to be talking to himself. "Do we behave in certain ways because we just can't help it? Are there some things we can't change?" He stared at nothing, stroking his mustache again. "Or, if we manipulate the environment, can we change whatever behavior we want to, when we want to?"

"I wonder what causes what," she murmured, but he did not respond as he stared into space. After a few minutes, a noise outside made him start reading again, so she left him in his office with his book and yellow note pad.

Disappointed that Cameron hadn't discussed it with her, she sat under her tree thinking about the nature-and-nurture concept, examining its facets from different angles the way a diamond merchant studies a gem. *How much of her parents' behavior was inherited and how much had their environments shaped them? What about Hank? Did he believe strongly in his mission because it was born into him as it would be for someone with innate perfect pitch? What about her own tendencies? Why did she want everyone to like her? Was it simply the southern custom, or was she born that way? What about Mira's influence?*

It took weeks, but Ellie got up the nerve to make the call. She planted her feet, picked up the phone, and dialed the number.

"Hullo—what's happenin'?" Susan demanded rather than asked.

"Hi, it's Ellie. Do you always answer that way?"

"Hey, Ellie! Like I said, what's going on?" Susan asked, ignoring the question.

"I'd . . . um . . . I'd like to go to a party with you. You know—one of those parties at your friend's apartment in the Ville. When's the next one?" Ellie's hands trembled, and she gripped the receiver tighter. She knew her parents would not approve, but that didn't matter because she wasn't going to tell them she was racing into new territory, taunting the panther on the precipice where it crouched, watching her.

"Yeahhh. He's having one tonight. Things won't get started 'til ten or so. How 'bout I pick you up somewhere around ten-thirty-ish?"

"Ooo, tonight? So soon?"

"That a problem, El?"

"No, no. Guess I don't need time to get ready. Sure—tonight's fine!" Ellie put the phone back in its cradle, then sank onto the couch and buried her head in her hands. She wondered if Susan was proud of her for deciding to go, but that didn't matter now. She was committed, and it was only hours until the party.

She was trying to figure out how to tell Patti about the event, but that problem disappeared when Patti handed her a letter in the familiar red and blue striped envelope Hank used.

"Your mother asked how you were doing when I stopped by to see her this afternoon," Patti mentioned while her eyes searched Ellie's.

Patti had agreed to stop by once or twice a week and retrieve Hank's letters from the parents' house for Ellie because avoiding them was the only way she could survive. Did Mom's question mean she was worried and wanted to repair past damages?

"Thanks," Ellie said and settled back to read the letter.

27 Mar 67
Quang Tri Province

Dear Mom, Dad & Ellie,

I may have a little time because we (Lima Company) are on Sparrow Hawk. That means we are the reactionary company so if anybody (usually a recon patrol) runs into trouble, we go in to help them. We are on 15-minute standby, and we don't know what we're gonna run into, but from the time of the alert, we have 1 minute to be in choppers headed for the action.

*We all (my plt and the others) have to stay on the ready in the
company area so we're available to go out. This waiting is bad
for morale because we just sit and do nothing. We wait. It's
OK for a little bit, but it gets to you after a while. That's why I
prefer to be on patrol. If it's quiet, I get pictures of the country-
side, which is vast, like some parts of the U.S. I don't know the
temperature, but I've been sweating all morning. We get some
rain, but not like it will be during monsoon season in late Sept
or Oct. Maybe earlier . . . no telling exactly when the rains will
start!*

*To answer your question about tents: Yes, I live in a G.P.
(general purpose) tent now, but when I was back in Dong Ha
I lived in what is called a "hard back" with electricity and
stuff. The working men (affectionately known as "grunts") live
in tents and "pogues" (support or non-combat staff) are in
hardbacks. I don't make a good pogue, and that's why I wanted
a platoon; tents are fine with me. They're a bit rustic, but comfortable enough after you get used to them.*

*I've been able to read recently because we've not been in the
heaviest action, but that could change at any time. Gio Linh
has been a center of activity, and we're in a different place farther away from where the enemy is concentrating. Finished 6
books since 1 Mar! See what I mean about waiting time? Next
time I get to Dong Ha I'm going to order a math correspon-
dence course. Didn't get a mechanical engineering degree for
nothin'! Gotta keep my mind exercised. Ha!*

Well, guess that's about all for now.

I love you and miss you,
Hank

*PS Hey, Ellie. Patti tells me you moved in with her. That's
GREAT! Glad she has company—plus, she says you have a
special arrangement for biology. I'm impressed. You're movin'
right along, learning how to get things done, huh? See ya!*

Ellie finished reading, then sat still for a moment, took a deep breath,
and forced herself to relax. Once again, Hank had cushioned the harsh-

ness of his circumstances and written about positive things, but she couldn't help wondering where Quang Tri Province was.

Patti hummed in the kitchen while fixing dinner, so Ellie got up and put the letter safely on the table as she helped her sister-in-law. "Sounds like Hank was kind of bored when he wrote that letter," she commented. "It's hard to imagine being bored in a war, though."

"Yeah," Patti agreed, "but isn't it just like him to order a math course in the middle of a war?"

"I thought so too!" Ellie smiled.

"He never lets things get him down, does he?" Patti put the salad on the table, then took her usual place and stared out the window.

"He's always been like that," Ellie took the hot food out of the oven and waited for Patti to respond, but when she said nothing, Ellie decided it was time to tell her about the party. "Guess what?" she said, leaning back against the counter, a dish in each hot-mitted hand. "I'm going to a party later tonight!" She hoped her voice was casual, but not too casual.

"Really? That's great!" Patti looked up and smiled. "You need to get out and have fun! Who are you going with?" She waited while Ellie brought their food to the table, tossed the mitts on the counter, and eased into her chair.

They bowed their heads and Patti said "Amen" before lifting her fork and taking a bite of potatoes. "Tell me all about the party!" she said.

"My friend Susan invited me," Ellie managed to say. "It's at her friend's apartment in the Ville."

Patti looked at her, fork in midair. "The Ville, huh? You'll be safe, won't you? I mean, I trust you, but that place does not have a good rep," she said. "Tommy told me the Ville is filled with hippies and dope, which is really something, coming from him."

Ellie swallowed hard. "Susan is okay. Her dad's a doctor too," she said, trying to push away doubt about her decision. "We have lots in common, so I think things will be fine. I'm going to wear my new skirt and top."

They ate in silence for a few minutes, and Ellie waited for Patti to tell her not to go, but she didn't. Ellie breathed easier when the conversation turned to other topics while they cleaned up the kitchen. Afterward, Patti settled in the living room to listen to Vivaldi with a glass of wine; Ellie showered and changed clothes.

Later, Ellie's nervous fingers and thumb made tiny circles on the nubby drapery fabric as she stood by the window and watched the street. Patti had wished her a good time and made her X on the calendar before disappearing into her room.

The universe—or maybe it was God—had moved Hank out of harm's way for a time, which was a relief. His letter had said he had time to read, so he must not be in the middle of heavy action, whatever that meant. He was okay nine days ago, and Ellie chose to believe he still was, which made it a good time to go to a party without worrying about his safety. She sighed and leaned against the window frame, determined to focus on watching for Susan, even though it seemed ironic that Hank was out of harm's way at the same time she ventured into unknown territory.

She heard a horn blasting before she saw the VW bug veer to the curb and screech to a halt. Ellie grabbed her bag, yelled "Bye!" to Patti as she ran out the door, and climbed in the car, barely getting her feet in before Susan stomped on the accelerator and roared away toward the Ville.

Fifteen harrowing minutes later, Susan curbed the car and pulled the key out of the ignition in one smooth action. She dropped it into her satchel and got out of the car, then walked around to the sidewalk and stretched. That's when Ellie saw that Susan had on a flowered mi-cro-miniskirt that barely covered her rump, a flimsy shirt, and a purple embroidered vest that vaguely obscured a clear view of her bare breasts beneath the top's fabric. Ellie felt out of place in her tailored A-line skirt and shell top, but she stepped out of the car and looped her own satchel across her shoulder. She wiggled her fingers, cramped from clutching the dashboard, and joined Susan on the uneven sidewalk. She looked around and tried to catch her breath, but the streetlights—some with broken glass, some dim—along the pavement didn't exactly calm her.

Rows of large houses wrapped in faded clapboard lined the street. Neglected and lonely, they faced the road like old ladies on nurs-ing-home porches. Large verandas of scuffed wood spanned the fronts, and peeling paint flaked from once-fancy curlicue gingerbread trim atop decaying columns. These houses were the Ville's history, left be-hind by former residents who had fled to a growing suburbia. The huge houses in the Ville were bleak reminders of grandeur abandoned for the convenience of shopping centers and the modern luxuries of central heat and air-conditioning.

Patches of grass grew randomly in small yards between the hous-es and along the sidewalk next to tall, stately trees that struggled to maintain some dignity through seasons of neglect. Ellie stared at the rickety staircases running up the outside walls of the houses like battle scars on a warrior's face. She and Susan both looked up when a weak breeze stirred Spanish moss draped from low-hanging branches that filtered the light. Dim shadows on the sidewalk made the Ville an eerie, uninviting place. The scene gave Ellie pause, but Susan strode up the sidewalk without missing a beat, so Ellie took one last look at the trees, smoothed her skirt, and followed her.

"Come on." Susan pointed to a house near the buckling sidewalk. "This is the one." She charged up three worn stairs onto the porch lit by a single light bulb dangling from an exposed wire in the overhanging roof. Scuffed wood creaked underfoot as she opened a dilapidated door to reveal an inside staircase that ascended into the shadows and disappeared.

Behind her, Ellie stumbled up the steps to a landing in front of a door hanging crooked on its frame. Susan put her hand on the doorknob and looked over her shoulder at Ellie. A fox's smile crossed her face as music, voices, and laughter seeped under the crooked door. The strangeness made Ellie want to run, but Susan pushed the door open and pulled her into the room.

A strong, earthy odor like two-day-old grass clippings reached out and grabbed them as Ellie trailed Susan into a dimly lit space filled with the soulful sound of a harmonica and a male singer's voice. The flickering light from candles around the room gave Ellie a creepy feeling. "Ah, getting high with Dylan," Susan breathed, and Ellie wondered if she was truly ready for this.

Several people with long, untamed hair and ill-fitting clothes lounged on a swaybacked sofa to the right of the door. Others stood against a wall to the left, somehow conversing in spite of the loud music. On the opposite wall Ellie saw an open doorframe with strings of beads hanging down. She stood motionless beside her friend, unsure where to look or what to do.

Susan went over and spoke to a boy and girl sitting in a dilapidated chair beside the beaded doorway. The girl had a pretty face framed by long dark hair parted in the middle, and she was wearing a long skirt and shapeless blouse made of filmy fabric that made it obvious that she, too, wore no bra. Ellie noticed the girl had straight, white teeth and used lots of eye makeup. She lounged across the boy's lap with her arm draped around his shoulders and her legs dangling over the chair's arm while the boy's arms draped around her, one behind her back, the other underneath her blouse.

"This is my friend, Paisley, and her friend, Rad," Susan said to Ellie, who had followed her. "I met her at a march last summer, and we met Rad at the coffee shop this afternoon."

"Hi," said Ellie, trying to smile as Paisley's eyes swept over her.

"You look new to this scene," the girl observed, adding in a voice dripping with sarcasm, "Nice, neat threads. Look, you gotta relax. Life is beautiful. The universe is free." She kissed Rad and nuzzled his cheek before her lips parted slightly and her eyes rolled back in her head. Was something wrong with her? Ellie inched closer to Susan until Paisley lifted her head to mutter to Susan, "There's some stuff in the other room that will help your uptight friend chill."

"Ye-ah-h," said Rad. "It's gooood stuff."

Susan nodded and flashed a peace sign before pushing aside the beads and walking through, Ellie at her heels. It was darker in that room, and Ellie had to pause while her eyes adjusted. She made out six or so people sitting in a large, raggedy circle on the floor. Some leaned against the wall, legs stretched out in front of them, and others sat close together, cross-legged, Indian style.

In the smoke-filled darkness, Ellie saw the glowing end of a wrinkled cigarette moving around the circle from one person to the next. The orange glow brightened as each took a pull, held their breath, and handed the thin white tube to the person beside them. Ellie watched numbly, her heart beginning to race. Wait a minute—this was a pot party! She remembered hearing kids in high school talking about these. The panther sprang and caught her by the throat, but she had no idea what to do.

Susan moved toward the circle, pushed on a boy's shoulder, and hitched her head to the side. He moved over and she squeezed in beside him, then said something to the girl on the other side of her. After that girl also moved aside, Susan patted the empty spot next to her and looked at her friend standing frozen in the doorway. Ellie hesitated but sat down.

Susan nudged her, nodding toward the cigarette. "That's a joint. Ever see one before?"

Ellie felt eyes on her. A blank-faced girl across the circle stared at her while Ellie looked around, trying to discern what was happening. Some people had their eyes shut and were half-smiling, and others raised their chins as smoke escaped their lips. A few rocked side to side, watching the joint making the circuit, and one or two, like the girl who watched her, had hard, angry faces. But most of them looked like children in front of a department store window at Christmastime, charmed by the whimsical scene.

"No," Ellie whispered, trying to sound confident. "I don't think I want any." Her mind spun as the joint moved closer—only three people away now and closing in on her fast. Her mind worked a mile a minute. Susan would get it first and then pass it to her. "Can't I just pass it on?"

Susan turned to her. "That wouldn't be very nice, Ellie," she said, her voice hard. "These people are sharing with you. It would be rude not to take a drag and pass it on." She held out her hand ready to take the joint, its tip glowing brighter when the boy next to her took a drag.

Ellie froze again. Her heart thudded and her breath caught in her throat. *I don't want to make them mad, but this is illegal!* She felt the panther's hot breath on her face as Susan reached for the joint, put it to her lips, and drew on it. A wisp of smoke passed in front her face, making her squint. She closed her eyes, tilted back her head, and held her breath. She held the joint in her fingertips—poised in front of Ellie—ready for her to take it.

Ellie's palms felt wet and the panther held tight. *I didn't know this would happen. Not prepared for it. Drugs are not good. Have to make a decision—fast.*

"I can't. I just can't!" Ellie shouted, then jumped up and ran through the beads. She kept going past Paisley and Rad, out the lopsided door, down the front steps, and across the veranda to Susan's car.

She stopped when she reached the car and slapped her hands on its low roof. Her breaths came in quick, panicked bursts as she put her forehead against the cool metal, but the Ville's eerie presence immobilized her. How was she supposed to get back to the safety of Hank and Patti's apartment?

Chapter 8

Still holding onto the car, Ellie tried to calm her breathing, then looked
up to a faint light above the trees. Campus must be that way. She had
to find a phone, so she began walking toward the glow, then started
running, stumbling on the uneven sidewalk.

She was out of breath and tiring by the time the campus buildings
came into view. She slowed to a walk, checked her watch, and saw that
it was 11:30. Her hands shook and her head throbbed, but she willed
herself to head for a bright spot ahead.

Twenty minutes later, Patti picked her up at the all-night gas station,
wearing sweats and bedroom slippers. Ellie climbed into the car and
murmured "Thank you," but that was all she could manage.

On the way to the apartment, Ellie was still speechless, slumped in
the passenger seat with her head down and her hands gripped tight in
her lap, while Patti shot quick, concerned, sidelong looks in her direction. When they got to the apartment, Ellie ran straight to her room.

The next morning, she felt like a hurricane survivor climbing out
from under the rubble when Patti put a cup of dark coffee in front of her
and sat down across the table.

"Okay, can you tell me about last night?" Patti asked, her voice soft
and her eyes intent.

Ellie took a deep breath but couldn't make eye contact. She started from the beginning and described everything while Patti drank her coffee, listening to every word of the story.

"I've never been so scared," Ellie concluded. "I was so relieved when you pulled up."

"I'm glad you called me." Patti clasped her hands around her cup. "I've heard about parties like that, and I suppose it's not surprising that people in the Ville use pot so openly. Did you think about that before you went?" Her voice remained gentle, sympathetic.

Ellie rested her elbows on the table and fiddled with her cup's handle. She stared at the dark liquid and let the steam warm her face. "I don't know. I should have, I guess. It . . . it's just that Susan didn't say anything about what the party would be like. I ran out like an idiot. I didn't say bye or anything, and she sits by me in class, so I'll be right next to her until finals are over. What am I going to say to her?"

Patti thought for a minute, then said, "Please don't fret over this because you can't know—no one can know—what the future holds. Susan's reaction will tell you a lot about who she is. All of us have to figure out for ourselves who our friends are and how we're going to live, Ellie. People make mistakes—bad decisions—all the time, and sometimes it takes making mistakes to figure out for yourself what you're made of. That's what Hank told you, right?"

"But why does it have to be so hard?" Ellie moaned. She paused a moment before looking up in a full panic. "Are you going to tell Hank about last night?"

"It's not my place to do that. You can tell him yourself when you're ready. You're new at being on your own, and you need to learn from this. Next time you can find out more in advance and decide whether or not you want to go into unknown territory."

Patti reached over and squeezed Ellie's hand. Her eyes held Ellie's for a moment before she stood up and put her cup in the sink, then grabbed her purse and said, "This is my Saturday to work a half day, so I have to head out. Please don't let last night spoil today, okay? Bye, new little sister, and take it easy. You'll be fine."

After giving Ellie's shoulder a reassuring touch, Patti left Ellie alone at the table. She needed to go to her thinking place, but she didn't want to see Susan under the tree on campus. There was only one other place to go at a time like this, and a warm April Saturday was the perfect time to be there.

The familiar sound of the old door scraping across the threshold greeted Ellie as she stepped inside and took in the magic of the lake house. In the summer, the rambling old building gave off the scent of the cedar-wood Grandpa had used so long ago, but now it was dark and musty, smelling of a Florida winter. Ellie left the door open behind her, went upstairs, and opened all the bedroom windows. She came back down and stopped at the bottom of the stairs to look around the great room with its exposed wood beams, plank floors, and timber walls. Two sets of board-and-batten doors on her left opened onto each end of the porch. The entire south wall was dedicated to a huge granite fireplace; across the room, Grandma had placed a dining table that ran parallel to the north wall, where Ellie now stood. She could almost smell the aroma of the meals Grandma used to set out on that table in the years before age overtook her.

Grandpa had built this house under the huge oak trees that shaded the spacious porch overlooking the lake. Grandma had furnished it with comfortable sofas and chairs made for watching the spectacular sun-sets. Ellie unlatched one set of the doors and threw them open, then did the same to the doors on the other end. The perfume from Grandma's camellias flowed into the house, and the lake and wetlands came into view. Ellie leaned against the doorframe, crossed her arms over her chest, and took it all in.

The oaks' thick trunks rose toward the sky and tapered into rough and knobby limbs that swooped downward in curves, nearly touching the ground before stretching upward again. The sight of the trees calmed her, and she remembered how Hank had said that this place was Gilead's balm for him. He had leaned back on the couch and said the lake was the portal through which he stepped away from reality.

She grinned when she thought of Hank—a big, strong, tough Marine—revealing his poetic side by saying his cares disappeared into the blue-green depths of water that he said looked like molten quartz.

"Maybe my worries will go away too," she said to the trees.

Last September she had come to the lake while Hank was at Basic School and Hurricane Greta wandered a hundred miles off the coast. The storm had pushed ashore warm late-afternoon breezes that made the lake ripple, sparkling silver in the sun, as the thunderhead loomed above the horizon, a shadowy hint of the massive storm at sea.

Back in the present, she looked over her shoulder at the stones around the fireplace. A dozen family photos in mismatched frames covered the thick, rough-hewn mantel embedded in the rocks above the hearth. Her grandparents' twin overstuffed chairs faced the fireplace, their arms touching. Grandma had said she put the chairs that way so she and Grandpa could sit in front of the fire and be by the lake at the same time. "It feels like you're outside when you're inside!" Grandma had laughed.

Ellie went over and put her hand on the mantel, leaning closer to study a black-and-white print of her parents. There was Dad, his hands in the pockets of 1940s-style pleated trousers, standing close to Mom in a flower-print dress. Her arm was linked through his at the elbow, and her head rested on his shoulder while her long, tapered fingers relaxed against his forearm. A dapper-looking couple, they smiled and leaned against a fancy car.

Another picture—this one in color—showed a skinny, tow-headed ragamuffin in a baggy swimsuit with her chin tucked down against her throat. Her round eyes, sad at the corners, looked upward toward the camera. Hank stood beside her in his swim trunks, standing a foot and a half taller, encircling her shoulders with his arm, while his solemn face looked straight into the camera. She thought about that terrifying day at the lake when she nearly drowned. He had always been beside her whenever she needed help. Until now.

Ellie's eyes stung as she shook her head and stepped back, then kicked off her shoes. She padded across the wide threshold to the old couch on the porch. She shook out the cushions, then put them back in place. Dust particles floated in the air, and without warning she sneezed, flinching at the loud explosion in the quiet. She stretched out on the worn cushions and sighed, turning on her side so she could see both the lake and sky.

She watched the clouds change shape, and their forms reflected upside down on the placid water. The trees whispered to her, and a warm breeze caressed her face, sweeping away the dust and soothing her to the edge of sleep, thoughts scrolling through her mind.

Hank had said Dad's disdain was not her fault. Mira said Mom loved her. But Susan told her she was naïve and needed to make her own decisions. Cameron said she was doing a great job, while Patti said making mistakes was normal and good because people learned from them.

Five people were telling her five different things, yet she didn't fully agree with any of them. *How can that be?* She had been taught to look right, to act right, and to think right, and Mom and Dad were the ones who determined what was right. Ellie wanted to be liked, even loved, so she had tried hard to do what she was told, but now the rules were changing. She thought she had understood them before, but everything was shifting, and she felt as if the rug were being pulled out from under her. Nothing made sense anymore.

A sandhill crane's bugle call woke her up, and she sat up, blinking. Two cranes were strutting along the shore on black, spindly legs, their long necks and small heads atop bodies too large for their legs. Their jet-black beaks and scarlet crowns seemed too dramatic for the mousy gray feathers below.

"You are strange and beautiful creatures, Mr. and Mrs. Crane," she yawned.

A red head near the water bobbed as if in response. The cranes paused and looked directly at her before one lowered its head and began to stride quickly along the shoreline. The second followed suit. They stretched broad wings and rose above the lake, their wings pumping smoothly before they sailed through the air, silhouetted against an orangey-pink sky. Graceful and lovely, they sailed effortlessly toward the wetlands. Watching them, Ellie marveled at the fact that oddly put-together things could be beautiful. She had never thought of that before.

She stood up and stepped over the threshold before turning to latch the porch doors back together. After closing up the house, she returned to Patti's apartment, satisfied that winter's stale air had been carried away and replaced by the clean scents of spring.

It was near the end of April, and the winter trimester would be over soon. Ellie was already in her seat waiting for the exam booklet when Joe plopped down beside her and stashed his notebook under his desk chair. He nodded and, as usual, favored her with a magnetic grin while she jiggled a pencil between her fingers, her mind on Hank and the jungles of Vietnam.

Joe leaned toward her. "How you doing? Ready for this exam?"

She tried to seem casual as she said, "I'm fine. Studied, so I think I'm ready." She lowered her chin and glanced at him, their eyes holding for a moment.

"What are your summer plans?" he asked, turning in his seat to face her.

"Nothing much," she said. "I have to finish up some biology research, but I plan to take a break until school starts again. I may try to find a job or something. What about you?" She looked away, then settled back in her seat and resumed fiddling with her pencil.

"I have to work this summer, but I've already got a job at a cool restaurant, so it'll be fun. Good tips. It's called Mary Jane's, but for most of us, it's MJ for short. You should come see me there sometime."

"Yeah, maybe." She looked at him. "So you'll stay here and work all summer?"

He put his hand on the back of her seat and tilted his head to the side while his bedroom eyes searched her sad ones. "Are you saying you're glad I'll be here all summer?' he asked, a wide grin spreading across his face. "I thought someone else was on your mind." When she didn't correct him, he continued: "Does that mean you're willing to have coffee with me?"

With Joe's eyes so focused on her, tingles spread through her body, her face warming the same way it had that first day in Cameron's office.

"Well, maybe—sometime, I guess." She looked away and focused on her pencil.

"I'll be more direct," he said. "Would you meet me at the coffee shop across the street from campus? You know, the Cuppa Coffeehouse—the one you can see from the pond next to the big, old tree on the corner." His voice became more insistent as his eyes continued to stare at her. "I have to finish a term paper, so I can't ask you to meet me today, but can we plan on meeting when finals are over?"

"Yeah, I know the place, but my last written exam is on Wednesday. Maybe you could ask me again after I get that off my mind." She kept her eyes glued to the empty desktop.

"Oh, you can bet I'll—" Joe didn't finish his thought but tapped her arm instead. "Our classmate doesn't look so good." He jerked his head toward the door, and Ellie followed his gaze.

Susan strolled in just as the professor called class to order and the teaching assistant started handing out exam booklets. Ellie's shoulders tensed and braced for the panther's strike. In the past, she and Susan had always chatted before class started and said goodbye afterward, but they had exchanged few words since the party. Since neither had mentioned Ellie's panicked retreat, an undeniable coldness had entered their relationship.

Because Susan had been her first and only friend on campus, Ellie wanted to explain why she ran out that night in the hopes some kind of explanation might save the friendship, but Susan had been in class only sporadically in the last weeks and didn't talk when she came, leaving Ellie no chance to repair the relationship.

Now Susan's eyes were surrounded by dark circles, and jailhouse-pale skin, messy hair, and wrinkled clothes completed her haggard look. She pushed her way down the row and offered Ellie an anemic smile just as Ellie bent over her exam and started writing.

Patti was already in her bedroom when Ellie came home after the exam and found three letters from Hank on the kitchen table. She poured a glass of wine and headed for her own room to read her brother's latest news.

Okinawa
25 Apr 67

Dear Mom, Dad & Ellie,

I know it's been quite a while since I've written, but things were pretty hectic. We (the whole battalion—3 /4) were pulled back to regroup and rebuild in Oki. Patti found out (through the wives' grapevine) that some of my friends from Basic

*School are near the DMZ or at least west of Dong Ha, so
they're in the thick of it. Lots going on there!*

*I was thinking this morning how important mail is to me. I
really live for my mail. I guess it must be the same for all of us.
Another thing I'm glad of is that Patti and I got married before
I came over here. It really gives me tremendous relief knowing
she's there waiting for me and looking forward to our future as
much as I am.*

*We've been doing a lot of training here. The other day we
(L Co.) went out to what they call "the jungle lane." We had
to walk three miles up with 85-lb. packs on our backs into the
mountains to get to the lane. They had all of these comman-
do-type climbs, etc., a booby trap trail about 1/2 mile long and
a pop-up target range. There was also a 2-rope bridge and a
3-rope bridge, which you had to cross above a 70-ft gorge. The
booby trap trail was about the best, not because of the traps,
but because of the terrain. It was really jungle, guerilla stuff.
At one point we had to climb down (by ropes) a 50-ft sheer
rock cliff. It really was wild and very rigorous. We're getting
ready for some rough jungle combat.*

Relief flooded through Ellie when she read that Hank was not in Vietnam. He had not mentioned the letters she sent at least once a week,
but that was okay because he had lots to say and she didn't have much
to write about. But he said he appreciated every one he got—however
mundane and dreary. She kicked off her shoes, stretched out on the
bed—her head propped up on the pillows—and kept reading.

*In response to Dad's question about liver flukes, etc., they
have everything, all of it, in VN. Many times in hot weather we
had to drink out of the rural streams, but I always use three
halazone tabs for protection. I think it's kind of dumb to drink
dirty water and expect to come out OK . . . without worms or
flukes or something. I have had no immediate ill effects from
the water, but my digestion hasn't been right (normal) for some
time, and although it doesn't bother me, it indicates something*

out of the ordinary. Don't worry (especially, Dad)—if it keeps up I will go to the doctor before we go back in country (that means back to VN for you civilians!)

In a day or two I'm going to do a little skin diving with a couple of buddies at Camp Schwab here on Okinawa. They have wide sand beaches like home and beautiful coral reefs to enjoy. You can also rent a boat, if you want to be on the water instead of under it. I like both, so we'll see. I'm planning on taking a bus ride down to Naha because they have some interesting outdoor markets where I might be able to find some things to send back home, but I'll let you know how it goes. It's been good to have a little R&R here, but in the long run it will be better to have some real R&R with Patti in Hawaii! That'll probably be in July, and, boy, am I looking forward to it!

Well, I'm about talked out for tonight.

I love you and miss you,
Hank

Ellie smiled and thought about Hank skin diving with his buddies. She couldn't wait to hear about his trip to Naha and made a mental note to look it up on the map.

Okinawa
8 May 67

Dear Family,

Well, I'm still here on Oki. Like I said, we've been training, but the Bn is here to refit and get replacement personnel so L company picked up 3 new Lts. I'll still have my platoon, which is good. We'll leave here late this month, make some practice landings, and then go back and do some in VN itself.

My trip to Naha was a little disappointing because I couldn't find what I wanted to send you, but I picked up some color- ful "fish" banners for everyone. Couldn't find a frog one for Ellie—ha! I wanted to get one of the exquisite silk kimonos for Patti, but didn't see one I liked so I found another one—not as fancy—but really pretty. Good thing I took a Japanese-English

*dictionary with me because I had a good time talking to the
people. They were very nice and patient. It was pretty interesting how all of the little shops run together, set up in such a way
that it was a complete honeycomb. You could walk down the
streets or narrow alleyways or through one shop into the next.
I heard about a tea-drinking ceremony and got a cab driver to
take me to a tea house, but the boysan (waiter) said they were
not open yet. So I went back to my quarters and took a nap,
then decided to write. We heard on the news that Dong Ha got
hit again. Things are really lively in Quang Tri.*

    Keep the cards and letters coming!

I love you and miss you,
Hank

She put the letter on the bed next to the first one and thought for
a minute. Hank kept writing about the action in Vietnam, but he was
still safe on Okinawa, and she'd rather think about that. She couldn't
wait to see Patti in the kimono. *Wonder what color it is?* A smile crept
across her face at the thought, so she picked up the last letter and started
reading, but the smile disappeared by the end of Hank's first paragraph.

Naha AFB on the way back to the VN jungle!
14 May 67

Dear Mom, Dad & Ellie,

    *This will have to be short because it's late and I am in need
of a little rest. The Bn is moving out tomorrow morning. It
really was a surprise to all of us so I guess it's just one of those
things. We are going back to Dong Ha then, probably headed
back to the Square.*

    *Things are pretty warm (lots of combat action, I mean) up
there, but we will make out fine. Better turn in. Full details at
the first opportunity.*

I love you and miss you,
Hank

Ellie reread the last letter and understood why Patti was in her room and had not greeted her when she came in. Hank was probably back in Leatherneck Square at this very moment, and he had been there for several days. That was not what Ellie wanted to think about, but not knowing what was happening to Hank was the cold reality she and her family had to face.

She wasn't sure if she could do it.

Chapter 9

Even though it was morning, Ellie was beginning to sweat as she hurried past her tree on the way to Cameron's office. Going to meet with her biology professor was a welcome distraction after the hours she'd spent brooding over Hank's letters. She was glad Cameron had convinced her to take an incomplete in the spring trimester and commit to a few more weeks of research because exploring publications kept her mind off worrisome things. Besides, she was eager to show him the significant article she'd found, so she bounded up the steps, yanked open the heavy door, and headed to his office, clutching several xeroxed pages with her notes scribbled in the margins.

The scent of his cologne met her at the open door, and she hesitated, unsure whether her excitement was because she had something to share or because she would see him. His back was to the open door, but when she knocked on the doorframe, he swiveled around in his chair. Their eyes met for a heartbeat, his eyebrows shot up, and he greeted her with a broad smile.

"Hi, El! I'm glad to see you." Cameron glanced at his watch and added, "You're early!" He stood up and moved a pile of lab notebooks off the side chair where she usually sat, putting them on top of another stack of books while she took her usual place next to his desk.

"Sorry to barge in, but I thought this was important enough to come over without calling first, and I wanted you to have it." She handed him the papers. "I found this article footnoted in a forensics journal article, so I looked it up and read it this morning. It's a discussion of a criminology theory related to genetic tendencies. The question is, Do innate factors influence serial killers?" She pointed to the note she had scrawled across the top: "Is the tendency toward homicide an inherited trait?"

"I thought this might fit in your book somehow," she concluded.

He took the papers and sat down as he studied them, all the while stroking his goatee.

She figured it would be a few minutes before he finished reading, so she stood up and stepped over to look through the big window, waiting for him to finish.

Her tree and the pond looked calm and inviting in the distance and cardinals romped with smaller birds among the trees just outside the window. The birds hopped from branch to branch, flew away, and came back to perch, chirping, cocking their heads, and looking at her. Absorbed by the colors and activity outside, she didn't know Cameron was near her until he put his hands on her shoulders and turned her around to face him.

"This is brilliant! You're amazing!" he exclaimed, towering over her. "This is the link I needed to make my theories relevant in nonacademic settings. This connection can be used in the real world, by psychiatrists or in forensic examinations. It's science applied in the real world—exactly the kind of pertinent information I want to publish." His voice was almost giddy, and his eyes shone, alight with excitement, as if he were an archeologist who had just made a discovery. He stepped away and pushed the door closed, then turned back to her.

Ellie smiled and opened her mouth to reply but never got a word out because he swept her into his arms and bear-hugged her. Purely by reflex, she wrapped her arms around him and found herself hugging him back, his tense muscles radiating desire.

His breath was warm against her ear, and the scent of his cologne—for so long only an occasional whiff of pleasure—now filled her senses and blocked out anything else. She stood still, breathing him in. Then she felt his mouth against her cheek.

Paralyzed with shock, she allowed his lips to caress her eyelid. His tongue teased her lashes, and his mouth moved closer to hers until, finally, he kissed her gently but with the confidence of a man. She had never been touched like this before. The boy who had kissed her in high school was tentative and shy, fumbling in his attempt. Nothing like this.

Cameron released her and took her face in his hands, his eyes inches away from hers. She stood still and mute, but her hands, as if separate from her mind, slid to his waist, and his body was so close she could feel his heart beating under his shirt. Hers was pounding when he kissed her again, this time with passion as his lips opened, taking hers with them. Her body was on fire as his left hand slid around to the nape of her neck and his fingers began caressing sensitive pressure points. Her body responded, tingling all over, and she was powerless to move.

When his lips came away, his face was not quite touching hers, but she felt his heat. "Since the first time you came here," he whispered, "I've wanted to hold you. To kiss you."

"You h-have?" she breathed, so stunned at his words that she was barely able to talk. She didn't—couldn't—object when his right hand slipped from her cheek and slid down her neck to the softness between her breasts. His warm touch against her chest made her head spin, and her body came alive in a way she had never felt. It burned from the inside out. As her breathing grew heavier, she looked down to see his long fingers unbuttoning her blouse.

The sound of muted voices in the hall brought her back from the edge when Cameron was starting to undo the second button. Sanity returned, and she stepped back, released him, then let her arms fall to her sides, shaking her head mechanically. She lifted her hands to rebutton her blouse as she took another step to the side. Time froze as he stared at her, his hands poised in the air.

"Ellie? What are you doing?" he asked, dropping his hands. When she didn't answer, he stood still for a moment before going to his desk. "You need to relax." There was no more softness in his voice, and a stern arrogance replaced the gentleness. "You don't know what you're missing."

"Cameron, I-I don't know what to say," she stammered, looking at the silver-framed photograph on his desk. "This is all new for me, and I don't know what's going on, but this . . . seems wrong." Even though her hands trembled and her heart pounded, a cog snapped into place in her mind, so she continued: "I'm sorry, but I have to go." She grabbed her satchel and stumbled toward the door, but when her hand touched the doorknob, she turned to look at him. "I don't know what to do. I'm sorry to disappoint you, but I have to think." She hurried out, leaving the door open behind her.

"You *don't* have to think!" he called after her. "Don't *think*, damn it!"

The sound of his voice chased her down the hall to the heavy outside door and echoed in her ears as she ran down the stairs, across the sidewalks to her tree. It took hours for Cameron's voice to dissipate into the sounds around her.

It was dusk by the time she walked into the apartment. Patti called out a hello, and Ellie answered, saying she'd be there in a minute. Shame and guilt enveloped her as she dropped her things on the bed and stood there, frozen. Her mind and emotions were a mass of knotted wires, jumbled and useless, because she didn't know what to do about the incident with Cameron. But she could not stay in her room all night.

Willing her thoughts to Patti's brightness, she stepped out into the hall, went to the bathroom, and threw cool water on her face. With water dripping from her chin, her image in the mirror was of a swimmer surfacing from a deep dive, desperate for fresh air. She longed for simple answers to her problems, but there weren't any, so she brushed away the droplets and made herself go to the kitchen.

Unable to relax and concentrate on dinner, she could not bring herself to say anything to Patti about what had happened with her professor. Neither of them had much to say, which Ellie assumed was her fault. But as soon as dinner was over, a serious Patti handed her a letter from Hank.

"He's back in the field," she said without making eye contact. "There's a note on the back." Patti stood up grimly and drew an X through the day on the calendar. As she headed to her room, she called back for Ellie to just leave the dishes until morning.

Ellie piled the dishes in the sink, stress making her head begin to pound when she picked up the letter and went to her room. She settled on her bed to read, but the muddle in her mind thickened with each word she read.

Thursday
16 May 67

Dear All,

Guess you can tell from the "FREE" postage on the envelope that I am once again in VN. I just finished writing Patti about my travels, but I'll spare her having to tell you what's going on and give you the details firsthand. We got the word to move out of Okinawa on Sunday morning, and by Monday night all 3 Bns (the 3/4, 2/26, & 2/9) along with their support and, of course, infantry companies had arrived back in VN. By tonight our supply and other rear elements will be here with us. That's thousands of men and a lot of equipment moving fast. Agility at its best!

We flew from Naha in a constant stream of Air Force C-130s. Before we left, I counted over 40 aircraft sitting on the tarmac at the ready, so I guess the total airlift was about 60. These planes are so big that they can carry a 6x6 trailer along with troops. Huge!

Now, we are living out in the bush, hunkered down in the grass because our tents—naturally—are a low priority. We pitched available shelter and dug foxholes this morning, got ammo, grenades, etc. We're supposed to be ready to move out by tonight, but it might be Friday before we actually do. Because of some problems with M-14 rifles, we got the M-16 while we were in Oki. It's a sweet piece of machinery, but I don't think it's going to make a major difference because the M-14 is a good weapon too.

One thing, though, my men are carrying 600+ rounds of 5.52 ammo, whereas 300 or so was the max before—that's about 20 extra pounds in addition to their regular gear. Bottom line: that's a bunch of weight to hump around. In fact, machine gun ammo humpers carry 1500 rounds with them.

It has been a beautiful day except it was pretty hot this afternoon. In a strange sort of way, it is nice to be back in the field. Maybe the nature bit has gotten to me! Old Dong Ha is about the same except for a lot of chopper activity—'cause they re-supply the field, but the big artillery has been pretty quiet. Last night some of the new guys—we call 'um a stronger name—FNG—cause they haven't had experience out here, but the F-word is Marine language—not for the ladies' ears! Anyway, the FNGs were bothered by the artillery. But as long as it's ours, it doesn't bother me. As a matter of fact, I slept like a baby!

I have to go. The XO wants us to do some PT—physical training—of all things! I'll write again soon.

I love you and miss you,
Hank

Ellie turned over the letter and found a hastily scribbled note on the back.

> *I write to my dear family as a whole because of the press of time. Things seem to be going pretty well, except at 0330 this morning 140mm enemy rockets fired on us. We hit the deck, but damage to men and equipment was done.*
>
> *By the time you get this it will be in the news . . . we got the word last night that we are going on a helo operation in the DMZ. There are several Bns involved so this will be quite a show. I feel confident that we can do well and will do so.*
>
> *I am thinking of you all always and miss you very much. I will write again ASAP.*
>
> *Hank*

Hank's note told the story of what was going on; he was under fire and surrounded by death. The letter was ten days old, so she feared he was still in the DMZ, but hoped—prayed—the DMZ operation was over, and he was someplace safer by now.

Ellie awoke the next morning and felt her world dangerously close to derailing, and there she was—alone and trying to regain control. After having read Hank's news and mentally reliving the scene in Cameron's office, she feared her life and her fledgling independence were coming apart.

Even so, something—maybe the anticipation of another, more reassuring letter from Hank—drew her to her parents' house. She eased into the driveway and stopped her car in the exact spot where Hank had parked almost seven months ago just before he said goodbye. Memories of growing up with him, thoughts of the moment, and apprehension about the future tangled in her mind like last year's Christmas lights pulled from storage. She sat in the car and looked at the house that was familiar yet foreboding. A strange sense of comfort descended on her because even though she was often unhappy in that home, it was a predictable place, and there was a comfort in knowing what to expect. She took a deep breath, clicked off the car, and started toward the front door.

Because she had not seen Dad's car, Ellie knew Mom was the only parent she would have to deal with, and at least she was aloof and non-confrontational, which was easier to handle than Dad's anger and criticism. If Mom was sober, maybe she could share a few cordial words. Ellie stopped to look at the gigantic magnolia tree near the steps; dozens of the huge white flowers dotted the soaring branches like clumps of cotton placed there by some great hand. Remembering childhood days, she gazed at the dark and cozy place under the branches where she had found shelter in the flowers' distinct, soft fragrance and the velvety petals that cupped protectively around the complex flower centers. She smiled when she realized Hank would be home by the time the blossoms produced their red seeds. Clinging to the thought of Hank's homecoming, she went up the steps to the front door.

The door was unlocked, so she pushed it open and stepped into a dim space, and an old feeling—something like dread—came over her. Then an image materialized in the shadows across the room. She didn't know what it was at first, but when it moved, she took a step forward and saw it was Mom slouched on the end of the couch with a cigarette dangling from her fingers. Spent ashes littered her rumpled blouse, and her skirt bunched at her hips in a way that revealed her knees. Ellie had never seen her mother so sloppy, so unkempt.

A tumbler most likely filled with her mother's favorite—Chivas and very little water—tilted half-on and half-off a crystal coaster on the side table, and a piece of paper with its top and bottom turned up at the fold lines lay next to the coaster. Ellie took a step farther into the room and saw Hank's familiar handwriting on the paper by the coaster, but a movement drew her eye back toward her mother, who shook her head and struggled to her feet, sending a mini-snowstorm of ashes spiraling to the floor. She took a few wobbling steps to her left and grabbed hold of the high-back chair next to the couch. Posing unsteadily with her eyes wide and unblinking, she stared in her daughter's direction, but as recognition spread across her mother's face, a deep, harsh scowl appeared. Neither said anything, but they faced off opposite each other like lawyers in front of a judge, and a pall descended around them, shrouding Ellie's hope of finding any kind of consolation here.

"Well, hullo, El'nor," her mom intoned, lifting her chin in a transparent attempt to muster courage and dignity. She raised her voice and blurted, "Where've you been, yun' lady? You haven't come to see us in a long time. You mus' not like us anymore, and all we've ever tried to do is help you become something." The stinging words found their mark, so Ellie stood still, heaviness filling her mind, body, and spirit.

Patti had mentioned her concern about Mom's state of mind, but Ellie had no idea Mom's drinking had gotten this bad. Something akin to pity took Ellie by surprise. She had never felt that kind of emotion when she looked at her mother, but now the woman's classic beauty and elegance were buried under drunkenness and disarray. Ellie's insides constricted as she realized it was a mistake to be here. She wondered what she was to do, but this was her family: Mom, Dad, Hank, Patti, and Mira—they were all she had. Something deep inside wouldn't let her abandon any one of them—good or bad—in spite of her own emotional turmoil.

After a few minutes of her mom's ravings, another cog dropped inside Ellie—like the one that had snapped into place before she moved out months earlier. Boiling anger came to the surface, hostility bubbling out before Ellie could stop it.

"I've been where I always am, Mom," she said in a loud voice she hardly recognized as her own. "I've been on campus. Looking right, acting right, thinking right—isn't that what you expect me to do? Acting like I want an education, but really trying to snag a man because I have to find a husband so I can get married so you won't have to put up with me anymore. I'm supposed to live happily ever after, like you— right? Oh, and by the way, that's even though I might want something different!"

The sharpness of her words stunned both of them. Her mother tee- tered as if pushed back by the blow of her daughter's honesty, but then she lurched forward. Ellie felt sick. How often did her mother get drunk like this? As quickly as it had erupted, Ellie's anger dropped to a sim- mer, and she immediately regretted snapping at her mother. More than before, she felt terribly sorry for her.

Speaking more gently, she said, "You need to drink some coffee and get straightened out before Dad comes home." She reached out for her mother. "Come on, let's go to the kitchen."

"H-home? You kiddin'? He's at th' hospital. Won' get here 'til I'm asleep. Same as every night!" She spat out the words, then tried to poke her blouse into her waistband with one hand while pulling at her skirt with the other in an unsuccessful effort to smooth it down. When she bent over to straighten the hem, she wavered and nearly fell down.

It was a sad scene, and Ellie dug deep into her heart to lay aside her irritation and try to respond as Hank would have. "Okay, then," she said, "come into the kitchen, and I'll make you something to eat." Ellie held her hand out to her mother for a second time.

"You don' even know how to cook. You thin' you can make me some- thin'. Ha! Tha's rich!" She stumbled toward the kitchen door. "I kin make my own food, thank ya, yun' lady!" She ignored Ellie's hand, and Ellie stood back to let her mother pass.

"Just stay outta my way!" her mother yelled without looking back as she disappeared through the door with a grand, queenly gesture cutting through the air.

Ellie stepped to the small table, grabbed Hank's letter, and put it in her pocket before walking to the kitchen door, where she abruptly stopped. Mom was at the table, her face buried in her hands, rocking, and moaning.

Ellie crossed her arms and leaned against the doorframe until Mom placed both palms flat on the table to push herself up. Wobbling to the cupboard, she yanked a glass off the shelf and pulled a whiskey bottle from inside the large flour canister on the counter.

Ellie stiffened. "Really, Mom? Hiding whiskey in the flour? Does Dad know it's there?"

Gripping the bottle partway down its neck, her mother filled the glass with liquid painkiller, then downed half of it in one gulp. Her face hard with resentment, she turned to her daughter, looked her straight in the eye, and finished off the drink.

"I don' know an' don' care what he knows." She grabbed the bottle again and poured more whiskey into her glass.

Her mother's self-destruction made Ellie's skin crawl, and she wondered if Mom was beyond help. The hope of a decent conversation dashed, Ellie turned and walked out the door as hot, angry tears threatened to spill over. She didn't try to fight the tears, and as she got in the car, they flowed because she could see no good future in store. Her mind heavy with doubt, she drove to the closest place of solace she knew—her thinking tree. She pulled the letter from her pocket in hopes it would somehow offer reassurances about her big brother's well-being, but the first thing she noticed was that he had written it from the DMZ.

18 May 67
Somewhere in the jungle!

Dear Mom, Dad & Ellie,

> *We have been in and out of the DMZ for days, but most of the heavy action has been to the south and west of our positions. Shelling is so loud it sounds like there are Bns of bad*

*guys around there, and there must be lots all around us; we
don't see them cause they're good at hiding in the jungle. Dad,
you can find Hill 117 on the map. Took us 2 days with lots of
casualties and wounded, but we took it. The VC dug in on the
south side and attacked H Co 2/26 before we could help them.
We put up a wall of arty all over the hill and finally secured it.
Lots of action, but I'm OK.*

*At the moment we are moving east through the jungle toward
Con Thien and 117 to block the enemy's escape to the north
where they can join the other Bns. We uncovered the enemy's
well-built and camouflaged fortifications. Found over 30 tons
of rice and 10 of ammo. We had to destroy the rice cause it
won't last in the heat, plus it's too far from anywhere to hump
out that much stuff. I'm used to the heat and humidity again so
I'm OK. Plus, we're well supported by air and arty.*

Time is passing rapidly and Patti—

Alarms went off in Ellie's head when she realized he had stopped
writing in midsentence and hadn't even had time to finish the letter. She
panicked at the thought of why. But true to form, Hank had scribbled a
reassuring phrase at the end.

Have to close. We're moving out. I'll be fine, don't worry.
                                            Love you & miss you,
                                                            Hank

Even though it scared her, Ellie reread the letter and, in the end, marveled at Hank's care to make sure—at a time when he was in grave
danger—that the message got to his family to calm them. Yet, here she
was, unable to tell anyone about Cameron and something as harmless
as a kiss. She held Hank's letter close and vowed to take a step and find
someone to talk to and hopefully find consolation, but who could that
be?

Chapter 10

After trying to absorb the information from Hank's latest letter, Ellie struggled to sleep that night. Between worrying about Hank, remembering Cameron's touch that she'd enjoyed too much, and trying to process her mother's rejection, Ellie's brain just wouldn't turn off. But she must have fallen asleep eventually, because early the next morning, bad dreams once again jolted her awake. She decided to go to the library to do more research, only this time she would do if for herself instead of Cameron DeMarco.

She had decided to research *where* Hank was fighting before moving on to why he was there. She pulled reference books and maps from their shelves, then lugged them to her favorite study spot and deposited them on the round table. In one of his letters, Hank had recommended an article in *Newsweek*'s December 1966 issue, so she started with that. Hank had said it was an accurate article about the Marines in Vietnam, and by cross-referencing it with the maps, she found the places Hank wrote about: Dong Ha, Gio Linh, Con Thien, the DMZ, and Leatherneck Square—places Dad had shown her on the map in his den.

The lengthy *Newsweek* article described how fierce guerrilla fighters—the Viet Cong—harassed Marine patrols with snipers, ambushes, and booby traps, then hid in the jungles. The Viet Cong, along with the North Vietnamese Army Regulars, were better trained than US military leaders had expected. Unsettled by what she read, Ellie stopped to catch her breath as she made her way through the article. She was even more disturbed when she remembered Hank had said the Vietnamese fighters moved back across the DMZ to regroup and refortify, then came across to ambush and kill American troops again.

Bending closer to the map, she saw a grayed, diagonal line labeled DMZ that followed the path of the Ben Hai River. A dark spot nestled next to the line was marked Con Thien. "Ah, the so-called Hill of Angels," she whispered. "Hank is probably near there right now."

She sat back and thought for a minute. Hank's first letters had been about Dong Ha, so she leaned over a map and found the camp, then picked up a picture of the large Dong Ha airfield.

"Now I see why Hank said it was a big target," she muttered to herself.

Leaning forward again, she found the South China Sea's jagged coast, then North Vietnam and Leatherneck Square, only three miles from the DMZ.

The reality slapped her when she read more articles and saw pages of pictures showing men in helmets, their fatigues covered with mud, slogging waist-deep through brown, opaque jungle water. There were others of troops in sweat-soaked T-shirts and combat pants sitting on haphazard piles of dirt or leaning against broken stubs of trees surrounded by ragged undergrowth. Images like these appeared on the nightly news. However, there was something more compelling about the faces captured in the still photos of men standing on craggy rises or in mud bogs, unshaven faces streaked with mud and sweat, holding rifles trained on something in the distance, cigarettes dangling from their lips. Some of the men seemed to be about her age—certainly not much older.

She stopped turning pages when she came to a picture of a Marine sitting on wet, brown earth under a rain-soaked scrap of drab-green canvas barely large enough to cover his head. He bent low, the nub of a pencil in his hand as he concentrated on a small piece of white paper spread on his knee. The caption read, "A Marine finds a minute to write a letter home." She sat back, transfixed by the realization that the Marine could be Hank.

A minute later, she found the place where Hank got the wound by his eye. One author said the Viet Cong wanted that hill so they could surveil and bombard Con Thien and its vital supply route. That route crossed the Cam Lo River on a sturdy wooden bridge built by the Sea-bees so the Marines could resupply their brothers holding Con Thien. With that, Ellie put aside hope of Hank finding any safe havens where he was.

"That must be why Dad said Hank was in the thick of things," she whispered.

The more she read, the more she understood why Dad was angry about the war. Nearly every author said American politicians and military leaders had misjudged the situation in Vietnam and the war effort was a mess—with Hank caught in the middle. She was angry now too.

Over the next hours, she learned that seek and destroy—move in fast and attack—was in the Marine DNA, but this war forced them into a holding pattern, and this new role of stalking the enemy in his jungle did not suit them. *So that's why Hank said that sitting and waiting was not good for his men's morale. Marines wanted to go and get, not sit and wait.*

Ellie's jaw ached, and a headache loomed, but there was one more article to read. She put it down when she read that a North Vietnamese official said they intended to make the Marines' capability stretch as thin as possible because they wanted to kill as many Marines as they could. She cringed, unable to read more. It was unbearable, thinking of Hank getting shot at, dodging explosions, and being bombarded with enemy fire, yet she was helpless. Her fist came down, thudding on the tabletop.

A hand touched her shoulder, and her head snapped around to find the library assistant leaning over her right shoulder, peering at her from under thick brows drawn together above his wide round eyes. "You okay?" he whispered.

"Oh, sorry," she said. "I didn't realize I made a noise. I read something that scared me. I'm fine." She tried to smile.

The assistant took his hand away and straightened up. "All right. Try to keep it down, will ya?"

She leaned forward, crossed her arms on the table, and rested her head against her forearms. She knew she didn't like the war, but she wasn't going to join any marches, because Hank's purpose—to keep a people from being overrun by others hungry for power—was just, even though it was in an ill-conceived conflict. She let that thought roll around her mind until the owlish library assistant announced closing time. She gathered up her things and left with a single thought in her mind: Hank was doing what he believed to be his purpose, no matter how dangerous, and now it was time to put her own life in order by finding her purpose, even though that seemed impossible.

Ellie's life looked no brighter as May turned into June, even though she had begun regularly meeting her new friend, Joe, for coffee. They talked about everything: Hank, her parents, her insecurities, and even Cameron. Joe had not made judgments or criticized her, and he didn't talk about other people, even though plenty of people nodded at him or flashed him a peace sign as a passing greeting. Moreover, she felt important when she was with him because he seemed to have a lot of friends, yet he chose to be with her.

"You miss your brother, don't you?" Joe had asked one day and reached over to touch her fingers. When she jumped at his touch, he pulled his hand away without a word of reproach.

The problem was that even though she enjoyed her time with Joe, Ellie couldn't stop thinking about Cameron, so now she was back at her tree, still kicking herself. Dad was right—she *was* self-absorbed. Hank was in Vietnam, in grave danger twenty-four hours a day, yet, in every letter, he took time to think of his family's peace of mind. In the meantime, all she was concerned about were her own silly, adolescent problems. *What a selfish person I am!*

Susan had called her naïve, and as if to prove that point, Ellie had allowed a married man to draw her into his force field. She should have known better. She should not have let him kiss her, and she most certainly should not have liked it. Even under her peaceful tree, the panther's black heaviness took over, and her body seemed to fill with cement. Shame and dread enveloped her, so thinking was impossible. She leaned forward, put her elbows on her knees, and buried her head in her hands. *What am I going to do?*

She wanted to go back to Cameron and feel him close to her again, but she knew it wasn't right. She liked being with him so much, but she knew she should not like it. He was married, committed to someone else. On the other hand, what harm would it do to enjoy his company? His wife didn't have to know, and besides, what she didn't know wouldn't hurt her. Ellie lifted her head and opened her eyes, "No!" she said aloud. "Getting involved with him is selfish, and even worse, it's foolish!" She slumped back against the tree and squeezed her eyes tight again. *What would Hank tell me to do about Cameron?*

"Ellie," he would probably say, "be careful and think things through before you do anything to damage yourself."

She knew Hank wasn't perfect. He made mistakes just like everyone else, but he had always handled his bad decisions on his own, learned from them, and kept moving forward. Now he faced life-threatening danger, and her worries seemed trivial by comparison. Even so, Cameron's temptations presented Ellie with a different kind of threat to the moral compass she tried to find, and she had to face that. It would help to talk to Patti about the struggle, but Patti's mind was filled with Hank's upcoming R and R—rest and recuperation—and Ellie couldn't bear to distract her with petty little college-girl problems.

Ellie smiled to herself as she recalled Patti's excitement the night before.

"It's definite that I'll be meeting Hank in Hawaii sometime in July," Patti had said, "but we don't know the exact dates yet. After he goes back, he'll have only a few more months in Vietnam, and then his war duty will be over. When he gets home, we'll be able to celebrate our first anniversary plus Thanksgiving and Christmas all at the same time!"

Ellie was glad her beautiful sister-in-law had something to look forward to over the coming months, but she, herself, couldn't imagine how to get through the next few days. "How . . . how do I . . .?" she began aloud, but the question dissolved when she sensed a presence nearby. She opened her eyes and found Susan taking a seat next to her.

"What's goin' on, friend?" Susan asked, as if nothing untoward had ever occurred between them. "You don't look good. Who are you talking to?"

Ellie gulped, unsure what to say; they had not said much since she ran away from the party. But as Susan seemed to carry no grudge, Ellie finally found her voice. "I have a lot on my mind," she said, her eyes straight ahead.

"What kinds of things? Your brother? Grades? Social life? Can't be a guy, can it? I noticed you and Joe talking before class a couple of times. He's cute and hip. Are you two gettin' it on?"

"No!. I mean—yeah—Joe's nice to talk to and everything, but we're just friends. We meet for coffee sometimes, but he's pretty busy since he works and shares an apartment with three roommates."

"Ha! What a bummer! I mean, how can he score with all that company? What's the point of free love if you can't enjoy it?"

"I'm telling you, Joe and I are just friends! Besides, that's not what's bothering me. There's someone else on my mind."

Susan grabbed Ellie's arm and forced her to make eye contact. "Oh, I knew it. Spill it—all of it!" Her face was alight with mischief.

Ellie squirmed and tried to think while Susan's eyes drilled into her. "There's not much of 'it,' really," she sighed. "But you have to promise you won't say a word to anyone. It involves someone on campus."

"Promise! Cross my heart." Susan's voice became hushed, conspiratorial. Her finger made an X over her heart.

Ellie felt as if she were back on the playground, sharing sixth-grade secrets, but she hesitated. Susan had befriended her when she needed a friend, and Ellie felt as if she owed her. Besides, Susan was not judgmental.

"Okay, Susan, here goes," Ellie said. "You remember I told you I had Dr. DeMarco for bio? Well, I've been doing research for him and . . . and, well, not long ago, he kissed me. He told me he'd wanted to do it ever since he first saw me but held back until he couldn't stand it anymore. I like him, but he's married, and I'm not sure what to do, and I have a feeling there may be more than kisses on his mind. I keep wondering, Who would it harm? His wife wouldn't have to know!"

Susan's lips became parallel lines, and she stared wide-eyed at her friend before she swallowed hard and fell back against the bench.

"Whew, I never thought I'd hear something like that coming from you!" she said, staring at Ellie. "Son of a bitch, you are full of surprises, chickie. DeMarco is your mystery man?" Susan blinked and turned to look into the distance.

"Well, yes," Ellie murmured.

Ellie expected her friend to say something, but Susan said nothing, which worried Ellie because Susan was usually open with her opinions. They sat in silence for a few endless minutes as Susan's face grew more and more stormy.

"Yeah, I know about Dr. DeMarco," she said at last. "I told you about him already, and you need to be careful! He's a scuzz, so take my advice and find a summer job or take a class, but forget about him." She chewed on her lower lip for a moment before her lips parted, and she sighed. Without warning, she slapped both knees and looked at Ellie.

"Well, here's my news: I flunked out," she said all of a sudden, her voice loud. "I haven't passed anthing, so my parents laid down the law and refused to pay tuition while I play around and party. They said they expected me to work toward a degree, which is not gonna happen, so I'm leaving school and won't be here this summer or when school starts in the fall. Have to find a job somewhere." There was finality in her voice, making it clear that no pleas or arguments would change things.

Ellie's heart fell. Susan, her only friend, was going away. Ellie didn't know what to say, but as Susan rose to leave, Ellie finally managed a question. "Will you keep in touch with me?" she asked. "You're the first straightforward, honest-to-a-fault friend I've ever had." Ellie mustered a weak smile and got to her feet to wrap her arms around Susan, who squeezed back for an instant before backing away a few steps.

"We'll see what the future holds, but I gotta motor on home now," she said, stretching her arms skyward. "I promise, my lips are sealed! No words about DeMarco to anyone—but if you're smart, you'll stay away from him." She covered her mouth with her fingers and winked as she turned on her heel and walked away.

Left alone, Ellie sank onto the bench and watched her only friend vanish from her life, their friendship ending as quickly as it had started.

Even though she was rarely home this early in the afternoon, Patti's car was by the curb when Ellie ran up the steps to the apartment door.

"Helloooo!" she called as she came through the door, trying to keep her voice light. She deposited her satchel in her bedroom and headed for the kitchen but stumbled to a halt when she saw Patti sitting immobile, staring out the window. Ellie had never seen her look like that.

Patti was at the table with her chin propped in one hand and her other hand clutching a wadded-up tissue in her lap. Her eyes and nose were red, and her lips curved downward, creating a picture of sadness. Sticking out from under the tissue, a letter with some sort of red emblem on the top of the page caught Ellie's eye.

Dread crawled up Ellie's back when she got a better look at the emblem and saw it was a cross—a bold red cross. Patti handed Ellie the letter and said, "This got here in four days because it came through the Red Cross."

> *29 May 67*
> *Phu Bai Surg Hosp*
>
> *Dear Patti*
> *(please be sure Mom, Dad & Ellie see this),*
>   *We've been out of the DMZ awhile, but yesterday afternoon I got hit by a mortar fragment that tore into my right calf. It was on the 28th when we found a huge bunker complex on Hill 174. That's about 4 miles to the southwest of Con Thien.*

Ellie's heart took off like a racehorse out of the gate, and she lowered herself into the chair opposite Patti, who stared into the distance while Ellie kept reading.

*The doc says I'll be back on full duty in 2 weeks so you can
see it isn't too serious. He opened up the wound entry & exit
points & put in a tube to let them drain. I get 1.2 million units
of penicillin every 12 hours or so (I think). I have full operation of my foot, but my ankle is numb on the inside. I had a
fever last night & my leg hurt, but I'm much better today.*

*Before I get too tired, here's what happened. We'd been on
the move doing sweeps in the Square when we made heavy
contact at Hill 174. The VC were dug in fortified bunkers
like the ones we'd found before. My company L (Lima) along
with M (Mike) went up the hill on attack, but we got hit with
small arms, machine guns, 57mm recoilless rifles and 82mm
mortars. I was hit going up, but there were thickets on top of
the hill and when another platoon (2nd) moved into them, 2
bunkers opened up on them and, at the same time, mortars
began hitting the rest of the column where I was & I was hit in
the initial barrage.*

*I was moving uphill when I suddenly found myself on the
ground with a numb leg and no idea where the blood was
coming from. I located the wound and cut off my trousers at
the knee with my K-bar because I knew I needed to stop the
bleeding and was starting to put on my battle dressing when
a corpsman found me. He said I'd be OK so he left me to tend
to a couple of more seriously wounded men. I found I could
hobble a little so I sent one of my squads further up the hill
to help 2nd plt, but the Capt radioed and told me to hold the
rest at the bottom. I told my SSgt to come up to me because
I couldn't move very fast. Together we maneuvered (me di-
recting, him helping me move) the other 2 squads to the side
of the hill, away from fire. In the meantime, SSgt had located
the mortar so we fired a couple of rockets at it, and we got it
because it was quiet after that.*

Questions whirred through Ellie's mind, but when she opened her
mouth no words came out, so she forced herself to keep reading.

Main trouble was the situation on top was so confused that the Capt didn't want us (not me, but my squads) to come up the flank because he was afraid we'd hit 2nd plt. along with the enemy fortifications. We could have carried the hill, but that was his decision. Later, the Bn operations office told us to pull back and evac the wounded after a 57mm recoilless fired and wounded several men in our mortar section. They were helo'd out first & I went out later with a couple of other med-evacs.

I'm angry at myself because I feel like it was my own darn fault I got hit. Should have been more careful and moved faster or something. But I did the best I could and that's what counts.

Someone said if Con Thien was The Hill of Angels, Hill 174 was where the Devil lived, and I believed them after yesterday.

Well, guess that's about all for now. The corpsman says I can get cleaned up since I haven't shaved or showered in 12 days—will keep you posted. I'm bushed.

I love you & miss you,
Hank

Patti's sigh filled the void. "I came home at lunch to get the mail because I was hoping for a letter from Hank, but the last thing I wanted was bad news," she said, her eyes filled with tears. "He got hit. I hate to think of him like that—in a field hospital—in that much pain. I can't do anything to help him. I guess this means he'll get another Purple Heart. That's two. The only good thing is if—God forbid—he gets one more, he can come home early because getting three purple hearts sends you home."

Ellie opened her mouth, then squeezed her eyes shut; still fighting to keep tears from flowing, she bit her lower lip to keep her chin still. Patti had enough to handle, and she didn't need Hank's kid sister blubbering like a baby, so Ellie studied a small drawing Hank had made near the bottom of the second page. It depicted his leg from thigh to foot, with a jagged tear below the back of the knee.

"He drew a picture of his injury," Patti said. "See?" As she talked, Patti put her finger on the drawing and traced the metal's path through Hank's flesh from his knee to a large spot above his ankle.

Ellie tried to wrap her mind around the fact that her big brother was injured and in a hospital somewhere on the other side of the world. "Where is he now?" she asked.

"He wrote us on May 29th—a day after he was hit—and he was in a hospital on a Marine base at Phu Bai, south of Leatherneck Square." Patti's eyes stayed on Hank's drawing, and she seemed to be talking to herself. "We'll probably get one or two more letters from the hospital, but we have no way of knowing where he is at this moment." She pushed her chair back and looked at Ellie. "It's only the third of June, and since he said the doctors had to send him back into the fighting as soon as he was fever-free and healing, he could already be back out in the field by now." Patti's face reddened, and her lips pressed together.

"Why does he have to go back to fight?"

"Because they need him. Besides, he wants to get back to his men. In one of my letters, he said they're working like a well-oiled machine, and as their platoon commander, he feels responsible for them and wants them to be safe. Plus, they've had each other's backs through rough times. Remember how he said the SSgt helped him after he got hit? Something happens to human beings when they face death together and have to depend on each other for survival. That's the Marine brotherhood."

"I wish he would come home. I hear so many things on campus about this awful war."

"I know, Ellie. I wish he could come home too." Patti took Ellie's hand. "But we have to wait until this combat tour is over. He said he would be okay, and I believe him, so please try to stay positive for his sake. Sorry, I lost it for a bit, but remember, he's a Marine, so he'll be fine, and so will we." Patti's voice gained strength as she talked. "The time will go by fast; you'll see. There's no reason we won't be on schedule to meet in Hawaii for R and R in July. Looking forward to that is enough to keep both of us going for now."

Patti stood up and opened the refrigerator, but Ellie remained motionless, thinking about Hank. She had to believe he would be okay and that he'd come home on time. Why is it so hard to believe? She felt empty—worthless—unable to help her big brother, but in spite of herself, she forced herself out of the chair and joined Patti as they went through the dinnertime routine, even though neither one was hungry.

"I'll do the dishes," Ellie said after the meal. She knew this was not the time to tell Patti what had happened with Cameron. Or that Susan had left. Or that she had found her mom hopelessly drunk.

Patti put an X over the day, said a polite good night, poured a glass of wine, and disappeared through the kitchen door.

Dishes tidied up, Ellie went to her bedroom and curled up on her bed. She stared into space, her mind refusing to wrap itself around the fact of Hank's injury. She fell asleep and immediately dreamed of an invincible Marine and his men towering above a lush, green jungle while anti-war protestors marched in circles around them.

Ellie awoke in a sweat, distraught from her dream, disoriented when she saw dim daylight fading into night. She threw her feet to the floor and looked at the clock by her bed. It was just before 9:00, but she had to talk to someone. She stood up, smoothed her clothes, and headed out the door when she realized there was only one person who could help her sort things out.

Chapter 11

Familiar campus buildings loomed gray and black when Ellie pulled into the unkempt parking lot of the restaurant where Joe worked. She parked in a spot facing the restaurant's entrance, switched off the engine, and sat back. Mary Jane's was a one-story, pitched-roofed wooden structure cowering beside the older, taller ones adjacent to campus, and the building's single distinction was a glass door imprinted with a picture of a steaming cup of coffee, its vapors rising and encircling the words Mary Jane's in fancy letters.

It was a late-night place, so she wasn't surprised to see people come and go, the weak light from the streetlamps making filmy reflections on the glass. She recoiled when a group came out looking like the people she had run away from in the Ville. *Don't freak about who's in there,* she said to herself. *Concentrate on finding Joe.* Feeling she had no choice, she walked to the dirty door and entered a smoke-filled din of rumbling voices, clattering plates, and the swirling odors of food and sweaty bodies. A thin haze hovered above a dozen or so oilcloth-covered tables, each with mismatched chairs, and Naugahyde booths along the outside wall, their backs cracked and split. Crumpled napkins festooned the piles of used dishes on several tables, as well as the filled tubs in the corners of the room.

Ellie stood motionless just inside the door and stared at the far wall, where heat lamps warmed steaming plates of food on the gray counter opening to the kitchen. The place was a beehive of activity, with cooks pushing plates through the opening and people in street clothes grabbing them in quick, purposeful movements to load up their large round trays. The servers' shoes clicked on sticky black-and-white linoleum, and a bicycle bell dinged intermittently, its shrill tone rising above the diners' voices and the servers' shouts.

"Order up. Get it now!" a voice boomed from behind the heat lights.

"On my way!" hollered a girl from across the room.

The only thing Ellie wanted to do was to find Joe—and fast—so she scanned the room and finally spotted him standing by a booth filled with girls. She didn't recognize him at first because his hair was uncombed, he was unshaven, and his clothes were wrinkled. He had looked completely different in class and when they met for coffee.

He grinned at the girls before leaning in to say something to a blonde as he tore off a sheet from his order pad, wrote something on it, and handed it to her. After they exchanged a few words, he moved to a nearby table, nodded a hello, and began writing on his pad. Ellie watched him leave the table, and head to the counter where he pushed a small rectangle of paper under a clip on a shiny metal turntable, then rotate it to the cook behind the heat lamps. Grabbing two full plates, Joe said something to the cook before starting toward the tables with a plate in each hand.

After a few steps, he looked up and froze with his eyes locked on Ellie standing by the door. He hesitated, then flicked his chin in a voiceless "hi" before he delivered the plates to a far table, wiped his hands on his jeans, and went toward her.

"Hey," he said with an edge in his voice. "What's goin' on? Why are you here?"

"I-I came to find you because I need to talk to someone and couldn't think of anyone else," Ellie said. "Susan's gone. Patti's busy, and I can't even consider talking to my mom or dad." The words spilled out like a torrent gushing down into a storm drain.

"I can't talk now, Ellie," Joe said. "You should've let me know about this, and I'd have met you somewhere else. I'm pretty busy at the moment."

Ellie cowered at the irritation in his voice. Her eyes pleaded, her shoulders drooped, and she shifted her weight from side to side. "Oh, sorry. I'm sorry. I shouldn't bother you." She stared at the floor and tried to force herself to leave.

"Okay, listen," Joe said after an awkward silence. "Meet me at the coffeehouse tomorrow morning at around 11:00. How's that?"

"Oh! Oh, sure—I'll see you then," Ellie stammered, then turned and flew out the door.

All the way back to the apartment, Ellie thought about how Joe had looked and behaved at MJ's. He was clean-cut when she first noticed him in class and when they met for coffee, but now he seemed different. She was confused about him, yet she still needed someone to fill the void left by Susan's departure and Patti's focus on R and R with Hank. Joe had become the only person Ellie knew well enough to talk to about her problems.

But now she felt as if she didn't really know Joe at all. Still disturbed by her visit to MJ's, Ellie stopped in front of Patti's apartment, wishing she could leap over the edge of the earth and evaporate, dissolve. *Oh, God, what am I to do?* she asked herself, but the only answer she heard was Dad's voice in her ears.

"You need to be a good girl," the voice said.

"Great advice, Dad," she said aloud. "I'd do that if I knew what that meant."

It was close to midnight, so she tried extra hard to be quiet when she unlocked the door and headed for her bedroom. She brushed her teeth and put on a light nightie, then fell into bed, hoping that tomorrow would bring her some relief.

Ellie wasn't sure what woke her up. Maybe it was the worry or another nightmare, this one about a drunk woman wobbling into the path of a car speeding down a dark, wet street. Ellie was a ghost in her dream, a bystander unable to move fast enough to pull the woman out of the way of death. Hank was a rain-soaked figure in ragged clothes that hung from his body. Ellie bolted upright with a gasp when the drunk stepped off the curb into the path of the car, and Hank turned to vapor.

She swung her legs over the side of the bed, rubbed her eyes before blinking in the morning brightness, and tried to clear her mind. Mom had always been aloof, but that day a year ago when Hank told them he was going to Vietnam, her mother's eyes had become empty, lifeless, as Hank talked about his future. Dad had slapped him on the back and said he was proud of him, but Mom had said nothing. In fact, she had kept quiet and had a drink in her hand most of the time since that day. A couple of months after Hank left for Vietnam, Ellie heard Dad confront Mom about how much she was drinking.

"Stop telling me I'm drinking too much, Mark!" Mom had demanded. "You have no idea what I'm going through! I've lived with an awful feeling ever since Hank said he was going overseas. I don't know what it is. All I can say is it is an unbearable feeling that something is wrong or is going to go wrong. You don't understand what it is to have a warning—it's a dread that never goes away!"

Dad had said he didn't understand, but he didn't want her to use Hank as an excuse for drinking too much. Mom was outraged and shouted that a suffocating blackness had come over her that day and strong drinks were the only things that helped her live with her dark premonition about Hank's future.

Ellie thought she knew the pain Mom felt but remembered the slap of rejection when she had reached out to help. Now, as she showered and dressed, she wondered if it was Mom's bad feeling or a rotten marriage that drove her crazy and caused her to turn to alcohol for relief.

Ellie appeared in the kitchen as Patti was pouring two glasses of orange juice. She greeted Ellie and said, "Tommy and I were talking about getting some help at Eden's Beauty while I'm in Hawaii for R and R. I suggested that you'd be a perfect person to fill in, and that you're a fast learner, so you'll be fine. What do you think?"

"Who? Me?" Ellie was stunned and sat back for a moment. "I could try to help out, but I wouldn't be as good as you are with the flowers. I've finished researching for my biology professor, so I guess I'm available."

"You'd be taking care of people who come into the shop, and that would give other designers time to do my work," Patti said with a smile. "I'll tell Tommy you're interested."

Ellie paced on the sidewalk in front of the coffeehouse until she saw Joe. He waved, waited for a car to pass, then jogged across the street to her. He looked neat and clean again, the way he had always looked until last night. He was certainly not the same guy she had seen in the restaurant.

"Hi—hope I'm not too late," he said as his eyes swept over her. He gave her a quick hug and added, "Shall we?" He bowed at the waist, pulled the door open, and waited for her to enter. As they walked in, he said, "I see our table is empty, m'lady." He flashed his dimpled grin, and they sat down across the table from each other.

"What's up, El?" Joe said after ordering their coffees. "You sounded upset last night."

"I am upset," Ellie said with a sigh. "Hank's in a Marine hospital because he got injured by shrapnel, plus I went home the day we got the news and found my mother so drunk she couldn't stand up. She wouldn't let me help her, so I left her that way, but I feel so bad. It seems as if I should do something to help, and I've been trying to figure out what Hank would say, but I'm at a loss." Ellie looked over at Joe and laid her open hands flat on the table. He leaned forward and covered her hands with his just as the waiter put down their drinks. She slid her hands out when the waiter cocked his head and said, "Aw, sweet."

"Thanks, buddy," Joe shot a not-so-friendly smile at the waiter.

"No problem, man. Let me know when you want to order food," he replied and flashed a peace sign. Joe raised two fingers in a V in response, then retook Ellie's hands. This time she curled her fingers around his hands and stared at him.

"Well," he began, "you can't do anything about your brother except know he's getting treatment, so let's talk about your mom. Your dad is there with her all the time, right? He must know what's going on. Does he want to do something about her?"

"That's the problem. I don't know what Dad wants, but I imagine things are the same as always, which means he's gone most of the time, especially at night, so she's in her room when he gets home, and he doesn't see her. I don't think she cooks or eats when she's alone." Ellie paused. "She hides the whiskey bottle in the flour canister. That's her secret place, and I'll bet Dad doesn't even know about it." Ellie's eyes drifted to the space between the table's edge and the window before she continued.

"My parents met in New York City in the '40s when they were both starting their careers. Mom grew up in an artist community in the Catskills surrounded by Bohemian artists who floated along like leaves in a stream, and Dad was raised to be a southern gentleman, which means he's in charge of everything, I guess. I think Mom resents what she's expected to do, and Dad doesn't like that, so he gets angry and critical. Hank told me I was not the problem causing their resentment and anger." Ellie picked up her cup and stared at it for a long moment before continuing. "I don't know how to help either one of them, but they are my parents, and I think I should try. Mom will be mad if I tell Dad how I found her, and he'll be mad if I *don't* tell him." Ellie shrugged her shoulders, frowned, then squeezed Joe's hand. "I'm wrong no matter what I do or don't do."

"You're so uptight about all of this," he said. "How can you possibly think straight?" He moved his cup across the table and swung his chair around to sit beside her. Then he put his arm around her and pulled her to him. Ellie could not help herself. She nestled against him, holding her breath to keep from sobbing.

"Hey." Joe's voice—gentle and coaxing—was close to her ear. "I have something that will clear your brain. Come home with me, and I'll help you unwind."

Ellie was beyond objection and mumbled an okay. Joe left money on the table, took her hand, and they walked outside. He kissed her fingers, then asked where she had parked. Joe drove them to his apartment in the Ville while she clutched his hand all the way there, but she shuddered when he stopped in front of a dilapidated old Victorian house. He clicked off the ignition, squeezed her hand, and pulled her toward him.

"I know you don't care for this part of town much, Ellie," he said into her ear. "But my roommates will all be gone until tonight, so everything will be okay."

The sun was high above the ancient trees when they started toward his apartment. The Spanish moss was less frightening in the daylight and made shadows that hid the cracked sidewalks as they walked to the porch steps. Mid-June heat and humidity made Ellie's arms and neck sweat, so the dark coolness of Joe's apartment felt good as he closed and locked the door behind them. He turned on a box fan in front of a small air conditioner humming in the window while Ellie stood in the middle of the room—dim even at noon—where oatmeal-colored shag carpet covered the floor and a rumpled couch faced the door.

Joe ushered her to an overstuffed chair opposite an old fireplace covered by coats of chipping paint. A nook by the fireplace served as a kitchen with a sink, small refrigerator, and stove squeezed together.

Ellie sat down, pressed her knees together, and crossed her ankles while Joe lit a thick round candle on the table next to her chair. The candle had burned low from previous lightings, and its edges had collapsed toward the wick. Soft yellow light filled the room when he lit two other candles on the mantel. He opened a cupboard, extracted two glasses, and filled them with garnet-colored wine, then put them on the table next to Ellie. He touched her cheek with his forefinger before disappearing through a doorway by the couch; a moment later, soft music—mellow and mesmerizing—filled the apartment.

He came back to Ellie carrying a painted container and a stack of thin, white paper squares, then sat cross-legged on the floor in front of her. Carefully, he put the box on the floor beside him, slipped her shoes off, and massaged her feet before lowering them to the carpet. Ellie leaned her head back, enjoying the carpet's feel on her bare feet. She watched Joe open the container and detected the same strong aroma she'd run away from at the party.

"I've smelled that before," Ellie said.

"That's good stuff you smell," Joe assured her. "Don't be afraid, Sweet Thing. I'll take care of you." He looked up at her. "These are rolling papers," he said, holding up one of the thin squares.

He spread it on his knee and smoothed it out with care, then reached into the box and pinched his fingers around some of the tiny, green-ish-brownish leaves inside. Ellie took in the earthy scent of day-old grass cuttings combined with the hayride smell of Christmas.

"And, this," he said with reverence, "is really good pot."

He picked up the rolling paper and cradled it in one hand, then sprin-kled the dried leaves in a line down the middle. Sliding his hands to opposite ends of the paper, he held it suspended between his fingertips, its contents hammocked inside. Then he wrapped the paper around the leaves, deftly forming a thin cylinder. With only his eyes visible above it, he held it up to Ellie and winked.

Joe touched the tip of his tongue to the unsealed edge of the joint and slowly moistened its length, his eyes never leaving Ellie's. Then he smoothed the damp seam against the paper and rolled it between his fingers again to secure it.. As he presented it to her, he said, "And there it is, my dear—a joint!"

She held it close to her face to study the thing. So this was a mari-juana cigarette—a joint. She had not gotten this close to the one at the party so she examined it carefully. Her father's cautions reverberated through her head, but the candlelight, the wine, the music, and Joe's eyes on her made her inhibitions crumble like a riverbank in a flood.

Besides, Joe had said he'd take care of her, so what was the worst thing that could happen?

Chapter 12

Joe held the joint between his thumb and forefinger and said, "You haven't ever smoked before, so filling your lungs will be hard for you at first, but you have to inhale and hold the smoke inside. Your throat will burn, and you'll cough, but don't let that worry you. You'll get used to it." His voice was reassuring as he added, "Here, I'll show you."

From out of nowhere, he produced a Bic lighter, flicked it to life, put the joint in his mouth, and drew the flame against the exposed tip. The cigarette burned instantly, glowing orange in the dimness, like the one at the party. Joe inhaled, then drew in his breath and closed his lips as he took the joint out of his mouth. Trickles of smoke escaped his lips and made him look like the man in the Marlboro posters. Joe turned the unlit end toward Ellie and carefully put it to her lips, then nodded for her to inhale.

Smoke curtained Joe's eyes and made him squint as he coaxed her into submission. Unable to resist him, she parted her lips enough to allow him to put the joint between them.

"Go, ahead," said Joe softly, puffs of smoke accenting his words. "Draw some into your lungs, and you'll see how good it makes you feel." He flashed his winning smile, and she took a timid breath through her mouth.

In a millisecond, she pushed the joint away, yanked her head back, and spat out the acrid smoke, her tongue protruding as if she were a baby tasting strained spinach for the first time.

"Ugh, that's awful," she said, shaking her head.

"You'll get used to it," Joe whispered. "Try again, Sweetie. Try another hit. It'll be fine."

Ellie sat forward and took the joint. With eyes on him, she held it the way she had seen Susan do at the party and took another hit.

This time she inhaled and let the smoke pass through her mouth to her throat, but she coughed so hard she almost dropped the joint. Smoke spewed from her mouth, and Joe offered her a sip of wine, taking another hit while she caught her breath. He handed it back and nodded toward it, wordlessly urging her to try again. Smoke drifted from his mouth as he told her to take another drag because they didn't want to waste good stuff.

She took it from him, and Dad's warning, along with the panther, slid deeper into the shadows. Feeling a bit light-headed, she turned the joint to study it again. Amazing how something that small and ordinary looking could tip the world sideways.

"Hey, Babe"—Joe's quiet voice broke in—"take a hit or give it back, okay?"

Ellie put the joint to her lips and inhaled, but this time she felt warmth enter her lungs. The smoke irritated her throat, but she kept her mouth closed when she coughed and opened her mouth only when she needed a breath of clean air. Her body felt out-of-focus, and she lay back, closing her eyes to let the new sensations take over her consciousness.

Her arms became light, her legs weightless, and her whole body relaxed. She felt as if she were floating above the chair. When she opened her eyes, a wondrous, warm glow filled the room. Her eyes fell on a lava lamp, the kind Susan had told her about. Ellie stared at the pink blobs rising, then falling, then rising again—up and down, over and over. Hypnotized by the images, she thought she had stopped breathing, but before she could call for help, Joe's voice bounced against her ears.

"Huh?" she mumbled. "What? Did you say something?" She giggled.

"Yeah, I asked how you were feeling, but I think I already know," Joe said, laughing. The joint was barely visible between his fingers. "Almost gone," he said, holding it up to show her. "But I'll take care of it—no more for you!"

"O-o-o . . . well, that's that, then!" She giggled again and put her hand over her mouth, eyes wide above it. After hesitating for a second, she reached out and slid her hand over Joe's cheek, tracing the side of his head to the back of his neck. Her fingers made tracks through the thickness of his hair. The rest of the world disappeared.

"I never felt like this before." She leaned forward and kissed him with more passion than she knew she had.

He responded and rose onto his knees as he pulled her nearer. His scent—woodsy and wild—made the room begin to move in slow motion, and parts of her body she had never known about came to life. Joe leaned forward and put his arms around her so his upper body pinned her against the chair. Her head spun and she held him, offering no resistance when she felt his hand sliding under her blouse, his palm warm against her skin.

He pushed her knees apart and pressed his open mouth to hers. Instinctively, her feet slid around the back of his thighs as he drew his head back a fraction of an inch and engulfed her in a bear hug.

Holding her close, he shifted his body and lifted her off the chair. The muscles of his shoulders and arms hardened under her fingers as he pivoted their entwined bodies and eased them down to the floor until Ellie was lying on her back against the carpet. Resting his weight on his elbows, he hovered an inch above her, teasing her lips and eyelids with his tongue.

She had never felt another person this close to her body and could not have imagined the thrill she felt. His heat, his essence, his hands on her skin sent quivers from between her legs to every inch of her. Joe must have felt it, too, because he sat up on his knees and pulled off his shirt, exposing a muscular chest. Ellie saw his jeans low on his hips, well below his navel. A trail of dark hair began at the top of the V formed by his tensed belly muscles and descended to below the top of his jeans.

She was paralyzed with pleasure in a world where the word *no* did not exist. Joe undressed her and spent the next few hours exploring her body—"magnificent," he called it—teaching her things about it that she hadn't known existed. She learned many things that after-noon.

Passion satisfied, Joe rolled onto his side next to her while she was still on her back with her eyes closed. He stretched his legs along her body and leaned on his elbow with his head propped on his hand, then traced her bare midline from her navel up to the hollow of her neck with his free hand. She breathed deeper, enjoying his touch.

"You know," he said, "we can't stay here much longer. I have to go to work this afternoon. Your car is here so you can drop me off, or I can walk—whatever works for you."

Ellie opened her eyes and turned her head toward him. "I-I don't know what to say. I never felt so relaxed, so . . . so something. I don't know what."

She had not felt embarrassed or self-conscious in her nakedness until she pushed up on her elbows and looked around to see the two empty wine glasses on the table next to a scattering of ashes. When she noticed clothes strewn on the floor around them, reality clanked into place, and without a warning, the panther got her. *What happened? What have I done?*

"Oh, no!" she gulped and grabbed her panties and bra. After slipping into her underwear, she pulled her dress over her head while Joe stepped into his jeans and zipped them up without speaking. Fumbling to cover herself while she smoothed out her skirt, she felt a hundred pounds heavier.

"I need to go home, Joe," she said, her face burning. They stood facing each other for a moment before he reached over and pulled her to him.

"It's okay, Ellie," he said, his mouth close to hers. "We had a great afternoon. You will soon realize that sex was meant to be just the way it was with us. It's to enjoy. Don't waste time feeling guilty about it."

"Sex was meant for *married* people," she said as black heaviness engulfed her. Even though Joe was close, she didn't look at him.

"You have to get over that archaic thinking and enter the 1960s, Ellie. It's hard to find a virgin anywhere these days," he said. "Free love is where it's at. Besides, having sex is the one thing you can do that no one knows you've done unless you tell them. It isn't a bruise or something that shows. You don't have to explain anything." His voice was hard, irritated, the way she'd heard it at MJ's.

She left him standing in the middle of the room with his hands on his hips. She rushed out the door to her car and sped away, but she could not outrun the panther. Its claws pierced her heart, and its weight held her down while its hot foul breath burned her face.

Shame stayed with her until Joe called her the next morning and asked her to meet him at the coffeehouse. She had intended to have coffee as usual, but they ended up in his apartment again. And then again the next day.

And then again and again.

June passed quickly with newsy letters from Hank that described his daily routine with the assurance that he had plenty of good food and time to rest during his hospital stay. Still, he said he was anxious to get back to his men because experienced replacement officers were not coming in-country regularly. Ellie relaxed a bit when she read that he was comfortable and well-fed, then tried to focus on remembering that Hank would be okay, but near the end of June, a letter came that brought back Ellie's worries.

15 Jun 67
In field-7 miles south of DMZ

Dear Family,

I'm all sewed up and healing enough, so I've been back in the field for a few days. Yesterday I had a 24-hr combat patrol in this area. It's north of Camp Carroll (a large artillery fire-base off Route 9) and heavily jungled. We had to cut our way through thick growth the whole time. It was the worst terrain I have ever seen. It was painfully slow going and made us good targets for the enemy.

We had to cross the Cam Lo River, but before we got there, we had to wade in the mud along the edge until we came to a fording point. Then we ended up in water up to our necks, and some men even went under, but we got them out. All our gear got wet, so anyone who had a camera lost the film to water damage. I have a good bandage on my leg, so it gave me no trouble on the patrol. After we crossed the river, we set in 3 separate, squad-sized ambush positions. It was miserable because we were wet, and our gear was soaked. Tomorrow

the company is going on a 3-day patrol to the northwest.
Don't worry, Dad, I'll get the medic to check my stitches.
In the field, we get only 2 meals a day (0730 & 1730) and
I have really been hungry. When Patti sees me on R&R I'll
probably weigh 180 pounds. Not long now!
Better go now, I'm a little short on sleep.

I love you & miss you,
Hank

Ellie didn't want to think about Hank in the field wading through muddy water and the infection that might bring, so she went to Joe's apartment for the afternoon.

On the first of July, Ellie waited for Patti and watched frenzied birds charging the feeder hanging from the gutter outside the kitchen window. Sunlight came in through the sliding door and made a wide, dazzling stripe across the floor where tiny bird shadows dashed and danced in random patterns. Ellie studied the images that entranced her the same way Joe's lava lamp mesmerized her and made her another person—another Ellie—who smoked pot and had sex with Joe.

Without warning, she felt the panther's hot breath on her neck. She should not have gone to Joe's apartment that first day, even though she liked the release, and the freedom she felt. *How could I lose control that way?* Before she knew it, thoughts and doubts began to invade the stillness. *What would people say about me?* The sunlight started to fade, and the birds got quieter as the afternoon cooled to an unusually comfortable eighty degrees, but Ellie shivered, and not because she was cold.

In the beginning, her new life was hard to handle, but the more she was with Joe, the less guilty she felt, and the easier it was to do what came naturally. After the first two weeks, it had felt perfectly normal, just like Joe said it would. Besides, her part-time job at Eden's Beauty filled her mornings—and her mind—with other thoughts. *But still—is this new life really okay?*

Troubled by her thoughts, Ellie welcomed the distraction when Patti walked in with three letters from Hank. "I picked these up earlier. They came all at once," she said. "The first one is worrisome, but the last one is good!

"Wonder why they came at the same time," Ellie asked and unfolded the first letter.

"Not sure what that means, but I'll ask him when I see him in Hawaii," Patti said. "I'm so excited! He said he can get R and R any time now, so it won't be long before we're together in Hawaii!"

Patti's happiness filled the room and overcame Ellie's angst. "Not long now!" she agreed and then started reading.

19 Jun 67
In the jungle near the Square

Dear Family,

I feel pretty bad today for no specific reason. My leg was hurting a little this morning but seems to be healing OK. Maybe I overdid it on patrol or something. Cameras and watches are taking a beating with this damp weather and all the sweating we do. My watch may quit soon. Guess everything kind of piles up.

It's really pretty country here and I want to send pictures, but we'll see. I have enjoyed your letters and know how you must work to get them to me so often, and I do appreciate it.

We are starting 2 patrols and 2 ambushes a day and that really makes it tough on the men. Tonight, one of my squads was moving out toward an ambush position and the leader radioed me that someone (enemy) was following them. It was kind of a mess because it was getting dark and the platoon didn't know exactly where they were. The enemy appeared to be a small element staying about 500 meters away, but one

*of my men saw movement in front and on the left flank. My
men had a dog with them and it alerted to the front so the
squad leader decided he was walking into an ambush. We
tried to get enemy coordinates, but couldn't, so I told him to
set in with a defense and see if he could locate the VC or the
follower. We sent in some artillery (81s) and I told him to sit
tight. So far, nothing has happened, so I don't think he has
anything moving to his front. He was a little shook, but the
experience will be good for him. We picked up a few FNGs
in Oki—they make me nervous—but most of my men are
well-seasoned Marines so we'll get the new guys up to speed
and be fine.*

> *Better go now. I have to brief my squads.*

I love you & miss you,
Hank

*Oh, by the way, I told Patti I can get R&R anytime, so we'll
need to agree on when I need to ask for it. I'll let her know
when the date is definite, and she can tell you.*

Ellie felt the panther near again as she read about the ambush and
the new men Hank had to train. He didn't sound too happy about that,
and guilt filled her when she saw Patti counting the days until she'd
see Hank, worrying about him and probably praying for him while
she—the other Ellie—was enjoying her newfound intimacy with Joe.
Was that wrong? Maybe the second letter would help her decide.

23 Jun 67
Southwest of Con Thien

*Well, I've had the plt 4-1/2 months already. In July, I'll be
working on 6 mo. in country. The time really has gone pretty
fast even though it seems like I've been here a long time.
We've been doing sweeps of this area since late May and
it looks like we've caused the VC to pull back, but they are*

sneaky so we'll see what happens. They want Con Thien to be theirs, so the attacks up there are relentless. Each battalion has to rotate in and out of there. We're tasked to keep it secure same as everyone so 3/4 (that's me!) will have our time up there, too.

Did you find Cam Lo on the map? We are working in the western part of that area, east of the Rock Pile. We had to cross the river to get here the other day because the VC have supply routes and large elements moving around here. We have to find them, or they will destroy our supply routes. We work all over the Dong Kio and Dong Ha mountains, and we're about 800 ft up so we see the South China Sea.

The Annamite Mountains are near enough to see too. The views here are tremendous. It's going to be pretty hot today, and there isn't a cloud in the sky. We have a clear visual of all the coastland east and north of here. There's a Naval destroyer firing into North Vietnam. Another infantry company left here on the 14th for a 5-day patrol up on Dong Ha mountain (to our west). I am glad the men had a rest for a while. Everyone is tired because we had 2 patrols and 2 ambushes at night and since we are short of men now with only 3 instead of 4 squads, we keep jumping!

We had a rest, but tomorrow we're going out on a company operation for 7 days. Good thing the doctor gave me a clean bill of health. I have 2 scars, each 2" long. One on the left inside near the front and one underneath the calf. You won't be able to see them when they heal.

We're going to be operating east of Dong Ha Mountain, northwest of Cam Lo on the eastern extremity of Mutter's Ridge. You can find them on the map.

Re Dad's question about the rifles: I know he was concerned because the reports you hear about them are not good, but the M-16 has been working fine for my plt so far. We had some trouble with jamming at first, but we think it's the ammunition that causes the malfunction. All of them are failure-to-extract so we tried 4 different types of ammo and found one with 00.1% failure. We've been using this type

only, plus carefully cleaning and maintaining our weapons so
they work like champs. I shot one the other day and I really
like it. You can hold it right in there, automatic or semi. Some
of the other Bn think it's another brand of ammo that works,
so there are quite a few experiments going on. Don't worry,
though—mine works just fine. Well, that's about all for now.

> *I love you and miss you,*
> *Hank*

Ellie let the letter drop to her lap. It didn't seem right to celebrate the upcoming July Fourth with Joe and watch fireworks while Hank was slogging through the jungle—hungry, dirty, and tired. She tried to shake off her guilt and remember that Patti had told her the next letter said Hank was in a better place. Surely that would help.

> *27 Jun 67*
> *Camp Carroll lines*

Dear Family,

We had steak tonight and it was about the best meal I've
had since I've been here, especially since we've been in the
field for 6 days! Lots of action going on. We encountered boo-
by traps in hedgerows, took sniper fire and dodged mortars.
We think the VC are quiet now cause they are getting ready to
infiltrate from the DMZ.

Hope you all plan a good July 4th with fireworks and good
food. Life has to keep going back home because that's what
we're fighting for! That's it for now. Gotta get some sleep.

> *I love you and miss you,*
> *Hank*

Ellie sighed and reread the letter, then folded it and put it with the other ones before going to bed.

Ellie had never expected to hear Susan's voice again, but there it was on the other end of the phone.

"Hellooo, friend," Susan had said when Ellie answered. "You didn't let it ring too long. Expectin' a guy or something?" Susan's voice was singsongy like the voice of a child who has just opened a Christmas present.

"Susan! Where have you been?" Ellie squealed. "I was worried about you because I haven't heard from you. You told me you'd write! Anyway, I'm so glad you called."

"Well, truth be told, I got into a little trouble, so I wasn't allowed to contact anyone for a while—" Susan's voice had turned grave, "but I'm doing fine now."

"What happened?" Ellie asked.

"It was inevitable, I guess," Susan sighed. "I did a little too much dope one night and someone dumped me—close to unconscious—on my parents' front porch. I was in bad shape when they found me, so they put me in a treatment program for alcohol and drug users. I'm clean now." She paused, then continued in a sad tone: "I want to tell you I'm sorry if I caused you any grief. I hope you can forgive me." Susan's voice trailed off, and the line was silent.

"Forgive you?" Ellie said with the phone in one hand and her forehead in the other. "I don't know what you did that I need to forgive." She waited for Susan to speak.

"First of all, I was wiped out most of the time at college, and I felt bad about taking you to that Ville party where you freaked out. You are so innocent, and deep down inside, I think I knew you couldn't handle it, but I took you anyway," Susan said. "I'm so sorry."

"Well, if that's all you want me to forgive, that's no problem. I forgive you." The panther began to claw its way up Ellie's spine. Not innocent anymore. If Susan only knew that smoking dope and making love with Joe were regular things for her now.

"Where are you?" Ellie asked, trying to stay focused on Susan.

"I'm still in treatment, learning to live the twelve steps. I can't leave yet, but I'm going in the right direction. My head's clear for once, and I haven't felt this good in a long time. I hated my parents at first, but now I'm grateful they loved me enough to send me to this place."

"Oh, I'm so glad for you," Ellie said. "But I do miss you myself!"

"That's nice to hear, my friend," Susan replied, her voice breaking. She cleared her throat and asked, "How's your brother doing? I think of him every time I hear the news about that stupid war over there, and I always worry for you." She paused. "I don't mean he's stupid. He's brave and committed. It's the politicians I don't trust."

"As a matter of fact, he and Patti are going to meet in Hawaii this month for R and R. They have two weeks together before he has to go back to Vietnam. But he'll have around five more months left before he comes home in January. I can't wait to see him."

"I know you and your whole family will be relieved when he's finally home . . ." Susan's voice trailed off, and she cleared her throat again.

"Yes, we will," Ellie said.

"What have you been up to this summer?"

Ellie felt darkness cloud her thoughts. She didn't want Susan to know about Joe, so she said, "I've been in training at Eden's Beauty— that flower shop on Main Street—because I'm going to fill in when Patti's in Hawaii," Ellie said. "I like working with Tommy. He asked me to stay on at the shop after Patti gets back, so I guess that means I'm doing okay."

"That's great news. How would it be if I come to see you when I get out of here?"

"I'd love that." Ellie heard a voice in the background on Susan's end of the phone.

"Gotta go, El. I'll try to call you again. Bye—see you soon!" The phone went dead.

Ellie was smiling, the receiver still in her hand, when she heard a light rap on her bedroom door. Patti came in, handed her a letter, and told her that her mom didn't look good when she picked it up from her parents' house.

"She didn't say anything when I told her I thought this would probably be the last letter before R and R," Patti said as she closed Ellie's door.

> *4 Jul 67*
> *In Annamite Mountains North of Camp Carroll*
> *Dong Tri Mountain, 3,000+ feet up*
>
> Dear Mom, Dad & Ellie,

> *Well, it's the old 4th again. Last night everyone was jumping because word came in to expect incoming artillery during the night. We rousted everyone at 0330 and stood on 100% alert until dawn. No problem, though. Life continues normally! I've been anxiously waiting for my math correspondence course to come so I can get started on it. Nothing like math to keep your world on an even keel. And your mind sharp. Numbers never change, no matter how high the seas!*

> *It looks like it will be a nice day and cool (enough) because the wind is blowing. Yesterday we watched a couple of Navy destroyers' big guns shooting support missions north of Con Thien. It's quite a sight—a lot like fireworks! This morning we are going to start setting out tanglefoot wire. I hope to have a bulldozer here to smooth out the lines.*

> *I hope by now the plans are set for R&R. I'm getting my shots today & I've been reading an interesting book about Hawaii. It looks like we're going on a Bn operation on the 10th. That means I should go on R&R as soon as we get back. It's required that the quota must be filled, so if you're in the*

field, they send a chopper to get you out. I think Patti & I
have the money part worked out, and she knows how much
cash to bring.

   Hmm—I think I'll just sit in the sun this year (heh!) instead
of going to the lake like we usually do on the 4th. I'll bet
you're out there right now! I'll be there soon, too.

             I'll close for now. I love you and miss you,

                         Hank

  PS These mountains are beautiful!

Hank's joke hit Ellie hard, and she cried when she thought about this year's Fourth of July at the lake. There was no celebrating, even though Mom had tried to act happy and make it a good day—for Hank's sake, she said.

Ellie and Joe had arrived in time for a swim and light lunch with Mom, but Dad had not shown up until after they finished eating. Patti was not there because her reputation as Eden's Beauty's event coordinator had grown, so she had to oversee a huge benefit celebration in town.

By midafternoon, Mom was stumbling and slurring her words, and Dad was angrily brooding on the porch. Ellie knew how the day would end, so she made an excuse and left with Joe. Before they left, Mom had made it clear she was not happy about Ellie ruining the day by leaving early.

Even after ten days, Ellie could still feel the sting of her mother's words. Since the Fourth, she had spent time under her tree, trying to figure out how—if it was possible—to gain her mother's approval, but she didn't see how that would ever happen. That's why the phone call she received over a week later astounded her.

Chapter 13

"Ellie, you need to come over here and tell me what this is," Mom insisted on the phone, and even though her words were garbled, there was desperation in her voice. "Some kind of strange thing came from Hank, and Patti's still in Hawaii or I'd call her."

Patti had gotten word about R and R the day Hank's last letter arrived, so she'd put her standby plans into action and left in a hurry. Now they had only a few days together before the war would pull them apart again.

Ellie's fingers tightened around the receiver because her mother had never asked for her help before. Unfortunately, she had other plans. She had gotten home a few hours earlier after being with Joe, and she'd planned to shower, clean, and do laundry before having a late dinner, so part of her wanted to say no, but something deeper made her say she would come over to Mom's after dinner. "I'll be there in about an hour," she had said before hanging up.

Ellie pulled up to the house next to Dad's empty space and walked up the steps into a house that smelled stale and felt lifeless. She found her mother in the kitchen standing by the counter with a drink in her hand.

"Oh, it's you," Mom said, nearly knocking herself off balance when she turned toward Ellie. "I don't know what this thing is, and your father didn't have time to look at it. Wait a minute—I'll get it." With one hand clutching the rim of the sink, she steadied herself, then wiped her hands on a limp kitchen towel, grabbed the doorframe, and disappeared through the opening while Ellie sat down at the table to wait.

Mom reappeared a few moments later holding a cardboard rectangle between her fingers. She handed it to Ellie, then stepped back, swaying a bit in the process. It looked as if she attempted to mask her condition by putting one palm flat on the kitchen table and the other on her hip, but she ended up leaning at an awkward angle with one ankle crossed over the other. After a precarious moment, she cleared her throat and stared at the brown object in Ellie's hand as if it were a tiny bomb.

Ellie turned it over, studying both sides. It was a small, flat piece of cardboard—jagged on one side and smooth on the other—about eight inches wide and six inches high with a rough surface. Three deep fold lines ran across the width of the cardboard, the first one below a small flap at the top. The flap had clean edges, and its corners angled toward the center, but the bottom edge of the cardboard was straight. The two other creases scored the card, dividing it into three sections, and there was bold, black machine printing on one side. Ellie flipped it over and saw Hank's handwriting on the other.

She refolded the cardboard from the bottom to the top along the creases, then folded down the angled flap like an envelope tab. Hank had written his return address—an FPO San Francisco notation—and Mom and Dad's address below the tab. Ellie held the card closed and turned it over where Hank had printed "COMBAT POSTCARD" in bold, black letters. The machine printing under Hank's writing said "MEAL, COMBAT, INDIVIDUAL," followed by B-1A-unit and "HAM FRIED."

"Ah," Ellie said, "He used packaging from his C-ration meal to write us. See? It's a makeshift postcard." She had read about the Marines making these postcards when they didn't have any paper for letters. She also noticed that Hank had added his personal comments about how to prepare his meal, concluding with: *"A meal fit for a king! This, John Wayne cookies & fruit cocktail make a good breakfast, lunch, or dinner (depending which one you happen to be eating!)"*

It was a make-do postcard from the jungle, written during war to make sure his family would know he was okay. Ellie smiled when she read how much he enjoyed this particular meal. It was so like him to find the best in the worst places.

Upon unfolding the cardboard again, Ellie found Hank's message on the inside, which looked as if he had written it when he didn't have much time. "True to his word, Mom," Ellie said. "He's letting us know he is okay, no matter what." She held the card open to read Hank's message aloud and hoped Mom would not see her hands tremble as she read.

> *12 July 67*
> *In the Annamite Mountains*

Dear Mom, Dad & Ellie,

> *We are moving up on to Hill 124 today. One of our plts found about 60 abandoned bunkers south of here on Hill 84. We blew them up this morning (so the enemy can't use them anymore) & the Bn is in a security status here for the time being. The situation has calmed down quite a bit now, but 60 bunkers means a lot of men were here, so we're not sure where or how close they might be. I will be leaving here soon so I guess Patti will be gone by the time this gets home, but I figured you might enjoy it.*
> *I'm running out of room so better close. I'm okay!*

> *I love you & miss you,*
> *Hank*

"Well? Why did he use cardboard?" Mom's voice was a mixture of concern and irritation as she tried to pour another drink. Her hands shook as her lips became a straight line and her face set, expressionless and hard.

Ellie waited until her mother looked up, then pointed to the date and said, "He wrote this on July 12th. See? That must've been a day or so before he was airlifted out of the field to meet Patti for R and R." Ellie thought for a moment, then continued. "And that means he was in good shape when he left the mountains, so that's why he hurried up and made this postcard. He wanted us to know he was stable and in no danger."

After thinking more about Hank's message, Ellie added, "He wanted you to know he was eating well so you wouldn't worry." Frowning, she looked up at her mother. "Sounds as if things had leveled off and he had a little time to write. I'll bet he thought you'd get a kick out of the improvised postcard that he wrote before leaving the war zone to meet Patti! That's what I think about it, anyway."

Mom took a long drink, lowered her glass to the table, and sat down. "Humph. Why din't your father tell me that after he saw it? Never 'nough time," She held out her hand, silently asking for Hank's card.

Mom's red-rimmed eyes stared at Ellie while one hand held the glass and the other reached for the only connection she had to her son—the light of her life. Ellie's heart softened when she saw dark patches under Mom's eyes and the infinite sadness on her face. She wished she could comfort her mother somehow.

"Can I get you anything before I leave, Mom?" she asked as she handed over the card.

"Yeah. Bring 'im home. Can ya do that?" Mom stared numbly at the card and said without looking up, "I'm fine. You can go on now."

Ellie left Mom in the kitchen, let herself out, and walked to her car.

The July heat covered Ellie when she flung open the apartment door and ran out to meet Patti as she got out of the taxi by the curb. Holding a wide-brimmed hat in one hand and a bag marked "Aloha Shop" in the other, she smiled at Ellie rushing down the steps. The sisters-in-law hugged while the driver opened the trunk. Patti's smooth skin was tanned, but Ellie noticed faint dark circles under her eyes.

"Can I help carry something inside?" Ellie asked, grabbing the nearest suitcase.

"Gosh, that's the big one!" Patti exclaimed and lifted a smaller valise over the trunk's edge.

"Ooooff!" The sound escaped Ellie's lips before she could stop it. "This is heavy. What's in it? Waikiki Beach?" She took hold of the case with two hands, wrestled it to the curb, and waited while Patti paid the driver.

"There might be, since we spent a lot of our time on the beach or having drinks—the kind with tiny umbrellas in them—on the lanai," Patti laughed.

"Lanai?"

"The patio outside our room," Patti said as they headed inside.

Suitcases stowed in Patti's bedroom, they looked at each other and sighed at the same time. "Let's have some coffee," Patti said, putting her arm around Ellie as they walked to the kitchen. Ellie had brought a short, big-leafed houseplant in a painted clay pot from Eden's Beauty to put on the kitchen table as a welcome-home surprise. Patti touched one of the deep green, shiny leaves and said, "How sweet this is!"

Ellie took a seat and blurted, "How is Hank?" She wished she had waited until Patti had gotten settled, but she simply couldn't wait to hear how he looked and how he felt.

"We had a ball," Patti said as she reached for the coffee canister.

"He was tired and wanted fresh, hot food, but otherwise he was in good shape," she continued, measuring the fine-ground coffee into the basket and flipping the switch. "He stayed in the hot shower for more than half an hour after we checked in. It felt so good to be with him, to hug him, to hear his voice," Patti said, her cheeks pinking. She eased into her chair and reached across the table to touch Ellie's hand as the coffee maker gurgled and filled the air with the savory scent of coffee.

"I know how close you and Hank are," she said. "He said to give you a special hug for him and to tell you he misses you."

Her heart heavy, Ellie turned away because she didn't want to cry in front of Patti, and when she looked back, Patti had her hands resting on the table and her eyes focused on something outside the window—something far beyond the sun and wispy clouds. Ellie shifted in her chair and said, "I'm so glad you and Hank had time together. Did his leg bother him at all?" She got up to pour their coffee and gave Patti her cup before sliding back into her own chair with her mug. *Is this the time to talk to Patti about Mom?* she wondered. *Maybe it's best to wait a few days until things get back to normal.*

Patti's attention was still focused outside when she replied. "I think it hurts a little bit, but he didn't say anything. He's gonna have a bad scar, though. But you know Hank. Would he ever complain about something like that?"

"Doubt it," Ellie said. She remembered how brave her brother had been when a pitched ball had caught him under his right eye during a Little League game. He fell down, held his face, and cried a little, but she never heard him whine or complain after that. Later, Dad said if the pitch had been an inch higher, his eye socket would have been crushed.

"Darn good thing you didn't lose an eye," Dad had said, and Mom had added that Hank must've had a guardian angel or something. Ellie remembered ten-year-old Hank sporting a black eye and a large, purple-and-blue knot on his cheek that hadn't stopped him from finishing the baseball season.

Patti's voice brought Ellie back to the present, and she listened as Patti explained that she thought the next few months would go fast. "Hank is proud of his men. He told me they're good Marines. They've been in some bad scrapes, but they've stuck together and taken care of each other." Patti's eyes were distant again as she absentmindedly sipped her coffee.

"That doesn't surprise me. Does it you?" Ellie asked.

"Not really. He said they keep up with enemy movements by doing what the Marines call 'sweeps.' That's when rifle platoons like Hank's follow a certain pattern of coordinates and go into the jungle looking for Viet Cong guerrillas and North Vietnamese Army regulars. He said that the triple canopy and high elephant grass make for slow going through the jungle. They have to cross hedgerows between large, open rice paddies. Our guys are sitting ducks in those areas because, in a jungle or crossing a paddy, Americans are larger and move slower than the Vietnamese."

When she finished talking, Patti raised her cup and took another sip. Ellie thought about what she had read and what Patti had said. "Did Hank talk about his platoon?" Ellie asked.

"Oh, he talked about his men a lot," Patti said. "There's something about seeing buddies get hurt or killed and being near death together that bonds people because they have to trust or go nuts. He said that's why they consider themselves brothers. He talked about the ones he trusted with his life, the ones he worried about not making it, and the ones who got killed."

Ellie reflected silently for a moment as the full weight Hank was carrying finally became clear. He was twenty-two years old when he left last winter, and Patti had said a platoon was four squads of ten or so men; that meant that as many as forty human lives depended on Hank's decisions. He took seriously his responsibility to make smart, tactical moves and to keep them—all of them—alive. She could not imagine the weight of the burden carried by someone just a few years older than she. How did Hank do it? It must be an awful strain to lead those men through one life-threatening situation after another while she, on the other hand, was smoking pot and having sex with Joe. The only real responsibility she had was trying to figure out Mom and Dad's problems. Ellie was embarrassed by her trifling life.

After studying the inside of her cup, she said, "I'm super glad Hank knows you'll be here for him when he gets home, Patti."

They sat in silence and sipped coffee for a long time while a setting sun cast its light through the glass doors and drew a wide, bright stripe down the wall and across the floor. The vivid band stood in stark relief against the shadow stretching across the room. Sun and shadows. Yin and yang.

Patti pushed her cup away and stood up, then walked to the door with her eyes fixed on the sunset. Her face had a soft glow in the light, and Ellie wondered how she could think of anything but Hank right now. Suddenly Patti broke the silence, saying quietly, "Hank told me that when he got back to Vietnam, it would be his company's turn to serve its time in the barrel."

"What does that mean?" asked Ellie.

"It's the time his battalion has to spend on Con Thien." Patti's eyes were still locked on the changing sky, and she seemed a million miles away.

"Oh, yeah," Ellie said, remembering what she had read. "That name means 'Hill of Angels,' doesn't it?"

Patti nodded, "It's not a high place by our standards. Only a little over five hundred feet. Not as high as the lowest spot in the Smoky Mountains. But it's high enough. From the top, anyone on Con Thien has a clear view for miles around, so our guys can keep an eye on enemy troops coming into South Vietnam from the north.

"That means our troops are exposed, easy to hit because there's nowhere to hide on top. Hank said the enemy has clear shots, like shooting fish in a barrel. Holding Con Thien has been up to us—the Marines—since the war began, so each battalion—that's upwards of 380 men plus their weapons support—takes its turn 'in the barrel' and they've lost a lot of men up there."

Ellie thought for a minute. "So he's already on Con Thien, right? I remember he wrote that he had to take his men up there as soon as he got back to Vietnam." Her arms felt numb and her heart raced. "How long does he have to stay up there?"

"He didn't say how long. Just that it would be their turn in the barrel." Patti sat back down at the table as the silence spread out before them like the lengthening shadows. "I worry for him, and it's good to talk about it a bit, but sometimes I'm just beyond words. Sorry, Ellie."

With the sun now gone, the earth plunged into life without light, but the two sad women sat at the table, each wrapped in her own world, until the room was fully dark. Lightning bugs rose from the grass and twinkled merrily in the dark just before the stars popped out in the black sky.

Eventually, Patti sighed, stood up, and walked over to the counter to switch on the light above the sink. The brightness startled them both. Ellie rubbed her eyes, then Patti turned to her with her eyebrows raised in surprise.

"Oh, goodness, I forgot! I have a letter for you that Hank wrote while we were in Hawaii. He asked me to give it to you as soon as I got back. I'll unpack the other gifts in the morning, but I need to get your letter now." She disappeared through the door and returned a minute later holding a thin, folded page, which she handed to Ellie before marking off the past two weeks on the calendar and saying good night.

Ellie took the letter to her bedroom and flipped on the lamp. She puffed up her pillow and settled back, eager to see what her brother had written especially for her.

20 Jul 67
Aloha!

Dear Ellie,

This letter is for you only. It's special cause you're special, even though you get lumped in with everyone else when I send letters. That's only because it's hard to find time to write, and I want to let everyone know I'm doing OK, so I usually address my letters to all of you. This is different because, and I don't know why, but something told me to write you your very own letter. It wasn't a little birdie who told me cause they all left when the war zone got noisy! And believe me, it's noisy all the time . . . hard to deal with when you're tired, hungry, and dirty, but that's the way it is.

There are blessed few times when we finish a sweep & get a little rest. That's when I try to relax & remember what it's like to be back home. I was thinking about you the last week. I thought about us at the lake and stuff . . . you were such a cute, sweet little sis. I'll never forget your towhead and skinny legs! We had fun, didn't we?

I hope you are remembering what I told you before I left. Never doubt you are a great person. I was thinking about how hard our family has been for you to understand. I realized your life at home must have been totally different from mine since I was away at school most of the time. Well, starting at 12, at least. You had to stay in the middle of Mom & Dad's mess, but I didn't. Anyway, I want you to know that I believe in you. Stare down anything that gets in the way of you believing in you! You're not a cute, skinny towhead anymore. You're a beautiful young woman.

Dad said Mom is having a really hard time. I can help more when I get home, but for now, you need to stay out of the problem and concentrate on your classes, on your life.

You are pretty, fun, creative, and sweet. Don't forget that. Get tough and don't let Dad's words bite your soft skin. Mom is hard to understand, but she does love you.

Last thing I want to tell you is that you'll make mistakes, but all you need to do is learn from them and keep going. You keep on with your life no matter what's going on with me or anyone else, ya hear?!

Remember when Pogo reminded us who the enemy is: ourselves. But he also said, "Looking back on things, the view always improves."

Pogo didn't say this, but I will: You can get past the obstacles
that hold you back. Keep up the good work, Little Sis. You'll get
the hang of being yourself. I know you will be OK.
   Patti tells me the apartment is working out well for both of
you. I'm grateful you are there with her. Thanks for that.
                                        I love you & miss you,
                                                    Hank

Ellie switched off the light and closed her eyes. Hank wanted her to
be herself, to be tough, and she was trying to do that. But what would he
think if he knew about her and Joe? Was their relationship the kind of
mistake he was talking about? He knew missteps were part of everyone's
journey. Did everyone wander in the weeds before finding their path?
Susan had wandered plenty, and look what happened to her!

Ellie held Hank's letter close and could almost hear his voice. Make a
mistake, but learn from it, he had said. She turned that thought over and
over in her mind as if she were looking through a prism, seeing its colors
from different angles, until Hank's words began to make sense and a tiny
spark flickered in her mind: the actual blunder was not as bad as letting it
hold you back. She held onto that thought until sleep took over.

Ten days later, the early August heat and humidity had started to climb
when Patti handed her another letter. She didn't say a word. She simply
drew a bold X through the day and went to her room.

                                              28 Jul 67
                                On Con Thien. . . Hill of Angels
My Dear Family,

   We've come to expect daily rifle and mortar fire, along with
artillery sometimes, too. Used to be early morning, noon, and
late afternoon, but now it is random. Someone yells "incoming"
at any time, any moment. Unnerving to some men. Add the rats,

*mosquitoes, ants, and minefields and you have an unpleasant
situation. We are standing security along the southern perimeter
of our camp. It's quiet for the time being, so time to write.*

*On the plane back from R&R, I started thinking about what
a great family I have. Mom & Dad: I was sad to think about
the times when I didn't understand you or was short-tempered
with you. But I am so thankful that's passed us now. Patti says
that you are doing OK—some things are rough, I'm sure. Don't
worry, things will even out before long.*

*Patti is really wonderful. She brought me up to date on ev-
eryone & said she tries to see you often. She says Ellie is doing
great! I'm proud of her.*

*I am so glad that we made the decision to get married when
we did. Patti is undoubtedly the perfect wife for me. I told her
that one of the greatest things in my life is the closeness of our
family & now she is truly a part of it. Being with her at the lake
is one of the greatest memories I have. I want to tell you how
glad I was that you came out before I left.*

I love you & miss you,
Hank

Ellie brushed away tears and rubbed her eyes. He was proud of her
and that meant he thought she was doing the right thing, but she didn't
deserve that kind of trust. *It'll be different when he comes home,* she assured herself. *I'll explain everything, and he'll be able to help me.*

Ellie asked Tommy if she could work a few more hours a week at Eden's
Beauty because working helped keep her mind occupied. She needed the
distraction—anti-war protests were more violent, people were burning
draft cards, and Hank's life on Con Thien was horrible. And then there
were her personal worries with illegal drugs and an illicit love affair.
Work was a welcome refuge until Hank's next letter arrived in mid-Au-
gust.

6 Aug 67
Con Thien

Dear Mom, Dad & Ellie,

I got your letters yesterday. Was fun to read them. I'm glad that Patti's reports of our time on R&R perked you all up. The break really made a bull out of me! I've felt so much better than before I left. I really needed a rest, the good company of my wife, and plenty of fresh food!

It's quiet again now. I sent Patti a picture of me at a bombed-out church at a place called Phu An. It's only about 1.5 miles southeast of Con Thien. The photo was taken a while back and developed while we were on R&R, but it gives you some idea of the amount of destruction here. The village was completely leveled on two separate occasions when we found VC hiding there. They use civilian settlements as camouflage quite often, so fights were deadly. I feel bad for the villagers caught in the middle.

Here's the story: We were doing sweeps around Phu An because it's not far from the MSR (main supply route) up to Con Thien. We needed to keep the road open so our guys up there got the ammo and other supplies they needed. I don't have much time right now, but I wanted to tell you about something that SSgt Mason and I found in the Phu An church. It was really something special.

We came out of low spot onto a small cleared rise after hacking our way through the jungle. The first thing I saw was the shell of a once-beautiful little church still standing in the clearing. I gave the men a break back in the jungle cover and told them to stay sharp, but to relax a few. Mason and I wanted to check the church. Probably was built by Christian missionaries—French Catholic, most likely. You could tell that it had been so pretty and well-used before the war because there was a worn path to the front doors. I thought it was a serene place even in this war. In the front, the bell tower still stood (somehow) above the rectangular shape where people once came to worship. I thought it was quaint; a simple monument to faith. It

*reminded me of chapels built by the Spanish in St. Augustine or
in the southwest.*

*I stood for a long time and looked at the structure riddled
with bullet holes, missing chunks of walls, but still standing—a
testament of God's strength even in this adversity. Fancier than
us Baptists would build, but a symbol of forbearance still.*

*After we cleared the perimeter, Mason called from inside.
He came through the opening where the door used to be and
said "Hey, Sir. Look at this." Coming down the path from
the church, he held up a brass figure of the crucified Christ,
untouched by bullets, big guns, or other things made to destroy.
He kept it & now humps it around with him. It must have been
attached to a wooden cross somewhere inside the church. We
thought it was quite a find. He's going to take it home to his
wife.*

*By the way, that day was Patti's birthday and Mason's first
wedding anniversary. What do you think of that?*

Gotta go. My candle is burning low.

I love you and miss you,
Hank

Patti had put on a Bach concerto, and its gentle, smooth melody
soothed Ellie's thoughts. Again, in the midst of total destruction, Hank
had found something of joy and beauty to write about. She wondered if
she could do that herself when it seemed as if everything in her life—
except Joe—was in turmoil; unfortunately, even that relationship had
begun to cause Ellie to worry.

Chapter 14

Calendars don't lie, but just to be sure, Ellie counted the days for the third time. *How could this be right?* She was never late! Her periods had been as regular as clockwork since she was in high school. Yet there she was—sitting in her bedroom counting and recounting the days since her last period. She bit her lip, then covered her face as she fell back across the bed. Her mind raced through memories of everything she had done from June until now. She sat up and counted the days again. It couldn't be true. The calendar simply had to be wrong.

She had read somewhere that pressure caused all kinds of physical problems, and now, in late August, she fought to convince herself that her period was two months late because her body was overwhelmed by stress and worries about Hank and Mom. Besides, even though she loved Joe, she knew they were doing things they shouldn't be doing together—so that weighed on her conscience too. There was also that other taboo she had embraced: smoking pot. *Surely that's the sort of thing that would make anyone's body get mixed up.*

"See?" she said aloud, "there are lots of reasons I might be late."

She had a fuzzy memory of Joe asking her about the pill—the little magic tablet that allowed free love to flourish. That must've been the

June afternoon they were in his apartment together the first time. She was sure she had said she was *not* on the pill, and he had assured her he would take care of things. After that, the subject had not come up again.

She told herself not to panic. Surely her system would cooperate, and she'd be back to normal. She sat up again and rubbed her eyes, then threw the calendar aside, willing herself to think about something else. Patti was at work already but had left a good-morning note on the kitchen table, along with a letter from Hank, so Ellie sat down to read Hank's letter while she ate breakfast.

> *14 Aug 1967*
> *C-2 Artillery Firebase*
> *4 miles south of Con Thien*

Dear Mom, Dad & Ellie,

> *We are down here (not far from the Cam Lo River) for 1 day and 2 nights so I might get some rest after 35 days on The Hill. They even have showers here! I took one this morning & I plan to take another one this afternoon! I washed my clothes this morning &, man, it really felt good to have cleaner things. I used a whole bar of soap on one pair of pants and a shirt.*
>
> *Tomorrow we are going back up to Con Thien. Lima is here because they started company-size rotations in and out of there when someone up the chain realized we needed re-charge once in a while. It's pure hell tryin' to survive up there in the barrel.*
>
> *The platoon really is working well. They are a well-oiled machine! Our mission is to provide security for Con Thien, which means we aren't moving around like we do when doing sweeps. We fan out on the parameter & watch for the enemy. We have a little slack time (just waiting and watching), so I'm hoping to have time for my correspondence course. It helps the time move faster.*

Ellie put down her toast and shoved her coffee cup away. Hank's letter—especially the part about trying to survive, quashed her appetite,

so she got up, leaned against the counter, and waited for her stomach to
calm down before finishing the letter.

> *I guess we'll be up at Con Thien until Sept sometime (I'll be
> making 1st Lt. on 8 Sept). Sorry I haven't written much from
> the field, but most of the time there isn't much to say and it's
> hard to write a clean letter because your hands sweat so much.
> Dust mixes with sweat and makes a mess. It'll be worse when
> the monsoons start! Plus, mornings and evenings are busy
> periods because that's when enemy attacks increase.*
>
> *Well, they are getting ready to pass out the beer ration (3
> beers per man) so I guess I will secure this letter until later.*
>
> *I'm back, with two beers down and one to go! Your letters
> are really good to get after the lapse caused by R&R. Patti said
> our pictures came out really well, and I'm glad because you'll
> see what a great time we had in Hawaii. Gave us both a good
> lift, like vitamins or something! I will try to write more often.*
>
> *I love you and miss you,*
> *Hank*

Ellie drove to work with the panther heavy on her shoulders because
her worries didn't compare to Hank's. He said Con Thien was a miserable place to be, yet he focused on the good things like his promotion
and letters from home. *Will I ever be that strong?*

Late August sunlight streamed in through the small window above
Joe's bed. Ellie opened one eye, stretched an arm over her face, and
reached out to touch Joe, asleep beside her. Her fingers searched for his
warmth across the rumpled sheets and found him on his side with his
back to her. His slow, regular breaths told her he was in a deep sleep.

Caught up in the soft, steady rhythm of him, she turned her thoughts
to his breath against her cheek a few hours ago. A quiver went through
her, and she pulled the sheet up to her chin, enjoying its softness against

her bare body. She caught a whiff of a flowery, exotic perfume she had smelled in the apartment a couple of times before. It was quite unlike the simple fresh scent of her soap and water.

She rolled onto her back and studied the dust particles swimming in the sun's rays. The specks swirled and floated in the light, only to become invisible in the shadows. She had never thought about sharing a bed with a man before, but, entranced by the particles above her, she realized how normal it felt to be like this with Joe. *Strange.*

Her thoughts turned to the first time she had shared her body with him, felt the soft carpet against her skin, and smelled the grassy aroma of the joint. To her surprise, the thought made her chuckle, because she wouldn't have done either of those things a few months ago. Her smile faded when her panther hissed from the darkness, *"Did you change for the good?"*

Ellie closed her eyes and remembered what Joe had said the day after that first time together, when he called to ask her to meet him at the coffeeshop. It seemed so long since she had sat down and confessed that she felt guilty about what had happened at his apartment the afternoon before. She'd said it was as if the world knew what they had done and wagged its finger at them. "It isn't right, that's all," she had said and hung her head.

"Why isn't it right? Because someone told you so?" Joe had replied. "People are made to come together. Why would God design us this way if he didn't want us to enjoy each other? You can't go through your life living the ideas your parents planted in your mind. Your feelings about me are natural. Normal." He grinned his imp grin at her, then scooted his chair close enough to drape his arm around her shoulders.

"Making love to you was simply the physical manifestation of deeper feelings I have for you," he continued. "It's perfectly fine to be close to the person you love." With a smile and a wink, he had finished by telling her that smooth pot and sex with her were the best things he had ever done.

She gave in to Joe's charms that day, and soon giving her body to him became part of her life. It wasn't long until guilt's growl became an annoying rumble she hardly noticed when she and Joe were together, so now there she was in his bed, waiting for him to wake up

Finally, Joe stirred and turned onto his back. "Gotta get going," he muttered as he looked up at the ceiling and stretched. "I'm working the supper shift tonight."

Ellie made sure the sheet still covered her breasts and raised herself up on her elbows. Joe got up, wrapped a towel around his waist, and walked into the hall.

Ellie knew his roommates would be home soon, so she swung her legs over the side of the bed where her feet landed on a rug so threadbare it would make her mother gasp. Ellie pulled on her clothes and tried not to notice the apartment's shabbiness or its boardinghouse character. Guilt nagged at her, but she pushed away the thoughts and tried to ignore them. *How silly to pay attention to those kinds of things.* Joe's apartment was that way because he was a man and didn't notice small things. Besides, she reasoned, she loved him, so it was okay for them to be lovers.

She slipped on her shoes just as he appeared at the bedroom door, fully clothed, smelling heavenly, and looking cute. He bowed at the waist while he held the front door open, and they headed out into the late afternoon sun.

"I want to go to the lake for my mom and dad's anniversary next month," Ellie said as they walked down the sidewalk to her car. "It's on September twentieth."

Joe nodded. "Um, so you want to go through that again, huh? Well, I'm game if you are, I guess."

She looked at the ground and took his hand. "What was that perfume I smelled in your room?" she asked.

"Uh-h-h, I don't know," Joe said, his hand flinching. "Maybe it's the new detergent I bought." He looked at her and flashed an off-center smile.

"Oh." An uneasy feeling spread through her. She had never smelled laundry soap like that. *Why does it matter, anyway?* Did she trust him? Sure she did. *You trust someone you love.*

They walked without talking until they got to the street where they had to go separate ways. Ellie started toward her car but paused to look over her shoulder at Joe. He walked away and never looked back.

After supper that night, Patti handed Ellie a letter postmarked eleven days before, then cleaned up and left the kitchen while Ellie read Hank's words:

20 Aug 67
Back on Con Thien

Dear Folks,

We're now set-in on our combat base perimeter just outside the south gate. Been here since the 15th. Our mission is to stand security and hold the perimeter around the south side of the mountain. We keep the perimeter secure with 20-man working parties to build the defense around us. Our safety requires digging trenches and fighting holes, filling sandbags that reinforce our bunkers, and stringing concertina wire around the whole boundary. Working on minefields to make sure the enemy can't penetrate our defenses on the ground and overrun our combat base inside the perimeter. The trench goes around the whole perimeter on all sides. The trenches and holes give us cover when the shooting starts so we live in bunkers behind the trench and open fighting holes.

Ellie cringed and closed her eyes for a moment. Hank and his men must be close to the enemy if they had to have trenches for protection. She remembered news photos of men fighting out of holes so deep that only their eyes could be seen peeking up through the dust and artillery smoke. Each man had a rifle raised out of the hole. "Ready to shoot," the caption had said.

We built a good bunker that sleeps 4. The NVA move around when it's dark so there's a man outside on watch all night. We get sleep sometimes, but it gets interrupted by the enemy's incoming mortar or big gunfire. Our howitzers are louder still when they return fire. Other companies go on patrols, or sweeps, and have found quite a bit of debris left behind by the enemy. Our guys destroy every fortification they find, but like mushrooms, enemy bunkers pop up again and again. Some are mined, but the ones planted fast at night are easy to spot. We are getting daily shelling, etc. and it seems to be increasing even more.

Ellie felt weak as the letter fell to her lap. She had read many questions about the American military command strategy to win the war. Some journalists even said the Marines and soldiers were making a strong effort but the war was unwinnable. An internal voice screamed, *Why don't they let Hank and his men come home?* Ellie was beginning to feel nauseous, but she compelled herself to finish the letter.

Looks like the monsoons are starting, and we found out that our bunker leaks a little. Had time to build a new roof though. It rains more and more as we approach Sept. when it will be steady rain 24 hrs. a day. Not as nice as a good old Florida afternoon rain, but it makes me think of being at the lake, sitting on the porch, watching giant raindrops pelt the water.

The dust turns into thick mud up here. Forget showers or shaves every day. We live in sweaty utilities, dirty boots, but gotta take care of our feet cause socks stay wet for so long. We're muddy, rough, lean, mean Marines for sure! Ammo crates get ripped open and parts of them are left all over the ground. Litter everywhere. It gets noisy when the NVA opens up on us and we respond. Not exactly a picnic.

    I'm OK though. I have tried to study on my math course a little each day because it keeps my mind active, but we don't have much light. We used our last candle—no flashlights allowed—last night, so I'm in a holding pattern on math at the moment.

    Gotta go. I'll try to write as often as I can.

I love you and miss you,
Hank

    Ellie folded the letter and put it back in the envelope. She left it on the table, went to her bedroom, and cried herself to sleep

Ellie awoke to the phone ringing. Her head hurt and she was groggy, but she reached over and answered.

"Hiya," said a familiar voice, clear and upbeat. "How's my sweet friend?"

Ellie gripped the receiver. "Susan!" she exclaimed. "Where are you? No, how are you? It's so good to hear from you!"

"Let's see," Susan paused. "Where to start? I'm out of the program and getting settled in real life again, so I want to come to see you in a week or so."

"That would be fantastic. Give me a date and I'll meet you. Or you can come to the apartment."

"Let's meet at the coffeehouse—for old times' sake, so to speak. I'll let you know when my plans firm up. We'll set a date then, okay?"

"Wonderful," Ellie said. "Can't wait to talk to you."

"Same here, but don't hang up until you tell me how your brother is. I need to know."

"Well, we're always behind on his news because it takes so long to get his letters, but his last one said he was okay and that the monsoon rains had started. He's in a place called Con Thien that's really close to the DMZ, so the North Vietnamese Army fires on them all the time. According to another letter, he'll soon be rotating from there to a place that's better. He was okay when he sent that last letter." Ellie felt her voice weaken and trail off.

"Well, thank heaven you know that, at least." Susan was quiet for a minute, then changed the subject. "Aren't you starting classes soon?"

"Yep, registration was a few days ago," Ellie responded. "I can't believe I'm a sophomore already!" They chatted about Ellie's classes until Susan said she had to hang up but promised she'd call again soon. Ellie wanted to jump up and down and clap like a child. Susan was back in her life again.

Later that evening, Patti eyed Ellie over dinner and said, "Something good must have happened to you today."

"It sure did," Ellie said. "Susan called and she's out of the treatment center. She's coming to see me."

"Great news! I know you've missed her," Patti said. They cleaned up the dishes and went to the living room. They both needed the regular time to sit, drink a little wine, listen to music, and talk.

Patti slid a black vinyl record from its cover, put it on the turntable, and lowered the needle into the groove. She adjusted the volume as the room came alive with Bach's genius. Settling back on the couch, Ellie let the combinations of instruments and counterbalanced harmonies fill her senses.

One evening a few months earlier, Patti had said the job she thought would be a time-filler was better than she imagined because Eden's Beauty, Tommy, and everything else about the job was right for her. Just as he said he would, Tommy had taught her what she needed to know and didn't interfere with her creativity because he said she had a natural talent for analyzing texture, color, shape, and size. From the looks of his event calendar and order book, her mismatched floral combinations pleased him—and the customers.

"Eden's Beauty is the perfect place to immerse myself in fresh flowers and beautiful scents," Patti said. "There's no tension and there's beauty all around."

Patti kept her eyes on her wine as she confessed she had not relished the idea of going back to work after R and R because she didn't want to have to talk about her two weeks with Hank. "Talking about it makes it harder to be here without him," she said. "I'd rather focus on him coming home. Actually, I'm glad I'm back in a work routine again, but things got complicated today. Don't worry—you'll hear about it next time you're there.

"Tell me now!" Ellie begged. "I don't know if I can wait!"

"Well, okay," Patti said and resettled her legs on the couch. "A well-dressed man came into the shop this afternoon when I was finishing up a banquet-sized centerpiece that took up my whole worktable. When I glanced up, I saw him standing there staring at me with his upper lip hidden under his lower teeth—underslung—he was like a bulldog in an expensive suit."

"Who in the world was he?" Ellie asked and leaned her head back.

"I had no idea, but Tommy told me later that he was Rocky Jensen, the convention coordinator for Masterson and Company. Anyway, he walked right over and without a pause or anything, told me he loved my use of texture and color. He said he'd never seen anything like that centerpiece before.

"To make a long story short, Rocky said he had flown in from Miami on an advance organizing trip for an important reception because there was trouble with the event's floral designer, and he needed to make a change—fast. He said a couple of the caterers recommended me and Eden's Beauty. Then Rocky told us Masterson was hosting a benefit for the hospital's pediatric unit in two weeks, and there was no need to haggle about cost because my work was so good. Next thing I knew, he handed me the color palette and told me to come up with something spectacular."

"Wow!" Ellie said. "What did you say?"

"I didn't say anything." Patti took a sip of wine and continued: "But sheesh! Two weeks? That'll be the second week of September."

"Hardly any time at all to get things together for a project like that!" Ellie said. "All kinds of stuff has to fall into place."

"Yeah, I just stood there with the color card in my hand," said Patti. "I guess I looked stunned because Tommy came over and right then and there agreed to do the project. Unbelievable—because we're already overcommitted this month.

"Rocky said the venue is that gorgeous restored hotel not far from campus. You know—the one with the huge ballroom. The Seminole, it's called. Rocky walked out the door, and all Tommy could do was fan himself and say 'Whew!' but I turned on him and asked why in the world he had agreed."

"I was wondering that, too. Didn't he wonder how you're going to get everything ready in time?" Ellie asked.

"He said the Masterson Company is the biggest and best, so it would be marvelous to have them as a client in the future." Patti turned to Ellie with a twinkle in her eye and said, "That's where you come in, Ellie."

"M-me?" Ellie asked, staring wide-eyed at Patti.

"I'll need extra help getting the ballroom set up, and Tommy agreed. So can you help me? I know you'll be back in school by then, but can I count on you?"

"Well, I'd love to help if you think I can," Ellie said.

"No doubt in my mind. I'll give you details later, but right now I need to sit back and enjoy Bach." Patti put her feet on the coffee table, then crossed her ankles and closed her eyes while she sipped wine.

"Which piece is this?" Ellie asked, eager to learn more about baroque music.

"Brandenburg Concerto, Number Four. It's in G Major—one of six in a collection he wrote in 1721. Typical Baroque: unlikely—meaning contrasting—combinations of strings, brass, and woodwinds." Patti swayed her head to the music. "In my opinion, baroque is the most beautiful music ever written. I think I convinced Hank to appreciate it too. Can't wait to tell him about Masterson. He'll never believe it," Patti murmured.

The plans for the Masterson benefit were complete and ready to come to life when Hank's next letter arrived, and it could not have contrasted more sharply with the beauty of Masterson's charity night. The letter was so grim that Ellie had to sit and catch her breath after she read the first sentence.

25 Aug 67
Con Thien—"Hill of Angels"

Dear Family,

> *I don't think we'll find any Angels up here. There was another B-52 run this morning. We saw and heard strikes with hundreds of bombs pounding the DMZ close to us. We believe there are large numbers of NVA moving south toward us from there. We've been told to expect an attack soon, so we used our new Starlight scopes last night. They are kinda neat and the ones for my platoon are signed out to me so you can imagine how careful I'm being to make sure all of my men have one. Last night we could see the B-52s dropping aircraft flares into North Vietnam as well as the enemy fire at the planes. We watched their red tracers and the flash when rounds exploded. The NVA is equipped with the latest and best Russian and Chi-*

*nese AA weapons, so their antiaircraft fire really looks mean,
but apparently, they don't hit many planes for the amount of
artillery they put out. Great equipment, poor aim, which is
good for us!*

*Our company tanks are our counter-attack force, and we
have one that lives beside our bunker. The crew has just come
in from their nighttime position; lotsa noise close by. The
nights are what I will remember most about being up here
because that's when I feel the most unsettled. Even though
we get hit by hundreds of rounds of arty, rockets, and mortars
during the day, we can at least see what's going on. Sometimes
it's sporadic and sometimes it's 104 rounds landing every 3
minutes, but we know where they come from. Not so at night,
and that somehow feels less secure.*

Ellie's head spun. Flowers and beauty here. Bombs, mortars, and
death over there. Mom drank, Dad doctored, and Patti arranged flowers,
but not one of them had anything except temporary relief from fear and
worry. Joe and his pot were Ellie's shelter, but nothing could provide
refuge from the realities of this letter.

*There's never a time when you don't wonder how close
the NVA really are. I don't know what it is, but the relentless
pounding during the day is easier to handle than wondering
where the enemy is.*

*We took over when the 2/9 got ambushed while they were in
the DMZ. That was a bad show because there is only one road
up there from here, plus they had tanks & Ontos with them, but
they had to use it to go up and come back. That's OK if you
provide adequate security along each side of the road. For
some reason, they did not do that.*

*The operation was supposed to be 24-48 hours long and
that was the big error. Moving in the DMZ you are likely to
encounter a large enemy force; therefore, you need good, stout
security. That's what we did last May in Operation Hickory
when we were up there (the DMZ). There has to be at least one*

rifle company on each side of the road moving along with the men and equipment to provide protection for them. You have to spread the men out because groups are easy targets, but that makes some of them feel isolated and vulnerable—since they have to be alone in the jungle when they move alongside the column. The 3/4 is a seasoned Bn because we've done things like that before, but the 2/9 operation was different, and they got ambushed from a hill. They lost a lot of men.

Well, so much for tactics—better change the subject. It's starting to cool off a little, but 3 days ago it rained all day. From up here we have a good view of the mountains to the west and Camp Carroll in the south. It's a really pretty panorama because you can see the mountains—The Annamites—stretching from north to south.

I should be putting on my silver bars soon. 8 Sept to be exact. That means I will be a first Lt. It's a promotion, in other words. We'll party when I get home, okay?

I love you and miss you,
Hank

Hank's letter was twelve days old, and even though he had tried to end on a positive note, the letter was darker than any had been so far. After a couple of days and two nightmares, Ellie tried to be upbeat by writing back to congratulate Hank on his promotion. She told him she was helping Patti at Eden's Beauty, and, trying to be newsy, she told him about her classes. She sealed the letter and tried to ignore the guilt that remained deep inside. She hoped Susan would call again soon because she needed to talk to her friend. *Maybe Susan will have good news to share,* Ellie thought. *I could sure use some.*

Chapter 15

Sure enough, Susan's call was a welcome distraction. Unable to control her excitement, Ellie bounded into the kitchen to tell Patti that Susan had called. "She wants to meet me in a little while at our old meeting place!"

"Go, go, go!" Patti looked up from the design and seating charts she had spread out on the table. "I won't expect you for dinner. The two of you will probably talk long enough to work up an appetite and get dinner out, anyway. Enjoy yourself."

Ellie settled under her tree and allowed herself to enjoy the anticipation of seeing her friend. A few minutes later, the familiar VW pulled up next to the curb across the street. Ellie saw a difference in Susan the moment she climbed out and headed for the coffeehouse. Maybe it was the way she carried herself or how she dressed. There was no more sauntering along in floppy sandals and a loose, wrinkly dress, and the slouch and shuffling steps were gone. Susan looked clean, neat—very London mod.

Ellie hurried across the grass with a million questions rushing through her mind, and by the time she entered the coffeeshop, Susan was sitting upright, not slouched, at their regular table by the window, with no cigarettes in sight.

"Hey, friend," Susan said, standing up to give Ellie a firm hug. They sat and stared at each other for a moment.

"How . . ." they said in unison, then laughed.

"Go ahead," Susan said, nodding to Ellie. "You first."

"Okay," Ellie responded. "You look so good! How are you?"

That was the start of an easy conversation—just the way their first one had been, only this time there was no evidence of Susan's got-the-world-by-the-tail attitude, and she laughed more than Ellie remembered. Her friend was the same relaxed person, but she seemed grounded or content—or something Ellie couldn't put her finger on.

They talked about everything that had happened since Susan left, and Ellie asked all her questions about what led up to the decision to quit school. Susan answered all the questions openly, not evading any. She explained the twelve-step recovery program she had been forced to embrace.

"My mom and dad took one look at me when I got home and said if I didn't get help, they would cut me off and I'd be without money or a place to live. They gave me two days to decide what I wanted," she said. "I pouted and fumed for a while—went to the basement and drank a lot—but for some reason I realized they were right, so I ended up in a treatment place for ninety days. I was locked away from temptation, not allowed to contact anyone or have visitors."

Ellie's eyes narrowed. "Wow, three months. That's a long time."

"Best thing that ever happened to me. After I quit acting so smart, I had to admit I was a pathetic fraud—a scared little girl trying to act grown up. I also had to admit I was—I mean, I am—an addict and alcoholic.

"I thought that was the hard part, but it wasn't," she continued. "After I faced myself, I found out that I—a human—am not the highest form of being in the universe. There is a power greater than me, and I had to accept that it's okay. When I understood those two things, I got on the right path, so I can live with who I am and what my life is to be from now on."

Ellie was dumbfounded because ever since the first time they had talked, Ellie believed Susan knew her way through life and, with all her antics, was simply enjoying college. Funny how a person can be so wrong about someone else, even a friend. They talked nonstop all afternoon and lost track of time until the server asked if they wanted a dinner menu.

"Gosh, yeah," Susan said to the server, then smiled at Ellie. "I'm famished, aren't you? Let's order."

After the server left, Ellie studied her friend's clear, steady eyes and said, "Well, the obvious question is: what do you want to do from now on?"

Susan cleared her throat and folded her hands on the table's edge, then with unwavering eyes on her friend, she said, "In a few weeks I am going to start my year of discernment to become a nun."

The world paused and its atmosphere thinned as Ellie's jaw dropped and she fell back against her chair. She was as shocked as she had been when she was ten and heard that the neighbor's dog had given birth to seventeen puppies.

"A-a nun? Whaaat? I didn't know you were religious or Catholic or anything," Ellie croaked.

Susan smiled and reached across the table to touch Ellie's hand. "I knew you would be surprised and you might even think I was kidding. The truth is, I know the thing I missed growing up, and—meaning no disrespect to my parents—it was the idea of service to others. I found out that helping other people frees us to know ourselves. I know now that it's not the establishment's traditions that keep us bound tight, but our own human egos and our need for power over each other. Real power comes from giving ourselves to benefit others, and as far as I am concerned, the best example of that is Christ. I understand now that helping people gives us focus and real—not phony—strength."

A minute went by before Ellie found her voice. "Not that I doubt you, but this is a lot to take in," she said. Susan withdrew her hand and started eating, but Ellie wasn't hungry anymore. All she could think about was Susan becoming a nun. Ellie had not been back to the Baptist church for months because the panther grabbed her every time she thought about going. She had never put Susan and Christianity in the same sentence, so the news—that Susan was giving her life to serving Christ—was stunning. *Should I tell her about Joe or about the pot and sex? Or about the pregnancy? The doctor at the campus infirmary—the only other person who knows about it—didn't judge me, but what would Susan—a nun or almost a nun—think?* Ellie stared out the window and focused on her tree, studying the gentle swaying of the branches.

"Susan," she said, "I want to talk about your decision, but I can't get my mind around it right now. Can we talk again in a couple of days?"

"Sure, that's fine," said Susan with a grin. "So, what about your friend Joe? Is he still in the picture?"

Ellie felt her cheeks get warm. "Well, yes, he is," she said. "We've been seeing each other since about the time you left. We have a good relationship. I mean, we can talk about anything. He's easy to be around."

Susan cocked her head and regarded Ellie with concern. "How do your mom and dad feel about him? And what does Hank say? Or your sister-in-law?"

"Umm, I don't know. They don't know he's my steady boyfriend, and I'm not sure it matters to Mom and Dad at this point." She looked up to see Susan's lips pressed together and a frown forming between her brows.

"Well, you've got yourself an honest-to-goodness boyfriend, I guess," Susan said and forked a heaping bite into her mouth. She swallowed and asked, "Is your dad still working as hard as ever?"

"As ever," Ellie sighed. "I don't think he'll stop 'til he dies. He's rarely home, and Mom's been drinking way too much, but that might slow down when Hank gets home. Things haven't changed much at the old homestead, and we're all worried about him." Ellie tried to sound light and newsy, but when she looked at Susan's empty plate and her own barely touched food, she exclaimed, "Boy, you were hungry! When's the last time you ate?"

"I'm a growing girl," Susan said. "It takes energy to discern what I am called to do. I have lots of nuns to talk to, convents to visit, and praying to do, of course!"

Ellie was struck by Susan's ear-to-ear grin until it faded and she turned serious. "How is Hank? I think of him often, especially when I hear news about the war."

Ellie poked at her food and didn't respond because the question triggered thoughts of Hank describing Con Thien and Patti's picture of him sitting on a huge stone in front of the destroyed church in Phu An where his sergeant found the brass figure of Jesus. The picture showed Hank in a sweat-soaked khaki-colored T-shirt with Marine utility trousers bloused and tucked into scuffed black boots. He looked straight into the camera with his elbows resting on his knees and fingers interlaced in front of him.

Ellie remembered magazine pictures at the library showing young, hard faces twisted by anger, pain, and misery, but Hank was different. Aside from his worn look, his picture showed the placid expression he'd always had—in spite of the church blown to bits in the background. She was sure, even though destruction surrounded him, he had not lost the ability to see the best in the worst.

"He's okay, but it's dangerous where he is." She looked up and said, "I mean, war is always deadly, but right now he's in an especially bad place because there's constant shelling and enemy attacks, so I'm afraid for him. Last May, he was wounded in the leg, but he went right back to the field, stitches and all, when the doctors released him. He said he needed to be with his men. What's more, Dad says the war is at a stalemate and the Marines are taking the brunt. I wish Hank were already home, but like Patti says, we have to wait a few more months." Susan's fingers tightened when Ellie looked away and murmured, "I miss him. I'm anxious to talk to him. I . . . I have a lot to tell him."

Susan looked at her friend as gloom settled over them. Finally Susan said, "I'm sure you are anxious to see him." Ellie heard Susan's voice quiver a little, but her friend kept talking after they paid for their food and walked out onto the sidewalk. "You told me he knows how to take care of himself, right? He's in God's hands, so be confident in that. All I can say is just keep being positive and doing what you are doing because you look great. I know you have Baptist roots, and as I understand it, that means you know prayers help, so don't forget to pray, either. Hank will be proud to see the person you are now."

Ellie tried to smile as they hugged goodbye, but the panther's weight squeezed her chest so hard she was breathless. *What kind of person am I?* She had told the infirmary doctor that pregnancy terrified and overwhelmed her. "I never thought of being a mother," she had said to him. "How can I be a good one?"

"Well, it's time to figure that out," replied the old man with kind eyes. "I've seen a number of students in the same trouble lately." Then he patted her arm and left the exam room.

The panther's hot breath rose within her and whispered, *if Susan only knew. How could she be proud anymore?* Ellie knew she was a disgrace to her family, and she couldn't remember the last time she'd been in church. She was pregnant, not married, and would become one of those unwed mothers she'd heard grown-ups gossip about ever since she was a little girl.

Dusk settled in as Susan drove away, and Ellie went back to her tree to reconcile Susan-the-hippie with Susan-the-nun. At least Susan knew what she wanted. But Ellie had no idea what she should do about her messed-up life. She massaged her temples and realized she had no answer about Joe, the baby, or their future. The only thing she had was a headache.

Suddenly a breeze ruffled her hair, and a strange feeling deep inside made her look up. She sat absolutely still and spread one hand across her belly, then closed her eyes and concentrated. There it was again: a flutter inside her, soft and quick—fluttery as an eyelid twitching. Transfixed by the new sensation, she stayed perfectly still, then frowned and waited. When it happened again, an innate understanding spread over her, and she smiled.

"Oo-ooh. It's you!" she murmured to the miniature life inside. She felt the flutter again. *How could a tiny life be a disgrace?* she asked herself.

"It's okay, tiny baby," she said aloud. "I don't know how, but I have to make everything fine by the time you get here." As if in response, the baby moved again, and Ellie's cares evaporated for a while, but it was getting darker. She'd have to head for home soon.

When she walked into the apartment, Patti handed her two letters. "I need to stay busy, so I'll cook dinner," she said. "You'd better go sit down when you read these. You'll need time with them." Ellie nodded and went to the couch to start reading.

31 Aug 67
Con Thien

Dear Mom, Dad & Ellie,

Last night we had some B rations for a change. They come from field prep spots and are served in the field instead of us

*getting individual cartons. We fixed up the fresh chili con carne
with C rat beans and franks. Plus, we had a big thing of green
beans. AND, earlier in the day we had ice cream flown in from
Dang Ha, and we had chicken noodle soup this morning so that
was good.*

Ellie's shoulders began to relax a bit when she thought of Hank's ice
cream. She smiled and read on.

*We're putting in minefields, etc. that will make Con Thien
pretty secure when it's all said and done. There'll be a wall
of company-size outposts all around here. I guess it'll be like
the iron curtain or something when we get finished. We need
to make a strong defense line from here to Gio Linh and down
to Cam Lo, so that it's difficult for the enemy to get through.
We'll be at the vortex of those lines, I suppose. We have to move
around to make sure our fortifications are in place and holding,
so we get shelled when they see any movement. We keep our
heads down, but the shelling makes fragments of junk scatter
everywhere.*

*I got cut on my shoulder from some of that flying debris. One
of my men, Jock Thibodeaux, is from New Orleans, and there's
no mistaking he's Cajun. He's long and lanky, wiry, strong.
Has small, intent brown eyes that move constantly, and big
eyebrows, a prominent nose, tight lips. Like the rest of us, he
has days-old scraggly whiskers! Best of all, he's a seasoned
fighter and quite a character, a good Marine—smart, quick,
disciplined.*

*Anyway, Thib was there when I got hit so he called for a med-
ic. The corpsman wanted to report my injury, but I said not to
'cause it's not bad enough for a PH. Not for #3 anyway. There
are lots of men worse off than me.*

Ellie's heart fell. Hank had turned down his third Purple Heart because of the other men who were hurt worse. If he had taken it, he might

be on his way home already. She read the last sentence with tears in her eyes.

> *I am getting anxious to get home, but at least we're past the halfway point!*
> *Well, guess that's about all for now.*
>
> > *I love you and miss you,*
> > *Hank*

Ellie sat and waited a minute to gather the courage to read the second letter, mailed separately five days after the first one.

> *4 Sep 67*
> *Con Thien*

Dear Family,

> *I know it's been a while since I have written, but things have been pretty rough up here so we have been busy. On the 1st, the NVA launched rockets from our west near Hill 174 (where I got my leg injury in May)—26 of them slammed into our position and wounded 4 Marines. For the next few days, they pounded us all day with barrages of arty, rockets and mortars. They aimed well and got 200 rounds inside our perimeter, so 24 more wounded and 2 lost. It was clear the NVA were moving in and would try to overrun us sometime around 3 Sep—we figured that was the day because it was when the South Vietnamese elections were scheduled—so we were ready for them. We're supposed to rotate out of here around the 10th, but all I can say is, "we'll see." Rainy season has started, and man, it's a soggy mess here!*

Ellie hated the thought of Hank on Con Thien. She feared the attacks, and rains had delayed the mail, so both letters came at once.

> *I know you must be worried since there are correspondents here and the newspapers have been writing about what's going*

on. We really are OK and, as a matter of fact, my shoulder is doing fine. Getting a little black and blue, but nothing to worry about. We have C-rats that we usually eat out of the can, so please keep sending the good snacks because they hit the spot. Like I said, they make sure we get everything you send, and thanks to my great family, things have been looking up in the chow department! Remember to send several small packages rather than one big one because large ones get bumped around and/or get wet so I'd have to throw it away. That would be heartbreaking. Well, that's all the news for now.

I love you and miss you,
Hank

Ellie read the second letter two times. Today was September 16th, and Hank said he was going to rotate off Con Thien—and out of the barrel— around September 10th. *Where was he now? A safer place, I hope,* she thought. But even so, when would it be the right time for him to get a letter from her with news of the baby?

She went to her room, opened her dresser drawer, and pulled out a letter she had written Hank after she'd been to the infirmary doctor. It was a long one about Joe and the baby, and she had told Hank everything. But instead of mailing it, she had put it in her drawer because it still didn't seem right to burden Hank with her problems. She held her letter for a moment, then put it back in the drawer. She would stick with her plan to send it later when she was certain Hank was in a safer place.

The next morning, Ellie woke up later than usual and found that Patti was already gone. Ellie sipped her coffee while she got dressed, hurrying because the Masterson benefit started in a few hours and preparing the ballroom would be demanding. Her responsibilities would keep her mind occupied, and she had no doubt Patti felt the same.

After parking in the Seminole's lot, Ellie stopped on the sidewalk to look up at the massive Collegiate Gothic–style structure. The elegant red-brick and stone fortress in its setting of flowering plants and paths laid out among stately live oaks took her breath away. Carved stone finials topped each corner of a thirty-foot tower with an ornamental parapet on top. Huge rectangular leaded-glass windows trimmed in stone fanned away from the tower in brick walls that stretched to each side below, the windows' beveled glass twinkling like diamonds in the sunlight. Every window was crowned by an ornate stone arch, echoing the tall arch over the entrance, where a large banner snapping in the humid mid-September breeze announced the benefit supporting sick children.

Somehow, Ellie felt secure in the shadow of the building, with its symmetry and timeless beauty. *Maybe there is permanence I can count on in the world.* She thought of the destroyed church Hank had described; unlike that church or the Ville's old Victorian houses, this building had escaped ruin and was refurbished—its brick and stone cared for by people who loved the past but knew life had to have a future. *What's mine?* Ellie wondered.

A delivery truck rattled by, interrupting her thoughts before it disappeared behind the building. She hurried along the stone walkway and pulled open the heavy oak door, determined not to let anything get in the way of doing what Patti needed her to do.

Cool, fresh air heavy with the scent of palms surrounded her as she stepped inside the lobby where she took off her sunglasses and waited while her eyes adjusted to the warm glow inside. Stretching in front of her, the entrance hall was a cavernous room with a twenty-foot-high ceiling held up by Corinthian columns crowned by rings of acanthus leaves and draping tendrils. Soft upholstered chairs and settees in shades of yellow, dusty pink, and blue clustered around the pillars like friends at a cocktail party. Floor lamps cast spheres of warm light around the room. Ellie allowed her senses to absorb the feeling of the old architecture—enduring and grand—proving that the past gave strength to the present.

The faint sound of voices reminded her that she was here for Patti, so Ellie followed the sound and stepped into a rectangular ballroom with a polished wood floor, a high ceiling, and brass chandeliers. Rows of round tables with pale-blue cloths filled the expanse, and people moved among them, placing stacks of china and piles of silverware on each one. Patti was in the middle of the room holding a clipboard and talking to Tommy. Carts of large and small floral masterpieces, tubs of greenery, and buckets of cut flowers surrounded them. Patti had shown Ellie the precise drawings of how the room would look when everything was in place, but now Ellie was exhilarated by her part in transforming the abstract concept on paper into reality.

Tommy's arms waved toward the ceiling while Patti looked up and scanned the room until she saw Ellie and waved her over.

"Hi," Patti greeted her. "This is quite a place, huh?"

"How're you doing, Ellie?' Tommy asked, hands draped on his hips. "This ballroom set-up stuff is new for you, but this one"—he jerked a thumb toward Patti—"this one has everything organized so we stay on time. You won't have any trouble, and you'll see why we think Patti is pretty special, not to mention talented."

"Thank you for coming, El," Patti said. "We're under the gun, and I knew I could count on you."

"Glad to help. This is a gorgeous place," Ellie said, looking around. "Someone did a terrific job of saving the building and giving it new life."

"Yup," said Tommy. "This is your first experience in a huge space like this, and you'll see how hard we have to work to soften the setting in such a large area. The ambiance is important, and the right flowers can make or break it, because if the guests don't feel comfortable when they walk in, they won't relax and engage with the cause, no matter what."

"See why Eden's Beauty is so well run?" exclaimed Patti. "Tommy knows his stuff!"

Tommy's face turned pink, and he took a few steps away when Patti turned to Ellie to review the design concept with her.

Ellie felt as if she were a part of something important, but even though she fought them off, worries seeped in like silt disturbed in a pond during the early morning. She wasn't sure how long she could hold the panther at bay as her fear of something dark in the future continued to fester beneath the temporary satisfaction.

After Patti finished explaining the evening's theme and the environment she wanted to create, she gave Ellie a pat on the back and said, "I have no doubt you'll get this right. Sometimes it's hard to explain to someone else what you want the room to look like, but you're a lifesaver because you get my vision! Thanks again for the help."

She turned back to Tommy, and they began positioning huge centerpieces on the serving tables while Ellie took charge of the smaller table pieces, pushed the carts from one table to the next, and chatted with the servers who were arranging place settings. Ellie watched with delight as a transformation took place around the room, and she loved thinking she had a part in changing lives—the lives of sick children in this case—even if she was just in the background.

Later, when the flower carts were empty and the servers were putting on their starched vests, Tommy, Patti, and Ellie stood back to admire the metamorphosis they had enabled over the past few hours. The room was magical, full of color, twinkling lights, and style, yet still inviting, elegant, and comfortable. Ellie glowed with pride.

Tommy said she had done a fabulous job, and without hesitation or self-doubt, she told him she'd be happy to help any time she was needed. When he told her he'd love to have her at Eden's Beauty full time, a new feeling she couldn't name flooded through her.

The sun was low in the sky and cast long, golden beams across the ballroom when Ellie took one last look around and headed out the door to her car, knowing something had changed within her. It was a feeling she intended to savor. Was it vitality? Satisfaction? Confidence? Or was it feeling she had been a part of something that empowered others? She couldn't put a name to it, but that didn't matter because this must be what Hank meant when he said she must find out who she was. Pleased by her newfound sense of purpose, she drove her car past the trees and bloom-lined paths and headed home, hoping the feeling wouldn't end too soon.

Chapter 16

Two days later Ellie walked into the kitchen and found Patti working on an event-planning sheet for anniversary day at the lake house. "I ordered your mom's favorite flowers," she said, "because I want this year's anniversary centerpiece to be something special. I won't have much room in my car for anything except the flowers, so you'll have to take the food in your car. It'll be up to you and me to make this a pleasant family anniversary party."

"You're right. It needs to be a nice party," Ellie said, even though she didn't share Patti's enthusiasm about it being a pleasant get-together.

"Did you want Susan to come too?" Patti asked.

"No, I don't think I'll ask her." Ellie wasn't ready to see her friend yet, because Susan would take one look at her and know something was wrong. Ellie had managed to put together a plan for telling Joe about the baby, and she didn't want to take a chance on the news getting out until she and Joe were married or had, at least, picked a date.

Patti stared at her for a moment before turning back to her papers. "Actually, that reminds me," she said. "Susan called and wants you to call her back."

Susan had said she was beginning a postulancy with an order whose convent was in St. Augustine, and because she was leaving soon, they had said their goodbyes a few days before. Ellie wondered what more Susan wanted to say. She chewed on a fingernail and listened to the phone purr in her ear. When Susan picked up, they quipped about her soul-searching journey until her tone turned serious.

"El, I couldn't leave without telling you something. It's important for me to say it, but I hope it won't cause problems for you." Susan's voice was soft, as if she were trying to shield her friend from something harsh.

"Okay," said Ellie. "Go ahead, I guess." She braced herself.

"You need to know about Joe," Susan said. "I've known him for longer than you realize, and I should have told you this at the beginning before you spent too much time with him." Susan was talking fast. "He was my pot supplier. That's what he does, and everyone who is a user knows it. Plus, he has a stable of girls he goes to bed with, so please be careful of him. He never got to me, but I know plenty of girls he seduced. You said he was easy to talk to and you got along well, but he's not who you think he is." Susan stopped, and quiet settled in on them like a thick swamp fog.

Ellie managed to say, "O-o-okay, Susan. Thank you for telling me. I don't know what to say except that I did keep going out with him after you left, so we see each other a lot. He works almost every dinner shift and dates me, so I don't think he has much time for anyone else. He must've changed since you left." She barely got the last words out before her throat closed and the panther pounced—clawing and compressing her chest.

"Maybe, but I want you to be safe and happy. That's all," said Susan.

"I . . . I'm sorry, Susan, but I have to hang up. Someone is at the door. Gosh, Susan, I hope everything goes well for you." After saying goodbye, Ellie put the phone back in its cradle, then grabbed the counter to keep from falling.

Patti looked up and said, "Are you all right, Ellie? You're pale as a ghost."

"I'm okay. It's just that Susan is leaving in the morning, and I'll miss her." Ellie felt Patti's eyes linger on her for a minute before she looked back at her papers. Ellie mumbled, "See ya" and went to her room.

She collapsed on her bed while her mind ran wild. *What did I just hear? Could it be true?* Her honest friend had told her Joe—the man she loved and shared her body with—was a fake. The father of her baby had deceived her. She would soon be in her second trimester and the baby was still her secret. *What am I supposed to do? Who can I turn to?*

It was the same old story. Mom was beyond helping herself, so Ellie could forget about going to her. Dad? No—that was too ridiculous to consider. Patti was worried about Hank, so no need to burden her. Hank was fighting for his own survival and didn't need her problems to think about. Mira was a possibility, but she was getting older and had her own problems. Besides, Ellie didn't want to disappoint her old nanny after not seeing her since Hank's wedding. There was no one—no one at all—to help her, so she sat on her bed and cried tears of fear and disappointment and panic. *What am I going to do?!* The words suffocated her and left her adrift in a sea of mistakes that had foundered her life, and she had no idea how to right herself.

Patti rapped on Ellie's door the next morning—September twentieth, the anniversary day—and handed her a letter from Hank.

"You went to bed before I could give you this," Patti said before heading out the door. "I'm on my way to Eden's Beauty. I'll bring the flowers and meet you this afternoon at the lake house."

Ellie was groggy and nauseated. She didn't feel like celebrating anything, much less her parents' marriage. She pulled on cut-off blue-jean shorts that barely buttoned and a long shirt to cover her tummy, then she picked up Hank's letter and stumbled into the kitchen for a cup of coffee.

7 Sept 67
Con Thien ("The Hill")

Dear Mom, Dad & Ellie,

Everything is going pretty well right now, but things were pretty intense for the last few days. We are supposed to pull out of here in 3 days, so maybe we can get some real slack after that.

At night or between shellings when it's calm for a bit, I can work on my math course. I have been trying to solve a problem (f'(x) of f(x)=1/√x). It's giving me a hard time, but eventually I should get it.

It may seem odd to do math up here, but math is a constant and it keeps me focused & centered, not jumpy. The randomness of the mortars and artillery is getting to some of the newer guys. Makes them edgy. So I told 'em you can't make sense out of things that don't make sense. Stay sharp, but don't waste your energy trying to figure out when to expect incoming.

Just got confirmation that we're moving out of here on the 10th. That's about all the news. I'll keep you informed about where I am. I'm OK.

I love you and miss you,
Hank

Ellie rechecked the letter's date and realized Hank had left Con Thien ten days before, and he must have gotten his promotion by now. That was the good news she needed. She yawned and stared at swirls of cream on the surface of her drink, then leaned back against the sink to watch the backyard come to life. The sun shone above the treetops in a clear sky, and tiny brown finches flitted from branch to branch while robins hopped in the dewy grass. Her favorites, the cardinal couples, chirped and flew to the feeder on the gutter. The bright-red male perched protectively on a branch while his mate ate her breakfast, and Ellie smiled when he looked directly at her through the window.

"Don't worry," she said to him. "I'll stand still so I don't scare her."

The kitchen table was obscured by baskets of dry ingredients and vegetables that Patti had packed the night before. All Ellie had to do was load the food baskets for the party in her car and take them out to the lake for dinner.

"I won't think about what might be or what Susan told me about Joe," Ellie said to the cardinals and rubbed her hand across her belly. "I've got plenty of things to keep me busy today!" Ellie dreaded the party, but it wouldn't last forever, and she could manage. Besides, Patti's sweet nature and compassion made all bad things tolerable.

She pushed off the counter, put her empty cup in the sink, then started through the living room toward the bathroom and happened to glance outside on her way past the big window above the couch, hoping for one last look at the wrens feeding in the front yard. But she stopped short, eyes fixed on a dark-colored sedan parked by the curb outside. There was a uniformed man inside—that was strange. And it was too early for visitors. Ellie stood still, watching the surreal scene unfold.

The passenger door opened, and a Marine stepped out. There was no mistaking the dress uniform. It was the same one Hank had worn when he and Patti were married—the deep-blue, high-necked, form-fitting uniform with red piping, a U.S. Marine Corps insignia on each side of the stiff collar and a crimson strip running down the outside of the trousers. A brass buckle on the brilliant white belt glinted as the Marine closed the car door. Ellie watched him stand still for a moment. He held a Bible with gold-edged pages that reflected the morning sun.

A second Marine got out of the driver's side with a manila folder in his hand. He flipped it open, nodded toward the apartment, then said something to the first Marine. They both put on crisp white caps with shiny gold insignia in the center front, above polished black bills. Their eyes zeroed in on the apartment door, and then the two men stepped up on the curb and headed toward Ellie.

Indescribable horror overtook her as she watched them walk straight to her door. There could be only one reason why these two Marines were here, but her brain raced as it tried to come up with any other possibility. By the time they knocked on the door, her mind had gone blank and her heart had broken in two.

She felt as heavy and hollow as a bronze statue, and her arm seemed to weigh a ton as she reached for the door. Although she couldn't feel the knob in her hand, the door opened to the two Marines standing straight and solemn on the top step.

The one without the Bible said, "Hello, I'm Major Garver, and this is Chaplain Stone. We need to talk with Patti Dennis, Lieutenant Hank Dennis's wife."

Ellie stared at them, unable to speak. A new wave of numbness swept through her, and the moment turned stark in its intensity. She heard a far-off voice say, "She's at work. At Eden's Beauty on Main Street. It's a flower shop." She heard her voice, sounding small and helpless, say, "I'm Hank's sister. You can talk with me." Blinking hard, Ellie fought to gain control, but her hands shook and her heart pounded. Even though her throat was dry, she asked the young Marines why they needed to talk to Patti.

"I'm sorry, but we need to talk with the lieutenant's wife first," the one with the Bible said. "We'll come back here to you after we've talked with her. We'll be back."

Ellie's body went numb, and she fell against the doorframe, but somehow—perhaps drawing fortitude from Hank's Marine brothers—she managed to give them directions to the flower shop.

"Will you be okay while we're gone?" Major Garver reached forward and lightly touched her arm. Ellie nodded but remained mute and frozen inside. She stood against the door and watched the Marines walk back to their car, get in, and drive away. Ellie was alone, and her brain refused to work.

Abandoning the open door, she lurched toward the orange hand-me-down couch under the window and dropped to the cushions to sit cross-legged, staring into space. A soft breeze found its way through the open door while the warm sun cast streams of light across the carpet of Hank and Patti's little home. Lost and all alone, Ellie knew the two Marines brought bad news—maybe the worst possible news. Panic took over, and her eyes filled with tears.

She sat there, numbly begging God to bring her beloved brother home. She adored Hank. He was her comforter. Her strength. Her wisdom. She closed her eyes and rocked side to side in the shrieking silence.

She didn't know how long it was until the Marines came back. The door was open, so they simply walked in and removed their caps in unison. Ellie looked up and saw them watching her with kind eyes and grave faces. The chaplain sat in the chair next to the couch while the other sat next to her. Their strength and steadfastness were oddly reassuring, as Hank's had always been. She took a deep breath, air catching in her throat, and looked at Major Garver, who delivered the message clearly and compassionately.

"Two days ago, just before dawn on the eighteenth of September, Lt. Dennis drowned in the Cam Lo River, Quang Tri Province, South Vietnam," he said.

The room turned gray, and Ellie's world became shadowy flickers, like a movie when it spins off its reel. Neither Marine said anything else—they simply waited.

"No," Ellie said quietly, shaking her head. "How could he drown? He's an excellent swimmer! He . . . he practically grew up in the water. It's not possible that he would drown. You're wrong. Maybe you've got the wrong file." Her mind floundered for an answer. They had to be in the wrong apartment. Hank couldn't have drowned. She squeezed her eyes shut and tried to block out reality.

"His company was guarding an important bridge, and there was a flood that no one expected would happen," the major said. "He pulled several of his men from the water and got them to safety before he got tangled in concertina wire that was deep under the surface. The commandant and entire U.S. Marine Corps asked us to let you know we grieve your loss. All his Marine brothers grieve with you. Your brother was a true hero."

Ellie began to cry. As she sobbed, tears flowed down her cheeks and dropped on the frayed edges of her cutoffs—a symbol of her generation's fight against tradition. None of that mattered now, and neither did her parents' problems or her fledgling independence. Her fight for freedom rang hollow as she sat there remembering the last time she had seen her one and only brother.

"I love you, Little Sister," he had said. He had hugged her and stood her on her own two feet as he had always done. Even now, he had left her the gift of his belief in her.

She didn't know how long she sat with the Marines, lost in her memories, until Major Garver asked, "Do you want to join your family at your parents' home? We took the lieutenant's wife there."

"She said she wants you to be there with her. She's waiting for you," Chaplain Stone added, with his hand resting on the Bible in his lap.

"Okay," Ellie mumbled.

The Marines stood and looked down at her. In a trance, she unfolded her legs and rose from the couch, then took a couple of steps toward the door. Major Garver asked if she needed her purse or keys to lock the door, so she stopped and pointed toward the kitchen and told him her purse was on the counter. Chaplain Stone disappeared through the kitchen door and returned with her satchel. She dug keys out and handed them to him.

Next thing she knew, she was walking between the two Marines into the house where she and Hank had grown up. The living room was dim and empty with no one to greet her.

"Where are my parents and Patti?" she asked.

"Through there," said the Major, gesturing toward the archway on the far wall. "In the family room." He went through the entry, and Ellie started into the room but stopped at the threshold.

Two matching leather chairs against the far wall faced the archway where Ellie and the Marines stood. Their anniversary forgotten, Ellie's mother sat in one chair and her father in the other. They did not look at each other, but tears rolled down Dad's cheeks, and Mom was emotionless, with a face of stone as if she were alone in a distant place. Patti was weeping, curled up against one end of the couch on the adjacent wall, facing the French doors and the impossibly beautiful garden beyond. Birds chirped outside, and a lawn mower clattered in the distance. The world did not know their family had been destroyed.

"I-I don't know what to do," Ellie murmured to anyone who would listen as tears streamed down her cheeks.

Patti looked up and patted the empty couch next to her. "Come sit here, El," she said. "My mother is coming in a couple of hours, and I'm going home with her. I've already told your parents the music I know

Hank wanted and that's all I care about. They can make the rest of the arrangements, and I'll be back before the service, but that's all I can tell you right now." She managed to finish talking before grief choked off her words.

Mom looked up but didn't make a sound. Dad held out his hand as Ellie walked toward him, so she touched it lightly before she made her way to the couch. Patti grabbed her hand as she sat down and sobbed with her head bowed and both feet on the floor. No one said anything until Dad broke the silence.

"Please sit with us, both of you," Dad said to the Marines in true southern-gentleman style. "Please? We all have to be strong."

The Marines brought in a couple of porch chairs and set them near the couch. They sat down as a cloud passed in front of the sun and shrouded the room in shadows.

"Where is Hank now?" Ellie asked, her voice sounding strange to her ears.

"We accompanied him home," Major Garver said. "He is now at the Gabriel Funeral Home. Do you want us to take you to him?"

"Yes," she said and looked at Patti.

"They said they'd take me," said Patti, "but I'm waiting for my mom to go with me. I want to see him. I can't leave until I see him." She covered her face with her hands, and her body rocked back and forth as her chest heaved with uncontrollable sobs. Ellie's heart broke. She tried to control her own weeping, but she failed, so she squeezed Patti's hand.

Dad looked up at his daughter and said, "No, Ellie, you can't go. We need to remember him as he was when he was alive."

Ellie turned to Dad and stared. She desperately wanted to see Hank again, but she could not think of a response to Dad's directive. Blinded by tears, she stood and stumbled out of the room. Chaplain Stone followed her. She made it to the living room before her legs quit working.

and she became immobile, unable to do anything but stare at the floor. She sensed the Marine beside her, then felt his arm on her arm, guiding her to the couch where she sat down heavily.

Her insides twisted and ached. "I can't make it worse," she said. "I want to see Hank, sit beside him for a while, but they'll get upset if I go. If I go, I'll cause more pain for them." She wiped away tears, but they kept coming, so the Marine put a tissue box beside her.

"Well, tell me if you change your mind. We are here for your family until after the funeral," the chaplain said. "I'll take you to see him if you decide to go, but I can't advise you what to do about your father." He stayed beside her for a few moments before taking a seat near the family room door.

Ellie managed a weak "thank you" smile. She blew her nose, mopped away tears, and crossed an arm over her abdomen as she held her head in her other hand.

The news of Hank's death hit the family like a volcanic eruption and flowed like lava through the community. Patti's mother came to whisk away her distraught daughter, and a short time later, Mira appeared, as if by magic.

Her dark skin rippled with tiny wrinkles, and her curls were gray, but she took matters in hand as if the last ten years had never happened. She didn't disturb Ellie's mother, but hugged everyone else, including the Marines, and said a brief word to each, before setting about her duties. She knew the way southern people grieved. They telephoned, sent flowers, and came to the house with copious amounts of food for the family. Without a word, Mira turned on the living room lights, then put into place a system for taking phone messages, storing and serving the expected mountains of food, and making a place for people to leave their names so Mrs. Dennis could later send a thank-you note. It was early afternoon when the phone started ringing and the first flower arrangement was delivered.

Ellie had not left the living room since the Marine helped her sit down, and she continued to be oblivious to her surroundings until she felt someone's eyes on her. She looked up expecting to see the Marine but instead saw Mira watching her from the kitchen doorway. A torrent of tears cascaded down her cheeks, and she held out her arms, asking Mira to wrap her in another warm hug.

Chapter 17

"I remember years ago when I started taking care o' you and Hank," Mira said as she held Ellie's hand and sat on the arm of the sofa. "You got the same sad eyes you had as a itty bitty girl, and I al'ays wanted to hol' you and not leggo, just as I does now. I ha' to he'p you be strong then, and I will he'p you now." She sighed and released Ellie's hand. "I think about my church friend, Ethel Rose. Years ago she ask me what it was like workin' for Dr. Dennis.

"I tol' her they was good to me and that you, the baby girl, had such a sweet disposition—a real soft core. You needed lotsa hugs 'cause you was gentle and sens'tive. I know, 'cause I ha' to hol' you 'n' wipe ya' tears when someone said harsh things or criticize the way you look.

"Ethel Rose ask me about Hank too. I tol' her he was a fine little man, 'n' I seen how much he love his baby sister. He took care a you too. I tol' her I didn't know what you would do without yo' big brother." Mira shook her head and looked at the floor.

When Ellie broke into loud sobs, Mira wrapped her soft arms around Ellie's limp body.

"Mi-Mi-Mira." Ellie lingered in the hug and buried her head against

Mira's ample bosom. "He d-d-drowned. Hank drowned," she whispered. "H-He's not coming home. It can't be that way. It should be me." The faint smell of bleach filled her nose and brought with it the memory of Mira's comfort and love that for so long had protected her feelings and wrapped up her soul. Ellie had always considered Mira to be pure love.

"I know, chil'," Mira said, stroking Ellie's hair as if she were a four-year-old. "You loved him 'n' he loved you. That why he be so good to you. I am so sorry about Hank."

Ellie felt Mira's chest heave as the old lady held her and rocked. Mira said, "Y'know I always thought a you as my white baby. 'Member when I taught you and Hank to say ya nighttime prayers? I loved listenin' to ya two tiny voices mumblin' words you din't understand. Loved to see yo' little hands together with yo' plump fingers folded over."

Ellie looked up and tried to smile. Mira squeezed her hand and continued: "I never understood why ya mama said she din't need my help anymore, but my place was not to argue. I had to make sho I didn't make her mad, 'cause that way she'd still call me to come babysit for you and Hank. And she did. I know ya family had problems, but I'm from the ol' school, so I had to keep my feelings to myse'f. But you knew how much I loved you and Hank."

"Yes, I always knew," murmured Ellie. "I was glad Daddy asked you to work at his office. I remember when Mom found out. I heard her ask him why he did that, and he said he needed you to keep his practice running efficiently and that you understood him—knew how to get along with him."

"I was at the office when I hear about Hank," Mira said. "All I could do is fall into a chair and cry my eyes out. I couldn' abide the news, but I couldn' stand by and do nothin', neither, so I put a note on the door and closed up. I needed to be here to he'p my baby be strong."

Ellie watched Mira's loving eyes fill with moisture and her lips press together in a line, but after another tight squeeze of Ellie's shoulder, Mira got up, smoothed her curls, and straightened her skirt.

She looked down at Ellie and said, "Chil', chil', chil'. You gonna have to stand up and be strong, cause ya mama and daddy won't be, that's fo' sho'. You gonna be the one to answer the door, say hello, and represent the family, cause I know they won't. I hate it, but you got to be the one what does it. Hank would wancha to."

A few minutes later the doorbell rang, and Ellie heard her father call out, "Answer the door, Ellie."

Mira looked toward the door, then turned her eyes—the color of melted chocolate—back to Ellie. Mira held out her hand, and Ellie stood up without another word, wiped her eyes, and went to the door. She opened it to a red-faced woman with mascara running down her cheeks.

The woman thrust toward her a gift basket of assorted cheeses and fruit while a man with downcast eyes and a trembling chin slumped beside her. Even though Ellie did not know the givers by name, she did what was expected. She thanked them, invited them in, and said the family appreciated their concern. It wasn't long until swarms of food-laden people began to appear. The living room began to fill with hushed conversation as most of the visitors stayed to talk, shaking their heads and holding plates filled with each other's comfort foods.

One person handed Ellie a basket with a big red bow on its handle and a linen napkin covering fresh-made bread inside, fragrant and still warm. Ellie held the basket and stepped back from the open door, but when she gestured the guest inside, the woman simply stood there and wept.

"Dr. Dennis saved my life," she said to Ellie. "I am so sorry his son died. It isn't fair."

Ellie's brave front—contrived and fragile—melted the instant the woman moved away and began talking to someone else in the crowd. Ellie clutched the basket and turned aside. She wiped her eyes and tried to stop crying, but the tears kept coming until the watchful chaplain came out of nowhere and asked if he could take the basket to Mira.

"I'll stick with you when I get back," he said. "People want to be nice, but most don't know how hard it is for the family to hear what they say. People simply don't know what to do."

"Thank you," Ellie said and told him his kindness was a comfort. She watched him take the basket, being careful not to crush the bow, and make his way cautiously—almost delicately—through the clusters of people. His size dwarfed the basket, but he carried it with care that reminded her of Hank—a gentle, loving giant. The image strengthened her as a cool breath of air passed over her. She sighed and blew her nose, then faced the door again.

The afternoon wore on and people kept coming without letup. Ellie knew a few—Tommy from the flower shop and a neighbor—but most of them were simply faces with familiar-sounding names that were artifacts from her childhood she'd heard mentioned at the dinner table.

The visitors wanted to express their sympathy and offer help, so Ellie listened and nodded when they said how sorry they were for the family's loss. She thanked them and tried to be cordial even though she didn't believe they had any idea of the depth of the family's sorrow.

Someone said, "I went to the funeral home to see Hank. He looks good. He's in his Marine uniform. There were flowers and plants all over the place."

"I wish I could see him, but my dad told me not to go," Ellie said and teared up.

"You better not then. Don't want to upset anyone," the neighbor concluded, patting Ellie's arm.

Another woman approached them and said, "What a waste. He didn't have to die over there."

The cruel statement made Ellie's belly boil and anger rise from deep within. *No one can say Hank's life was a waste! No one should ever say that.* She wanted to say as much but kept quiet. Her cheeks burned, and she wanted to turn her back on everyone, but instead, she responded with a whispered, "Not really a waste." The two neighbors drifted away and were absorbed by the crowd, so Ellie went back to her safe place by the door. The house buzzed with conversation, and she was sure her mom and dad heard, but they never left the family room, talked only to Major Garver, and did not greet their visitors. Ellie did her best to talk, nod, and hug people, but there was no relief for her, and she was left on her own—alone among scores of townspeople.

Ellie felt the same way she had the time she was too far out on the lake with a hole in her pink rubber float, only this time Hank was not there to rescue her, and the reality was he would never again be nearby to make her safe. She shifted her weight and frowned. *I don't want to be here. If only I could go away.* As if reading her mind, the chaplain came over and began talking to the people around Ellie. His presence drew them away and created breathing space for her. She caught his eye, nodded, then drifted away, thankful to escape at last. She fled to the kitchen, where Mira moved quickly amid the abundance of food items. Ellie sidestepped around the table, darted to the phone, and called Joe.

She was sure he was home because it was still midafternoon and not time for work yet. Joe's groggy voice came on the line after the fifth ring. "Can you come to my parents' house?" she pleaded. "Come quick. It's Hank." Her voice sounded frantic and little-girl helpless.

"What happened? What's going on?" Joe asked. "Give me a minute. You woke me up from a dead sleep."

"H-he . . . d-drowned," she said, struggling to get her breath between sobs.

"Oh, my God, no," Joe said.

"P-please come to M-M-Mom and Dad's house. Hurry!" Ellie said and hung up.

Hours later Joe had still not shown up, and Ellie was tired and numb when an unfamiliar woman came to the door, introduced herself, and put her hand on Ellie's arm. After explaining she had lost her own son in Vietnam the previous year, she held out a piece of paper containing her name and number.

"There are a number of us who've lost children in this war," the woman said. "We're called Gold Star Mothers, and we share the pain that only a parent can feel when their child dies. Please give this to your mother so she can call me if she wants to. It may help her to talk to one of us."

Ellie took the paper, thanked the woman, and asked the chaplain to take the note to her mother. "Please let Mom know they want to help her. It's more likely she'll listen to you than to me," she said. She asked the woman to come in and have a bite to eat, but she politely declined and left quickly.

The minute Joe appeared at the door, Ellie wrapped her arms around him. She pressed her head against his neck and held tight. He let her cling for a minute and then guided her a step or two into the house, but when he looked at the crowd filling the room, he stopped moving.

"I'm stunned," he said. "I had no idea there were this many people here with you. I don't know what to say." Ellie rested her head against his shoulder and sobbed, but moments later another visitor came to the door, so Ellie had to wipe her eyes and move away from Joe.

"I have to talk to people, so why don't you go sit on the couch? I'll come sit with you soon," she said. She watched Joe eye the Marine and then Mira as he made his way across the room. Susan's warning about

Joe played in Ellie's mind, but she was exhausted and pushed her fears away. Joe sat rooted to the couch with a glass of iced tea while Ellie greeted a steady stream of people, but once in a while Ellie caught his eye, and he offered her a smile. She noticed that a few people tried to make conversation with him but gave up when he didn't return their interest.

The afternoon dragged on with no sign that Ellie's parents would come out to greet the guests, so she was forced to wait by the door and make excuses when visitors asked about them. The sun was low on the horizon, and she felt as if she had crawled a hundred miles without water when the visitors finally stopped coming and Mira told her to sit down and relax.

She sank onto the couch next to Joe, and he put his arm around her—an invitation to rest her head in the curve where his neck met his shoulder. She sighed heavily, leaned on him, and stifled a sob, then sat still in the warmth of him for a long time.

"Why do you cover for your parents?" he asked without warning. "They should be out here too. I don't understand why you make excuses for them."

"I don't know. It's what I do. That's all." She pressed closer to him and whispered, "I need to tell you something important, but this isn't the right time." Her chest heaved and she sighed again. After they sat still for a moment, she sniffed his neck and said, "You smell good. What is that—a new aftershave?"

She heard him gulp, but all he said was, "Uh-h-h, well . . ."

Before he had a chance to say anything else, Ellie's eyes widened and she jumped up and ran to the door. Susan rushed in to meet her. They embraced without a word and cried together until Susan stepped back and took Ellie's hands in hers.

Susan wore plain black shoes and a dark, one-piece, shin-length black dress with a white shoulder-length veil that framed her face. She wore no makeup, yet her skin and hair below the veil were radiant and smooth.

"I'm so happy you're here," Ellie managed to say.

"I know you are beyond sorrow," Susan said and hugged Ellie again. "I thought maybe I could do something to help you."

"You have no idea what this means. My parents are in the family room and have not come out to see anyone, so I've been on my own," Ellie said and nodded toward Joe. "But he got here a while ago."

Susan's head turned sharply, and her gaze settled on Joe, her eyes blazing with intensity. She walked toward him with Ellie beside her.

"Well, look who's here," Susan said without emotion. She stood looking down at him with her feet planted a few inches apart.

"Hello, Susan," he said. "I guess you heard about Hank." He made no attempt to rise or reach out to her.

"Yes. I heard a few hours ago, and I wanted to be here with Ellie." Susan looked at her friend. "I'm sure she's been attending to everyone's feelings and neglecting her own."

"Glad you're here," Joe mumbled, looking like a fox caught heading to the henhouse. He stood up and turned to Ellie.

"Susan is here now, so how about I go to work for a while? The two of you can talk, and I'll be back later." He touched Ellie's hand and kissed her cheek, then fled through the door without waiting for a reply.

"He doesn't know what to say, I guess," said Ellie as she watched him striding down the front walk. His quick retreat reminded her of his manner the afternoon he had unexpectedly met her parents when Ellie had asked him to take her to their house to pick up one of Hank's letters. Joe hadn't wanted to stick around that day, either.

Susan harrumphed and linked arms with Ellie just as the chaplain entered the foyer.

"Can I get you something to eat, Sister?" he asked.

Susan dipped her head and turned pink. "Thank you. Actually, I'm just a novice, so technically not a Sister yet," she said, smiling at the Marine.

"You're right," said Ellie to the Marine, "she must be hungry." Ellie turned away from Joe's retreat and said, "Come on, Susan, there's plenty of food. Besides, I want you to meet Mira."

The house was quiet when Ellie, Susan, and Mira sat together and talked until the two Marines excused themselves and left for the night. They said they would be back the next day to help her parents finalize Hank's funeral arrangements. Mira also prepared to leave, saying she planned to check in at the office in the morning, but she promised she would be back in time to make sure everyone had a good lunch.

After a while, Ellie's mother and father appeared and brushed by, not uttering a word on their way to their rooms. Ellie watched them disappear up the stairs and let her eyes fall to her hands, folded in her lap. As tears dripped from her chin, Susan covered Ellie's hands with her own.

Ellie looked up. "Can you stay the night, Susan?" she asked. "You can have the spare room. You won't even have to share a bathroom. Please? It'll be good to have you here."

"How can I refuse the only thing you've asked of me?" Susan said, looking deep into her friend's bloodshot eyes. "Sure, I can make arrangements." She paused, then continued: "But I'll need to call and tell the Sisters where I am and why I need to stay here. They'll understand."

"Susan," Ellie said with a catch in her voice, "thank you for coming. Hank would have . . ." She stopped, unable to finish what she was going to say.

"Shhh. No need to say anything else. I'm here because I want to be with you. Maybe I can bring comfort somehow."

Susan finished her phone call, and Ellie showed her to the guest room,

212

then said good night. Ellie went to her old bedroom and fell against the closed door, leaning her head back on the hard, cold wood as new tears streamed down her face.

If only Hank had come home when he was hurt the third time. If only he had not gone far away to fight for an oppressed people. If only he had not been a Marine. If only she were not pregnant. If only Joe had called or come back to be with her. But he had not.

If only she had not been born.

Two days later, townspeople packed the old Florida Gothic-style church as "Jesu, Joy of Man's Desiring" flowed from the majestic pipe organ, filled the sanctuary, and echoed around Hank's family seated in the front row. Enormous stained-glass windows surrounded them, but sniffles and whispers punctuated the melody as Mom and Dad sat next to each other without touching. They shared a front pew with Patti, who sat close to her mother, and Ellie beside Joe at the end of the row. Susan and Mira had chosen to sit together in the back pew with their heads bowed and eyes closed. Dark wood and glass images of Jesus in prayer bordered the room, but Ellie kept her head down, barely listening to the preacher pronounce comforting words over Hank's family.

Patti cried quietly and clutched her mother's fingers while Ellie stared through tears at the flag-draped coffin. Hank's body was in there, and she would never see him again. She kept her arm wrapped tightly around Joe's and didn't try to hide her grief. A stone-faced Joe looked straight ahead with his jaw working rhythmically.

Ellie was not surprised that her parents never touched each other at the church. After the service, the organist started Bach's Toccata and Fugue in D minor, and bathed in its minor tones, everyone stood while the family filed out of the church. The grand melody seemed to flow from the church and fill the air as the funeral director ushered them all into a long, black limousine that took them to the cemetery.

The day was clear with a bright sun in a sapphire sky embellished with pure white clouds as it had been the last day Hank spent at the lake with his family. Ellie stared out the window of the limousine, remembering the many days she and Hank had enjoyed at the lake. At the gravesite, the family members took their seats in the front row of chairs arranged under a large tent. Their row faced a polished walnut casket that held Hank's body. The vivid red, white, and blue of a pristine American flag covered the coffin.

Even though the chaplain had again offered to take her, Ellie had not gone to see Hank at the funeral home. To avoid upsetting her parents, she had buried her goodbye inside her heart and had thereby ripped herself in two. At the sight of the coffin, however, regret weighed her down because she had missed the chance to see him, to tell him she loved him, and to say she would be okay. She wanted to wake up from this nightmare and tried to stare through the flag, willing herself to see her big brother for the last time, say goodbye, and tell him how much she loved him.

From somewhere behind the chairs, four Marines in dress uniform joined Major Garver by Hank's casket. They formed a line on the far side and included the chaplain who had stayed by Ellie's side ever since she had learned that Hank had died. She caught his eye a moment before he faced Hank's casket, saluted, and mouthed the words "Semper Fi, Sir."

The Baptist preacher said more words, but Ellie's heart and mind dwelled somewhere a million miles away. She was numb, but she ached as memories of Hank came and went like the changing cloud patterns she had watched from her float so long ago at the lake.

The burial ceremony concluded with a twenty-one-gun salute and "Taps." The bugle call carried across a sea of headstones—cold granite symbols of once-vibrant lives. After the last note faded, two Marines carefully removed the flag from Hank's coffin and folded it into a neat triangle with only the stars showing against the field of blue.

A solemn and reverent Major Garver carried the flag between his gloved hands, one palm holding it underneath while the other rested face down on top of the cloth. In measured steps he walked to Patti, then leaned over, stretched out his hands, and presented the flag to her.

"On behalf of the President of the United States, the Commandant of the Marine Corps, and a grateful nation, please accept this flag as a symbol of our appreciation for your loved one's honorable and faithful service," he said.

Patti mouthed a thank-you and held the flag against her heart. Streams of tears ran down her cheeks and dropped onto the flag, marking Old Glory with dark splotches.

In time—Ellie wasn't sure how much—the Marines moved to the sides of the casket. At precisely the same time, each grasped a velvet cord running underneath and up through the brass handles on each side. The metal glinted in the sun as they lowered the coffin into the ground. Ellie's heart broke when the shiny lid disappeared from view. *No, no, no! This is not real!* She wanted to scream, but at great cost, she kept the crushing agony inside.

Mom and Dad made their way to the limousine as the crowd of mourners thinned out and the Marines said their goodbyes before going on their way. Ellie and Patti lingered under the tent next to Hank's resting place with the delicate scent of flowers and the strong smell of freshly turned earth washing over them. Patti looked tired and pale, but she reached out and clutched Ellie's hand. Patti's mother said she would wait in the car before walking away. The sisters-in-law stood together and held each other's hands beside Hank's grave.

"It's just too painful for me to stay here," Patti said at last. "I have to find a way to get on with my life. Hank and I agreed that if something happened to him, I was to go to my mom's house. He and I never expected he would not come home, but here we are. Hank made me promise to keep going with my life. He didn't want me to give up even though he was not with me."

She swallowed hard before withdrawing her hand. Then she brushed her cheek and looked back at Ellie. "The night of the benefit, Rocky asked me to work full time for Masterson's. He wants me to do all their conventions and benefit galas, and I've decided to do it. The company isn't that far from my mother's house, so I plan to commute to work."

Ellie stared at Patti and tried to adjust to what she had just heard. "My life won't be the same without you here," she finally said.

"I'm so sorry, Ellie, but I can't live here. I'm not sure when I'll see you again, but I'll try to stay in touch somehow. I'm so sorry." Tears once again began rolling down her cheeks.

"I understand how hard it would be for you here." Ellie tried to hide her disappointment with a forced smile.

"I paid another six months' rent in August," Patti said, "and I could get a bereavement refund, but I don't want that. Why don't you stay in the apartment for now? You'll have a place of your own until after Christmas. I know Hank would want that for you."

"Thank you, Patti," Ellie whispered. "You have no idea what this means to me."

"No need to say anything else," Patti said and grabbed Ellie's hand. She squeezed it and they hugged, then parted.

Ellie and Joe were walking from the tent when a redhead got out of a nearby car and waved to him. He waved back and said she was a coworker who was going to take him to work that evening. Something didn't ring true when he said that, but Ellie was too numb to think about it, so she followed her parents to the limousine that took Hank's silent family back home, followed by Susan in her car with Mira beside her.

Mom and Dad disappeared upstairs as soon as they entered the front door. Susan and Mira took Ellie to the screened porch and sat down among the plants and ferns. Susan found a rocking chair and folded her hands in her lap, then bowed her head. Ellie and her beloved nanny were side by side on the wicker settee when Mira took Ellie's hand.

"It will take a lot of time, baby, 'n' there'll be a hole in ya heart forever," Mira said, "but you has to get on with yo' life. Hank would want that."

Ellie clutched the dark, soft hand in her own freckled one. "But it's so hard," Ellie said. "I don't think I can do it."

"I know, chil'," the old woman said. "But ya have to or ya won' su'vive. First, ya has to accept that he's not gonna be here in person, but remember: he is here! He is in yo' memories, 'n' no one can take them from you, and that makes him a part of who y'are. He gave ya a priceless gift: he believed in you. Don't forget that. That was for you and only you. Remember what he did f'you—learn to live it and go on."

"Mira's right, El," Susan whispered.

Mira went home that evening, but Susan agreed to stay for another day, and Ellie planned to return to the apartment after Susan left. At least she had a place of her own to live—thanks to Patti . . . and Hank.

As Ellie lay in bed, an image of the Marines moving in disciplined unity at Hank's funeral appeared in her mind and a whiff of cool air crossed her brow, bringing with it an awareness she could not explain. She knew she had to let her memories of Hank be her treasure. Maybe her life and the new life she carried could be her gifts to him, but how could she make that come true?

Chapter 18

A fitful night's sleep left Ellie in a fog the next morning as she stood beside Susan's VW while her friend toyed with the keys in her hand. Tears filled Susan's eyes when she turned to Ellie and took a deep breath.

"I pray you will be okay," she said. "Please think about what I said about Joe. You have to get on with your life, and I simply don't think he's the person you should do it with."

Ellie was numb and wooden, but she said she would think about everything her friend had told her. Then Susan, waving as she drove away, left Ellie alone on the driveway. She had already put her things in her car and was ready to go back to the apartment, but for some reason, she decided to get the mail from Mom and Dad's mailbox, hoping her effort might help them, in some small way.

When she opened the silver box and reached in, her hand closed around several envelopes. She removed them, and noticed the corner of one sticking out partway down the stack so she pulled it out, but froze and let the other mail fall from her grip and flutter to the ground. The envelope in her hand had red and blue stripes marching along its edges and an FPO San Francisco return address written in Hank's familiar handwriting. The Navy postmark said it had arrived stateside four days ago—September 19th—the day after Hank died.

Ellie nearly lost consciousness when reality sank in. She was holding the last letter Hank had written. She fell against the mailbox and tried to get her breath as she stared at the envelope, but her mind was blank, unable to figure out what to do. *Should she take it inside and give it to Dad? Or Mom? Should she read it first and then give it to them? Would they be upset?* Fighting for control, she gathered up the fallen letters, staggered to her car, then wrestled the door open and collapsed into the seat.

Hank's letter in her hand, she tossed the rest of the mail onto the passenger seat, then closed her eyes and breathed deeply. Later—she wasn't sure how long—a wisp of cool air made her open her eyes and look at the letter. She gripped each end of the envelope as she stared at the oh-so-familiar handwriting.

Something deep inside told her to open the letter and read it before giving it to her parents, so she turned it over and carefully pulled up the flap. She took out two sheets of onionskin paper covered in Hank's familiar script. Her heart sank when she saw it was dated a week before he died.

> *11 Sept 67*
> *The Cam Lo Bridge*
> *7.5 miles south of Con Thien*

Dear Mom, Dad & Ellie,

> *It's almost dusk, and here I am, watching the sun's reflection on the water. It looks the same way the lake did so many years—seems more like eons—ago. I'm by a river, not the lake, but at least it's water—a welcome sight after being in the barrel for nearly 40 days. I have time to bring you up to date about what's been going on.*

We got used to (if that's possible) getting bombarded, being dirty, hungry, and sweaty most of the time on Con Thien. Enemy incoming & ground contact had increased before we left, so we decided the NVA were gaining momentum & getting ready to isolate and/or try to overrun us. Their force was possibly regiment-size (1,000 or so men) plus artillery support—maybe even more—and they were getting ready to attack, so 2 battalions replaced us—we were the only Bn—up there. Now, they will be on high alert, and I feel for them.

We started walking out of Con Thien at 0830 yesterday. The MSR (main supply route) is a dirt road—the same color as Georgia clay, by the way—wide enough for the tanks & Ontos—so it took a while for a group as large as our battalion along with all of our support to move out. That many men with that much equipment moving together make a great target so, when we were on our way out, NVA mortars started hitting everywhere around us. On instinct, we hit the deck, which by that time was nothing but mud! VC must have been hiding in a vast rice paddy near the road because when the shelling started, they rose out of the paddy like a wave at Waimea Bay. Every one of us with a weapon opened up on them as we fought for our lives. I'm sure after surviving a month of relentless bombardment, hunger, rats, mud, and casualties, none of us wanted to die face-down in the mud on our way out of Con Thien. What an irony that would be! After the skirmish ended, we headed out again, and I don't know a man who was hesitant about leaving that hell-hole.

After that, we spread apart (to make the target smaller) with men flanking each side of the MSR and kept moving south in column toward our firebase (C-2). A couple of companies stayed at C-2 to secure it, but my Co (Lima Co) continued south along the MSR until we reached the river—the Cam Lo River, where I'm watching the sun go down.

So, we finished our time in the barrel, and now we're the reserve force in case they need us to go up there again. Our mission down here is to keep open the bridge over the River. Believe me, we know how important it is for Marines to get what they need up there in the barrel. Got a little shrapnel

scratch during the attack this morning, but it was minor. The
medic dressed it, but it's not PH worthy so I told him to ignore
it on his report.

They treated us well when we got down here. Hot showers
and even fresh food. Pretty good after 49 days of hell on Con
Thien. Even we had to admit we looked pretty rough, but now
I'm nearly human after showers, shaves, and food!

Ellie had to stop reading because tears blinded her. She let her head
fall back against the headrest and did not attempt to stop crying. Hank
had lived through the horrors—through hell as he put it—and when he
wrote this letter, he thought he was going to get a break.

I'm so proud of my men. They worked professionally and
stayed disciplined even in the thick of it. I want to stay with
them 'cause I don't want them to have to deal with a F'n New
Guy Lt. after what they've been through. Good replacement
officers are few and far between these days. Besides, I got my
promo papers, so I'm an old guy, a 1st Lt!

I've heard worries about the monsoon downpours dam-
aging the MSR, and it's washed out in one place already.
The rain has been bad up there lately. You can't imagine the
downpours at this time of the year. Never seen so much come
down so fast! Monsoon season at its best.

Not raining much here, though, so the Captain put our new
camp on a stretch of sand (sort of like a beach) along the
north side of the river. Our tents are on the beach at the base
of a riverbank that has a road running along the top of it. I
can see a small (6 or 8 feet high) pagoda on the far side of
the road beyond our wire perimeter at the top of the bank. We
always set concertina wire around camp no matter where we
are so, it runs alongside the road all the way to the bridge,
then goes under it a ways. Sleeping will be different here
'cause we're not getting direct shelling. It sounds strange, but
now we have to get used to the quiet!

We can hear our artillery pounding in the distance to the north & jets overhead on their runs, so there is still noise, but it's quieter than before, and I'm planning on getting a lot done on my math course while we're here. I'll have time to solve that problem I showed you.

Even though this is not the lake, it is relaxing to look at the river. What is it about water that's so soothing? Does my soul good to be near it. Hey, Mom and Dad, isn't your anniversary coming up? It's 27 years, right? Bet you're all going out to the lake house to celebrate this one! Wish I could be there, and I can't wait to get back out there to sit on the porch under the oaks. That will be Heaven!

Gotta go for now. More later, I'll have more time to keep you posted. Don't worry, all is well, dear ones. See you before long . . .

I love you and miss you,
Hank

Ellie pressed the letter against her chest and cried the tears of a lifetime. She reread the letter over and over, wanting to memorize every line. After what seemed like hours, the bright sun hurt her eyes as she walked into the lifeless house and left Hank's letter and the other mail on the kitchen table. She simply didn't have the strength to face her parents. Somehow, she managed to drive to the apartment where—blinded by tears and paralyzed by loneliness—she collapsed on the orange couch.

In the weeks that followed, Ellie lived inside an exoskeleton that kept her separated from the world and protected her from living in the reality of Hank's death. She managed to follow her class and work schedules, but deep in her soul, she wanted one of the Marines to rush in and tell her there had been a horrible mistake. She wanted to hear that Hank was not dead but had been found alive somewhere in the dense jungle. She so desperately hoped that would happen, but reality smacked her hard in the face every time a person unaware of her fantasy uttered a word of condolence or kindness. Those innocent words made her return to grief as debilitating as it was the day the two Marines came to her door with news of Hank's death.

She was a hollow body with a mouth that produced weak smiles, numb hands that went about doing mundane tasks, and eyes that cried when she thought of her brother or saw a man who resembled him. Her afternoons with Joe had stopped, and with Patti gone, Ellie felt forced to do what was expected and check on her parents more often than before. She kept the visits short and tried to put her emotions on the shelf when she saw her mother, who was at home alone most days.

Hank's death had dismembered their family. Mom stayed home drinking until she was catatonic and didn't even attempt to do volunteer work or go to club meetings. When Ellie tried to console her, she angrily said that Dad was at the hospital or his office all the time because he needed to play God. Her mother—in a voice unsympathetic and bitter—said he worked all the time because sick people came to him for help, and he couldn't turn anyone away—not even when he needed to be with his family.

Ellie simply occupied a seat in campus lecture halls. She shuffled in and out like a windup toy, jostled by crowds of students, and carried a yellow legal pad but never took class notes. A few classmates from her freshman year recognized her and said hello, but she didn't encourage conversation with anyone. Even though she tried to concentrate on her studies, her mind was elsewhere. *How can everyone act as if nothing has changed when everything is ravaged, scattered in the rubble of my life?* She lived in a deep cavern without the presence of a living, breathing Hank to lean on, and most afternoons she wandered to her tree—the miniature sanctuary where she tried to make sense of things.

Mom is an alcoholic, and Dad is a workaholic, Ellie told herself. *They've found ways to run away from grief. What can I do to make the pain go away?*

She and Joe had not seen each other since Hank's funeral a month before. Even so, she knew she had to tell him about the baby because they had to get married. She was nearly five months along, and the pregnancy was getting harder to hide. No doubt about it—marriage was expected under the circumstances.

"You're *what*?" Joe shouted. He leaped up and began pacing around the shabby apartment. Ellie was in the same chair she had sat in months ago; only now all she could do was watch him rage. He had been so seductive before.

He had offered her a joint when she came to the apartment, but she refused it and told him she didn't want any wine, either. He had looked at her and asked why not. It took her a minute to gather her nerve, but she finally told him about the baby. He shouted at first, then stared at her—speechless, redness crawling up his cheeks—before his fury exploded.

"How could you let that happen?" he demanded and stopped pacing to stand in front of her. A frown creased his brow, and he glared at her with his lips pressed together so hard they disappeared. Then he raised the joint, drew in a long hit, and turned away. He held in the intoxicant longer than usual and began another round of pacing as smoke escaped his lips, encircled his head, and dissipated in his wake.

Ellie sat immobile, her eyes glued to him, not knowing what else to say. She flinched when he whirled around to face her. "I'm not ready for a kid! I have too much to do to be saddled with a family. You should have taken care of things yourself, so this wouldn't happen. Are you trying to ruin my life?" His face was twisted and ugly as he spat out the question.

Ellie doubled over like a boxer taking a fist to the gut. She covered her face with her hands and began sobbing. *How can he think I want to ruin his life—the man I love and gave my body to?* She expected her father to blame her for getting pregnant, but not Joe.

Susan's warning was right, but it had come too late. She wondered how she could have been so dumb, and the dark, familiar presence pounced, finding its mark in her softness, and made her body heavy with guilt. A blinding whirl of thoughts took over in the simmering brew of Joe's rage and the panther's accusations.

Hank and Patti were both gone now. Susan was back at the convent. Mira was near and would help, but she was getting older, and Ellie didn't want to burden her. *Why did Hank have to die? Why did I live? Hank has given so much, and I so little. My life is useless.* Guilt purred in her ear and told her the family would have been better off with her gone instead of Hank.

Out of the blue, something—perhaps Joe's fist against the mantel or the flutter of the life inside her—made Ellie sit up and wipe her face. Her heart pounded as she took a breath and dug deep for the words. "I thought you would be happy or intrigued at least," she said to Joe's back. "I didn't think you'd be thrilled, but I never imagined you'd be angry. I thought you loved me. Besides, you told me to relax, and you would take care of things, remember? You said you would handle birth control." The forcefulness of her words surprised her as she waited for his response.

Joe turned and faced her from across the room. "Well, you were wrong. Let me fill you in on some things." His voice was cold, his face expressionless, unreadable. "I work at MJ's for a good reason. The place is busier than a beehive during gathering season, and most of my customers are young, good-looking kids supported by their parents.

I'm surrounded by teenagers anxious to establish their independence, so they live like they want to and not the way their parents tell them to. Translation: they're open to experimentation. That means my pot supply business is good—lucrative because the underground network knows I can get my hands on plentiful amounts of good stuff.

"You and I *were* an item because you didn't ask questions about what I did in my free time, so I stayed in the dating game. You were manageable and easy to keep in the dark, and our sack time was during the day, so I had late nights after work to be with anyone I chose."

He finished off the joint and smashed its remains in an already full ashtray, then leaned back against the fireplace and crossed his arms over his chest. His face turned smug, then became arrogant, like a predator surveying its territory. "Don't get me wrong, Ellie," he continued, "I never got tired of your innocence. You were so willing to please me, and that made it easy to keep you from knowing about my business or the other girls. We didn't even fight because you didn't seem to have opinions about anything. My life was good with you, Ellie, but that didn't stop me from wanting other women. I'm not dead yet."

Joe's cruelty just didn't stop. "As a matter of fact, I've found someone who interests me a great deal. She has long, gorgeous red hair, blue eyes, and freckles across her nose. Her pouty mouth says 'Come and get me.' She's a real Mona Lisa who intrigues me and makes me want to find out what's going on with her." He pushed away from the bricks and smiled. "By the way—that's her perfume you've smelled on several occasions."

Ellie stared, but Joe wasn't finished yet.

"So, Ellie, you're going to have to take care of this . . . uh . . . problem. You can't have this baby, and I know places you can go to get rid of it." His diatribe complete, he turned his back to her and grabbed the mantel.

Ellie felt her insides solidify. Joe wanted no part of her or the baby, and he had told her to kill the tiny life she carried. Nauseated, she put her hand over her rounded abdomen. Escape was her only choice, so she dug deep and found enough strength to gather up her things, walk to the door, and yank it open. She stepped across the threshold just as the baby moved, a shy reminder of its vulnerability that gave her the power to leave Joe behind with his pot and his brutality.

It was well past midnight, but Ellie lay awake and stared at the blue-black ceiling in her apartment—silent and empty, just like her heart. She had hoped that somehow Joe would get used to the idea of having a baby and call her, but after three long weeks, she knew better. She had to come to grips with the fact that he simply didn't care about her or the baby. *Do I have a future? What would Hank say?*

The thought hit her between the eyes. What would Hank have said?

The question hung in her mind all through the next morning and blurred everything the professor said in her class lecture, so she decided that going to another one was pointless. The baby had been restless since the wee hours, and she needed rest, so she cut her last class and went to her tree, hoping to find peace on her bench there.

A Florida chill filled the air, so she pulled her sweater close and stretched out her legs to let the pond's bubbling spring mesmerize her. She smiled as she thought of Susan's call weeks ago, saying she had begun serving in a classroom of children who lived in poverty. She was eager to help them prepare for their futures.

"That's kinda ironic since you didn't seem interested in college when you were here," Ellie had replied. "You bombed out before the end of your freshman year, remember?"

Susan laughed. "Yeah, I gotta finish college first and get my teaching degree, but the Sisters reminded me that there are multitudes of different God-given gifts, and the most important thing—after loving God and having faith—is to use our gifts to serve others. I've spent hours in prayer, and I believe in my soul that loving others means serving them as Jesus did. I believe Hank understood what commitment and service meant because he didn't run away from them." She added quietly, "Serving is what I want to do. I can help young people who are just as confused and angry as I was."

Susan's passion was clear and defined, and Ellie gave her friend credit for knowing where she was going. *That's more than I can say about myself,* she thought, but a tiny, soft kick against her belly interrupted her thoughts. She looked down and spread her fingers over her baby bump.

"Are you reminding me about something?" she asked aloud as she looked at her outspread hand. "Do you think Hank would tell me that I need to love you and not run away from you?" Ellie felt the little life roll once more, then settle down to rest.

Her mind began to clear, and a thought emerged as plain as a cloudless, summer day. Joe and his anger didn't matter because her commitment was to the baby. Hank was right—she must try to believe in herself and find a way forward.

Even though Ellie slogged through her classes, she wasn't doing well with her grades. Her part-time work at Eden's Beauty offered some relief, but not enough. The Thanksgiving holiday loomed ahead, and Ellie had tried not to dwell on the fact that Hank and Patti would have celebrated their first anniversary soon after the holiday. At the moment, Ellie's mind was on her mother, who sat in a wing chair, holding a drink to her lips.

Her mom had called her, and during a rambling, stream-of-consciousness monologue, said someone wanted to talk about Hank. She made

some garbled comment about Hank, another Marine, and the night of
the Cam Lo flood. The call was so incomprehensible, Ellie decided it
was best to go in person to try to make sense of what her mother was
talking about, since it was impossible over the phone.

"He called and said somethin' like he was there. Thin' his name
sounded French—Thib-a-something . . ." Her mother's thick-tongued
voice trailed off.

"Did you ask him to spell it for you, Mom?"

"Yeah, may have," said her mother, fishing a slip of paper from her
bathrobe pocket. "Here." She handed the wrinkled scrap to Ellie before
closing her eyes and letting her head drop back against the chair.

Ellie smoothed out the paper and saw *Tribdow* and a phone number written in her mother's uneven handwriting. Ellie remembered
Hank had mentioned a Marine from New Orleans in a recent letter,
and she knew her father saved all the letters after Ellie returned them,
so she rushed to his den and grabbed the file from his desk. Ellie riffled
through the letters and scanned for the name, which she found in one of
Hank's September letters. She took it back to the living room with her.

"Mom, did it sound like he said 'Thibodeaux?'" Ellie pronounced it
slowly, watching her mother's reaction.

"Coulda' been," she murmured, then raised her bloodshot eyes to
Ellie.

"Thibodeaux," Ellie repeated.

"Uh-h. Yeah, tha's it," she said. "He wanted to come and see us, but
I tol' him not to. Like I tol' that Gold Star woman who called me after I
buried my only son—don' wan' anything to do with people who wanna
talk about Hank dyin'. I want to 'member him alive."

Ellie looked at the scrap of paper again. There were ten numbers. "Is
this a phone number he gave you? Thibodeaux's number?"

"Hum? What? Oh, yeah. He said to call if I wanted to talk. I tol' him

I din't, but he made me read it back to him anyway. Said I had it right."

"Okay, Mom. Thank you for calling me about it," Ellie said. She returned the letter to its place in the files and headed to the front door, pausing as a mix of pity and anger swirled inside at the sight of her slack-mouthed mother asleep in the chair. Ellie knew there was nothing she could do for her, so she let herself out and headed home to the apartment with the note safely in her pocket.

A Vivaldi concerto filled the apartment as Ellie stared at the phone and told herself to make the call. She swallowed hard and pulled out the scrap of paper. With trembling hands, she picked up the receiver and dialed Sergeant Thibodeaux's phone number. She listened, dry-mouthed, while rhythmic hums filled one ear and violins sang in the other. The phone rang eight or ten times, but just as she was about to hang up, a clear, resonant voice answered.

"Thibodeaux," it said.

Ellie cleared her throat and replied, "H-Hello. I'm Ellie Dennis. My brother is—was—Hank Dennis. My mother said you called and gave her your phone number."

A sharp inhalation came over the line. "Uh, yes. Yes, ma'am, I did," he said. A few seconds later, he continued: "I told your mother I could tell her about what happened if it would help to know how Lieutenant Dennis died. She said she didn't want to talk about it, and I understand. It sounded as if she was having a bad time of it." Thibodeaux's voice had a cadence and accent new to Ellie's ear, although she recognized a few southern-sounding words.

"Yes, our whole family is having a hard time, but I appreciate that you called," Ellie said.

"Your brother was my lieutenant, and it was a privilege to serve with him. I was the one who found him that morning, and it nearly killed me. He was the finest officer I ever came across in my Marine career—and it was a long 'un. I want you to know that we all respected and cared for him, ma'am. None of us has been the same since that awful day. It shouldn'a been him."

Ellie held the phone tight in one hand, and her temple with the other. A brief muffled sob came over the line, making tears flow down her cheeks. "Thank you so much for calling," she gasped. "I never got to say goodbye to him. And I-I do want to know what happened, but I don't think I could get through a conversation about it. Could you please write everything down?"

Thibodeaux told her he had already written what he wanted to say, and that he would send it in a letter soon. Ellie thanked him again, and they said goodbye.

Thibodeaux's letter arrived the next week.

Chapter 19

Ellie's hands quivered as she turned over the envelope, slid her finger under the flap, and began reading Thibodeaux's bold script:

> 13 Nov. 1967
> Abbeville, Louisiana
>
> Dear Miss Dennis,
>
> I was glad to talk to you, and I hope this letter will help you. Your brother died a hero, but that won't bring him back. Even so, I wanted to tell your family why he was a hero because that might help a little. Besides, I found out it is better not to keep everything inside and stay quiet about the war because doing that makes you rot inside—and believe me, that's experience talking.
>
> I think you need to know what things were like before the flood so you can understand the greatness of Lt. Dennis's sacrifice.
>
> Vietnam's wet season starts with mists in May and lasts through September when it pours. We were in Quang Tri Province, and our rain increased from late July on. That sort of rain dumps gallons of water into tributaries and rivers that swell to overflowing as they go east from the mountains toward the South China Sea.

*I was on Con Thien with your brother, and I remember
when the rains changed from mist to solid sheets of water that
started without warning and lasted for days. Con Thien was a
muddy swamp, and moving out of there was a welcome change
after all those weeks of hell in the barrel.*

Ellie stopped reading and closed her eyes, trying to remember the
maps of Quang Tri Province and what she had read about it.

*We were in a country that was once beautiful. When we
looked west from Con Thien, we could make out the jagged peaks of the Annamite Mountain Range that ran north
and south above the Cam Lo river basin. We all thought the
landscape was eerie because, in the mist, the gray mountains
loomed like giants marching in the distance.*

*The boys from western Carolina figured the peaks we saw
were close to three thousand feet high and gave birth to a
watershed that ran down slopes to cut centuries-old stream-
beds deep into the valleys. The streams came together to form
rivers where the land flattened near where we made camp at
the Cam Lo River.*

*I never heard Lt. Dennis complain about the rain, the mud,
the humidity, or soaking-wet utilities (our work uniforms). We
were Marines, so we lived with the discomforts and dangers
of war, but he kept reminding us that it was only temporary,
and we'd be back home in time. We all looked forward to that,
and I know he was looking forward to getting home because
we talked about our families a lot.*

*We left Con Thien on 10 Sep and went south to the Cam Lo
River. Our new mission was to secure the bridge across the
river not far from a small village called Cam Lo. If you look
on a map, you see our position was the southwest anchor
point of Leatherneck Square.*

Ellie nodded and chewed on her lip, then kept reading.

The bridge was important because it was a vital crossing point for vehicles carrying supplies to Con Thien. The Seabees had built the bridge about four-and-a-half meters (fifteen feet) above the water. The bridge was what we called a "stout bridge"!

Our company commander, Captain Drake, picked a place for our camp that he believed was strategically advantageous. The spot was where a one-hundred-meter expanse of dirt abutted the riverbank on the north side of the river and west of the bridge. We called the dirt spot "the beach" because it sloped a little and ended in the water. We set up—tents and such—on the beach, and from there we could keep good eyes on the bridge.

Above our camp, a gravel road ran along the bank and formed a T-intersection where the bridge met the bank. From our tents, we could see a small pagoda (where people used to worship) on the far side of the road, so it was like having a friendly neighbor.

We established listening posts near the water where we had unobstructed views of both sides of the river, up and down it, the underside of the bridge, plus keep an eye on the gravel road.

We always secured our camps with wire fences. At Cam Lo, the wire went along the top edge of the bank next to the road. Just so you know, Marines use concertina—a coiled wire embedded with razor-sharp pieces of metal because it was harder than ordinary barbed wire for the enemy—once caught—to get out of.

We built a gate in the fence atop the bank near the T-shaped intersection at the foot of the bridge, which meant we had to walk up the beach to go in or out of our camp. Lt. Dennis and I thought it was kind of a pinch point, but that's the way it had to be.

Ellie closed her eyes again and tried to form a mental picture of the bridge, the river running under it, the riverbank and road, the beach, and the camp near the water. It was hard to imagine, so she found a pencil and paper and drew a picture.

> *It rained hard off and on when we settled in, but our camp was more or less tranquil (well, compared to Con Thien, anyway,) and once we secured it, the flat sandy area was our home-base. We'd only been there for six days or so, but Lt. Dennis found a couple of crates and made a low table outside of his tent. He even made chairs out of two smaller boxes. When he wasn't in briefings, he sat there in between rain showers and looked at the water or worked on a math book. I remember telling him he had regulation patio furniture! He said, "Damn straight, I do!"*
>
> *One day I asked him about the booklet, and he told me he was a mechanical engineer, so doing math was his way of unwinding after the hell of Con Thien. He said numbers didn't change, didn't threaten to kill you, and were predictable. I had to hand it to him: he was right, we needed predictability after Con Thien!*

Ellie smiled. She remembered Hank leaning over the table doing homework when he was in elementary school. He had always been good at math—something she hated.

> *I'm a Louisiana bayou boy, Cajun born and bred, so I've fished, hunted, and lived all my life where it rains nearly twice as much as anywhere else in the U.S. I thought I knew about rain, but these monsoon rains were different. I could sure do without them! It was hard to believe that the river was quiet after the days of heavy rain we had before pulling out of Con Thien, and the daily report said torrential rains still pounded up there.*
>
> *The lieutenant and I talked about Con Thien and the thick, sticky mud that clogged machinery, covered our faces, and*

caked everything we wore. It was new to both of us, and after we left, we heard that the main gate where the supply route entered the perimeter had washed out, trapping vehicles in quagmires of the mud and muck. Getting supplies past that was impossible, so we felt for the Marines still up there defending the hill.

We had had a week of rainy but tolerable weather at our camp, yet the Cam Lo still flowed gently, and we had no idea why. It seemed unreasonable that the water level had only risen a small amount, not enough to cause concern.

Each platoon took its turn on night watch, and when it was our turn—your brother's third platoon's turn—to stand night watch, he made assignments and gave the order to commence watch. He knew we were a good platoon, but I'm confident he slept with one eye open and his T-shirt, utility pants and boots on. Most Marines do. We knew we could count on him to be ready if things got rough.

On 17 Sep it was my turn to stand night watch. I will never forget talking to him that night. It was nearly 2300 (11 p.m.) when I headed down the beach toward the listening post that was half a football field down the bank from the tents. Lt. Dennis was outside his tent, and when I went by, he asked me how I was doing. I knew he was interested—not just making conversation. He reminded me that the river looked a little swift, but the moon was out, so it should be a good night. Then he asked me if this rain made me feel at home.

I told him I had never seen so much rain. I was glad there weren't any gators or copperheads in it, but I wouldn't mind seeing some of those good ole American snakes—never thought I'd say that.

The Lieutenant asked, "You're a short-timer, aren't you?" I said yes and that I was looking forward to home, but I'd miss the jarheads cause they get in your blood.

He laughed and said, "I know what you mean, but don't worry about us. You get yourself home to your wife and kids!"

I've thought about what he said that night, and I realized he was as concerned with my family and me the same as he was about his own. I learned a long time ago that a good officer

knows his men and lets them know he cares, but he maintains
good discipline and insists on men doing their best.

Ellie put down the letter. "So like Hank," she said aloud. She sat holding it for a few minutes, then wiped her cheeks and continued reading.

I relieved one of those tired jarheads at the post, then
patrolled along the water's edge for a while. Two hours later,
I decided it was time for a little variety, so I found a good-size
boulder sticking out of the sand a meter (roughly three feet)
away from the water's edge. The rock was almost two-and-
a-half meters high with a flat spot jutting a couple of meters
above its base. There were rough steps that other guys used
to climb up because the spot was big enough to stand on and
keep watch for a while. There was a place farther up, but the
flat spot was high enough to get a clear view of everything.

I turned my back to camp, faced the river, and got comfort-
able with my M16 in the crook of my elbow. My job was to
scan the surroundings and be alert for signs of enemy activity,
so my strategy was to scan in all directions by turning three
hundred sixty degrees in an hour.

At 0130—that would make it 18 Sep—I heard lapping
sounds against the rock. I looked down and saw the water
level just below my boots.

All I could think was, "Damn, that water came up fast!"
I figured the rain in the mountains north and west of us was
causing the rise. Then, just as gray clouds covered the moon
and stars, it started to rain hard at our beach.

I repositioned myself higher on the rock, adjusted my hel-
met, and pulled my poncho closer around my neck. I figured
I'd be drenched by the time my watch ended at 0600, but
by 0230, the river had reached my boot tops. By then, I was
balancing on top of the rock. I'm not one to panic, but I knew
something was wrong.

I thought, my God, the water had come up at least six feet
in the past hour. I decided I needed to get Lt. Dennis, so I
jumped off the rock and made my way up the beach as fast

as I could. I won't forget the sound of the water sprays from my boots hitting the sand when I finally got to the shallower water.

I raced to your brother's tent and rapped (tried to keep from pounding) on his tent post, then glanced over my shoulder and realized I couldn't see the rock I had been standing on. That's when I started yelling. "Lieutenant, Sir! You gotta come quick. The water's gonna flood us out!"

He came out right away, but by then, we were both standing in several inches of water. He told me to get Sargent Flagler and get the men moving toward the gate, then Lt. Dennis went to tell the Captain we were flooding.

By now, the entire camp was knee-deep in water, and the river's main channel water had started getting close to the bridge's supporting under-beams. It wouldn't be long before the water covered the whole roadbed above. I didn't see Lt. Dennis for a while but found out later the Captain had told him to take two men and find a way to get everyone out of the gate and onto the road.

Dirty water was churning across the beach when I saw Lt. Dennis again. He was near the gate, so I went over to help him. The water rushed toward the bridge from the west, and the current was strong, fast, and washed away everything in its path. It was loud and chaotic in the darkness, which made everyone desperate to make sense of what was happening.

The last words Lt. Dennis said to me were, "I'll find us a way out."

He yelled something else to me over his shoulder and started pushing his way to the gate, a football field's width away. The gate's stabilizing posts were rapidly disappearing, and he had to go through rushing water to reach them.

I struggled to stay with him—we had to dig our boots in the sand to fight our way up the bank. It was like running in a swimming pool with muck on the bottom, and it sucked in our boots like the ocean's undertow.

But Lt. Dennis was strong, determined, so he never stopped until he reached the gate. He grabbed hold of a post, wrapped

*his arm around it, and held on, then clutched my arm with the
other. He yelled for the men to grab each other's arms and
make a human chain. I grabbed the man nearest to me, then
the others down the line stretched out their arms, groping for
each other. We clutched forearms and hung on for dear life.
The chain was the lifeline to the road where we'd be safe.*

*Your brother gripped the gatepost and anchored the chain.
I was next to him, and our systems worked: together, we'd
grab the next man in line, pull him up to the gate, and push
him through. Several men made it and began to drag others
through the opening from the other side. Everyone yelled
about hurrying. The system was sound, but the current was
getting stronger. Even so, your brother pushed one exhausted
Marine after another through that opening.*

*Then someone slipped and lost his footing and started
yelling for help. I reached out for the man, but the water got
him first and swept him out of line. I dug my fingers under Lt.
Dennis's belt, and the man behind me locked his hand onto my
belt so the chain would not break.*

Ellie thought of the time she was out in the lake, yelling for Hank to
help her. She knew how desperation felt and what it was like when she
saw him coming for her.

*Your brother, still hanging onto the post with one arm,
reached out and lunged toward the man who was flailing, trying to keep his head above water. Lt. Dennis let go of the post
and grabbed him with both hands, but I still had ahold of the
Lieutenant's belt with one hand. I grabbed the gatepost with
my free hand and hung on tight.*

*The current was savage, but Lt. Dennis got a piece of the
man's utility jacket and, with a mighty heave, pulled back him
toward the line. Several others reached out and grabbed him,
so the lieutenant and I pushed him through the gate, clear of
the wire. I saw the man stagger up a few feet then fall against
the road. I found out later that he couldn't swim.*

Lt. Dennis retook hold of the gatepost, and we used our technique—me the anchor at the gate holding Lt. Dennis's belt, and him reaching out—to pull two more men to safety.

The flood was getting worse, but we kept getting more men to safety. By now, water covered the underside of the bridge, and we could barely get our breath, but we thought we had the upper hand. I thought we were all gonna make it.

Without warning, a surge of shoulder-high fast-moving black water came out of nowhere. It must have grabbed the Lieutenant's legs and swept them out from under him because he went under. We made eye contact above the water for a few seconds and reached for each other's hands, but something happened, and we could not get a hold.

I didn't see him again but figured he'd found a handhold and pulled himself out of the water. I just thought he was fine and was somewhere near the bridge. My mission was to finish getting men through the gate, and I was the last Marine to get through. Up on the road, someone said we had lost eight men in the water, but I wasn't sure who they were.

By dawn on 18 Sep, the water was back down the bank, and the beach exposed again. I had a hard time understanding what had happened—it was tranquil, just like before.

A fluke of nature, the flood had taken everyone by surprise. Now, a few hours after I ran up the bank to sound the alarm, the river flowed gently again and was calm, beautiful. I was sprawled on the ground, leaning against the pagoda, smoking a cigarette when another lieutenant told me to take my team and recon the riverbank. He said we needed to assess our situation and account for everyone. Marines never leave anyone behind, so I knew what he meant. We were to find the casualties and bring them back.

I said, "Aye, sir," and asked if Lt. Dennis had already gone out. Like I said, I figured he was okay because we had lived through pretty bad scrapes before, and he'd always kept going no matter what.

The other Lieutenant said he didn't know. Then he said that everyone knew Lt. Dennis had done a helluva job getting us out.

*By then, it was sunup and the sky clear, free of clouds. I'd
never seen dawn like that. Translucent golden beams came
first, and then the sky turned cardinal red, so the river reflected gold and red. I remember thinking no human hand could
duplicate those colors.*

*I gathered my gear and, with three other Marines, passed
through the crooked gate with the wire still attached to it. We
set out down the bank, going east toward the bridge, across the
beach strewn with debris and marked by curvy indentations
made by the current. We moved slowly, studying the damage
and looking ahead for signs of life along the way.*

*About thirty meters from the gate, I stopped. I could not be-
lieve what I saw. I wanted it to be a hallucination, but it wasn't.
It was Lt. Dennis's body entangled in the concertina wire that
ran along the riverbank.*

Ellie put her hand over her mouth to keep from screaming. She
couldn't do anything but sit back and sob. Thibodeaux's letter made
Hank's death so real it took minutes before she could bring herself to
finish it.

*I was empty and spent. All I could do was sink to my knees
and wail. The rest of my patrol was silent, but they were good
men and knew what to do. They went to the wire to begin the
solemn task of untangling the Lieutenant from the sharp teeth.*

*There's a Cajun saying: "Defan Papa, a sainted man has
died." Another says, "M'su Diable is very vain." They mean
the Devil can't let such a good man live. This old Cajun believes the flood was evil-doing that took away a sainted man—
took away your brother.*

*Miss Dennis, I think of him every day. I cry every day and
wonder why . . . why him? I can't stand it but have no choice
but to keep living. He'd say to get on with life. I came home,
then retired because I couldn't imagine serving alongside anyone else. Lieutenant Dennis was the best leader we ever had.*

*I pray that this account helps you somehow. Please call me
anytime you need to talk. Talking and remembering seems to
ease the pain a bit.*

*Semper Fi,
Jock Thibodeaux, USMC (ret)*

Ellie put her arms on the table, laid her head down on them, and let tears flow. Jock Thibodeaux had been there with Hank and witnessed the fact that other people lived because he died. Her brother was a hero, and knowing what happened that night blunted the pain of losing him, but nothing would ever bring him back, so grief was part of her life forever. Thibodeaux and Patti grieved for Hank, too, but somehow they had kept going. Ellie kept wondering how she could get on with her life the way they had? Or *if* she could do it.

The questions stayed with her after she pushed away from the table and walked through the dark apartment to her bedroom. She didn't bother to undress but collapsed on the bed with her eyes closed. As she began to drift into restless sleep, a framed cross-stitch picture in her grandmother's living room came to mind. She had pondered the words as a child and was never sure what they meant, but she was beginning to understand now. The cross-stitch message said: What we are is God's gift to us. What we become is our gift to God. She fell asleep with one last question on her mind. *Can my life be part of Hank's legacy?*

She was tired and in a daze when a sunbeam shone through the window and woke her up. She faced a long, demanding day on campus, and she was already a half hour late for class when she remembered Thibodeaux's letter, and a cloud passed over her. *Why do I have to go to college?* But she was sure Hank would have told her to get up and go— let the baby live, finish college, and get on with life, so she swung her feet to the floor and sat on the side of the bed, trying to clear her mind.

She needed a shower, coffee, and a good breakfast. She shuffled to the bathroom, turned on the shower, peeled off yesterday's clothes, and let them drop in a pile to the floor. The baby nudged her as she let the warm water flow over her head and body.

"Hang on, baby. We need to try, at least," she whispered. "I'll get us going."

She stepped out of the shower and glimpsed her reflection in the foggy mirror on the back of the door. Her shape—a steamy apparition in front of her—was changing. She turned to the side and stood on her toes. Subtle though it was, a delicate, smooth bump behind her navel had begun displacing her disappearing waist. It was slight now, but she'd read somewhere that pregnancies are evident at six months, so she would not be able to hide the facts much longer. She would have to tell her parents—soon. Trying not to think of their reaction, she pulled on an oversized dress and sweater and slipped on her shoes. She grabbed some coffee and a piece of toast, climbed into the car, and clipped the safety belt across her lap, intent on making herself go to campus.

The route included an intersection where her street met a broad thoroughfare used by fast-moving morning commuters. The traffic light was red at the intersection, so Ellie—barely aware of anything else—pulled up and stopped. When the light turned green, she started to cross the busy road. Halfway across, there was a deafening crash. Her car jolted sideways. The sound of metal on metal was on her right, somewhere close. Disoriented and confused, her head jerked oddly toward the noise as breaking glass showered over her.

For an instant—brief as the click of a camera lens—her mind registered the front end of another car in her passenger-side window. A massive hole in the spider-webbed glass framed the image, and bits of shattered glass lay on the empty seat, the floor, and her lap. The armrest next to her bent inward and pressed against her right arm. *How was that possible?* It didn't make sense.

Then she perceived something else. Her car should be moving straight ahead, but it was going sideways in the wrong trajectory. Habit said to squeeze the steering wheel and jam on the brakes, so she did, but nothing happened. The car was still moving sideways, and the smell of burning rubber hurt her nose as pain shot through her neck and head. Her hands flew back from the steering wheel and covered her face; her lap belt gripped tight across her belly. Sharp, intense pain deep inside pierced upward from her abdomen, then passed through her chest to her shoulders.

She screamed and clawed at the belt, trying to make it let go, but she could not pry it loose. The car rocked side to side, then tipped up on its two left wheels. Finally, as if in slow motion, it fell back down onto all four tires. Black spots popped in front of her eyes, and a whooshing sound filled her ears. Then it became deathly quiet. After a moment, she heard wailing sirens and people yelling. Hands pulled at her body as the voices became distant, indecipherable echoes. The black spots fused just before everything went blank.

Someone was moaning. Ellie tried to open her eyes, but the lids were heavy as lead, and there it was again—a faraway sound of someone in pain. *Why doesn't anybody help?* She raised her eyebrows in an effort to drag open her lids. She forced a few blinks until a ragged slit allowed white brightness to burn consciousness into her brain. Finally, a huge, bright white chrysanthemum bloomed above her head, and she perceived low murmurs among the fading moans and the ringing in her ears. A moment later, she made out a familiar voice.

"She's coming around," it said. "Ellie. Ellie? Can you hear me? It's Dad."

She blinked again and again, trying to clear her eyes. The bloom's petals slowly disappeared and became a big, bright, blinding circle. She squinted and turned her head away from the brightness. An image came into view, and she made out Dad's face surrounded by what appeared to be a lion's mane. A few more blinks made the golden fur begin to diffuse. *What's happening? Why is he standing sideways?*

Before she could say anything, a stabbing pain hit and took her breath away. She had never felt pain this intense, pain that came from deep inside, knotted her entire body, and made her breaths short like those of a panicked child. She squeezed her eyes shut, scrunched up her nose, and gritted her teeth until the pain began to subside. Then she forced open her eyes once more. The voice, closer now, said she would be okay. The warmth of a hand against her face calmed her.

She became aware that she was flat on her back in a high bed with metal rails along the sides, and Dad wasn't sideways, he was beside her, standing over her, reaching over the rails to lean close to her with his right hand holding hers. Her eyes focused on him and the fuzziness around his face fell away as he squeezed her hand.

"Glad to see you, El," Dad said in a voice softer than any she remembered. He wore green hospital scrubs and had a stethoscope draped around his neck. Dark circles underlined reddened eyes, and a five-o'clock shadow smudged his cheeks, but despite that, a tender smile appeared and pushed up wrinkles at the corners of his eyes.

A childhood memory of Dad flashed across her mind. Dressed in white scrubs and leaning on the car door, he was talking to Mom through the open window. Hank was next to Mom in the front seat, and Ellie was in the back of a black car parked at the curb outside a big brick building that cast a large shadow across an expanse of grass. Mom handed Dad a piece of paper and looked straight ahead over the steering wheel while he read it. Dad's face was stern and harried—unapproachable. He crumpled up the paper and handed it back to Mom. The memory faded when another pain shot through Ellie's abdomen, making her head ache and her whole body throb. Again, Dad's warm touch on her cheek helped her fight the pain and regain her bearings. She began to understand that something somewhere had gone wrong, and she was the one who moaned.

A voice on the other side of the bed said her name, and another soft hand touched her, so Ellie rolled her head toward the sound as the hand rested next to a white bandage taped to her left arm. When her head moved, the room turned fluid, objects floated in space, and collided unnaturally. Nausea flowed over her, and she gagged, so she kept her head still and squeezed her eyes shut until the room settled down.

When she managed to open her eyes again, a pouch of red liquid on a rod above her head came into view. There was a woman's face next to the bag, and plastic tubing carried the opaque liquid from the pouch and disappeared under white gauze wrapped around her arm.

"Well, hello," said the woman, her voice gentle in Ellie's ringing ears. "You're in the hospital with your dad, and I'm Dr. Vaughn, the emergency room doctor. A car ran a red light and crashed into the passenger side of your car. You had a close call, but we think you're going to be okay in time."

"Thaaat's good," whispered Ellie, trying to smile, but not knowing if she had or not.

"You have severe bruises," said Dr. Vaughn, "and a couple of lacerations that we had to suture, a mild concussion, and a cracked rib. You'll need lots of rest while you mend because we don't want that rib to puncture your lung."

Dr. Vaughn's image was fuzzy—like looking through unfocused binoculars. Even so, Ellie made out a smile until the face changed and the smile disappeared.

"I'm so sorry," Dr. Vaughn continued. "You miscarried because of the trauma during the accident. We lost the baby—a girl. I'm so sorry." Dr. Vaughn's eyes softened, and she looked away from Ellie toward her dad.

Ellie squeezed her eyes shut, and a sob, then a moan, escaped her throat. More and more came out, but she couldn't stop them. Her body shook, and her chest heaved, and she wanted to hide—to wake up and not be a part of this nightmare. The baby—her baby girl—had vanished.

She hadn't known whether to think of it as a boy or girl, but her baby was gone before she had seen the small face or touched her tiny fingers. Ellie slid her hand across crisp white sheets toward her tummy, but the tubing attached to her arm stopped her hand short. She reached out to hold Dad's hand—the only steady thing in the room.

"Oh, El, I'm so sorry," he murmured and bowed his head. Ellie felt a tightening of his hand on hers but heard no barrage of criticism about the pregnancy. The fingers of his left hand passed across her forehead and came to rest on her right cheek, his thumb wiping away the tears flowing down.

A cool draft passed over her, and the voices grew fainter until her eyelids—independent of her control—began to close. Blurred images and soft but clear sounds surrounded her while a heart monitor beeped steadily in the background.

Ellie felt her breaths become slow and steady. The last thing she heard as she fell into deepening sleep was her daddy's voice. It was barely discernible, but she understood every word. "How could I save so many others and not save my own son?" he asked. "I don't want to lose you, Ellie. I won't leave you. I'll be right here." She fought to keep her eyes open, but the light dimmed, then disappeared.

Chapter 20

Ellie woke up later in a hospital room and had plenty of time to think during the week she spent there. Nights were hardest, when remorse hit first and heartaches followed. Most nights, Ellie put her hand on her flat stomach and let tears flow when the halls quieted and took on that special kind of echoing stillness found only within a hospital's walls. It was her fault the baby was gone. Hank was gone, but she'd survived. Joe didn't care and left only grief, guilt, and shame to stay with her.

The days were not so bad because people came and went randomly. Tommy delivered flowers from Patti, and the nurse brought encouraging cards from Susan. Mira stopped in or sent notes to her, and Dad came in at least twice a day. He even brought lunch for the two of them when he had a little extra time. He told her Mom would probably come to see her soon.

One day over pastrami on rye sandwiches, he said, "I've not seen Joe, and you have not mentioned him since you've been here. I thought you would want him here with you."

"Thanks for asking, Dad, but I don't think we'll ever see him again," she whispered.

Dad had looked up from the thick sandwich poised near his open mouth. Instead of taking a bite, he pursed his lips and frowned, but he didn't ask her to explain. He looked at his sandwich and seemed to consider something before taking a bite and staring into space, lost in his thoughts.

He never uttered a judgmental word during his visits, and his turn-around left Ellie baffled. Could she trust it? Would he start criticizing without notice? Berate her the way he had before she moved to the apartment? She wanted to believe his transformation from judgment to compassion was real. One night when darkness settled in and the night nurses' voices became cooing doves, Ellie remembered Hank's words about their father: "You are not the cause of his criticism," Hank had said. He had explained that there was something within their father that he needed to put away or perhaps forgive himself for.

"Thank you, Big Brother"—she spoke into the darkness—"You were right. I was not the cause, but I'm not the cause of his change, either."

A few days after Dad had asked about Joe, Ellie was in an easy chair by her bed when Mom came to the hospital. She stood in the doorway and shifted uneasily with one hand on the doorframe and her purse in the other. She wore a simple, stylish dress that needed ironing.

"You look dreadful," she said while scanning her daughter's ban-daged arm and face with its bruises turning deep purple, green, and yellow. "I mean, I don't mean that in an awful way. I mean, just that it looks like you . . ." She looked away and took a breath then started again: "Well, I mean you were in a terrible wreck and got hurt badly. Yet there you are looking sweet even with stitches, bruises, and all." She tried to smile but managed only to lean against the door and fix her half-closed, rheumy eyes on her daughter.

Ellie repositioned herself and tried to get comfortable, but her heart ached at the sad lifelessness of her mother. *Where had Mom's familiar anger gone? Was it there, under the surface, just waiting to bring more pain? Did the alcohol extinguish it or feed it?* In any case, for reasons Ellie did not understand, she wanted to reach out to this pathetic woman who was so clearly suffering.

"You can come in, Mom," Ellie said from her chair by the window. "Why don't you sit with me for a while?" She pointed to a chair on the other side of the bed. Her mother moved unsteadily and sat down. She asked Ellie how she was doing.

"I get up while they change my bed," Ellie said. "After I sit for a while, I'm able to walk in the hall. I'll probably go all the way to the lobby today, so I could walk with you when you need to leave."

"Okay, that would be good, but I can't stay long. I don't want to tire you out." Mom perched on the edge of the chair with her purse on her lap, like a person waiting in a bus station. She took a breath and asked, "Where are you going once you're discharged?"

"Back to the apartment. I feel pretty good, and the bruises will be gone soon. The ringing in my ears is gone, but the neurologist said I need to limit my activities for a few more weeks. I'm just sore and a little stiff."

Mom did not mention the baby, and Ellie wondered if she even knew about the miscarriage, but she didn't want to deal with her mother's unpredictable reaction, so she kept quiet.

"I wish I could help you, but you're right," Mom said, fidgeting with her purse handle. "It's best that you go back to your own place, not to our house."

Ellie didn't remember saying it would be best to be at the apartment, and after the stab of rejection subsided, she tried to let it go and said, "Susan is coming up from St. Augustine, so she can drive me home when I'm released. She told me she could stay a day or so to help me get settled. Mira said she would check on me, too. She can help if I need it."

"Oh, Mira. Yes . . .well . . . that's good, then," Mom said. "I wish Hank were here to help you."

"I do, too, Mom." Quiet settled over them like a predawn mist on the lake. Ellie shifted in her chair again, and Mom focused on the cold, shiny floor. She didn't move a muscle until—without a word—she rose and patted Ellie's hand. Then she abruptly turned, walked through the door, and disappeared into the hall. Tuneless, bland music from a distant Muzak speaker oozed from the hall into the void that filled the room.

Ten days after the accident, Ellie was sitting in the chair waiting for Susan to pick her up. The stitches were gone, and her arms were free of bandages, so Ellie could move without help and go home.

Dad came quickly through the door clutching a clipboard. When he saw Ellie, a smile spread across his tired face.

"You look terrific, El! I'm so glad you've been liberated." He took his stethoscope from around his neck, put it on the overbed tray and hugged her. "I was doing rounds and wanted to see you before you checked out." He was a breathless giant standing over her.

"It feels pretty good. I took a real shower this morning and even washed my own hair at long last," she said. "I stayed under the water as long as I could."

"Don't stay in there too long. Your fingers will get all pruney like when you were a little girl at the lake, remember?"

"Yeah, I remember," she said. The memory of those days spent diving, swimming, and playing in the lake made her smile. "We'd be in the water all day, wouldn't we? Our wrinkly hands and feet scared me at first, but Hank told me it wasn't permanent."

Dad pulled up a chair and sat next to her. He leaned forward and grasped her hands in his strong, agile fingers, drawing her hands to his knee. Ellie felt his warmth but noticed a nearly imperceptible quiver. He sat quietly for a moment and looked at the floor before he began talking. "I've been waiting until you were strong enough to say this to you." His earnest face turned to his daughter's. "I want you to know that I'm sorry for being so hard on you—such a bad father—all these years."

Ellie opened her mouth to speak, but he kept talking: "Shhh. Just a minute. Let me get this out, okay? Hank told me you had grown up to be a strong, competent person, and he was right.

"I was too pigheaded and too focused on building my practice when you were little. I didn't pay attention to you or Hank. Mira told me more than once to let up and pay attention to my family, but I attended to my patients more than to the two of you or your mother. I'm afraid I missed your growing-up years, but I don't want to miss anything else. I didn't have enough time with your brother, and I know I wasted what time I had." His eyes filled with tears, and his face was no longer an impenetrable mask.

Ellie was stunned—speechless. Her mind took her back to second grade, when she was a skinny, freckle-faced seven-year-old with hair that refused to be tamed. Clear and oppressive as an August afternoon, a memory flashed in her mind—his harsh words telling her to fix her scraggly hair. She remembered the sting in her eyes and a lump that closed her throat. How many times had she bit her lip, rubbed her eyes, and escaped to the comfort of Mira's arms?

Now almost thirteen years later, he had apologized to her and said he wanted to be in her life. Was this the real person Hank had seen? She leaned forward and put her cheek against his hand clasped around her own, still on his knee.

"Oh, Dad," she said, her own tears moist on his skin. "Hank told me you only wanted the best for me. It's okay. I'll be fine."

Dad swallowed hard and said, "Even though you never held your baby, you have lost a child, so you know how that changes your life. Part of you is gone, and you can't bring it back. There's no one to blame, and no justice can prevail. My son is gone—it's final—no going back to say I'm sorry or remake memories. Losing my child rocked me to the core. I loved him so much, but I'll get no second chances to do a better job. Somehow, I know you understand. I don't know how your mother and I will continue without Hank . . ." He released her hands and straightened in his chair.

"I do understand," Ellie said quietly as she put her hand against her flat abdomen. She knew her baby girl had had distinct facial features when she died and that her round head had been the biggest part of her body. Her little arms and legs had completely formed with ten toes and ten fingers. Ellie grieved, knowing that she would never be able to count those toes or feel the tiny fingers wrap around her own. The absence of the small life inside her hurt more deeply than her superficial cuts or bruises. Those wounds would heal, but she feared her heart— twice wounded—would not. Her father didn't have to say another word about losing a child. She already felt his sorrow.

Dad leaned back and ran his fingers through his hair, interlacing them behind his neck. "Your mother told me I had a god complex and that I thought I was in charge of everything and everyone. When you and Hank were in elementary school, she said she wanted to send him away from home to a boarding school because she had to get him away from me. She thought my influence was bad for him." He paused. "I don't know. Maybe she was right." He leaned forward and put his elbows on his knees with his hands still hugging his neck.

Ellie could not think of anything to say, so she simply stared at her father. It was as if layers of bandages had been removed to expose his emotional cuts and bruises and the scars he would bear forever. How had he come to grips with the past? Did he feel responsible for Hank's military career or for his death? Ellie reached out and touched her father's shoulder.

"I have a letter you need to read," she said. "It's from a Marine who was with Hank at the river when he died. I think it might help you." Neither moved or spoke for several minutes until Dad sat up and patted her hand. He reached for the stethoscope and winced, then rubbed the left side of his chest with his other hand.

Ellie watched his face. *Had he turned pale for the briefest moment?* She couldn't tell. He stood, and in one deft move, the stethoscope was back in place around his neck.

"Your mother is an incredibly strong woman," he said. "She's simply different from most people. We had so much fun when we were first married. You don't know how she was before we came back to the South. We loved each other from the beginning, but somehow we got on the wrong foot and stayed there, so we became adversaries.

"I've never seen her cry," he continued. "One contrite word from her or any indication of regret for missteps in our marriage over the years would have gone a long way toward rebuilding our relationship. We should have gotten closer after we lost Hank, but she started drinking to anesthetize herself when he left—and now that he's permanently gone, she's lost in it. She keeps her grief inside, but it has to come out sometime, some way. That's a fact."

"What do we need to do to help her?" Ellie asked.

"I'm not sure," he shrugged and opened both palms at his sides. "I've tried to convince her she needs to stop drinking or admit that she can't stop on her own, and I'd pay for the best treatment program we could find. You can imagine how that went. She doesn't want to hear anything from me."

"Can I ask Susan to talk to her?" Ellie asked. "She and Mom are kind of the same, but Susan went for treatment after she dropped out of school and said it was the best thing that ever happened to her. I could talk to her about helping when she comes to take me home—to the apartment, I mean."

She waited, wondering if she had gone too far. *What will he think? Will he approve?*

He surprised her when he said, "That's a good idea." He put his hands on his hips and was quiet for a minute. "Susan, huh? Your peace-marching nun friend? Guess it couldn't hurt. How could things get worse? Yes, go ahead and ask her. Your mother needs help."

"Yes, she does," Ellie said. "Susan will be here soon, and I'll have plenty of time to talk about options for Mom."

Dad left with a wave, but the warmth of his hand stayed on hers, and his presence was strong even in his absence. She leaned her head back and looked out the window. Dad's words played over in her mind, and she got lost in the clouds floating outside.

Pale amber and yellow, star-shaped leaves crowned the sweetgum trees, and spiky brown seed clusters fell all over the ground underneath the branches. Across the landscape, the orange leaves of Florida maples mixed with the sweetgum and evergreen foliage, while the bare arms of dogwood trees reached to the sky. The dogwood's cross-shaped blooms had died and fallen away in the early Florida spring many months ago, and now the last of November's breezes announced autumn was becoming winter, but still the dogwood's crimson berries brightened this gray season.

Susan had stood beside Ellie when she hugged the nurses and promised them she would take care of herself. Later, at the apartment, they had talked about Mom, and Susan had promised to contact her and try to help her. Then Susan had cooked a large chicken and announced that it would be their Thanksgiving dinner since Ellie had missed a real one when she was hospitalized. Mira had shown up with a fresh-baked pumpkin pie to top off the meal and had assured Susan she would check on Ellie every few days after Susan went back to the convent.

A day or two later, when Ellie was alone, she tried not to think about Hank and Patti's wedding day the year before. Deep sadness filled her when she realized their first wedding anniversary—sweet but uncelebrated—had come and gone while she was in a hospital bed covered with bruises and stitches and mourning her lost baby girl. Patti had sent flowers and a note saying she missed Ellie but coming back to visit would make too vivid the memories of her life with Hank at the lake and the apartment. She said it was still too painful for her to be there, but she hoped she'd be able to come back sometime.

Ellie slogged through the following week as if she were in leg irons. Her injuries were healing, and she had gone back to class after the Thanksgiving break because it seemed the right thing to do, but she ignored grocery-store ads and banners across dress shop windows that hinted of Christmas celebrations.

Her physical injuries were less painful, but her emotional pain was intense as she sat stoically among giggling, self-absorbed students who talked of little except the partying they planned to do during the Christmas holiday break. A couple of classmates had exchanged looks and commented on her absence, but no one asked questions after she told them she had had an accident. Only one person mouthed perfunctory words of encouragement. Ellie smiled and thanked her for her concern but said nothing more. Class lectures became droning soliloquies, and academics were meaningless—hollow in the light of Hank's death and her lost baby.

One cool afternoon, Ellie sat bundled underneath her tree and came to grips with the fact that college was not important anymore and she had little in common with her chattering classmates—their problems were minor compared to her reality. She decided that continuing her education was a waste of her time and Dad's money, so she went to the administration building and withdrew. She called Tommy to ask if he still needed her help in the shop. He was delighted to hear from her, then said he had plenty of work for her since Christmas was not far away. Later, Dad listened to her explain why she'd quit college, and as if to solidify the truth of his transformation, he did not object to her decision.

Even though her body had healed and she had Dad's validation, the damage to Ellie's soul felt permanent. She hid her sorrow and went to Eden's Beauty with a heart that ached with the same force it had when the two Marines delivered their devastating news nearly three months before. She didn't understand why she had lived, but Hank had not. Her baby's death was a brutal kick against that open wound. *Why am I alive, but they are not?*

Christmas peeked over the horizon. The solitary light in Ellie's life was the reborn relationship with her father. But even with that new hope, she faced a future along a path obscured by loss and guilt the way fallen leaves hide a forest trail.

Her doctor had said mild exercise would help her recuperate faster, so every morning, after a lonely breakfast, she put on a jacket and went to the campus for a walk before going to work. Most students had cleared out for the holidays, so she had the ribbons of sidewalks all to herself, but no matter where she started, she ended up sitting for a few minutes under her magnificent live oak by the pond.

It was comforting to pull her wrap close and look up at the sapphire sky through the leaves. Her tree's new leaves remained green even as its older ones had dropped and other neighboring trees prepared to go dormant for the months ahead. Her tree had weathered many a deadening season, yet it remained vibrant and hopeful for the end of winter. *Is it possible for me to hope too? Is there an ending to this season of my life?*

Hank had looked forward to coming home after Christmas when the magnolias dropped dark red, pineapple-shaped seed pods to the ground. She had planned how to tell him about her pregnancy when he got home, but that release was impossible now. *What would you have said about the baby, Hank? Would you and Patti have started the family you both wanted?* She had no answers and never would.

"Hello!" Ellie said with the phone in one hand and a newly opened can of soup in the other. Dad had gotten into the habit of calling her a few times a week around dinner time after he had finished attending to patients at his office, so she expected to hear his voice. But it was someone else this time.

"Come to the hospital quick!" Mira's voice was urgent. "It's yo' daddy. He had a heart attack. Git yo' mama. Bring her here." The line went dead.

Panic seized Ellie and she dropped the soup can. She ignored the spill spreading across the counter and ran to get her satchel, grab her jacket, and start out the door. She was about to slam it shut but rushed back into the bathroom instead. She pulled a brown medicine bottle from a drawer next to the sink. The bottle contained the twenty little blue pills Dad had given her before Hank's funeral. Dad had said they would help her stay calm. She had thanked him but later stashed the pills in the drawer so all twenty were still in the bottle. She jammed it in her pocket and ran for the door, fumbling for the car keys on her way out.

Why did this happen to Dad just when we were starting to repair our relationship? She pleaded with God even though she was not sure He listened anymore. She didn't want to lose Dad, too. Heart pounding and hands trembling, Ellie slid behind the wheel and tossed the satchel onto the back seat, then started the car Dad had given her to replace the wrecked one. A moment later, she pressed the accelerator and the engine roared, but the car did not move. She held the wheel and pushed down the accelerator again, but still nothing happened. Shaken, she checked the gauges and found that the car was still in park. She was a fool, and it was a good thing she had remembered the pills because she sure did need one.

"Get a grip, Ellie," she said out loud to herself. She grabbed the shift lever and focused on easing the car into drive. A cringe rushed through her when she came to the intersection where her life was crushed an eternity ago. She took a long look in both directions and when the light turned green, she crossed under it and drove away from the scene as fast as she could.

She jumped out of the car at her parents' house and ran up the front walk. It was dusk, and the sun drew long shadows across the lawn, but the house was already dark. Ellie was not surprised to find the door unlocked, so she threw it open and called out to her mother, who would be in rough shape by this time of day.

"Mom! Mom!" Ellie shouted. "Where are you? Something has happened." She stood, listening for a moment. The sound of skin slapping against a hard surface came from the family room. "Mom! Mom!" she called again, moving through the shadowy living room toward the sound.

"Good grief, Ellie. What're you yellin' about?" Mom's voice was thick with alcohol and irritation. "I'm in here—in the family room. Wha'd'you want?"

Ellie ran toward her mother's voice and started through the door but halted. She gripped the frame, reached toward the light switch, and flipped it up. The instant brilliance contrasted sharply with the darkness and blinded her briefly until her eyes adjusted. The scene ahead was what she had feared, and her stomach knotted as her skin began to crawl.

Her mother, clad in rumpled clothes, squinted her eyes and pinched up her nose under a head of messy hair. Her mouth was a lopsided sneer, and she struggled to stand up with one hand holding a drink and the other gripping the arm of the couch. She wavered sideways before planting both feet wide apart on the floor.

"Good God, Ellie," she growled. "What in the world are you doing? Can't you see I'm busy?" She released her hold on the couch and attempted to run her free hand through her hair but lost her balance and had to grab hold again.

"Mom, you have to come with me. Dad's had a heart attack, and we need to get to the hospital. Now." Ellie reached deep down inside to keep herself from judging the person who stood in front of her. She worked to stop from frowning.

"Oh, Ellie, dear," her mother said, her voice edged with sarcasm. "I can't go anywhere. I'm not dressed to go anywhere. Can't you see that? Besides, your father has plen'y of people to take care of him. They all love him a' the hospital. He has them fooled. They don' know what a horse's ass he can be." Mom's face was hard and unforgiving as she fell back onto the couch.

"You *have* to come. No matter how you feel, he's your husband. He's my father," said Ellie, taking a few steps into the room and reaching toward her mother. "I'll get you some coffee."

Mom raised the glass, tilted it, swallowed, and looked at the ceiling before lowering her contentious eyes to glare at Ellie. "My, my, my—if you aren't the most righteous one!" she said. "What makes you think you're so smart? You're always sayin' I need this or that."

"I'm not so smart, Mom," Ellie said, trying to keep her voice steady while the dark weight of guilt pressed on her chest. "I thought it would be better if you went with me instead of getting a call from the hospital."

"Lea' me alone, Eleanor. Stop botherin' me. You never knew when to quit. You act like you're better than me. Don' be so self-righteous. You can go to him by y'self." Mom took another swallow and turned away from her daughter's downcast face. "I'll go later. You have no idea what I put up with. I haven't been able to do anything to please him for a long time. He pro'ly wouldn't miss me, anyway." She held the half-empty glass with one hand and swirled the liquor that numbed her pain but left her devoid of compassion. "B'sides, I'm enjoying my independence!"

"It doesn't look like you're enjoying much of anything," Ellie said and heard her own voice turn granite-like. Her mother glared and waved Ellie off without another word. The conversation over, Ellie turned, switched off the light, and left her mother in the darkness, drowning her sorrows. The sharpness of her mother's contempt had torn open Ellie's emotional wounds and left her bleeding. She flew down the front steps and ran to her car with hot tears burning her cheeks.

Chapter 21

Ellie put her hand on the outside of the glass wall enclosing the intensive care unit where her father lay pale and motionless. He seemed to be sleeping, but the oxygen mask and the bags of liquid hanging at his bedside and tubes taped to his arms revealed the truth. She stared at him, the warmth of her fingertips making foggy outlines on the cool glass. He was one of several patients in a large open area divided into smaller spaces by short curtains hanging from ceiling rails. His curtains were open, affording her a clear view of him. He was in a semi-sitting position, surrounded by machines he had used to save other people's lives. But his life needed saving now. The rise and fall of his chest was so shallow it was all but invisible. Only the incessant beep, beep, beep of the heart monitor and the rhythmic hiss of the respirator proved he was alive.

She remembered his reassuring words when he shared her sorrows that day she lay in her hospital bed. That connection had lightened her load somehow, and since then, she had allowed herself to hope she could get to know her father, spend time with him, and learn about him. She had even dared to hope a bond could grow between them, yet here she was, watching as Dad slipped into the depths and was about to disappear the way her pink float had so many years ago.

After Ellie left her mother, she had rushed to the hospital to find Mira sitting on a Naugahyde-and-steel settee in the family lounge next to the door outside the ICU. While Ellie stood staring through the window at Dad, Mira sat with her head bowed.

"Why don't you sit down, chil'?"—Mira's voice broke into Ellie's thoughts—"You're gonna wear yourself out if you don't sit for a bit. They's takin' good care of 'im cause they love 'im here, 'n' they'll let us go in 'fore too long."

Ellie sank down on to the settee, and Mira took hold of her hand but said nothing. "He's going to be all right, isn't he, Mira?" Ellie whispered and rested her head on Mira's shoulder.

"I don't know, baby," Mira said. "We jus' have to keep watchin' and prayin'."

Ellie was nauseated. If Dad didn't pull through, she would be alone in the world with only Mira as a lifeline, and Mira had said it herself: she was getting old—too old—to keep up. Ellie felt as if she were stuck in the mud, watching a coming flood, knowing she would soon be under water. *How will I ever be able to move on from here?*

A whooshing sound caught her attention, so she sat up and released Mira's hand as she jumped to her feet, fine lines of worry creasing her face. A pleasant-looking nurse held open the glass door.

"You can have a little time with him," the nurse said. "No more than fifteen minutes, though."

As Ellie stood up, she felt—more than heard—the faint rattle of the tranquilizers in her pocket. She wondered if she should take one, then remembered Dad's warning that taking too many could kill you. A dark voice in her head whispered that maybe she should take all of them, for they would let her slip away and leave behind this world of loss, grief, and pain. She would simply go to sleep, then disappear. No more finding a path, being strong, or anything else. The dark thought held her captive until a wisp of cool air passed over her face and brought her back to reality. She followed Mira into the ICU, where the smell of antiseptic surrounded her on the way to Dad's bedside. There was a chair on each side, so Mira took one and Ellie took the other.

She took hold of Dad's hand, but he didn't respond to her touch. Seeing him this way—dependent, helpless, and motionless—was simply not natural. He had been judgmental and harsh, but he had never been weak or helpless. He could be insensitive and demanding, but he was always strong, decisive, and invulnerable. People's lives had depended on him, so he kept moving no matter how he felt.

But now . . . Ellie stared at her dad's slack skin and the five-o'clock shadow beginning to show under the oxygen mask. Hank had said Dad was driven to heal others even if that meant he must deny himself, but it was Mom's needs and desires that had been denied, leaving the entire family as broken as a ship against a rocky shoal. Now that Hank was gone, the family had no anchor, and Ellie felt adrift and very alone.

When the nurse came over to fiddle with one of the machines, Ellie looked across the bed at Mira. She was holding Dad's other hand, her head lowered while she murmured a prayer. She looked up and asked the nurse how long it would be before he woke up. Instead of offering assurances, the nurse said something about it being impossible to know what to expect.

"Dr. Dennis had a massive heart attack," she added, her face solemn and mask-like. "We simply have to wait and see."

The moment Ellie heard those words, something sucked the air out of the room, and she couldn't get her breath. Like a crystal goblet against cement, her world crashed into so many pieces she couldn't see how to put it back together. She wanted all this to go away so she could escape her pain, loss, and guilt. She couldn't stand it. She had to get out of there.

"I can't . . . I just can't!" Ellie said and sprang up from her chair. She thrust her hands into her pockets to hide the trembling.

Mira's head jerked up, but she did not say anything. Instead, her dark eyes—clouded by cataracts visible in the bright lights—turned sad and stayed on Ellie, who blurted out that she needed a breath of air. She hurried out of the ICU, rushed down the corridor with the hidden pill bottle clutched in her hand, ran to her car, and then roared out of the parking lot. Hot tears blurred her vision, so she bumped over the curb and sideswiped a bush on the corner, but she clung to the wheel and headed to the only place in the world that never changed—the place where quiet cocooned her, the place where she wanted to be at the end.

On the familiar road out of town, she passed a new housing development scarring the once-rural landscape that seemed part of her. Hungry earthmovers churned up palmettos along with the natural undergrowth and spat out healthy pine trees unlucky enough to be in their path. Everything along the way was the same—but everything was also different, the same as Ellie's life. The sun flickered through scrub pines close to the road as Mira's voice echoed in Ellie's head.

"Yo' daddy wanted me to hep with you and Hank 'cause he trusted me," Mira had said when Ellie was in the hospital, recovering from the accident that took her child. "Yo' mama's hidin' from everyone behind that devil alcohol, makin' a shield out of it 'cause it's easier for her to push us away than take our comfort. She can't admit why she's angry or even that it started a long time ago. I tol' yer daddy he needed to stop criticizing so much and hug more, but he was workin' too hard 'n' didn't get 'nough sleep so he on'y made things worse. Still, yo' mama has a good heart, Ellie, so you gotta forgive her. I wonder sometimes if she mad at God or if she blames yo' daddy for Hank's dyin'. Mebbe it's both . . . I dunno. But I do know losin' yo' brother's been a torment for y'all. Hank was always such a good li'l boy who wanted to hep everyone—you, 'specially. Taking care was his nature, so that's why he wanted to hep them people fight the communists. First, he want to hep them hep theirselves, 'n' then he just wanted to take care of his men."

Mira was quiet for a moment before going on to tell Ellie about the two small children—one strong and full of confidence, the other shy and scared—who absorbed her love and care like dry sponges soak up water. "Let go, chil'," Mira had said. She said she thought sorrow was like wicked currents hiding underneath the ocean's surface as the waves come and go. If she wasn't careful, Mira had said, the currents would carry her away quick as a riptide, then sweep her out to sea. She would vanish in a flash, just like her mother.

Back in the present, Ellie drove past the familiar scenery near the lake house and decided Mira was right. Sorrow—the hole in her life— was always there below what others saw, but she was confused when she recalled the rest of what Mira had said. "I learned thin's don' always make sense," Mira had concluded, "but if you lose hope, the unde'tow buries you deeper and deeper in de sand, and pretty soon, you disappear. When yo' daddy and I was little kids playin' in the surf, I tol' him to keep changin' his feet and find a firm foundation.

"It's harder for yo' mama. She gonna need hep now that Hank's gone. She don' want us close, but if we jes keep a-holt a her, sooner or later she'll get better. You gotta believe, Ellie."

But Ellie didn't believe—she simply couldn't. When the preacher had shouted about faith and asking for God's blessing, Ellie had tried to hope, and she had prayed for God to protect Hank. But neither her faith nor her desperate pleas had kept him safe. Nothing had helped. So why would it be any different now, with Dad?

The thought haunted her until she had to jam on the brakes to keep from passing the hidden dirt road that led to the lake house. She rounded a gentle curve, and the stone chimney's silhouette came into view among the trees in the dusky sky. Beyond the house, the lake's beauty spread to the horizon, and the colors of the late afternoon sky reflected on its glassy surface. She pulled onto a worn patch of ground by the house, turned off the ignition, and looked up at the chimney, a welcoming sentinel among the mighty oaks that had been the same since she could remember.

She stepped out of the car and paused to listen to the frogs and crickets. The house, dark and two-dimensional, like a woodcut print on the sky, loomed in front of her. Fall had yielded to winter and—even in Florida—that meant building a fire in Grandpa's granite fireplace. She gathered sticks, twigs, and broken branches on her way to the door.

She wrapped an arm around the kindling and found the hidden keys. After unlocking the door, she walked into the main room, crossed to the fireplace, and stepped around the twin easy chairs to deposit the small sticks on the hearth beside the woodbox. Her father, and his father before him, had closed the house at the end of every summer and left the woodbox filled with large pieces of seasoned split wood and an old newspaper for starting the first fire of the winter season.

When she opened the double doors to the porch, she felt a fresh cool breeze brush over her arms and face. The oaks peered through the porch screens like curious elderly neighbors, and she stood enjoying the moment until a shiver went down her arm—a reminder that it was time to set the fire the way Hank had taught her.

With twigs and sticks piled on the andirons, Ellie poked wads of crumpled-up newspaper into spaces under the stack and topped it with a split log. She double-checked her work, then found the big wooden matches on the mantel. She lit one and touched it to the paper until a fluttering flicker appeared. The flame sputtered and crackled but caught the twigs, so she straightened up and turned toward the lake while the fledgling fire grew and fought off the chill in the room. She put another log on, adjusted the fireplace screen, and strolled out to the porch.

Leaning against the doorframe, she took in the muted images of wispy clouds mirrored on the surface of the lake. Twinkling lights from other houses around the lake and a rising moon provided enough light to outline the oaks, pines, and palmettos along the shoreline. Her thoughts disappeared among the night sounds and glistening water until she shoved her hands in her pockets and her hand closed around the pill bottle. After pulling it out, she went back inside and settled into one of the soft chairs in front of the fire. She leaned back in the chair, held the bottle up to the light, and gave it a shake. The pills rattled like a snake's warning.

She wrapped her fingers around the bottle and popped off the top with her thumb. The top flew up, arced downward, bounced, and rolled across the floor. "Think of that," she said, "a simple flick of the thumb, and here they are—the little blue answers to my troubles." She gripped the bottle and lowered it to her lap, then grasped her head with her other hand. Her insides torqued and choked her.

It would be easy to tip the brown cylinder to her lips, swallow the pills, and drift away from her life. There would be no more guilt. No more struggling. Someone else could be the strong one—she was tired of fighting, tired of trying to be strong, and tired of learning how to go on with her life.

An owl hooted in the distance, and a whippoorwill called to its mate, while tree-frog sopranos and bullfrog basses sang near the house. The familiar sounds enfolded her, and the gentle timbre of the natural world lulled her eyes closed as the fire warmed her body, and the music of the creaking lake house sang to her. With exhaustion taking over; she lost her grip on the bottle and drifted into sleep. In a moment, her fingers twitched, and the bottle tipped over, spilling its contents on the floor. She began to dream while the flames burned yellow and orange, consuming the wood that had given them life.

In her dream, Ellie was on a foggy path lined by family artifacts. She saw remnants of her grandmother's house from her early youth, and she could hear her boisterous cousins coming in for dinner after spending all day in the water. Warm, homemade bread, bowls of fresh vegetables, and a platter of fried chicken filled the table. There was Grandpa in his chair at one end of the dining table and Grandma at the other end, with the family gathered on sturdy benches along the sides waiting for Grandpa to say grace. When he finished praying, he smiled at Grandma as their children and grandchildren filled their plates with crispy chicken and buttery mashed potatoes. Another image of Grandma materialized: she held the chubby hands of a young cousin and kissed away tears from a plump cheek after the child had dragged a footed tray across the tabletop and left deep furrows in the smooth surface. The child's mistake had left permanent scars, but Grandma had told the child not to feel bad because she knew it was an accident.

Those were fond memories of good times before Ellie was old enough to notice her parents didn't say loving things to each other or to anyone else. There had been good times at the lake before her shameful mistakes, before Hank had died and she was alone, afraid to go on. Even in her sleep, sorrow moved through her body the way a drop of ink spreads in a glass of water. Her dream turned into a nightmare, and she was suffocating.

Her need to breathe jolted her awake. Just as her eyes flew open, she heard a sound nearby. It was the rustling of a bird—perhaps a great blue heron—spreading its wings in flight. At the same moment, a breeze crossed over her face, and an incense-like smell—smoky and exotic—permeated the air. Tears had collected along her lower lids and obscured her eyesight, but she lifted her head, blinked, and tried to clear her vision. She startled when a log in the waning fire burned in two and popped in the stillness as its middle ends flamed brighter for an instant.

Ellie's heart raced when she felt something or someone nearby, shrouded in silence. Her skin prickled, and a quivering sensation flowed in waves down her back, out to her arms and legs. Not knowing if she was still asleep or if a night animal had crept in, she was ready to bolt, but she didn't move. She was afraid that if she moved, the thing would grab her and rip her to pieces.

Moving only her eyes, she looked toward the sound and then, as nonchalantly as possible, rolled her head slowly to the left. What she saw in the adjacent chair took her breath away. She forgot about being nonchalant, and her hands flew up to cover her eyes as she sobbed uncontrollably. *Who is playing tricks? What's going on?* An overwhelming need to double-check made her lower her hands and look again at the chair next to her. She held her breath and gripped the arms of her own chair as her eyes widened.

It was impossible, but there he was—Hank. Her brother was right there beside her, close enough to touch, with his skin glowing in the firelight. He sat with his feet planted shoulder-width apart on the floor, his arms resting along the chair's arms. He looked real—*so real*—but she knew he simply couldn't be there. Hank was dead.

Unable to stop it, a flood of tears cascaded down her cheeks. Her breath became rapid and shallow even as she realized she was no longer afraid. She felt something she'd never experienced before. The firelight danced lights and darks across his open and sincere face. He looked so natural, so normal, that she could not do anything but stare at him as he looked back at her with concern in the same way he had when she was nine years old. As their eyes met, the corners of his mouth turned up.

He held her gaze for a moment, then turned his face back toward the fire. He leaned forward, rested his forearms on his knees, and interlaced his fingers. She was sure she had heard the chair creak when he moved, but she was not sure of anything else.

Hank had a luminous quality about him, and the room filled with a feeling she could only perceive as pure love. He looked at her again, and his gentle and compassionate eyes stayed on her until she blinked, at which point a wide smile spread across his face. Tiny wrinkles radiated up from the corners of his eyes.

"How ya doin', Little Sister?" he asked, his voice exactly as Ellie remembered it.

The world stopped, the same as it had when she'd ridden a roller coaster and her car had crossed over the top of a steep peak. When her car descended, she had risen off the seat, suspended for an instant beyond the pull of gravity. Now she was feeling that same sort of sensation, except this time, as she sat in front of the fire at the lake house, it was time—not gravity—that was momentarily paused.

Ellie opened her mouth to say something, but ordinary words seemed silly. She heard herself stammer, "Wh-wh-why are you here? How can this be?" She buried her face in her hands and shook her head, trying to wake up. "This has to be a dream," she moaned, her voice muffled against her palms.

She sat for a moment, waiting to wake up, but when she took her hands away to look, Hank was still there beside her, still as clear as spring water. His hair was cut high and tight, and he wore the Marines' khaki-colored service uniform. Firelight glinted off the silver first lieutenant bars on his shirt collar, and she noticed a small half-moon scar near his eye.

"Don't worry, you're awake," Hank said. "I know it's hard to believe, but I'm here. I'm here for you, El, and it doesn't matter how I got here, exactly. What matters is why I'm here." He settled back and crossed his right ankle over his left knee, resting his chin on his hand, his elbow on the arm of the chair. His eyes stayed on her face.

Chapter 22

Silence slid over them as a full moon appeared above the trees. Ellie took a deep breath and willed her eyes open for the third time. There he was—Hank—leaning back in the chair with his eyes still on her. She decided to say something to see if the vision or dream or whatever it was disappeared.

"I . . . I love that you're here," she began. "I wanted you to come home. I needed to talk to you. It's just, just . . . now that you're here, I don't know what to say." She waited for him to fade away, but instead, he smiled sympathetically and spoke to her.

"Maybe you don't have to say anything right now." He turned his head back toward the fading flame, leaned his cheek against his closed fist, and spoke in a rather distant way. "Maybe it would be best if I tell you why I'm here with you, okay?"

"Yes. I would like that," Ellie said, trying to understand what was happening. "It feels odd to talk to you. It's as if you never left. I can't believe this."

"I'm here for you, El. Do you remember how it was when we were kids? Grandma and Grandpa enjoyed every minute of their life together, and I can feel their happiness in this house."

"Uh-huh," Ellie said. She looked at Grandma and Grandpa's picture in the line of family photos on the mantel.

"Our family had good things going at first," Hank continued. "We had great times back then, but somehow we got derailed and fell completely off-track. Maybe it was pride, fight for control, or plain boredom. The reason isn't important. But the result is that Dad and Mom simply lost sight of joy. They retreated into their separate worlds and turned against each other.

"Their anger with each other took the space intended for us. I was sent away, and you were pushed away. We were the collateral damage of their personal battles." Hank went quiet, uncrossed his legs, and turned to look at his sister.

Ellie thought for a long moment before she responded. "I could never please them," she whispered. "You kept telling me I wasn't the problem, but I never believed you, even though I wanted to. I don't think I understood anything."

"I know, El. I felt so bad for you," he commiserated. "I spent so many hours wishing I could have taken you away with me."

"I did too. I wanted to get away more than anything," she said. "But at least you were home for holidays and in the summer after you were in high school and college, but it all changed when you went to Vietnam. There was so much I wanted to talk to you about—Mom's drinking, my mistakes, my baby, Dad."

"I know about those things, Ellie. And I'm sorry you felt alone," Hank said. "But the truth is that everyone walks their path alone."

"Jock Thibodeaux wrote a letter about the flood, and to be honest, I was not surprised that you helped so many men. I don't think I'll ever get over what happened at the bridge, but what about after you were swept away? How did you get here?"

"Are you sure you want to know, Ellie?" he said.

"I have to know."

Hank sighed and leaned his head back against the chair. He steepled his fingers, then rested them against his chest. "I dozed off with a bad feeling that night," he began. "It was the premonition Mom had had about me—did she tell you about it? She told me. And it turned real when Thibodeaux ran up the beach yelling about a flood.

"The sky was black. No stars. No moon. The water was muddy and savage when Thib woke me up. By the time we organized the human chain, the water was chest high and moving fast under the bridge. I tried to catch my breath, but a huge wave filled with debris swept me off my feet. I tried to grab something I could hold on to, and by some miracle, I was pushed into a place in the bank where a root stuck out. I kicked and clawed and tried to wrap my arm around that savior root. I had it, but a Judas force pulled it out of the dirt, and the water took it out of my hand.

"Somehow, I got a foothold and started fighting my way toward the gate when I caught a glimpse of Thib's face. He was hanging onto the post with one arm and reaching out for me with the other. One more push, and I would be close enough to grab his arm. I was within a finger's length of him when another wave took my feet out from under me again. I'll never forget the look on his face when I went under. The force swept me downstream toward the bridge. I was alone. On my own to save my life.

"I grabbed for something else to hang on to, but concertina wire was all I got. It cut my fingers and palms, but I held on. I heard Thib calling me, but I couldn't answer because I was chin-deep in water, fighting to get my feet back under me. But my boots were blocks of stone."

Ellie sat forward and covered her face with her hands. "Oh, Hank," she sobbed. "I'm so sorry."

Hank let her cry for a few moments before continuing, his voice soft but steady. "The wire ripped into my legs and felt like piranha in a feeding frenzy. The water grabbed my shoulders and threw me off balance. I went under again, and a force as fierce as a demon somersaulted me along the bank and slammed me against the concertina wire we'd strung out under the bridge.

"I knew I had to get out of there, and I tried to move, but one leg and the opposite shoulder were pinned, tangled in the wire under the raging water. Swells rose and tore over my face, so I held my breath and shook my head. I kicked, squirmed, and jerked, and I fought against the wire, but the water was filling up my mouth and nose.

"There was a moment when the water ebbed, giving me one last chance to get loose. I blew out so hard the water sprayed out in front of me. I took a huge gulp of air and jerked my shoulder hard. The barbs ripped my shirt and skin, but my arms were free. I reached down, grabbed my leg, and tried to pull it away from the wire, but I was starting to get weak. Then I realized what was holding me. My boot lace was twined around the barbs, and the teeth would not let go. They held tight like the devil attacking a faithless man. The lace was too tangled to untie, and I couldn't reach my K-Bar to cut it, so there was no way to free myself."

Hank sighed, looking at Ellie sadly. "I was so tired, El. Spots started to appear in front of my eyes."

As Ellie wept, Hank's voice became a whisper, "Strange what goes through your mind at a time like that. I thought about how I'd survived Con Thien's horrors and this strange, humid, sweltering country with jungles and rice paddies, living through nine months of hell. That's why I believed I could survive this. I had to survive this. This Marine wanted to go home.

"Then someone on the road must've trained a light on the gate because I caught a glimpse of the men silhouetted in the brightness as they splashed their way through to the high ground by the pagoda. I thanked God they were safe. But by then my heart was racing, and my ears were ringing. My lungs burned and felt like they were exploding. My muscles spasmed, and I knew I was running out of air. I never thought my life would end that way, Ellie, but I knew it was ending. Just then a peace came over me, my muscles eased, and I watched crystalline bubbles with tiny rainbows inside escape from my nose and rise through the water. It had turned clear and pristine like the lake." Hank and Ellie both looked out at their beloved lake as he continued.

"The water surrounded me, softly cradling my head, wrapping its velvety arms around me, and my body went limp. The thing is, Ellie, I wasn't afraid or angry or desperate. I was full of sorrow, and I grieved my life, my mission, my family. I was in darkness, but a presence stirred my soul, and a tunnel lit by red and gold rays materialized ahead of me. A glow came from an opening at the far end of it. A man, Jesus—I knew it was Him—took me through the tunnel, and I found the place I am now."

A breeze passed over them when Hank finished his story. Ellie sobbed and reached toward him. "I'm sorry, so sorry," she managed to say. She took comfort in the fact that even though his last moments were brutal, he hadn't said the words fear or pain. When her tears ebbed enough to allow her to look at him again, she saw he was content, but she was angry. Their parents had driven Hank to a career that had killed him, and her mother's rejection had left Ellie riddled with doubts and fears. What was worse, she had shamed herself by making foolish mistakes. Her story contained those words *fear* and *pain* plenty of times, but it couldn't compare to what Hank had just told her.

Hank's clear, strong voice broke the silence. "Ellie, you must get past your grief and throw off that guilt you carry around. Life is not to be feared, but to live—no matter how long or short it is. Stop blaming yourself for everything. No more fearing or avoiding the future." Hank paused. "It's okay, Ellie. I'm okay, and I'm here to tell you that you will be too."

"Jock said you were a hero," she said, sniffling. "Does that make it all worth it?"

"I'm not really a hero, and I'll tell you why," he said. "My Patti made a music lover out of me. She taught me to appreciate the classics, especially Baroque masterpieces, and now I understand life itself is baroque, like a misshapen pearl made of people and personalities that—from the human perspective—should not be put together. Think of life like music, made of ensembles and solos, counterpoint and harmony. No matter how small the parts may be, the combination of them creates the beauty of the whole melody. Life is God's concerto—a masterpiece of contrasts."

Ellie leaned her head back and closed her eyes, listening to Hank and trying to understand what he said just as she had all of her life.

"The universe is composed of contrasts," he went on. "The most insignificant of us adds to the whole of creation, and as different as we all are, each of us is important to the finished composition."

He stretched his legs toward the fire, crossed his ankles, and concluded: "People cry when they hear a four-minute cantata by Bach or when they hear one of Vivaldi's longer pieces. What I need you to understand is that no matter how short a life is—mine or your baby's—each plays an important part in God's plan. Joy is finding out what our part is . . ." His voice trailed off, and the room filled with quiet.

The fire's embers glowed red beneath the ash of burnt wood, and the frog voices began to fade. A sigh of wind rustled the oaks as limbs creaked, and the moss whispered.

"What you're saying makes me think of the fish in your aquarium," Ellie muttered thoughtfully. "There were all colors, sizes, and shapes swimming in one tank. We watched them because of the differences among them. The difference was the beauty. Having one fish, alone in the tank, didn't make sense, right?"

"That's it exactly, El. I wasn't a hero because I did not save my men alone. Going after them was a small act in contrast to what we were fighting for. I had an obligation to the welfare of the others—my Marine brothers—and that's what my actions represented. The meaning of my sacrifice was the importance of commitment, honor, and caring—even love—for my men. 'Semper Fi' meant something to me.

"What I'm saying, Ellie, is that you should let your life add to the concerto whatever it's supposed to add. I played the part I was given, and your part represents something important too."

Eyes still closed, Ellie tried to wrap her mind around Hank's words. Fear had defined her, and fear fueled the self-doubt that had bound her actions. Fear had kept her from playing her part.

"A drop of water is small and seems insignificant," he said. "But think what a *trillion* drops will do. Then think of the strength in *three* trillion drops of water. That's about the size of our lake. Think of that much water—three trillion tiny drops—going in the same direction. That's a force more powerful than we can easily imagine.

"So, here, Ellie, is the message I am here to deliver, and I hope you're ready to hear it." Hank paused and trained his eyes on her. "Find your part and play it. Fight for it. And when you stumble, you must not stop looking for it."

The room grew lighter the second Hank's last word reached her ears. Ellie was refreshed the same way she was when she burst through the water's surface among millions of tiny bubbles into the fresh, warm air and her lungs filled with oxygen after she had stayed underwater too long. Hank's words had left her alive, light, and free. Fear lost its grip and shame fell away in one piece the way a snake sheds its skin.

"Semper Fi, Little Sister," Hank whispered. "I'm right here for you."

Ellie wanted this time with Hank to last forever, but when she reached out to touch him again, her fingers found only the chair's soft fabric. Tentatively, she opened her eyes to a predawn sky and an empty chair next to her. The fire was ash and memory, so, trying to shake off disappointment and accept reality, she sat in the quiet for a moment before switching on a small lamp nearby. The light reflected off the small blue disks dotting the floor at her feet. She sank to her knees and picked up each pill, then she looked at them cradled in her palm.

"My secret way out of here," she said out loud, glancing at the family of faces on the mantel.

Her hand closed tight around the tablets, and she rose, then crossed the porch and walked across the yard toward the lake. She stepped up onto the dock's familiar weathered boards and strode out to the end, where she stood above the still water, turned to look at the house, and watched the morning sky turn cardinal red over the roof top. She faced the water again and wondered how many times she and Hank had dived off this dock, back when they were carefree and joyful. She opened her hand to look once again at the twenty pills nestled in her palm. Then, curling her fingers over them, she shifted her weight backward, raised her arm, and cocked it high above her shoulder. Just as Hank had taught her, she reared back on one leg and raised the opposite one in front.

"Get your body behind you if you want to throw far," he had said.

Like a Big-League pitcher, she brought her foot down hard, swung her weight toward the lake, and threw her arm forward. The pills flew far out into the placid water and made faint *plunk-a-plunk* sounds as they hit the water one by one and disappeared, leaving nothing but small concentric circles on the surface. She waited until the ripples dissipated and the surface smoothed out again, then headed toward the house.

Back inside, the faint, smoky aroma of Hank's visit lingered, and she knew what she had to do, no matter how hard it was. Her burden was gone, and she felt unbound. The sun peeked over the house and sent golden rays into a cloudless pink and red sky. It promised to be a glorious day.

Ellie's drive back to town was different from the previous day's ride out to the lake. She was not running away; she was running *to* something. She went to the hospital first and pushed open the heavy door into the lobby. The antiseptic hospital smell hit her, and that smell brought fear that tried to shake her resolve. She stepped to a window overlooking the landscaped entrance where an older woman sat smoking a cigarette on a bench by the door. Ellie let Hank's words echo through her mind: she had to find her part, however small it was.

After a moment, she turned, walked to Dad's glass-enclosed room, and dared to look in. She stopped short and her eyes filled with tears. Dad was sitting up in bed with Mira still in the chair next to him. Ellie pushed open the door and started toward him, and her movement caught his eye. Even though he was pale and drawn, he reached out to her. Mira looked up and beamed when she saw Ellie.

"Things are looking better for me," Dad said, his voice weak and raspy.

"I'm so thankful, Dad," Ellie said as she took his hand and sat down in the chair she'd vacated the day before. After only a few moments, he drifted off to sleep. She stayed by him until the nurses came to tend to him, and Mira suggested they both go home and relax.

"Bes' we leave him to rest fo' a bit. That'll hep him heal," she said on their way down the hall. "Lord, chil'. . . I wondered what happened to you last night. Guess I didn't need to worry, 'cause you look fine. Rested or somethin'."

"I went out to the lake. You won't believe what happened. It was a miracle and I want to tell you all about it, but you look tired, and I need a shower, so we'll talk later—okay?"

They stopped in the lobby, and Mira took her hand. "You bet," she said. "Oh, and Susan called and tol' me she needs to talk to you. Ya mama tol' her about the heart attack, so Susan got hol' a me here. She said she had gone to visit ya mama a couple a times, 'n' she wants to tell ya 'bout them visits."

"I'll get in touch with her," Ellie said. She was quiet for a moment, then said, "I don't want you or Dad to worry, because we're gonna help Mom."

"I know you will, Ellie. You a fine person," Mira said. "You're jus' like Hank." She kissed her white baby on the cheek before they hugged and left the hospital.

Ellie went back to the apartment and threw open the windows. Cool, fresh air filled the room, and she wrapped herself in a throw blanket. She sat on the couch to listen to Vivaldi and Albinoni for a long time.

The next day, Ellie went to her mother's house. Her fears tried to stop her, but she ignored them, determined to make sure her mother knew she wasn't alone, the same way Hank had reassured her. Ellie climbed up the front steps, paused, then pushed open the door. She went to the dark family room and found her mother in her usual place, in her usual condition.

"Hello, Mom," Ellie said, her voice soft and shy. She took a seat in the side chair where she had sat the day Hank announced he was going to Vietnam.

"El'nor. What're you doing here?" Mom's voice was harsh and unwelcoming.

"I wanted to stop by and say hey and let you know that Dad is doing better."

"Oh, well. That's nice." Mom's cold tone did not match her warm words.

"Do you plan to go see him?" Ellie asked.

"Oh, so you're checking on me, huh?" Mom's words exploded and spewed bitterness. She picked up her drink and sipped, eyeing Ellie over the rim of the crystal tumbler.

"No, Mom, I'm not doing that. I wanted to . . . to . . . make sure you were okay. That's all." Ellie looked down and fidgeted with her hands.

"Don't you worry about me, li'l lady," Mom said.

"Well, I wanted you to know I care about you," Ellie said, trying to sound confident.

"You seem to thin' I need some kinda help. You have no idea what it's like living here or the way it is for me." A frown creased her face, and a sneer formed on her lips.

"No, I can't know exactly what you feel, Mom, but I believe I do have an idea," Ellie replied, her eyes steadily on her mother.

"There you go again. Soundin' like you know it all. Well, you don't. Your brother's gone, your father's impossible to talk to, 'n' you're na-ive and self-righteous about everything."

"Well, I'm sorry you feel that way, Mom. And believe it or not, Hank is still here with us, in our hearts. I know that for a fact. And I know he wants you to go on and try to find happiness. He doesn't want you to be angry." Ellie braced herself as her mother cleared her throat.

"El'nor, I know you must mean well"—Mom's voice softened—"but I don't want to talk about this. I'm sorry, Ellie, but I never knew what to do with you. I never knew what to say to you. I wasn't a good mother, so it's better if you leave me alone. Just leave me alone."

No wonder Mom was hard, Ellie thought. *What an awful burden she's been carrying!* Tears blurred her vision until Hank's words came back to her, so she stood up and looked down at her mother.

"Okay, Mom. I'll leave, but please remember you can call me anytime. I'll be here when you need me." Ellie quietly let herself out the front door and fought to stay focused on Hank's message. She had to stay on the right track, do what she thought best, and not let Mom's words discourage her. If she did that, it might be possible to kindle a relationship with her mother in the future—but not quite yet.

"Your mom's beginning to let me get a little closer," Susan said when Ellie called her the next day. "She says she doesn't have a drinking problem, but that's what we all say until we realize we do have a problem. Good thing we recovering alcoholics aren't easily put off when we hear that."

"Thanks for sticking with her, Susan," Ellie said. "Dad appreciates it too. I simply can't help her right now."

"No problem. Been there myself. I'm working on convincing her to go to an AA meeting with me. I'll find one that's convenient for her, and we'll go together. I don't mind driving up from St. Augustine. I'll keep you posted on how that goes. But for now, she's stuck in anger and grief."

"I guess so," Ellie said.

"El, I want you to remember that when she says awful things to you, it's the alcohol speaking. Do not take anything she says personally." Susan's voice broke as she continued. "She's in a tough place, and she has to leave there to learn to live with her grief. She has a lot of anger to get rid of, and that will be hard. But nothing's impossible. We just have to let go and let God."

"She doesn't want me around and won't listen to Dad or me," Ellie said and paused, then continued. "Mira said Mom told you my dad had a heart attack, so at least she remembers I told her that. He's still hospitalized, but it looks like he's getting better—thank God. He gave me a scare. I don't know when or if Mom will go see him."

"Oh, I'm glad to hear he's doing better," Susan said. "I lit a candle for him when I found out he was ill. I'll try to see him next time I'm in town."

"I'm sure he'd love to see you, but he'll be in ICU for a bit longer, and they only allow family. I'll let you know when he can have more visitors. He and I had a wonderful talk when I was still in the hospital, and we've been working on our relationship." Ellie said. "By the way, what do I call you? Sister what?" Ellie asked.

"Nothing different yet. Still just Susan—your friend. When it's time, I will be Sister Susan Rita."

"Oh, I see, but why the Rita part?"

"That's after Saint Rita of Cascia—there's an Italian basilica named after her. She's the Saint of the Impossible because her mission was devoted to bringing forgiveness and reconciliation to people in impossible relationships. She did miraculous things to bring peace to families. I'm sure you get the significance of my name choice!"

"I sure do," Ellie smiled. "I have something pretty miraculous to tell you about, too, but it needs to be face to face, so let's wait until we have lots of time." After chatting a few minutes more, Ellie hung up and smiled, poured a glass of wine, and put on Telemann's classics. She turned up the stereo and let his melody and countermelodies fill the room and her heart with beautiful sounds that should not go together.

She thought about Hank, miracles, and her future. *What should my next step be?* It took a while, but the cogs eventually dropped into place, and she picked up the phone.

Chapter 23

Ellie walked into Eden's Beauty and found the whole place newly painted, cheery, and alive with the holiday spirit. Even the plants seemed to pick up the vibe and respond with deeper greens and brighter colors, their leaves and blossoms stretching toward the sun that streamed through the front window.

When he saw her, Tommy put down a handful of red carnations and rushed over to enfold her in a hug. The beaded leather tassels on his jacket sleeves rattled when he wrapped his arms around her, and he radiated the scent of patchouli and roses. His hair—longer than she remembered—was tamed by a multicolored headband, and he sported a bushy mustache.

"Oh, my gosh, girl! I haven't seen you in an age," he said. "I'm so glad you called!"

"I was happy you agreed to see me," she said, her cheek against his thin chest. He released her and stood back to study her at arms' length.

"You look good," he said, then dropped his arms. "Have you heard from Patti? There was a write-up in Florida Florist Review about a huge convention she did in Miami that created quite a splash. She's making a name for herself." True to form, Tommy didn't wait for a response before pivoting to another topic. "And what about you? Are you doing okay?"

"I feel good, and I'm getting along. But I do miss Patti. I heard from her when I was in the hospital, but that was it." Ellie paused for a moment before adding, "I'm not surprised, though, because she told me it would be too hard for her to stay in touch with our family."

A cloud passed over Tommy's face, but he shook it off and moved toward his desk. "Come over here—I have a plan to show you." Ellie followed in his wake and inhaled the smell of fresh flowers permeating the air.

He picked up his calendar, showed it to Ellie, and said, "Look! This Christmas and New Year's season is the busiest we've ever had, so I need you to come back to work. Are you up for that?"

"Yes, I'd love to help," she said softly, even though her heart soared, and she wanted to jump for joy.

"The pay will be pretty good, and as a matter of fact, there's a high-profile party coming up, and I want everything to be perfect. Think you can handle it?" He handed her a thick notebook. "It's a huge buffet dinner to benefit a charity organization, and its director knows that having a fundraiser on December 23rd is a bit risky. He told me that's why he wants us to manage the evening, and that's why I agreed to do it. I do love a challenge! We only have weeks to get it together, so I'll give you more details in the morning. Then you can go look at the venue." Ellie barely had time to say thank you before he was called away by a floral designer, but he turned back to Ellie and said, "That desk in the corner is all yours. Enjoy!"

After looking around the place, Ellie sat down in her designated chair and pulled out her calendar to circle the date of the event. She walked to the door, and like old friends at a reunion, the potted plants and cut flowers in buckets reached out to touch her as she brushed by. She was struck by a sense of serenity, and something inside her said this was a beginning—a trailhead complete with an arrow pointing toward good fortune.

Susan called a week later and announced, "Your mom and I went to an AA meeting. She was withdrawn and didn't want to talk with any-one, so we sat on the back row and listened. I wasn't surprised when she wanted to go home right after the meeting ended. She told me the people were a bunch of losers, and she wasn't about to spill her guts to strangers." Susan's voice faltered on the last word.

"Gosh, that was rough," Ellie said and asked herself if her mother's wounds would ever heal enough so she didn't just lash out at everyone.

"Yes, it was disappointing," Susan agreed, "but alcoholics like us can see right through her because we've been there! Your mother has to admit she is an alcoholic before she can get better, but she's not ready to confess it yet. I'll keep talking to her, El. I don't give up easily."

After a moment, Susan added, "She has to hit rock bottom—be in the gutter—and then she has to take the first step and admit she has no control over alcohol. That first step was the hardest for me, but the second—acknowledging a higher power that leads us to sanity—wasn't a problem. I've always been a believer, but up until that point, I don't think I ever understood the depth of God's love."

"Well, I hope she gets help somewhere soon," Ellie said, "because right now it's miserable for Dad and me."

"Okay, kiddo, you brought it up, so I have to tell you this is not only your mom's problem. It's is a family disease, which means you and your dad are part of it, so you both need to admit that."

"Bu-but what did I do to cause this?" Ellie murmured and sank into the chair with her head in her hand. She felt the panther's acrid breath for the first time since Hank had visited her at the lake. All her life, she had tried to be good and do what Mom told her, but her mother had always rejected her and still did, even now that Hank was gone and she was the only child Mom had left.

"I didn't say you *caused* it. I said you are *part* of it," Susan said softly. "Women with alcoholic mothers have all kinds of trust and confidence problems, so, if you want to change that, you need to look into your heart of hearts, Ellie, and understand the old tapes you've got playing in your head." Susan paused then continued. "There's a family group called Al-Anon that has weekly meetings to help people like you—people who've lived with an alcoholic they love. You can call your church to find out about the meetings, or I'll check with some of my friends to find a list of meeting places for you."

"Hank said he wanted to help her. He said he wanted to help me."

"Yes, and if he were here, he would say what I'm saying. Find out about yourself, and with God's grace, you'll find your purpose. And you do have a purpose, my friend," Susan said confidently.

"I thought I'd found that in my work at Eden's Beauty." Ellie's voice was weak and confused.

"But are you doing that work for the right reason, Ellie? Is it for yourself, because it's something you want to do, or are you doing it because you want to please other people? I want to hear you say you are doing what Ellie—the person I love and the person God loves—wants to do. It's okay to please yourself. You don't have to prove yourself worthy to anyone else." Susan's tone left no room for argument.

Ellie was nauseated and begged off the phone, but she promised to call back soon. She thought she had conquered her doubts—her demons—but Susan's questions had opened new territory that Ellie didn't want to enter. *Have I made any progress at all?* The thought rocked her, and she wondered if she simply did things to make other people happy, to be a good girl like her mother wanted her to be. Ellie enjoyed her job, but was there something more? *Do I need to look deeper? Can I look deeper?* Hank had told her to fight for her part and not give up the search when she stumbled. Ellie guessed he'd been talking about times like these, so she ignored her fears and her sick stomach and reached for the phone book.

Christmas rolled by two days after the charity dinner raised a great deal of money, and the new year looked bright with plenty of events for Ellie to manage. Dad was steadily gaining strength, and he had begun going with Ellie to Al-Anon meetings. As a result, their father-daughter talks had been frequent and intense, so their relationship was improving every day.

One day in late January, Dad brought sandwiches to the place where Ellie was supervising the setup of a large ballroom for an upcoming benefit. They settled on a bench along the wall and ignored the pandemonium of people coming and going, delivering items, setting up tables, or laying out linens and dinnerware. The kitchen staff contributed their own commotion in the kitchen.

Dad handed her a chicken salad sandwich, winked, and said he knew her type—she forgot to eat when she was working.

"I'm tired, El," he said above the din. "I've decided it's best to slow down a bit, so I'm going to cut back my medical practice."

"You've had enough sleepless nights helping sick people," she said with a grin. "As far as I'm concerned, you've earned the right to go easy.

"I will take it easy, but that means Mira's life will change, too," he said. "She's worked for me for a long time, and the office is her life."

"I hadn't thought about that," Ellie mused. "But surely she needs a rest too."

"She and I have talked about my plans several times," he said, "and she's all for them. She just wants us to be happy. She stayed here in town because of us even though she has a sister in south Georgia." Ellie noted the sadness in his voice, but she wasn't sure how to respond. The moment passed, he seemed pensive, and then he changed the subject. "This place looks beautiful! You're doing such a grand job!"

"Thanks, Dad. I love what I do, but I worry about disappointing you or Mom." She watched him as she continued. "I don't intend to get a college degree, and you may never have grandchildren, either. I'm sorry because I know you wanted them." She looked at her half-eaten sandwich and waited.

"Do you remember Dr. Vaughn?" he asked. "From the ER after your accident? She told me she went to a charity affair that you—Eden's Beauty—put together, and she couldn't say enough about how magnificent it was. I knew you made it happen the minute she described it to me. So let's not worry about college or grandkids. You're doing good things, and I'm proud of you, El."

"Thanks, Dad, I appreciate that," she said and touched his hand. She was a young woman, but it felt good to hear Daddy say he was proud of her.

The next few months marched by in a parade of successes. Tommy was a big-hearted yet shrewd businessman who endlessly praised her ability to plan and bring together the many moving parts to create a successful event. Her practicality brought to life his vision, and before long, the shop's specialty became events that raised money for causes of the heart. Over time, Ellie grew familiar with every large and small charity organization in the area.

"You and I are 'purpose' meeting 'creativity,'" Tommy declared one day when they stood munching on snacks in the middle of a cavernous banquet hall echoing with pre-event hustle-bustle.

"I feel that way, too." Ellie had to raise her voice over the noise. A smile crept over her lips as she thought of the first time she saw Patti and Tommy in the middle of a different chaotic room. Now Ellie was the one orchestrating the delightful chaos.

Even though bringing about synergy was demanding, Ellie felt energized in the hours before an event. Her favorite time was when everything was in place with the tables set just so with Eden's Beauty floral creations in place. To Ellie, that's when the metamorphosis occurred. The flowers were the crowning touch that transformed ordinary spaces into whimsical, dreamy places, places where people forgot reality's sharp edges for a time, places where they shed their outer shells and professional facades to reveal generous or giving—even tender—natures. The magic of an evening satisfied Ellie as she had never imagined it could.

One night while she was at home double-checking details of an upcoming event, a thought came to her in the pre-midnight quiet. She was curled up on the orange couch with a glass of wine when she realized that her job was more important than simply having the right color flower in the right place. The thought struck her with enough force to make her drop her pen and lean back against the soft fabric. She was a part of making something out of nothing and that, in turn, became a part of something bigger, and the results of her part touched people far away from her—people she would never see. The impact of her work was like the wavelets spreading across the water after Hank cannonballed into the lake each first day of summer. The power of the ripples she made overwhelmed her—but humbled and gratified her at the same time.

Through her work, she was fighting for the poor, aiding the helpless, comforting mistreated children or animals, and bringing joy to a deserving person. Her part of those efforts was nothing more than a drop of water, but when combined with other drops, her drop gave hope to people she would never know in person. She understood now that it was her part in God's concerto, and her work at Eden's Beauty wasn't simply a job. Her work was the part she wanted to play in life's symphony.

Dad moved out of his house in the spring. "I'm afraid I'll make a deadly mistake and hurt a patient if I don't get out from under the weight of your mother's grief and anger," he told Ellie. "Even though I cut back on hours, I'm still a surgeon, and the stress at home has simply become unbearable."

The strain was obvious in his eyes, but his voice was steady as he continued. "I don't want to hurt your mother, but I can't be around her any longer. I remember the beautiful woman I married. She was so full of fun and energy, but she's different now. I love her, but I can't live with her. I'm sorry, Ellie." Dad had said the words as tears formed in his eyes. "We both loved Hank so much, but she has to grieve in her own way, and I need to honor his legacy in my own way."

"I understand, Dad," Ellie said, and hugged him.

After that, Ellie watched her mother sink deeper into the gutter every day. Things got so bad Ellie had to tell her mother she was not going to visit anymore. "Maybe I can come back when you're sober," she had said because she simply couldn't watch while Mom destroyed herself. The decision was validated when Mom's response was to tell Ellie to leave and not come back until she apologized.

Mira came to Eden's Beauty a month after Dad settled into his own apartment. Ellie took a break and went outside to talk with her, the person who had been by her side—at least in spirit—since she was born.

"Yo' daddy's slowing down now, and I'm glad about that," Mira began. "He needs the rest, but I know he's sad that he can't stay with yo' mama. I hope you understand that, baby." Mira touched Ellie's arm.

"Yes, Mira, I do now," Ellie said. "It's time I gave up trying to make them happy."

"Tha's right. You can't carry that burden." Mira kept her eyes steady on Ellie's. "I'm tired, too, baby. And I'm old. I needs to go to my sister's in Georgia where I have hep. But I wanted to tell you in person."

"Oh, Mira, I can help you!" Ellie cried as she reached out to her beloved nanny.

"I knew you'd say that, but no. You is a sweet chil' same as always. You doin' fine now on yo' own. You and yo' daddy're fine, too. You'll never know how thankful I am for that. I'm so proud a you, Ellie." Mira's face was soft and loving, then her eyes filled with tears. "I don't want you to stop doing what you're doin'. Besides, my sister needs me and I need her. So it's time to go."

Ellie knew from Mira's voice that no amount of talk would change her mind.

"I have all the arrangemen's made. The young men from my church are gonna pack me up and drive me to Georgia." Mira gave Ellie her new address and phone number and said she'd be sure and come by before she left.

Ellie stood on the sidewalk and waved as Mira got in a car driven by a younger woman, who pulled away and drove out of sight. Tommy met Ellie at the door and let her cry against his bony shoulder. After a moment, he reached his arm around her shoulder and guided her back into Eden's Beauty.

A few days after Mira came to see Ellie, Susan delivered surprising news on the phone: "Maybe the fact that you refused to be around your mother pushed her to admit she had a problem," Susan said with excitement, "but, for whatever reason, she called me and asked me to help her find a treatment place!"

By the beginning of summer, Susan said Mom was adjusting to living alone and being sober, but Ellie knew she had to face the fact that, even though her parents loved each other, they could not live together; they were just too toxic for one another, as Hank had said. Susan said Mom was even allowing a Gold Star mother to visit, and they were slowly getting to know each other. Ellie was growing hopeful about her mother's future.

"Mom will need other Gold Star mothers to help through the years to come," she told Susan. "The war is more unpopular than ever, and this is the worst year for casualties since the beginning. I've heard that 1968 is shaping up to be a turning point, and, more and more people say the war is unwinnable."

Shortly after that day, Ellie quit reading newspapers because the burden of grief and anger was unbearable when hostile crowds maligned sons, brothers, grandsons, or husbands who had made the ultimate sacrifice. Those who lived to come home from Vietnam were treated just as poorly. These things made life even harder for families like Ellie's, so she grew uneasy as September 18 approached, but there was nothing she could do to make the grim anniversary easier for her parents.

Chapter 24

On the anniversary of Hank's death, Ellie did her best to console her parents, then met Susan—now Sister Susan Rita, working toward a degree in counseling—who came over from St. Augustine to spend the day with Ellie. They laid flowers on Hank's grave, then sat on a little stone bench under a tree nearby, sharing memories for hours. It was a hard day, but Susan's presence brought peace and calm to Ellie, especially after the tearful, but short conversations with her parents.

"Eden's Beauty is my refuge, but dating is my problem," Ellie said later over dinner. Her mood had lightened a bit, so she told Susan about a couple of disastrous dates and declared that she was not cut out for even casual relationships.

"Did you ever think it's not you that's the problem, but the men you pick, the ones you find attractive, that create the problems?" Susan asked, leveling her intent eyes on her friend.

"Ummm, never thought of it that way," Ellie said. "But how do I change that?"

"First, believe you're worthwhile," Susan replied. "Then, be with someone who feels the same. Like Hank said, you need to find your essence that's buried under years of debris left by others defining who you are. It's your turn now. You did it with your career. Now it's time to do it with your personal life."

"Why must that always be so hard?" Ellie put her elbows on the table and flopped her chin into her hands. "I'm afraid having to prove myself worthy will always be a part of me. Maybe it would be easier for me to just stay single."

"Don't look so dejected, El," Susan said and reached across to squeeze Ellie's hand. "Don't let the childhood scars of self-doubt and fear trip you up. Trust me—people don't like other people because they're perfect. There's been only one sinless—perfect—person ever who walked the earth, and you can't be Him. People will like you because of who you are, my sweet, dear friend! Don't forget that, because you never know what's around the corner!"

October had come and gone when Tommy called Ellie into his office and gestured to the wicker armchair next to his cluttered desk where he had laid out event organization plans. He called it his "disorganized organization" strategy.

"What's up?" Ellie asked and sat back with her pen and pad ready. "Is there another big party or event coming up? Was there something wrong with an order?"

Tommy studied her for a moment. "No, it's nothing to do with events, unless you call my health an event." He looked her in the eye and sighed. "I'm going to step aside for a while—I don't know how long—and you're the only person I trust to run the place while I'm away."

Ellie felt her mouth drop and her eyes widen. "W-what?!" She stared at him. "Why are you leaving? Are you okay?"

"I know you. When I tell you this, you're going to worry, so I'm asking you, please, don't get hung up on what I'm about to tell you. Promise?" He sat forward and folded his hands on the desk with his eyes on hers.

"Uh, I'll try," she said, hoping she sounded convincing.

"I had an X-ray last week, and my doctor found suspicious spots on my lung," Tommy said. "I don't smoke cigarettes, but both my parents did, so I was engulfed by smoke all my life. The doctor wants to do some tests, and the fact is, I've not felt good for a while, so it's time to find out why."

Ellie fought to fulfill her promise. "Uh, okay. And you want me to run Eden's Beauty while you are gone, right?"

"You got it. You're going to run everything from flowers to ballroom layouts to caterers to event registrations. Everything!" he said, sitting back.

"Take over for you. Right?" Her voice said the words, but her mind whirled. "You want me to run the place."

"Yep. That's what I said!" He grinned at her. "How many times are you going to say that?"

"Oh! Uh . . . well, I . . ." She cleared her throat and tried again. "I . . . uh . . . wondered when you were going to . . . I mean how long are you going to be here to teach me?" She looked down and squeezed her eyes shut.

"Teach you? What's to teach? You know most things already," he said. "But I'll be here another week at least."

"I . . . uh . . . I guess I can do it," she said and looked up, but Tommy was already back at work organizing the disorganization atop his desk and muttering to himself.

Tommy's matter-of-fact approach helped Ellie veer away from the pit of self-doubt. The first thing they did was set a plan for her transition to management, so she gained confidence. By the time Tommy was gone, she felt good about being in charge for a while. After all, it was only temporary. But after a month, Tommy came in to tell her he had been diagnosed with a fast-growing form of lung cancer, and he would not be returning to work. He hugged her and said he would be fine, but, to her surprise, he also said he didn't think he'd ever want to come back to work, even if the cancer treatments were a complete success. He asked if she wanted to make things permanent and buy Eden's Beauty from him.

With the help of a loan from her dad, Ellie bought Eden's Beauty, and three years passed in a blur of learning to run a business while meeting endless deadlines. Her specialty remained causes of the heart, and business was so good that when the office space next door became available, she expanded the shop to include unique gifts and hired another designer and a part-time assistant. But she remained the one in charge of the conventions and benefits she loved so much.

After a hard stint in rehab and years of follow-up therapy, Mom had finally overcome the grip of alcohol and confronted the pain that had led her to it. At this point, she and Dad were still living separate lives, but they had at least developed a workable relationship that was cordial, if still tainted by shared loss. This was a great relief to Ellie, who was finally able to spend time with either of her parents without the warning growl of the panther making her stomach churn.

Late one afternoon, she rushed home from the banquet hall to put on her favorite midnight-blue sheath and crystal beads for the evening's events. "Yup, Ellie girl," she said to herself in the mirror as she finished her makeup, "Hank said you would be okay when you found your path, and now you are!" She took one last look and turned away from the mirror. She slipped on her heels, grabbed her briefcase, then headed for the front door because she needed to hurry, or people would arrive before she got back to the venue.

She dashed out the door and across the wide, open porch running the width of the Craftsman house she—along with Dad's cosignature—had purchased eleven months before. The bungalow was clapboard painted gray, with a red front door and white wooden railing on the porch anchored by substantial, square columns. She had fallen in love with the house partly because of the yard, where a large oak tree spread its mossy arms to shade the front walk and porch steps, while a magnolia towered above the rooftop in the back yard. She did not think it a happenstance that she found the house for sale in September—the month her life had changed forever nearly five years earlier.

She climbed in her car and glanced through the windshield at the house in front of her. It was her house, bathed in the afternoon sunlight. She leaned back and sighed, remembering that she had not been afraid to sign her name and commit to the mortgage because buying the bungalow was what she wanted to do. There was no emotional shutting down or self-blame and no fear of being alone or that she might not be able to take care of it—because it was hers. She had her own porch where she could sit and collect her thoughts. She even had a new thinking tree of her very own! She was home, and she had no doubt that Hank would approve.

Ellie put the key in the ignition, and when the car roared to life, her thoughts turned to the evening ahead. She wanted it to be perfect because the gala was launching a newly created home for single, pregnant young women, and the evening included recognition of community volunteers who were instrumental in getting the home started. This gala was especially significant because it honored one of the board members in charge of education for the residents: Sr. Susan Rita. As it happened, the gala was at The Seminole—the same place she had first helped Patti and Tommy years before, and everything there was the same, except she was a different person walking under the stone entryway.

Inside, she stood near the registration table by the entrance to the ballroom and focused on the final touches, while her assistant checked in the guests. She ran her finger down her list of details and crossed off the ones that didn't need her attention anymore. Microphone working—check. Caterer all set up—check. Flowers looking stupendous—check.

Susan and the others at their table and comfortable—check. Ellie was double-checking the registration forms when a voice interrupted her thoughts.

"You must be the person in charge," said a voice with the deep, rich timbre of a temple gong.

Ellie nearly dropped her pen, then looked up to find herself lost in a pair of deep azure eyes, fringed by thick, dark lashes set in the face of a man she had never seen before.

His skin was the color of creamed coffee, and a hint of five-o'clock shadow smudged his strong jaw, while full lips heightened his dramatic, European look. His shiny brown hair was wavy and tousled, but somehow he managed to look stylish and put-together. Custom-cut trousers and a dress shirt didn't hide the lean, well-proportioned body that emitted masculinity like steam rolling off an athlete on a cool day. A bit nonplussed, she jerked her eyes back to her list and tried to concentrate on her work before answering.

"Oh, well, I don't know how the recognition presentation will go, so I'm not completely in charge," she said, "but I do know enough to be confident that this will be a grand evening!" She looked up and attempted to appear composed.

"Good to hear! I'm Azai." He pronounced it "as I," and even though she kept looking through the registrations, he continued, friendly and relaxed. "And I'm the guy who will make the presentation. Plus, I have to manage the unmanageable tonight."

"Unmanageable? What is unmanageable?" she asked as alarm bells went off in her head.

She had only heard his name mentioned, so she didn't understand why she felt as if she knew him already. An awkward moment went by as she tried to regain her bearings, and Azai, taller than she, tilted his head and kept his eyes on her.

"Unmanageable people," he said. "Honoring volunteers is a bit like herding barn sparrows. They move fast, but you don't know where they're going. Except for Sr. Susan Rita, most of our honorees are self-made, wealthy, and used to following their own star, and it's my job to know which ones want credit for their good works and which ones work to benefit others instead of gaining attention.

"I have to know who wants what credit tonight," he continued. "Have to give the right person the right amount of celebrity. I walk a thin line because a misstep can be disastrous to our support base."

As Ellie listened, she felt herself smiling, inside and out. "Oh, I see what you mean," she said. "That's your balancing act! Don't worry—I scheduled a roving photographer and a reporter from the *Tribune*. You'll have to brief them on whose ego needs to be in newspaper pictures and who wants to stay out of the limelight and behind the potted palms."

"Ah, thanks so much," he said, thrusting his hand toward her. "Azai MacAlpin. You must be Ellie. You've communicated with my assistant, who told me you were exceptional with details. Happy to meet you."

"Yes. Ellie Dennis," she said and shook his hand firmly and professionally, the way Patti had taught her. "Glad to meet you too. You have an unusual name that I'll bet most people don't forget." The words slipped out before Ellie could stop them. *Did I overstep? Was that too personal?* Oh, well. Too late. She had said it.

"Well, yes, thanks to my Hebrew and Scottish-Gaelic ancestors. I have a family that is proud of its heritage on both sides," he said as he smiled and leaned against the table. He and Ellie talked until someone interrupted with a question, at which point he held up a finger to the person, then turned to Ellie.

"I don't want to lose track of you, Ellie Dennis," he said. "I've enjoyed talking with you, and I'd like to talk some more. Can we have a drink later?"

"Yes, that would be fine," she said and hoped her surprise didn't show. "I usually stick around for the whole evening in case something happens that needs fixing, so you can find me afterward." She watched Azai walk away and couldn't keep herself from looking forward to the end of the evening.

After the gala was over, Ellie hugged Susan goodbye and was lingering by the buffet table littered with bread baskets and casserole dishes when Azai came across the shiny wood floor. She heard his shoes click and looked up from the collection of centerpieces, while the servers removed dirty dishes and bundled up tablecloths around the room.

"What happens to those gorgeous flowers now?" he asked as he touched one of the roses.

"Tomorrow's Sunday, so we'll take them to nursing homes or the hospital for people who don't have families," Ellie said. "My former boss started doing that years ago, so it's sort of a tradition."

"Are you too tired to get a drink with me?" Azai asked.

"No, I'm wide awake. Takes me awhile to come down after something like this. By the way, what did you think of the evening?"

"Wonderful—being able to talk with you, I mean," he said. "As for the gala, it was fantastic."

Even though the bartender was gone, the bar that had served the guests was still set up, so Azai stepped behind it and fixed drinks for himself and Ellie. Then, drinks in hand, they went to the lobby, chose a cozy sitting area under a huge palm, and talked through the night. The conversation was easy, and Ellie found herself telling him about Hank and Patti and the college days when she had met Susan. He told her about his childhood growing up in a large, loud, happy family.

"That's hard for me to imagine," Ellie said. "Mine was the exact opposite, except for Hank because he made things okay. I'll tell you about my growing-up years someday, but I have to know you better."

"I'm looking forward to that," Azai said with a grin.

The sun was just about to rise above the horizon as they walked to their cars. He asked if would be okay to call her, and she gave him her phone number. She drove home, kicked off her shoes and changed into her robe before making a cup of coffee. She took it out to her porch, settled in the swing, and sipped her brew while the sky grew bright with sunrise colors.

Thoughts rushed through her mind like minnows schooling in the cool water under the dock at the lake. Azai had listened to her and nodded while she talked, but she wondered what he would do if she told him everything about her family's problems, her baby, and the pills. *What would he think if I told him about Hank's appearance at the lake house?*

"What does that matter?" she said to her new thinking tree by the sidewalk as sunbeams outlined its branches, turning it golden. "My life is what it is. I am who I am. God made me who I am."

When she looked up, she was not surprised to see Hank sitting in one of the wicker chairs across from her. He smiled, looking at her with his head cocked a little to the left in that particular way of his. She noticed laugh lines radiating out from the corners of his eyes as his smile broadened and lit up his face. His forest green eyes looked deep into her soul, bringing the same warmth and peace to her every time she saw him. They didn't need to say anything to each other because the message was clear, but when it was time, they always spoke aloud the words that crystalized their lives together.

"Semper Fi, Little Sister," he said as an orange sun sent rays of light into the sky.

Ellie watched a bright red cardinal take wing from a branch high in her tree. "Semper Fi, Big Brother," she whispered.

1LT Dennis Babers, USMC

1Lt Dennis Babers pictured on the sandy bank of the Cam Lo River after leaving the horrors of the Con Thien battles. This picture was taken between September 11, 1967, and September 17, 1967, the few days before the flood when he was able to relax and recoup with his men by the bridge. Even though surrounded by warfare, destruction, and loss, he looks at peace in this photograph.

Life is like a river carving its course in the landscape,
relentlessly finding new paths; finding nothing to deny its force.

—cbs

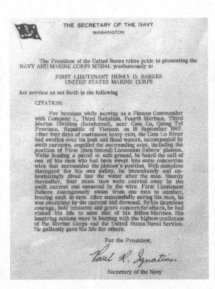

ACKNOWLEDGEMENTS

This story is from my heart. It took years to unlock the places I'd stored it for safe-keeping, but I'm thankful that I finally did. It is a work of fiction except for Hank's letters, which are actual letters from my brother, 1 Lt. Dennis Babers, USMC. Some of the book's scenes are my recollections of what happened to me (the two Marines coming to tell Ellie about Hank's death, for instance), but I created most of the narrative. I never had a friend like Susan, but I think she, like Ellie, typifies a young female searching for self and purpose in the 1960s.

The story first came to life when I met the men who served with Dennis in Vietnam. Three of them were at the Cam Lo bridge when he drowned during the flood. I talked and cried with them when I attended the 2007 Third Battalion Fourth Marine Association Reunion, where they told me about my brother's heroism during the Cam Lo bridge flood. Thank you to Don Matthews, Bob Siems, and Carlos Saenz for your transparency as you gave me the details surrounding Dennis's death. "The flood was a fluke," they said. "No one expected it." Bob told me the last thing my brother said to him as the floodwaters rose was, "I'll find us a way to get out of here." I treasure the brass crucifix that Don restored after finding it in Phu An's bombed-out church. I know it was hard for all of you to remember and re-live that time.

Thank you, too, to Michael Madden for your gracious hospitality, for making me feel welcome and a part of Lima Company's Gold Star Families. I learned what the Marine Corps brotherhood and Semper Fidelis meant when I heard all of you talk about Vietnam.

There is no adequate way to express my gratitude to my friend and mentor, KB Laugheed (*The Spirit Keeper* and *The Gift of the Seer*), who was always honest, straight-forward, and fair in her critiques, guidance, and enthusiasm. Thank you, KB, for holding me accountable and making me disciplined through a long process. You made me know I could write this book. Everyone needs a friend like you!

I am grateful to Lindsay Heider Diamond, my cover designer, who captured the novel's theme and understood its emotion from the very start of our collaboration. My appreciation to editors Cindy Marsch, Nita Robinson, and Alison Imbriaco for helping me polish and refine my storytelling. I owe a debt of gratitude to Patricia Moss and Sharen Ritchie for proofreading. The book is better for your help.

Another thank you goes to my critique group in Indianapolis. Arlene Barker, Mariah Julio, Gail Mehlan, and Andrea Dunn waited a long time to read this book in its entirety. Still, they never stopped encouraging and inspiring me to continue no matter how long it took to get it right.

Love and gratitude to my own family: my husband, Steve, who stuck with me, never complaining about late or cold meals, household projects put on hold, or dust bunnies in every corner of the house. And to my children, Dennis Feaster and Andrea Husiden, who never failed to encourage me even as they cared for their own families. Your Uncle Dennis would be proud of you.

Finally, I need to acknowledge every Gold Star mother, father, sibling, and family member in our country for their fortitude in the face of immeasurable grief because there is something unrelenting about the kind of sadness we face. Life is a hard and deeply rutted road to travel, and so often it takes others to keep you going after you lose someone to war. Unfortunately, there will always be families who must accept their new reality of being Gold Star families like ours. We said goodbye to our sons, daughters, brothers, or sisters, but the memory of them will not fade from us no matter how long we live without them in our lives. I pray this book will provide some solace and God's peace for each of you.

Semper Fidelis.

CPSIA information can be obtained
at www.ICGtesting.com
Printed in the USA
LVHW030504141021
700296LV00006B/26